THE CLIMAX
TO AN EPIC STORY
OF LOVE AND CONQUEST
ON A GALACTIC SCALE

The Second War of Energy is over, but hurtling
toward Cluster is a million-ship spacefleet
from the enemy galaxy of Amoeba—and only
Herald the Healer can stop it! From the World
of the Jets to the Galaxy of Pinwheels to the
diabolical kingdom of the Solarians—where
a laser duel can win a woman's love or
seal a man's destruction—he must outrace
time to unravel the sacred puzzles of the
Ancients ... the only means of vanquishing
the looming space menace.

But first Herald is summoned to Kastle Kade
to heal the unthinkably beautiful Psyche ...

KIRLIAN QUEST

Piers Anthony

AVON
PUBLISHERS OF BARD, CAMELOT AND DISCUS BOOKS

KIRLIAN QUEST is an original publication of Avon
Books. This work has never before appeared in book form.

Cover illustration by Ron Walotsky.

AVON BOOKS
A division of
The Hearst Corporation
959 Eighth Avenue
New York, New York 10019

First Avon Printing, July, 1978

AVON TRADEMARK REG. U.S. PAT. OFF. AND IN
OTHER COUNTRIES, MARCA REGISTRADA,
HECHO EN U.S.A.

Printed in the U.S.A.

Contents

Prologue

He never looked through a telescope. He was perhaps the leading research astronomer of Galaxy Milky Way: experienced, capable, intelligent, and of high-Kirlian aura. He formed an ear-horn to listen to audios, and an eye-stalk to view the graphics, and he pooled comfortably in his basin while he worked. He was a creature of repute, but by no means a hero; there was little in his makeup to suggest that he had the capacity to become involved in Cluster adventure. In fact, his type went into shock at the mere threat of extreme danger.

He specialized in Fringe-Cluster phenomena. The major galaxies of Andromeda and Milky Way did not really interest him, and the lesser structures like Pinwheel and the irregular galactic satellites were hardly more intriguing. It was the far-out fragments, dwarf ellipses, and globular star-clusters that compelled his attention. He knew more about "wild" globs and nongalactic stars than any other creature of the Cluster.

Now his attention focused on the Amoeba—a tiny pseudonebula hardly a hundred light-years in diameter. It was a nonluminous, diffuse, vague shape hidden behind the dwarf ellipsoid called Furnace—itself worth contemplation as the "missing link" between the tiny globular clusters and the small elliptical galaxies. Yet the fifteen-thousand-light-year diameter of Furnace loomed monstrously compared to the tiny haze of the Amoeba. In fact, the Amoeba had not even been discovered until the past century, as it was virtually invisible to all conventional observation techniques.

1

The astronomer formed a second eye and contemplated a holograph of the Amoeba. It appeared to have a number of projecting pseudopods, each curving slightly; this was what had given it its name. Overall it was amazingly regular; the pseudopods seemed individual and evenly spaced.

Its discovery had been largely serendipitous, a result of the Cluster survey program instituted after the Second War of Energy. After twice narrowly averting destruction of their galaxy, the coalition of species of the Milky Way intended to keep fully informed of all future developments in the Cluster. The most powerful Segments— Qaval, Etamin, Knyfh, Lodo, and Weew—had pooled their resources and manufactured the largest fleet of spaceships ever known: 125 billion strong. But they were very small ships, any one of which an average-sized sapient could have lifted in a single appendage without effort. Each contained perceptive apparatus, mainly optical, and a tiny molecule mattermitter. They were dispersed around the entire outer surface of the Cluster, accelerating to one-tenth the speed of light and then drifting outward until they were, theoretically at least, eventually recovered by the gravity of the Cluster. Every ten years each unit mattermitted back what was visible from its quota of space. Each ship was about ten light-years from its neighbors, and so was responsible for a surface area of a hundred light-years; its report was normally current within about seven years. Thus no major intrusion into the Cluster could escape detection; the Net would report it long before the light reached the nearest galaxy.

The Net had been in operation for almost a thousand years. As the fear of alien intrusion had abated, the main beneficiaries of this expensive program had been the astronomers and stellar cartographers. The entire Cluster had been mapped with phenomenal accuracy—retroactively. For the Net reported what it saw—and it saw what the Cluster had looked like up to a million years before, because of the time it had taken the plodding light of distant stars to travel.

The section of the Net launched from Furnace had penetrated a hundred light-years into space—and picked up the Amoeba. Only two specific reports on it existed, and neither was remarkably clear, for it remained at the

2

fringe of the Net's awareness. Only specialized research astronomers such as this one were able to perceive anything of significance there. To the untrained eye, it was only a faint haze against the backdrop of deep space. Perhaps merely a smear on the image, or some distortion of the lens.

He substituted the second holograph, taken from the same units ten years later, or one light-year closer. The image was very similar and a bit sharper, but a trifling discrepancy caught his attention. He reactivated the first holograph, projecting it in modified color, and superimposed it on the second. He grew a third eye on a long stalk, so that he could study the superimposition from three directions at once.

The two images differed, even after adjustment for slightly differing ranges. There seemed to be a slow rotation of the subject. He compensated for this, aligning the curved arms of it precisely, magnifying the smaller image until its absolute perspective exactly matched the scale of the other.

There was no doubt. *The Amoeba had expanded.* The projections extended some five light-years farther than before.

What constituted the substance of this obscure, minor formation? Not gas. The refraction indices of the wan light of distant background galaxies were wrong. Not dust; that would have blotted out such light entirely. The indications were so fuzzy; there simply was no way to properly analyze a dark obscuration without *going* there, and it would take the local units of the Net the better part of another century to pass through the physical Amoeba. Mattermission directly to the Amoeba could not be used until the first receiver was delivered, and Transfer required a living host already present. A number of attempts to Transfer there had been made, all without success. There appeared to be no sapient life in the Amoeba. And why should there be? Life normally required the services of a sun; it could hardly evolve in the great abyss that was intergalactic space.

The holographs did not resolve any bodies of planetary size. Indications suggested that the Amoeba consisted of perhaps a million fragments of rock, none larger than a planetoid. An assemblage of meteoroids, like a mon-

3

strous comet, way out in Fringe-Cluster space. An anomaly! Which was what made it so intriguing.

Possibly it was the remnant of a planetary explosion, and its expansion reflected the continuing impetus of that cataclysm. Even so, there were questions. The planet could not have been formed in deep space; it had to have coalesced or come from *somewhere*. This cloud of fragments had not been traveling, for the two holographs would have shown the change in position that marked that velocity; instead the Amoeba was virtually stationary with respect to Furnace.

It had not coalesced; prior holographs going back a thousand years showed no dust cloud there. A dust or gas cloud was easier to track than a planetary body, because it spread over a much greater volume of space and obscured far more background light, however faintly. Instruments could analyze this, though it might be too subtle for the naked sapient eye. Not that such an accretion from gas or dust could have occurred in so brief a period. No, the planet had to have been there before, invisibly small, and exploded approximately two hundred years ago, after remaining quiescent for at least a hundred years.

But there had been no explosion of that magnitude. The sensors of the Net would have picked up such radiation within a few decades, instead of having to wait to come into dark-body perception range. In fact, the telescopes of Sphere Furnace would have caught it within a century—and they had not. So there had been no explosion—at least, none of the force required to propel elements of the planet outward at a significant fraction of the speed of light.

Yet the Amoeba was there, and it was growing. It could not have resulted from an explosion anyway; it was not an expanding shell of debris, but a growing semi-material structure. The arms were elongating, or extending from the center, almost like a living thing. Yet it was only gravel—wasn't it?

A mystery indeed! There had to be some explanation, for the thing existed. The astronomer did not propose to wait decades for new evidence from the Net. He was the Galaxy's leading research astronomer, and he had all the information anyone had. This was the kind of challenge that gave his life meaning!

For days he labored over his references, checking and

4

rechecking. He did supplementary research, seeking new insights. He meditated, and viewed the holographs with as many as six eyes simultaneously, and put them on sonic translation and listened with several ears. His well-trained, subservient maid brought him food and carried away his refuse; he never moved from his basin. He would crack the riddle of the Space Amoeba before he left here!

News circulated, for nothing the ranking experts did was entirely private. A tremendous breakthrough must be in the offing! Other astronomers studied the Amoeba, hoping to upstage the master, for this was a highly competitive field. But they could not solve the mystery; data were insufficient, and there was much more pressing business. It was not as though it were an important subject, this far-distant tentacular system of dead pebbles.

Suddenly, in the privacy of his office, the researcher stiffened. @The Space Amoeba is—@ he exclaimed in his native language. Then he sank into shock.

His loyal maid summoned the authorities, and they rushed him to the medical center for treatment. But the astronomer lay puddled in his basin, oblivious. They could not revive him.

They knew that the force of his insight about the Amoeba had done it. His species was subject to such shock when faced with overwhelming danger. It was a defensive mechanism that had often saved individuals before, rendering them insensate and pliable enough to survive severe abuse. Obviously in this case there had been no direct physical threat. They knew the matter had to be supremely important, for no minor revelation would have had this effect on such an expert. Therefore it was necessary to ascertain the specific nature of the intellectual shock, in case it affected others of the culture.

No doctor of the Segment could bring the astronomer out of it. They could not fathom how the distant Amoeba could threaten anyone here, but they dared not gamble on their ignorance. So they made an arrangement with the leading shock-technician of the Cluster: a super-Kirlian entity of Sphere Slash, Andromeda, named Herald the Healer.

PART I

KIRLIAN

1

Abatement of Honor

&All units drift by for geographic review.&
0Action units 1 through 9 drifting by.0
XResearch units A through Z drifting by.X
&Target Cluster now in range. Geographic unit report.&
GTwo full-scale Galaxies, one small Galaxy, all spiral, six ellipses, seven irregulars, assorted lesser fragments. Overall, typical small Cluster. Nomenclature of local sapients: Milky Way, Andromeda, Pinwheel, Furnace, Sculp, Cloud 9, Cloud 6.G
&Dispense with detail listing; local species identifiers will shortly become passé.&

His host-body was a peculiar amalgam of loops. He was not certain whether it was all in one jointless string or whether it branched and rejoined at twisted intervals. It had no disks, feet, or treads; on a flat surface it would have been a disaster.

There are no plane surfaces here, the host-mind informed him. *No flatnesses. Do not be concerned. I shall convey you safely wherever you wish.*

/Appreciation,/ Herald replied, employing his own mode of intonation, though of course he used the language of Sphere Ast. /I come to encounter Whorl of Precipice./

Immediately the body moved. It twisted up and through a lattice of stone, spun around an angled ceramic column, and tied into a metal basket-frame. This in turn moved, following a flexible line through an astonishing network of shapes. Commercial transport, of course, but a far beam from the forthright geometry of Herald's own Sphere.

They came into a cavern laced with stalactites. The host halted abruptly and withdrew his personality, yielding full control to the Transferee. Herald realized that he had arrived.

An entity that was superficially like his host convoluted up to meet him. A loop of its body touched Herald's form, and moved in the sensation-language of this species. This one had a good aura of about fifty. *Welcome, expert of Slash,* he pulsed. *I am Whorl of Precipice.*

Herald's normal mode of expression, modulated laser, was even less well suited to inter-entity communication than to internal-host dialogue. But a certain perverse pride of origin caused him to employ it anyway. The result was a tactile rendition that seemed affected.

/I am Herald the Healer./

Your incredible aura needs no introduction! Just what rating, if I may ask, is it, precisely?

/Two hundred thirty-six./ Herald was used to such queries, and suffered from no sense of intrusion of privacy. He had the most intense Kirlian aura ever measured, higher even than those of the famous historical characters Flint of Outworld and Melody of Mintaka, from whom it was said he was deviously descended. Their auras had come to historical prominence in the Wars of Energy; there was now no war, so he had made his aura part of his profession.

Two hundred and thirty-six times normal! Whorl exclaimed in a violent vibration.

/You have purchased one unit of my time,/ Herald reminded him. /It commenced when we met. You will not wish to waste it./

Your fee is high, but I feel that only you will be able to help me.

/I do not guarantee it. Some maladies are not amenable to my art./

This one surely is. I require the answer to a single question—and you, as the greatest living blazoner, surely have the information.

/Surely,/ Herald agreed. /I shall of course blazon an Achievement for you. That is the other facet of my profession./

9

*Unnecessary. I *have* my Shield of Arms. I merely wish . . . an interpretation.*

/You have wasted your fee! Any heraldic scholar of your own Sphere can give you an interpretation at the merest fraction of what you are paying me, and it will be quite as accurate. Heraldry is a fixed art; there is little leeway for interpretation. Perhaps even a text can provide what you require. Surely your Planetary Library—/

I queried the library once. Not again!

Herald perceived fluctuations in the entity's aura. There was an emotional charge to the matter. So it was not a strictly routine query, as quite often his cases *weren't*. Herald's fee was high because he brought extraordinary ability into play. Still he affected a certain modesty. /If you feel my particular interpretation is worthwhile, you shall have it. Yet it will not differ materially from—/

Let me explain. The Family of Precipice is of recent formation. It required some difficult maneuvers on my part for me to gain . . . are you familiar with the hereditary mechanisms of our Sphere?

/My business requires me to be conversant with the derivations for Shields of Arms in many Spheres. Beyond the legal procedures I become vague about specifics, until some particular case requires my spot education. I do not, for example, comprehend precisely how your five-sex mode of reproduction operates; I have not felt it necessary to pry into such private matters. Is this information necessary for proper application to your question?/

Perhaps not. I mention it only passingly, then. We do not, despite widespread belief in other Spheres, possess five sexes. Rather our quintuplets consist of four complementary males and one female. Our procedures for the selection of particular types of males for family continuity depend on the types of interfamily liaison desired. Suffice to say, the matter can become complex, and at times certain family lines must be legally discontinued and new ones constituted. Development of a new family therefore requires a new Shield of Arms, with impalements representing the critical ancestral elements.

/This is elementary, Whorl, though I point out as an aside that your use of the term 'impalement' is imprecise. Impaling is the specific process of marshaling arms together by mounting them side by side on the Shield; it can only be done *by pairs*. Thus your shield is actually—/

Please, I am not conversant with every technical detail. Otherwise I would not need to summon an expert.

/Of course. My apology, Whorl. But this being the case, I trust you engaged a competent heraldic artisan to design and execute your Achievement?/

I insisted on the very best. It cost me a great amount of value, for there was resistance, but I brought sufficient twist and constriction to bear, and it was handled personally by the King of Arms for Sphere Ast.

Herald flashed an internal beam of exclamation. Whorl must indeed have applied political and economic pressure to command performance by such a figure. The top echelons of legal heraldry were known to be extremely jealous of their prerogatives, and notoriously resistant to the urges of outsiders.

/I have had occasional dealings with your College of Arms and found it quite competent. I am sure your hereditament is more than sufficient. Be assured that you may display it without apology./

*I am *not* so assured. There are those who . . . who have sniggered.* A snigger, in Ast terms, was a most expressive and borderline-obscene ripple of implied meaning, the depth of bad taste.

/An Achievement rendered by the King of Arms is not to be sniggered at,/ Herald assured him. /Such entities only demonstrate their own gross ignorance./

They are not ignorant. They are— Whorl broke off. *This is why I require your service. There is something wrong.*

/We appear to be at an impasse, Whorl. I assure you that I am unlikely to divine any error of substance or detail in your Shield of Arms. For one thing, the Spherical Colleges of Arms *define* legitimacy in hereditaments. Their records are public, and their Grants are valid across the entire Galactic Cluster. The Universe, as much as we know of it, accepts the authority of your Family Shield. As far away as the Milky Way and Pinwheel, aficionados are contemplating your Achievement and considering its merits. If you are unsatisfied with the actual design or execution. . . ./

No, both are magnificent. I was most pleased.

Herald considered briefly. /Perhaps I have overlooked

a nuance of Ast meaning. I perceive no service I can offer./

All I require is that you examine my Shield and give me your completely candid opinion.

/I shall be gratified to. I offer no other type of opinion than candid./

Whorl twined to another section of his convolute residence, and Herald followed. Here in the living rock bordering a corkscrew chamber was emblazoned in relief a creature-sized Shield of Arms.

It was beautiful. The outer shield was in the shape of an ellipse set at an angle, representing Galaxy Andromeda, bordered inside by a wreath of intertwining serpents to designate Sphere Ast. Within that were the Family Arms of Precipice, resembling an ornate overhanging cliff. Herald moved his loops across it, savoring its aspects. It had superior form, texture, and color, and was, in its fashion, a genuine work of art. The King of Arms of Ast was certainly a master!

What do you find? The query was urgent.

/I find an excellent and flawless emblazon./

Did you not say 'blazon' before?

The tedious questions of amateurs! But Herald repressed his annoyance, for courtesy was vital to his profession.

/I did, Whorl. The 'blazon' of a Shield of Arms is the precise linguistic specification of its elements. To 'emblazon' is to render this description into physical actuality./

I comprehend. The one is the description, the other is the carving. I feared for a moment there was something wrong with it.

/No, your Achievement is quite in order. Azurine, a cliff of thirty-seven rocks and forty-two rills, alternately thirteen, twelve, thirteen, seven, eleven, twenty-three, pearline, all within a bordure of the Serpents Rampant./

Herald winced inwardly as he communicated, for the old-style heraldic term "rampant" was restricted to certain quadrupedal beasts of prey, standing erect on the left foot, raising the right foot in stride, balancing with the left forefoot outthrust, the right raised to strike. It was technically impossible for a legless serpent to be "rampant." But the broadening of the system to include diverse Cluster cultures had forced the fudging of some terms. However, as he had informed Whorl, the local Colleges of Arms defined legitimacy. So he had to accept it, nonsensical as it was in derivation. Regardless, this remained an excellent Shield of Arms, in concept and execution.

But as this chain of thought proceeded on the surface, something more insidious was percolating in the depths. Abruptly it surfaced. Herald suppressed a quiver of sheer incredulity.

Continue, Herald, Whorl vibrated anxiously.

But Herald could not continue. He was too busy stifling an emotion that threatened to overwhelm him.

You perceive! Whorl shuddered. *You are aware!*

Herald controlled himself with difficulty. /I regret I may not help you. I shall refund your fee./

*No! Every knowledgeable entity to whom I have so proudly displayed this Achievement has *laughed!* None will tell me why. It is as if some huge private joke exists at my expense. All say the Shield of Arms is perfect, yet they practically uncoil in their obscene mirth. Now you do the same. I have paid—I insist to know— you must perform service, by the honor of your profession. *What is wrong with my Shield?**

Herald writhed away. /Nothing is wrong. It is completely accurate in execution./

There you go again! That cannot be! I demand to be advised!

Herald quivered carefully. /There *is* one qualification. But it is unusual, of no technical account. You would prefer not to know. I void your fee and depart./

Whorl flung himself into an anguished knot. *Accept your fee or void it—that matters not! I charge you by the Lot of Asterisk—*tell* me!*

Herald paused. The Ast had invoked a powerful convention that required the truthful exchange of information. But there were certain key reservations.

/By the Lot of Asterisk I may not tell you, for I now perceive the answer would harm you./

I absolve you of all guilt for that harm, Herald! Tell me, lest I lose my sanity!

Herald was not certain of the proper course. Would the telling do more harm than the withholding? Whorl did seem to be on the verge of nervous collapse, yet the truth. . . . It was a problem of ethics he had not en-

13

countered before. /I know not where expediency lies. Therefore I accept your release of guilt, and accede./

Thank you! Thank you!

/I fear the thanks is undeserved. Your Achievement is perfect in every respect but one: it possesses an abatement in Stainand. This is the handsome color of *tenne*, or brown./

Yes, I have taken great pride in that hue, and pointed it out to important visitors.

/Unfortunately, in heraldic terms this signifies a question of honor./

I do not comprehend!

/I fear it has reference to some scandal in the roots of your family, perhaps a claim to an improper honor. One that is technically legitimate, but morally suspect./

The Ast was stricken. *The King of Arms has damned me! I thought no one knew of that matter!*

If all Whorl's friends had sniggered, many must have known!

/It seems the King has a subtle way of advising you of his research and opinion./

Shame! Shame! I am undone! Now everyone knows! My friends, my business associates to whom I described that very aspect of the Shield! My potential family-mates! Sapients all over the Galactic Cluster! I am a laughing-stock everywhere, everywhere!

Herald tried to alleviate the creature's concern. /On the contrary. Few know. Ordinary entities neither seek nor comprehend the significance of heraldic devices and conventions, do not know shield from crest. Had there been justification for any legal action against you, your Achievement would have been voided from the start. Obviously your family honors are valid. This merely . . . diminishes their impact. In fact, the very concept of hereditary abatements is suspect; I have never seen it done before in a recognized Achievement. I believe you could initiate a formal challenge on that basis, and perhaps have the abatement nullified./

And bring my shame into Cluster Court for all the nonheraldic sapients to perceive too? I'll be damned if I do that!

And Herald realized that the Ast was not indulging in vernacular; he meant quite literally that his cherished

14

honor would suffer damnation. Pride of family was a thing quite apart from law.

/I will lodge a protest on your behalf,/ Herald offered.

No, the damage is done. My only recourse lies beyond the auspices of heraldry.

Yes, it was serious! *Should* he have refused to tell? What was Whorl going to do now, assassinate the King of Arms? What mischief this Achievement had wrought!

But Herald could not afford to interfere further; this was no longer his business.

/As you wish. I deeply regret bringing this news upon you./

The Ast recovered himself.

I thank you, Herald. Please accept your fee; you have earned it. There will be no complaint. Parting.

Further dialogue was pointless; the noble of Precipice had made up his mind. /Parting,/ Herald said, and writhed away toward the transporter. He did not feel at ease.

As he left the domicile, he thought he perceived a faint pulse in the rock, echo of a distant tactile exclamation: *The whole Cluster! Shame!* The anguish was horrible.

Even before Herald transferred out, the news of the suicide of Whorl of Precipice and the dissolution of his nascent family was pulsing through Sphere Ast. The reason for this act was a mystery, but Herald knew the truth. He shuddered with anger and remorse. He had tried to honor his profession and deliver honest service for his fee, but had been forced into being an accomplice for an execution. If he made any protest now, his share in it would be exposed, and he might well be liable before the Cluster Court. Therefore he had to maintain silence, for there was no way he could benefit Whorl at this stage.

The King of Arms of Sphere Ast had gotten away with murder. One day he would have to settle for that crime.

2

Child of Grief

&Research units drift by for assignment.&
XDrifting by.X
&Research Command make assignments.&
XAssignments as follows: one unit per local cultural division. Units lettered, cultures symbolized.X

Milky Way: B ♀ E" F♂ K% L□ N$\sigma\sigma$ Qδ T ::: W@ Zι

Andromeda: A* C $^0{}_0$ D— P :: S/

Pinwheel: R ⋏ Uθ

Other: G$ J= M¢ V# Y§

&Action units drift by for assignments as invoked.&
0Drifting by.0
&Take samples of life and verify for aura and sapience.&

Herald's next host was a creature of treads and powerful hammering chisels, adapted for life within the rock wedged between the frozen ammonia of the surface and the superheated lava of the depths. This creature moved by drilling the stone ahead, and ate by sifting nutrients from the crushings. It was a pleasant enough livelihood when the region being mined was good. This was a planet in Sphere Quadpoint, halfway across the Galaxy. Herald went where his business took him.

He explained his mission to his host, and was conveyed with surprising speed through the rock. The material pounded from the front was cast back to block the passage behind; it was bad form to leave an open tunnel. A predator could come up from an exposed rear, or the

16

hole could interrupt the rhythm of another sapient entity. Of course, one of the planetary shifts would soon collapse everything and make way for a new cycle, but still, a self-sufficient creature cut and filled his own way. Soon he arrived at the territory of his client, Bore of Metamorphic.

Like most of Herald's clients this was a wealthy and powerful representative of his Sphere. It was not that Herald sought riches; rather, he could not afford to travel the universe for a pittance. He sought some way to serve the most needy, but at present it was necessary to serve the rich needy first. Once he had developed a retirement fund, he would do what he could to improve the lot of the downtrodden masses of Sphere Slash, struggling under what was ironically termed the "Curse of Llume."

Or was he, like so many he dealt with, merely a hypocrite? He thought he was storing up wealth in order to promote good, yet he had seen how easy it was to forget the latter part once the first had been accomplished. He hoped his life, in its entirety, would benefit his Sphere and his Cluster, but he could not be sure of that, yet.

Bore came right to the point, as was characteristic of his kind. : :My offspring will die. It is a malady of mineral insufficiency, incurable. For your fee you will enable her to knock out with grace, without pain. We are informed you have done this before, with other immature entities.: :

/I have, and with mature entities, too. However, each case differs./

The Lady Bore was more evocative. : :It is said that you interviewed a dying little bird of Sphere Dash, and that before you came the chick was in such depression he would not flap at all, but that afterward he glowed and consoled his parents with all three wings and then died in simple peace and comfort. And when they asked him what the Healer had done all he said was—He touched me!—and so it was never explained, but they were satisfied more than they could convey.: :

/True,/ Herald agreed.

: :If you do not do this for ours, we shall revoke your exorbitant fee,: : Bore said gruffly. : :I permit your intrusion in this hour of our bereavement only at the muddlebrained behest of the Lady. We have no use for your kind here.::

::Bore!:: the Lady protested. ::We have no prejudice against the Slash, even if they did betray the Galaxy. We are enlightened sapients.::

Prejudice? No, not much! thought Herald. The Curse of Llume marked his kind indelibly, as it had for a thousand years.

/You are assured of her condition?/

::Assured, Healer. Do your job.::

So blunt about the incipient demise of his young! But Herald knew better than to react to the seeming inadequacies of his client's manner; his profession required understanding and tolerance. He knew that often a gruff manner masked a tender sentiment. Creatures accustomed to smashing through hard rock all their lives might be forgiven their hard-hitting personalities.

/Convey me to Smallbore./ All Quadpoint immature used the diminutive of their parents' titles. /And then leave us alone, please./

Both adult Quadpoints seemed a bit taken aback at the expletive "please," but honored the request. The child rested in her small cave, too weak to carve her own tunnels anymore.

/Hello, Smallbore,/ Herald said. The child did not respond. /I have come to bring you peace./

::Then you are Death or the Devil,:: she said, evoking an image from his host-memory. Death was simple oblivion, but the Devil was a lithic monster who gleefully collapsed crushing layers of rock on trapped entities, or opened cracks to let ammonia snow pour in on the innocent. Smallbore sounded much like her father.

/Perhaps. Will you play a game with me?/

::I don't feel like playing 'Spaceship,' and if I did I wouldn't play it with a Slash!::

Herald produced a stack of thin stone panels. He had specified that his Quadpoint host carry these in his reserve hopper. /A game of guesses, Smallbore./

Despite herself, the child evinced interest. ::Guesses?::

/I shall lay down a card, and you shall guess its meaning. If you succeed, you keep the card./

::What the crush do I want with a crushing card? I am dying!::

Herald ignored the cursing. He moved close, and the

potent fringe of his aura touched her. /To die is unfortunate, Smallbore. To die without meaning is tragedy./

She made a sandy sigh. ::Oh, lay down your card!::

He shook the deck in his front tongs, shuffling it, and flipped out a random card. The mica-thin leaf landed face up on the floor between them.

Smallbore considered it. ::A picture of three entities rising from a deep pit, beneath a representation of Galaxy Andromeda,:: she said. ::Oh, I know what that means! It is the Andromedan Council of Spheres summoning the Slash for judgment. See, the creatures don't want to come!:: There was a certain malice in her tone.

But Herald accepted the slur against his Sphere without rancor, having had a great deal of practice in this sort of thing. These cards had pictures, true, but the pictures served to evoke suppressed reactions, to dredge up interpretations that reflected the most fundamental concerns of those who considered them. The animus against Sphere Slash was very strong in Sphere Quadpoint, which was natural. The Bores of Metamorphic had performed an act bordering on ignominy when they summoned a Slash to heal their child.

/You have guessed it, Smallbore. The card is yours. But do you know why the Slash are so poorly regarded?/

::They committed a crime against our Galaxy. They betrayed us to the enemy.::

/Yes. That crime is known as the Curse of Llume. May I tell you our side of it?/

::Slash has a side?:: she asked incredulously.

/Strange as it may seem, it does./

::Oh, all right,:: she said, pleased at her success in winning the card she didn't want. ::We Quadpoints are enlightened sapients, after all.::

Uh-huh. /In the time of the Second Energy War, a thousand years ago, there was an agent from Sphere Slash who, on the verge of success in her mission, renounced it and defected to the enemy galaxy, Milky Way, thereby enabling Melody of Mintaka to reverse the course of the war. The situation was very nearly saved by the fine general Hammer of Quadpoint.

::Hammer!:: she cried, recognizing the hero instantly. ::*Admiral* Hammer!::

/This Slash agent was called 'Llume' because that was the local identifier of the Milky Way host she first took in Transfer. It was a Spican Undulant of Segment Etamin. Llume became enamored of Melody of Mintaka, whose aura was very like hers but almost as strong as mine. Thus she was the arch-traitor of Sphere Slash, just as another female Slash, whose name history has refused even to record, had been in the First War of Energy a thousand years before that. The Sphere did not endorse the treachery of either female, but it nevertheless suffered the stigma of it, and the idea developed that the sapients of Slash were somehow traitorous by nature. Ever since, we have labored under that onus. The irony was, both females thought they were doing right, granting parity to the Milky Way so that it would not be destroyed. Llume prayed to the God of Hosts that Sphere Slash might one year redeem itself in honor./

: :Didn't Andromeda seek to destroy the whole Milky Way?: : Smallbore seemed unaware that the thrust of her question had changed.

/Andromeda merely sought to harvest the energy of the enemy galaxy for better purposes. That energy was needed to promote the level of civilization itself./

: :At the price of sapiencide? I do not see that Llume, was such a criminal, or that the Sphere she represents is necessarily cursed. She sought a *blessing!*: :

/Thank you, Smallbore./

Startled, she sputtered sand for a moment. : :You— I—you *are* from Sphere Slash?: :

/Yes./

: :Is your aura like Llume's?: :

/Perceptive of you to guess that! Perhaps I shall have to give you my aura, like the card! Yes, it is like Llume's, and like Melody of Mintaka's, and perhaps like Flint of Outworld's too, at least in intensity./

: :Then you must be the one to abate the Kirlian Curse!: :

/All things are possible, if unlikely. Would you like to trade places with me?/

: :Never!: :

Herald reshuffled the deck, preparing to flip out another card. The first had done very well. But Smallbore stopped him.

: :What is this set of pictures that you use?: :

He hadn't intended to go into that yet, but decided to answer honestly.

20

/It is called the Cluster Tarot. The roots of it date back some three thousand Sol years (as you know, we use this alien measurement of time because the conquerors imposed it on our whole galaxy, along with much of the rest of their dubious system of measurements) to educational pictures made by an obscure cult. Sibling Paul of Sol revised the deck and popularized it among Galactic species. The cards have changed many times in form and meaning, but have persisted to this day, owing largely to the continuing influence of the Temples of Tarot, which in certain periods have been very pervasive. Normally a Tarot cube is used, showing images on each of six faces, but individual cards have been used as emblems for many cultures. Spaceships are still designed along these lines, falling into five broad types after the five suits, resembling Wands, Cups, Swords, Disks, and Atoms. The Milky Way Society of Hosts used the card of Temperance, an entity transferring fluid from one vessel to another—/

::Transfer!::

/Yes. They used to supervise matters relating to it, caring for both hosts and the vacant bodies of Transferees. Because they used to use only Kirlian-vacant bodies as hosts, you see./

::Zombies! Ugh!::

/It certainly seems primitive today! But Kirlian science, like other sciences, had to progress from primitive origins. After control of the body passed to the host, regardless of the strength of the visiting aura, the Society's power faded. There is no longer any such thing as involuntary hosting, so no creature need worry. This Quadpoint host of mine can assume control any time, but since he earns his living by serving as host, he would not do so unless extreme circumstances warranted. But that is off the point. Other Tarot images occur elsewhere. The Queen of Energy—the Thirteen of Wands—remains the symbol for Galaxy Andromeda. That is the chained lady, about to be consumed by a monster of the sea. Since she is of the Suit of Fire, this is a hideous fate indeed./

::I've seen that! I did not know it derived from Tarot!::

/Actually it derives from pre-Tarot Solarian mythology. It—/

::Show me another card.:: She was a child; her attention-span was short.

This time Herald sorted through the pack and selected a particular card. Sometimes Tarot worked best by seemingly random examples, but in the critical areas he preferred to choose his symbols. He flipped it down. It showed a Quadpoint male doing tricks with colored rocks.

::A magician!:: A picture instantly recognizable to any child of the Cluster, whatever species might be represented.

/You are correct again, chip of Metamorphic!/

::I may be young, but I'm not stupid. I know I don't know enough about this image. Who is this magician? Is he you? Are you going to do a trick?::

Very intelligent child! Such a pity she could not survive. /I am the magician, at the moment, and I am going to do my trick. This is how I earn my fee./ Herald extended his tong and touched her nearest tread.

The child reacted. ::What is this? Suddenly I feel so good!::

/I have lent you my aura, Smallbore. I am Herald the Healer, and this is the way I heal./

::Oh, I . . . I never knew this . . . this . . . what *is* this aura? I feel it, yet I do not comprehend it.::

/The nature of the aura is cumbersome to explain, Smallbore./

::No more cumbersome than knocking out in ignorance, Healer!::

How eager the young mind was, once given the taste of health and knowledge! /Perhaps not. The aura, according to Zlqx of ¢, who authored the earliest surviving study, is a composite para-electronic complex that—/

::You confuse me already!::

He had been afraid of that. She was a bright child, but nevertheless a child, lacking the background for technicalities beyond her immediate experience. /Well, in my own flashes, it is an aspect of bio-pseudo-luminescent energy that manifests in all living—/

::I am just a little Quad, Herald.::

Herald made a beam of good-natured resignation that translated into a rattle in his host's treads. /I hesitate to offend you by flashing below your level./

::Oh, please offend me, Healer!::

Her attitude had been transformed by his aura, but he

22

knew it would not last unless he reached her inner belief. Aura combined with intelligence: that was the key.

/In that case I shall tell how the simplest and most recent of the great Cluster species discovered and named the aura. That would be the—/

: :I know! The Solarians!: :

Herald had actually been thinking of Segment Thousandstar, in neighboring Milky Way Galaxy. But he was also conversant with the similarly brash Solarians of Segment Etamin, so he obliged her by orienting on that instead.

/Yes, the infamous Solarians, who somehow obliged the rest of the Cluster to employ their nonsensical system of measurements. Two and a half of their millennia ago—that would be about thirty-five Quadpointers—before they strayed from their small dense homeplanet, there was a man named Kilner of London. He was a special kind of healer called a 'doctor' who worked with primitive radiation called 'X rays.' He became interested in stories of a nimbus or invisible aura around living creatures that he thought reflected their states of health./ Herald paused. /This is not insultingly simple?/

: :It *is* somewhat simple. But I like stories about primitive cultures.: :

/So do I, Smallbore! Kilner made colored lenses through which he was able to perceive this aura. He found that it consisted of three or four layers, a very narrow band that exactly followed the contours of the body, that he called the 'Etheric Double,' and a deeper layer beyond it he called the 'Inner Aura,' and a more diffuse and irregular layer outside that called the 'Outer Aura,' and sometimes an extremely tenuous outer band that faded away indefinitely. These bands tended to be broader and clearer in healthy individuals, and distorted or intermittent in unhealthy ones. He catalogued and described all variations and published a text on the subject, but other doctors did not believe him, and he died without recognition for his fundamental research./

: :I knew Solarians were stupid, but not *that* stupid! No wonder they were so late to master Transfer!: :

/They were ignorant, not stupid, Smallbore. They did not like to change their ways of thinking, which is why they were so late to achieve space. So in essence you are correct. Thirty years after Kilner's observations, another man named Kirlian of Krasnodar managed to photograph the aura, that is, to make a sort of two-dimensional holograph of it, very crude. *Then* the Solarians began to believe. As they put it, 'Seeing is believing.' So they named it the 'Kirlian Aura,' in this manner managing to avoid advertising their mistake about Kilner's work, and now that term is known throughout the Cluster./

::Funny how the terms of the primitives displace those of advanced cultures such as Quadpoint.::

/It is one of the anomalies of nomenclature. A Solarian maxim covers the situation, perhaps: 'Bad money drives out good.'/

Her mirth rattled the full length of her treads. ::Bad terminology drives out good! Bad maxims drive out good! Bad cultures drive out good! Bad life—:: She broke off.

Herald continued hastily, to interrupt that thought before it undid all that he had accomplished so far. /The Solarians developed more sophisticated methods of analysis in due course, and soon learned what others in the Cluster knew: that the aura is not merely a force that permeates and surrounds living creatures, but that it is the very *essence* of those creatures. If the aura is moved to another host, it induces its typical patterns in that host, much as a magnetic field induces its current in the output coil of a transformer. That host *becomes* the original entity, in mind and memory and emotion. In this manner, instantaneous travel across galactic distances becomes possible, for the Transfer of an aura requires much less energy than the mattermission of the entire host. But since the aura fades slowly in an alien host, only those personalities with auras more intense than the norm can travel this way. A normal aura would very soon fade out; in effect, death. Intensity of aura thus becomes an advantage—/

::And you have the most intense aura of all!::

/Yes. The stronger auras fill out, until at my level they become perfect spheres, except when specially focused. But it is intensity and type that count, rather than size or outline. There are many families of auras, distinct from species associations, and close aural affinity is regarded as more significant than genetic relationship. Thus I can claim relationship to Melody of Mintaka and to Flint of Outworld, though neither entity was of my species. The very strong auras also can help strengthen weaker auras, and a strengthened aura improves health

24

and outlook. Thus we become healers. Anyone can heal somewhat; those with very high auras heal much more dramatically. And this is the power I have, Smallbore. I cannot make you live longer, for your malady is of the physical body, not the aura. No amount of faith can make you well. But I can enable you to accept your fate with grace./

::You have done so, Healer! Death is no specter, now.::

/Unfortunately, there is much we do not know about the aura. We can measure it by color, type, intensity— a complex science of aural analysis has been developed —yet this has never approached the level the Ancients possessed. They alone knew the ultimate secrets of aura./

::The Ancients! I know about them! They died out three million Sol years ago.::

/And that is about as much as anyone *does* know, Smallbore. I cannot answer the next question you will ask. I don't *know* how it was that the greatest healers of all could not save themselves from extinction./

She made a tread-clacking chuckle. ::No, I was going to ask about the other part of your name. Why are you called Herald, if what you do is Healing?::

/I am called Herald because I also practice the art and science of heraldry. This is a Cluster convention of increasing popularity as divergent sapient species mix. There are so many types of sapience, in so many forms, in so many alternate Transfer hosts, that it becomes difficult to find common reference points. Heraldry satisfies a certain part of that need./

::But isn't it just drawing little pictures, like those Tarot cards?::

/Ah, but they are very special pictures, my dear! They are symbols, representing most specific identities, and are fundamental to the unification of the Cluster./

::Herald, I don't understand.::

/Do you really want to, Smallbore?/

::Yes! I have so little time, I want to know all I can before I know nothing at all. I mean—::

/I understand. We must *do* in life, and *learn* in life, and *feel* in life, for in death it is over./

::Yes, Herald! You understand so well!::

In a moment she was back on the subject. ::How did heraldry start?::

/Many species, in their pretechnical phases, wore special apparel to protect them from the attacks of physical weapons. This apparel was called 'armor,' and it was so encompassing that it became impossible to recognize the individual entity within it, the 'knight,' which figure is also represented in the Tarot deck. Therefore it became necessary to decorate his shield with some characteristic design, typical of his household and affiliation, so that friend could be distinguished from enemy. This eliminated the awkwardness of a knight lining up behind the formation of his enemy, supposing he was among friends. Or even attacking his friends, thinking they were enemies. The markings on the shield made everything instantly clear, even when the knights were not personally known to each other. This was the origin of heraldry. Today, all great families of all species in the Cluster have their registered Shields of Arms, even though they may never engage in combat./

: :My family has a Shield! I never knew what it meant.: :

/Come, I will explain what it means./ Following her directions, Herald located the Metamorphic Shield and placed it against the wall where both could view it./Note that the shape of this Shield is elliptical, a kind of angled oval that signifies Galaxy Andromeda./

: :But Andromeda is a spiral!: :

/So it is. But from Milky Way it appears elliptical. (Since Andromeda lost the Wars of Energy, we suffer the additional humiliation of the ellipse. The Milky Way Shield is the fundamental shape, flat across the top, round or partly pointed across the bottom. Other Galaxies have other shapes.) Within this is the band of prints, the little four-point patterns, signifying Sphere Quadpoint. In Milky Way there are two bands, since that Galaxy is organized into segments and Spheres, but it is the same idea. Then the main design, the symbol of Family Metamorphic: a lump of edible rock superimposed on the geologic flochart of its derivation. A distinctive Achievement—that is what the complete affair is called—recognizable anywhere in the Cluster./

: :Can you recognize any Shield of Arms in the whole Cluster?: : she asked, a bit awed.

/Within certain broad categories, yes. It is my business. And this is true generally. Two completely alien sapients

26

could meet on a barren planetoid, perhaps shipwrecked from different vessels, possessing no common language, form or status, and they could recognize each other by their Shields of Arms. That would provide their common experience. Each would know the other was sapient and civilized, and where he was from, and that he honored Cluster conventions of behavior./

: :How wonderful! Both would be like modern knights in armor, only one might be from Quadpoint, and the other from Thousandstar. Are there still knights in armor today?: :

/Indeed there are! It happens that my next client resides in a genuine medieval-Solarian-reconstruction society. No modern weapons, only swords and bows. No motorized transport. He needs me to exorcise a ghost in his castle./

: :Oh, I wish I could go with you! *Are* there such things as ghosts? I mean, really?: :

/Perhaps. I would lose business if there were not. This seems to be a Kirlian ghost, a manifesting aura of strong intensity. At any rate, I shall soon find out./

Smallbore paused, concentrating. : :Oh, be careful, Herald. I just got an awful feeling about this ghost. I perceive terrible pain for you, worse than that of death itself. You cannot save *my* life, but you can save—: : She halted, unable to grasp the full concept. : :Three million years,: : she finished. : :Does that make any sense at all, Herald?: :

/That sounds like the Ancients,/ he said, uncertain what to make of this. Was it his future or her own she had glimpsed? /Of course, I *am* searching for the legendary 'Kirlian Crest,' or the Shield of Arms of the Ancients themselves—there is a distinction between shield and crest, but that does not matter in this context—that will reveal at last their actual nature. But of course this is chimerical./

: :No, not that, exactly. Oh, I have lost it! Something about the ghost host, old, old, that will destroy you—Herald, my mind blanks it off, it is too horrible. Do not go—but no, you *must* go—oh, I can't face it!: :

What could be too horrible for a dying child to face, when death itself no longer frightened her? Herald had a premonition that this was no idle warning, but he had no way to grasp its nature.

Smallbore changed the subject. : :May I deal a card now?: :

Herald presented her with the cards. Here he had come to heal her, and she was trying to heal him! Yet such interactions happened on occasion. It was one of the mysteries of aura. Some entities placed a religious interpretation on such things; Herald did not, but it left him without adequate explanations.

Smallbore mixed the cards inexpertly and flipped one down. : :What is this?: :

/The Universe./

: :I don't understand.: :

/Certainly you do, Smallbore! There is a whole geography of stars and planets and galaxies and clusters in space out beyond these tunnels. That is the Universe. Everything. More than we can even imagine./

: :You mean the Milky Way is not just another tunnel?: : she inquired facetiously. : :Have you traveled the Universe, Herald?: :

/The Universe, no. The Cluster, yes, but the Cluster is merely a rough ellipsoid in space, a sort of flattened ball, with Andromeda at one end and Milky Way at the other, each with its satellites or associated lesser galaxies. Andromeda has a couple of cute little spiral galaxies in attendance, and Milky Way has a couple of irregular blobs./

Smallbore's laughter rattled her treads again. : :You're making that up!: :

/No, it is really true. The larger blob is ten parsecs through. And that's about thirty-three light-years—oops, multiply those figures by a thousand; I'm trying to make dwarfs of giants—over thirty thousand light-years through, called Cloud Nine. The sapients of Sphere $ reside there. The smaller one is Cloud Six, and it contains Sphere ¢. Both cultures are very sensitive about their status. They point out that superficial regularity has nothing to do with cultural merit, and that there are many remarkable constellations within their clouds, some quite beautiful. They say that if Milky Way had not thrown its weight about for the past few billion years, distorting its satellites, they would by now have formed into perfect elliptical galaxies, and not the smallest ones in the Cluster, either. I think they have a case./

28

::I'm sorry. When I knock out, I will Transfer over there and apologize to the two irregular blobs.::

/That would be nice,/ Herald agreed gravely. /It is merely a matter of rotation. All galaxies start as blobs; those that have sufficient rotation evolve into more orderly disks in due course. Andromeda is one of the most scenic galaxies in the Universe, but we have our shame, too./

::I know. We lost the energy wars.::

/Our shame is not that we lost, but that we instigated the wars. We tried to destroy our sister galaxy, the Milky Way./

Now she argued the other side again, as he had thought she might. This was a good, positive, juvenile reaction. ::But we needed their energy to promote our civilization!::

/Civilization promoted by such means would not be worthwhile. We must never again consider the horror of galacticide./

::You know, if we had tried it against a smaller galaxy, we might have won. There would still have been plenty of energy.::

/*Which* galaxy? Pinwheel? It has two major sapient species, Sphere Pin and Sphere Wheel./

::Pin and Wheel!:: she exclaimed in delight. ::No, we couldn't destroy that galaxy; it's too cute.::

/Well, what about one of the dwarf ellipsoids or irregulars that fill in the volume of the Cluster? There is Sculp with its Sphere §, or Furnace with its Sphere # . . ./ he trailed off.

::Why are you silent, Herald? Have you traveled there? What do you know about them?::

/Oh, Sculp and Furnace are very special in their way. They resemble globular clusters, which are little balls of stars perhaps eighty parsecs in diameter, very tightly packed with about a hundred thousand old red stars. But Sculp is two thousand parsecs in diameter, and Furnace four or five thousand parsecs. They are grossly oversized for globs, yet too small to be galaxies. They actually represent the 'missing link,' the intermediate stage between—/

::You are evading my question, Herald. I feel it in your marvelous healing aura. Would you lie to a dying child?::

Herald paused, shaken. /Yes, child, I do evade. I have traveled to Sculp on business, but will never go to Furnace./

::Why not?:: She sensed a mystery here, and was excited.

/I think this is not a thing you would understand./

::That is exactly the kind of thing that interests me most! Please, Herald; I will keep your secret. Tell me what keeps you from Furnace. Is it very hot there?::

/The sapients of # are hot, but that would not dissuade me, as I would naturally go there in Transfer./

::Come on, tell me—or I'll condemn Furnace to be destroyed for our energy supply!::

/You bargain ruthlessly! Therefore I must confess: my betrothed is there./ He dealt a card: the Devil.

::Oh, I am sorry, Herald. I would not really have destroyed Furnace! But—how could you love her if you have never been there? Did she come to Andromeda?::

/No, we have never met. It was a birth-betrothal, decreed by the Cluster Council. We are the two highest Kirlians living in the Cluster and so by law, we must mate with each other before we take any other mates./

Smallbore finally took note of the card. ::The Devil? Now I really *don't* understand, Herald. Why is this law? Where is the Devil? You are not even of her species, are you?::

/I hardly understand it myself, Smallbore. There is a body of experts who believe that the mating of two high-Kirlian entities is more likely to produce high-Kirlian descendants. Many other experts doubt this. The available evidence lends itself to differing interpretations. But for the past few centuries, that law has been in force; it applies to all auras of one hundred fifty or above. Thus I am betrothed to this devil female./

::So you have to marry this hot one! Why is that so bad?::

/Just how old are you, child?/

::Old enough to snoop on my parents, some. I know what the words mean.::

Herald sighed, hoping he wouldn't get in trouble with the older Metamorphics. Some cultures still had regressive notions about what was fitting for children to know.

/I have to mate with Flame of Furnace. After she

conceives by me, I am free to mate and marry elsewhere. But I refuse to honor this dictate, so I shall never Transfer to Furnace, or permit Flame to Transfer to me./

: :But she might be a nice girl!: :

/That is irrelevant. It is a matter of principle. The Cluster Council shall not dictate my personal life./

: :Won't that get you in trouble with the Cluster Council?: :

/Not so long as I don't marry elsewhere. I shall remain celibate./

Smallbore considered that. : :But you might have a child like me. Would you deny me my short life?: :

Herald was silent, struck by the ramifications of the question. A child like her?

: :Oh, I have wounded you,: : Smallbore cried contritely. : :I am sorry, Herald. Forgive me!: :

/No fault in you,/ Herald replied quickly. /You have caused me to examine my motives, and they are unworthy. I would not deny you life./

Smallbore looked through the deck, found a card and laid it down: Death. She considered it for a long moment before speaking. : :Strange, Herald. I know it for what it is, yet I find no terror in it. How can this be?: :

/Many things in life are worse than death. Not long ago I analyzed the Shield of Arms of a noble Ast, and he charged me by the Lot of Asterisk to explain its fault. When I did, he died. For him, abatement of honor was worse than death, though in truth it was the fault of the vengeful King of Arms of Ast./

: :Oh, the poor entity! I must comfort him, when I enter that realm.: :

/That might be appropriate,/ Herald agreed.

: :And after that, I shall go haunt the King of Arms of Ast!: : she said with a return of childish malice.

/Perhaps that, too, would be appropriate, / Herald said. If there were any reality to life after death. . . .

When Bore returned, Herald had gone. Smallbore remained too ill to drill, sinking toward death, but now there was a special brightness to her finish, a kind of metallic radiance all about her, and she was at peace. : :I will die very soon,: : she announced. : :Isn't it wonderful?: :

31

Bore was suspicious. Had the alien drugged her? ::Tell me what passed between you and the Healer.::

::He touched me, and he showed me pictures, and he told me stories,:: she said simply. ::It was such a wonderful conversation! Daddy, I love you!::

::Did he give you funny rock to eat? Did he flash compelling patterns on your receptors? Did he make subtle threats?::

She laughed, her whole body vibrating. ::None of it, Daddy! No poison, no hypnosis, no warnings. He made me feel so *good!*::

Now an even darker suspicion occurred. She was, after all, old enough to snoop on her parents and to know what the terms meant. ::Did he touch you . . . in a certain way?::

::Daddy!:: the child exclaimed with mock shock. ::I'm way too young to know what you mean, let alone to breed. And anyway, do you think I'd do it with a Slash?::

Embarrassed by his daughter's perception and humor, Bore desisted. ::It is only that you were so sad, and now you are so happy, yet nothing has changed. If the Healer did nothing but talk to you, I paid—uh—::

::I know you paid him a lot of mineral, Daddybore. He is a very expensive healer and he is very good. But I am sorry if it was not worth it to you.:: And she began to dim.

::It was worth it!:: Bore vibrated quickly. ::It was worth the whole punctured planet! I just don't *understand* it!::

Her treads clinked cheerfully. ::He said you would not, Daddy. He explained how sad you would be after I died, because you don't understand about apologizing to irregular blobs or haunting Kings of Arms or Devils having little girls like me.::

::I certainly *don't!*::

::But he told me how to make you happy again, in the little time I have left. May I do that?::

Amazed, Bore vibrated acceptance.

And for the few days that Smallbore survived, she made her parents happy, for *she* was happy. After she was gone, a plaque to Herald the Healer was erected in the Metamorphic household, and no slight to Sphere Slash was permitted.

There was of course no possible connection, but the King of Arms of Ast became indisposed shortly thereafter. Forced to retire from office, he was heard to mutter, *Damn that child!*

3

Kastle of Kade

*0*Samples taken and inspected. All are aural nonsapients.*0*

*&*As always. Any association with the sapients?*&*

*0*Yes. The sapients control them, breed them, utilize their products, and slaughter them for food.*0*

*&*They employ aural entities—as cattle?*&*

*0*I have consulted with all my units. There is no question. These samples are animals, bred for docility, production, and potability of flesh. *Not* for intelligence.*0*

*&*Surely this culture must be expunged from the face of the Universe! We shall give this Cluster to the animals, letting the meek inherit. As we have done before.*&*

*0*As we have done before.*0*

*&*Research units report in order, routine reports omitted.*&*

*D*Our assignment, Sphere Dash Andromeda, contains several operative ancient planetary sites. One on planet £ has been penetrated, circa eleven cycles BP, but no evidence of exploitation, and site was resealed.*D*

*&*Planet £? This has a familiar aspect.*&*

*D*Its designation is taken from its formerly dominant species, the tripeds. Sapient but nonspacefaring, owing to their extreme bulk.*D*

*&*It was this species that penetrated the site?*&*

*D*Correct. Two £ entities died within it. Presumed malfunction of admittance procedure, corrected by site computer when intruders were analyzed.*D*

*&*Orient action unit.*&*

*0*Action unit 1, orient on that site.*0*

1Oriented.1

&Act only if site is reactivated by Cluster entities. It is necessary to prevent ancient technology from falling into their capability, but destruction of a secure site would be wasteful, and waste is abomination. This site has historical relevance, and its level is parallel to our present technology.&

1Clarification of assignment: should the site be reactivated by local entities—1

&This would indicate a repeat activation, highly suggestive. Destroy it, and extirpate life on that planet.&

The item on Herald's schedule said "Exorcism," followed by a Shield of Arms. One glance at that Shield gave him the address, for it was the shape of Galaxy Milky Way, inset by the dragon of Segment Etamin, itself inset by the disk of Sphere Sador, one of the so-termed circular cultures. The specific Achievement was that of Planet Keep, inset by the device of the Duke of Kade. Beyond that, Herald would have to research; he was not conversant with every device of every planet in the Cluster. There were, after all, in the neighborhood of a million sapient-populated planets, with new ones being added and old ones being closed down constantly.

Herald was eager to get the job finished, so he could go home and relax for a day in his own body. His aura suffered only trifling depletion on his excursions, but still he liked to keep it at optimum strength, and that could only be done at home. The interview with Smallbore of Metamorphic had shaken him, coming so soon after the suicide of Whorl of Precipice. Had her warning of the hazard of this mission been a true manifestation of the paranormal? Powerful but incomprehensible forces seemed to swirl about him, settling in to wreak he knew not what. He had been a creature without evident destiny; was that now to change?

The way Smallbore had forced his rethinking about his fiancée, Flame of Furnace . . . would it be better to abate his foolish pride, go and mate with her and perhaps produce a child like Smallbore? It would not matter to him if that child had no significant aura; she would still be a charming individual. But it would be hard, very hard, to admit so dramatically that his prior stand had been wrong.

35

He could picture the half-veiled flicker of contempt of Flame of Furnace when he came to her.

Best to get this exorcism done with rapidly, so he could relax and sort out his private thoughts. He proceeded to Planet Keep of Milky Way without delay, not bothering with the spot research that would normally have prepared him for the immediate detail. He would learn what he needed while on location; this was not a matter of heraldry anyway.

He arrived in a Solarian host, an upright quadruped creature formed of bone, cartilage, tendon, and meat, ambulating on two digits and employing the other two for manipulation. Its primary senses were optical and auditory and tactile. He had utilized a humanoid host once before, so had no real problem adjusting to its oddities. This was not as convenient a body as his own, but it would serve.

He sat—that is, his body was partially supported in a folded position—in a plushly padded chair in a chamber hung with elegant tapestries adorned with heraldic motifs. He was clothed in a loose tunic with holes for appendages to project, emblazoned with the Achievement of Kade.

/I am present, host,/he announced. /Please conduct me to the assignment./

Immediately the body shifted weight, brought the solid head forward, and lifted with the large muscles of the thighs so as to balance on the legs. It leaned forward and thrust out each leg in turn to break the incipient fall threatened by its unbalance; a precarious but effective mode of propulsion. One arm stretched forward and drew aside a fiber panel, providing access to another chamber.

A genuine Solarian turned from his contemplation of a window-aperture, startled. He was solid for his species, seeming to possess some superfluous avoirdupois, but seemed nevertheless powerful.

"I am Herald the Healer," Herald said, noting with interest that his communication was not manifested in his normal slashes. He generally stayed with his natural intonation as a matter of pride, but in some hosts the set language patterns were too strong. It didn't really matter; this was a good host, not intruding in any other manner.

He was used to the surprise that his rapid adaptations evoked. Most entities seldom Transferred, even those of high aura, so they took some time to adjust to their alternate hosts. Herald's whole business involved Transfer, so that he was able to make an adjustment in a minute that might have required an hour or even longer for another entity.

"Please produce the subject for exorcism," Herald said, still faintly bemused by the way his words emerged in quotes. No doubt he would grow accustomed to this, as he would to the other oddities of this situation.

But it was not to be so easy. "I am Duke of Kade," the man said, extending his right hand.

Herald took that hand with his own right, honoring the custom of digital contact common to many species, and a boon to those checking on aura. The Duke's aura was a strong one of seventy-five. The man was of middle human age, with pale blue-green hide color and orange disks around the black pupils of his two eyes. Since the Solarian base-stock had been black, white, yellow, or shadings between, Herald knew that this was a galactic offshoot, modified by generations of life aboard other planets. Most sapients suffered similar variations as they settled on alien worlds; local conditions inevitably had their effect.

"There are things you must know before you proceed," the Duke said. "Your presence was imposed on this house. I shall grant you the amenities of guest status, but it is my wish to be rid of you as soon as possible. Do not allow my politeness in company to mislead you about my basic attitude. Do we understand one another?"

Now Herald felt the hostility that permeated the man's aura, worse than that of Bore of Metamorphic. He was at the same time aware of a fundamental integrity and strength of purpose that he had to admire.

"I am not always welcome, but I always perform proper service for my fee," Herald said. This entity's animosity did not appear to be rooted in anti-Slash prejudice, but in some local matter of principle. Could it be similar to Herald's own refusal to mate with Flame of Furnace?

"I do not desire your service," Kade said bluntly. "I regard you as a charlatan. But I have made a covenant with my enemies that requires your participation. I shall now summon the enemy representative, who shall serve witness to the fact of your presence. Upon his arrival, you shall proceed to your ritual. I shall be pleased if it is brief."

"I appreciate your candor, and shall be as brief as possible." This fitted nicely with Herald's own preference; the mission should be over soon.

Kade made a snap with his fingers. A servant-Solarian appeared, garbed in a plain tunic: a contrast to the ornately embroidered robe of the master. Clothing, in this culture, made the entity. "Fetch the Witness," the Duke said.

The servant disappeared. Kade turned to Herald with grim formality. "Now, as befits a good host, I shall show you the grounds," he announced.

Herald was momentarily startled by the use of the word "host," but realized that in this context it lacked the usual connotations. To those who did not Transfer, a host simply meant the proprietor of a domicile. "It is not necessary," he said.

"One does not permit the agent of a malign influence to wander the premises unattended."

The antipathy was strong indeed! But there was no element of hypocrisy in it. This man hated him, but Herald knew he was quite safe from molestation in this residence. This was heraldic honor of the old style.

Herald shrugged, hoping the enemy witness would arrive promptly. "May I say, sir, that I feel better at ease with an enemy of your integrity than I would feel with a friendly hypocrite."

Kade gave him a bleakly appraising glance. "Thank you."

Kastle Kade was an impressive fortress. It was roughly circular, as befitted an artifact of a Disk culture (though this was still an oddity, since this was evidently a Sword-culture enclave within the Disk-culture Sphere), with outer walls about eighty feet high. These were braced by a triangular pattern of towers extending upward another twenty feet. Within this large enclosure was the keep: a massive stronghold substantially taller than the main wall, overlooking an entire lake—for the castle was an island in a lake formed by the damming of the River Donnybrook. Beyond the lovely water the mountains rose into the sky, their peaks snow-girt. To the east the ascent was virtually vertical, with cliffs the height of the castle plunging into the water. Only to the south, where the dam was, and to the north where the narrow river emerged, was there room for a level road.

"The stables," said Kade. He showed the way through a

passage lined with chambers containing multiply wheeled creatures. "Planet Keep is within the old Sphere Sador, as reflected in the Shield of Arms. Sadors are wheeled entities, from the sapients to the sentients. But these are good steeds, as strong and responsive as the horses of ancient Earth." His suppressed ire could not conceal his pride in his stock.

Herald was unable to visualize how such creatures might be ridden, as their wheels projected in six directions. But he nodded affirmatively. The remainder of the premises were similarly intriguing, but he really was impatient to complete the mission.

At last the Enemy Witness arrived. He was a sapient wheeler, who superficially resembled the wheeled horses, but he was smaller, and his wheels differed, being smoother and finer. The topmost wheel spun rapidly, making vibrations in the air as its angled spokes tuned in. "I am Whirl of Sador, Earl of Dollar," he said, poking one side wheel forward.

A "dollar," Herald remembered, had once been a circular unit of currency formed of metal. So this designation was consistent with the culture. He touched the rim of the wheel with one hand. This, too, was a strong Kirlian entity, with an aural intensity of about fifty. High-aural individuals tended to gravitate to positions of power or responsibility. "Herald the Healer, of Sphere Slash, Andromeda."

Privately, he marveled at the similarity of name-concepts; he had not so long ago interviewed an entity called "Whorl." But this was a different planet, and a different species, and a different language. Only the coincidence of his recent experience in the other galaxy made the analogy apparent. Herald had a natural tendency to integrate diverse factors; that was part of his skill as a healer and developer of Shields of Arms. But he also had to recognize when a juxtaposition was meaningless, as in this case. Whirl ... Whorl ... perhaps a multilingual intellectual riddle could be fashioned from it!

"Now we shall meet the subject for exorcism," Kade said stiffly. He snapped his fingers again. "Advise the Lady of our approach," he said to the servant who appeared.

They proceeded to an upper room. Kade lifted a heavy fiber bar from its crude catch which freed the door to swing open. So the Lady was a captive!

Inside, a small figure stood facing the narrow window.

39

She did not turn or react as they entered. To Herald she conveyed an impression of forlorn indifference rather than anger or fear. She wore a sleek tunic shaped to be subtly feminine, and light slippers on her dainty feet. A female child, reminiscent of Smallbore of Metamorphic, but somewhat older. Certainly no demon!

"My daughter, the Lady Kade," the Duke said.

The figure turned, and Herald saw that she was indeed a lady, albeit a young one, barely nubile by the standards of the species.

"Herald the Healer, the exorcist," Kade said tightly. "Whirl of Dollar, Enemy Witness." His irony verged on discourtesy, but no one took overt notice. "If I may now absent myself from these proceedings. . . ."

Now the Lady reacted, albeit timorously. "Father. . . ." Her voice was thin and sweet, tinged with fear. The breast of her tunic pulsed slightly with the beat of her human heart beneath it, another hint of the tension that gripped her.

"Herald is a Cluster-famous healer," the Duke told her, his voice abruptly softening. "He would not destroy his reputation by harming you. The Earl is a creature of honor; he rests in judgment of the proceedings, not of you. When these two entities ascertain that you are innocent, they will make their reports and depart, and all will be well again."

"It has never been well," she said. But she seemed reassured.

Kade turned an inscrutable look upon Herald and the Witness. Without further word, he spun on his feet and departed.

Whirl settled on his side wheels. "I merely witness," he said. "I do not interfere."

Herald understood that there was a great deal he had not been told. But he preferred to obtain his information in his own fashion.

"Lady, may I touch you?" he asked, unsmiling. A smile was a stretching of the human mouth to suggest happiness or good intent, but at this stage it would have been hypocritical. He had been presented as an agent of the enemy, tolerated only because of terms imposed. Already he knew that the social or political situation was a large part of the problem. This girl might be an innocent focus, attacked by the enemy because she was dear to the Duke.

She put out one delicate hand as though suffering its amputation, while averting her gaze. Herald extended his own hand slowly, so as not to startle her into flight, and touched the tips of her small fingers.

She had a respectable but not remarkable aura of twenty-five, its type typical of a rare but established aural family. It exhibited the patina of stress, but was essentially normal and healthy. She was certainly not possessed by any alien aura.

She felt the tremendous healing power of his own aura, like none known in the Cluster for three thousand years—and melted. Her face turned to him, the large eyes focusing. They were orange, like her father's. The sunrise of hope emerged from the vacant gaze and seemed to illuminate her golden hair. In that slow moment she expanded from the forlorn child into a shining young woman, a truly regal Lady.

The Earl lifted on his wheels. "Supercircular!" he exclaimed. "With one touch you have transformed her! Even I, alien to your form, can perceive the miracle!" Then he broke off, stopping his communication wheel. And spun it again, momentarily. "Apology. I promised not to interfere."

The Lady turned to the Sador, but retained contact with Herald. "How is it that you, the Enemy Witness, react so positively to my pleasure? Do you not wish to burn me?"

"No, Lady, no!" the Earl exclaimed. "I wish you *cured*, that this unhealthy strife may be gone from fair Keep. Kastle Kade was ever the bulwark against deceit and oppression, the strongest and truest wheel of the King. Only this—this misfortune prevents it from being so again. I am enemy not to you or to your father, but to the demon possession that took your illustrious mother and threatens you. Be as you are at this instant, and we are all friends."

There was no mistaking the sincerity of the Earl's expression. Yet this was strange, for there should have been no need to summon a healer if the opposing factions were so eager to settle their differences.

"This girl suffers no possession," Herald said. "Her aura is rare but normal."

But now the Sador became adamant. "She is normal *now*, Healer. And perhaps with your help she will be normal always. But she has been possessed, and this is our concern."

41

"Perhaps we suffer a confusion of terms," Herald said. "By 'possession' I refer to the inhabitation of a host by a hostile, malevolent aura, what was historically termed 'hostaging.'"

"Precisely."

"This is not the case, here. Since an aura can be removed from a given host only by Transfer, the Lady cannot have been possessed—unless there is a Transfer unit in this castle. Then of course the hostile aura could have directed her to that instrument, and departed. But normally a good host is not given up so readily. And of course a foreign aura cannot control a host without the acquiescence of that host—"

"A demon can," Whirl said. "We of Keep know of cases."

Local superstition, Herald was sure. "Still, the other restrictions remain. Without a Transfer unit—"

"There is no Transfer unit here," the Earl said. "As Witness, I brought equipment to verify this."

"Exactly my point, sir. Since an alien aura could not have departed, and since there is none present now, possession cannot have been the case."

Still the Sador wheeled his ground. "It *has* been the case. I do not attempt to explain it, I merely affirm that it is so."

Herald returned to the girl, whose hand he still held. "Do you know whereof he speaks, Lady?"

"No, sir," she said. "I have never suffered siege by a hostile aura, though it is true that here on Keep such things can occur. My father believes that our enemies seek to harm him through me; to terminate the lineage of Kade, that they may accede to the spoils. Therefore this charge."

Herald nodded; the same suspicion had occurred to him. Heraldic manner often accompanied heraldic politics, the other face of the coin.

"False!" the Earl cried, his wheel seeming almost to fly off with his vehemence. "We are no part of such dishonor. We care only for the repute and welfare of our fine planet!"

Herald removed his hand from the Lady and stepped toward Whirl. "May I touch you again, Dollar?"

"I insist!" And the Sador extended his front wheel.

The contact showed considerable agitation of aura, but there was no deceit in it. The Earl was completely sincere.

"This is a problem," Herald said. "Your position seems unreasonable, yet you uphold it honestly. Is this typical of the forces you represent?"

"It is typical, Healer. It is not unreasonable. We have had experience. There is a demon among us, and the Lady Kade is now its focus. We do not profess to comprehend its mechanism; that is why we summoned you."

There might be a demon about, Herald thought, but it seemed to have possessed the enemy, not the Lady! He returned to her. "I cannot heal what needs no healing. Unless this demon manifests itself for me—"

"It will," the Sador said. "You have merely to remain here until it happens."

"I had expected to return within hours to my own Galaxy."

"If you do, and the demon manifests again, we shall have to burn the Lady," the Sador said. "Please do not force this course upon us; we regard it as an abomination."

"Burn her! In the Lady's presence, the Enemy Witness speaks thus!" Herald remarked with edged reproach. "Burning is characteristic of demons, not of Ladies."

"The Enemy Witness is a creature of honor," the girl said coldly. Much of her glow had faded when Herald's contact ceased, but she retained some spirit and now regarded him as an ally, not an alien technician. "They burned my mother."

"Not we!" the Earl cried. "That was an act of dishonor. We executed the perpetrators. Now we seek to abate the problem positively, amicably."

Herald raised his two hands. "This is too much for me to comprehend in fragments. Allow me to speak with the Lady more gently."

"Yes! Yes!" the Sador cried. "I remain only because I must. I shall be silent, as I am supposed to be."

"Talk with me as long as you want," the Lady said to Herald. "Only hold my hand while you do. It drives away the fear."

Herald took her hand again. "This is because I am a healer." He led her to the couch, and they sat down together. "What is your given name?"

"Psyche." She smiled, and her face shone, the light blue complementing the gold. "Oh, I know you do this for money, Herald, but I wish you could stay with me always. Then the horror could never come near."

43

The horror of burning—or of possession? There was certainly something strange here, and it reminded him again uncomfortably of Smallbore's warning. What dread was he about to encounter? But he concealed his doubt. "When you are healed, you will not require such support," he told her. "Please tell me, in your own way, how this situation came about. I am an outsider, and there is much I do not know."

Without further ado, the Lady told her story.

"I was aged twelve years of Sol when the demon came to Kastle Kade. It possessed the body of my mother, the Duchess of Kade. She was a striking woman, with fair tresses falling to her buttocks and a piercing orange gaze, her skin the delicate color of our world of derivation, Planet Kade. Men said she was the most beautiful human female of Keep, and that I would one year resemble her.

"But when the demon took her, she flashed fire. She took a laser sword and slew our steward, saying he had made improper advances to her. My father believed her, for otherwise he would have had to put her on trial. But I knew the steward was innocent; he had a mistress who would have slain him herself had he considered another woman. I think it was my mother who made the advances —and I know she would never have done it had she not been possessed. The demon, for what purpose we cannot grasp, had desired to compromise the man.

"Possession is a very real threat here on Planet Keep, for we have many powerful and malignant auras. We are a kind of prison planet. Political criminals and the incorrigible partisans of dangerous sects are Transferred here and given animal hosts. It was once thought to be impossible for a sapient to occupy a subsapient host, but modern techniques have made it possible. If the sentence is death, the prisoners are allowed to remain in their animal hosts until their auras fade entirely. If it is merely exile, they are recovered shortly before their auras expire, assuming their hosts have not been killed by other animals. Sometimes a Pretender will be renovated when the political situation on his home planet changes to favor him. It can take years for a high-Kirlian mind to fade.

"There is little proof of this, but circumstantial evidence suggests that some of these prisoners learn to control their animal hosts, perhaps by conditioning their inferior minds to obey directives that make life easier and safer for the animals. Our legends claim that a few of these high-aura entities are capable of Transferring spontaneously from their animal hosts to human hosts, and that they then condition the sapient minds in much the fashion as they did the subsapient minds. Since these entities are desperate schemers, often criminals, such possession leads to much mischief. This would have explained what happened to my mother. But my father would not hear of it. He has ever been blindly loyal to his own. He treated her with even greater deference than before; indeed, it seemed he preferred her this way, for she did have much enhanced personality and will.

"For two years my mother's machinations continued. I had been very close to her, but now I was not. There was no doubt her character had altered. She conspired almost openly to gain the crown itself. My father tried to restrain her from such treachery, but she had woven such a tangled web of deceit and promise that he had little effect. Perhaps the spirit that possessed her was fading, for there were brief moments when her old personality manifested itself and I could feel close to her again. In its desperation that spirit resorted to ever-harsher measures to obtain its objectives before it was rendered defunct by time and its alien host. Only the return to its natural body could restore it, and if that body were hidden from the knowledge of man, perhaps imprisoned in some oubliette far from the light of day, that return would be pointless until by political machination that body were freed. So the full power of the Throne of Keep might have been necessary to its purpose.

"Then my father was summoned for a conference with the King. The reason was not stated, but everyone knew it was to answer privately to a charge of treason. My father was known to be loyal to the King, so the matter was circumspectly handled. If he should turn over his wife for trial, no onus would attach to him.

"My mother—I call her that, though I know she was no longer that—knew the peril she was in. She waited only until my father was safely on his way, then she departed for another castle, intent on further mischief. I wished there were something I could do to stop her and save him, but I was restricted to the castle. She had bribed and threatened our servants, and in his absence they obeyed her unwillingly but certainly.

"Then her party was ambushed, and she was captured by an outlaw band of knights with covered shields. They took her and burned her at the stake.

"When my father returned and discovered what had happened, he organized his forces for vengeance. Kade is the most powerful dukedom on the planet. Only the Duke of Qaval can marshal similar forces, and Qaval is far away. No one in this region could stand against Kade. But just before he marched, the outlaws were trapped by the Marquis of Maryland and slaughtered to a creature. Their heads were impaled on lances and set before Kastle Kade by way of apology for the act.

"I became Lady of the estate, and there was peace. It was whispered that my father, knowing of his wife's treachery, had permitted himself to be called away so that the execution could occur without his seeming sanction, and that the Marquis of Maryland had further acted to protect the reputation of Kade by preventing any possible interrogation of those who had done the King's business. I do not think my father would lend himself to such deceit, but I do not know for sure. Perhaps it was planned without his knowledge, and he lacked the means to substantiate his suspicion, so held his tongue. But I am quite sure he would not suffer himself to be so manipulated a second time.

"A few months ago the mutterings began again. Now they said the demon had not died, but had somehow Transferred itself to a new host—to me. Perhaps this is the way of such possession: The alien aura can move only on the death of its prior host. My father never speaks now of my mother; I believe the King showed him such evidence as could not be denied, and that my father was returning to yield her up for trial when she was killed. But now he is freed from the onus of doing that, and will not admit that there was ever a shadow on the House of Kade. He knows that there is no demon in me, and he protects me more closely than he did my mother. He locks me in my room at night, that no one may even suspect me of mischief, but he does this from his great love for me. Perhaps the enemy did have cause against my mother, but they have no cause against me.

"Yet they have persisted, and when my father refused to let me be interrogated by their experts, they took up arms against him, a coalition controlled by Prince Circlet of Crown. The King did not actually commit himself. But before it came to battle, a compromise was reached: The leading Healer of the Cluster, one whose expertise could not be questioned by either faction, would be summoned to perform an exorcism in this castle, abolishing the demon. If he were successful, all would be well again. If not, I would be delivered to the King for interrogation and treatment. If that proved I was subject to demon Possession, I would be destroyed, for such potential hosts cannot be tolerated in our society."

She turned to face the Earl of Dollar. "Witness, have I omitted aught?"

Whirl spun his wheel in momentary confusion, taken aback by the sudden question. "Naught, Mistress," he said, embarrassed. "You have spoken more than I preferred to have you know."

Herald considered this remarkable history, delivered so lucidly despite the aspect of innocence of the narrator. The young Lady of Kade was neither stupid nor ignorant!

"But I *am* that healer—and you are not possessed," he said.

She smiled. "I think I *am* possessed—by you."

Now he was on better ground. "There are perturbations of aura that occur in Transfer hosts," Herald said. "I have analyzed such cases many times. It is not an effect that is deleterious to the host, merely an involuntary signature left behind, the imprint of the visiting aura upon the hostaura. This occurs regardless of the comparative strength of the two auras, or who controls the body. Your own aura has no such imprint. I speak as an expert in this regard: You have never been host to a foreign aura."

Psyche turned to the Sador. "How say you now, Witness?"

"I regret to say the expert is mistaken," Whirl declared.

Herald made a human shrug. "You are free to summon another exorcist. I doubt his verdict will differ."

"We are *not* free to do this," Whirl said. "By the covenant, your verdict governs. Yet you are mistaken. On your wheels be the onus."

"In my Sphere of Slash, such a statement would constitute a challenge to laser combat," Herald said. "Still I am aware you mean no offense. How may I satisfy you as to the validity of my verdict?"

"Only remain long enough to perceive the nature of your error. Perhaps a few days will suffice."

"A few days! I intend to be home in Andromeda in hours!"

The Sador was unmoved. "Is it convenience that guides you—or truth?"

Herald sighed inwardly. This round, wheel-spinning creature had considerable force of personality! "I shall consult with the Duke."

"He will be in the trophy room," Psyche said, taking his arm like the Lady she was, and guiding him along. The Sador rolled after them unobtrusively. Herald noted that though the castle stairs were not fitted with ramps, the wheeled creature had no problem negotiating the steps. He was able to use his front and back wheels as stops while maneuvering with the side wheels. A wheel set crosswise to the direction of motion was quite effective as a brake, and Dollar was physically constructed so that two wheels were always sidewise, easy to drop into place.

The trophy room was filled. Cups, helmets, swords, lances, and other weapons lay on tables and under glass, and Shields of Arms covered the walls. The Achievements of families of far-flung Spheres were much in evidence. Even at a glance, Herald recognized several, and knew them to be authentic. This, more than anything else, demonstrated the power and galactic awareness of the Duke of Kade.

The Duke turned to face them, evincing some of the same tight mannerisms his daughter had. "Your verdict?" he asked Herald coldly.

"The Lady Kade is not now, and has never been, possessed by any foreign aura," Herald said. "I testify to this as an expert in aural matters, and will so report officially. I recommend that you verify this by obtaining an aural printout for computer analysis. My visit here has been an unnecessary expense for you."

If the Duke was gratified by this report, he did not show it. He turned to the Sador. "Witness?"

"Protest," the Earl said. "I do not question the expert's sincerity or competence; indeed, I have been extremely impressed by his power of aura. But he has examined the subject at a moment of quiescence and has not perceived the nature of the Possession. Neither can this be verified by any machine printout. Were it an ordinary case, we should have had definitive evidence before this."

Kade placed his five-fingered blue hands behind him, linked, and paced in two small circles, forming the pattern of a lemniscate, the symbol of infinity used in mathematics and the Tarot. Unconscious symbolism, surely!

"Witness, you are aware that the expert was summoned at your behest, not mine, and was chosen by your group, not mine. I abstained entirely from the examination. Now he has ruled against you."

"I am aware. But in the performance of my duty as Witness, I must ask that the expert be retained until the Possession manifests."

"There *is* no Possession!" Kade shouted explosively. "He would have to remain until my daughter died of ancient age." But he calmed himself immediately, exerting the personal discipline of his station in this society. "Apology. It behooves me to see that the Witness is completely satisfied. Set us a period for Herald of Slash to remain. If he still aquits my daughter, then you must needs be satisfied."

"This depends on the time allotted," Whirl said dubiously. "I am certain that Possession will manifest, but uncertain *when*. It might occur within the hour, or as long as a Keep-month from now."

Herald's host spoke briefly, internally, sensing confusion. "A Keep-month is the period of revolution of our largest moon, which is ten Sol days or one point four Andromedan units."

/Thank you,/ Herald replied to him.

"Then we shall retain him for a month!" Kade was saying. "As far as I am concerned, Possession will never manifest. But a month it is—for your satisfaction."

"I cannot stay that time!" Herald protested. "I have other appointments—"

"I shall reimburse you for your lost fees," Kade said dryly. "I believe I command sufficient resources to accommodate such a commitment."

"*We* shall reimburse him," Whirl said. "He remains at our behest. But he must accompany the Lady continuously, that the manifestation not be missed."

"Not at night, surely!" the Duke said.

"Night is the most likely occasion. He must be there."

Herald shook his head, aware of the possible complica-

49

tions this invoked. "This is not entirely a matter of fee or human propriety," he said. "I have commitments. Other creatures require my help. Some may die. I cannot allocate so much time to a single case."

"I shall pay their way here to see you!" the Duke cried, as if dealing with a spurious objection. Then, to Whirl: "My daughter is nubile. The presence of a man in her chamber at night would militate against her honor."

"I *must* be present," Whirl insisted. "I am the Witness. I assure you I have no dishonorable interest in—"

Herald suppressed a smile. "Witness, he refers to me. I am an alien creature, but I am at the moment in human form. I believe Solarians of opposite sex are not encouraged to share night facilities unless they are married."

"Precisely," Kade said. "My daughter's repute must be chaste, for potential marriage. The presence of a man in her room at night, however justified, would cast a shadow."

"Who would she marry, unless she were free of the demon?" Whirl asked. Then he quickly qualified himself. "Of the suspicion of Possession?"

"Would any of your scions be available as grooms, were she so freed?" Kade demanded.

"We do have human allies," the Sador said. "The Scion of Skot, for example. Historically the Klans of Skot and Kade were once united, serving with honor in the Second War of Energy. The young Solarian Skot may not be averse. Your daughter is mooted to be very pretty by the standards of your species, and an alliance between Klan Skot and the Dukedom of Kade would be politically—"

"Enough, Earl. You have made your point." The Duke returned to Herald. "You will remain here a month, and my daughter shall not leave your presence. The Enemy Witness shall stand chaperone. Your forthcoming appointments will be conducted to you, or granted the services of other healers, fee covered by Planet Keep. Satisfactory?"

Herald spread his human hands. "If this is so important to you—"

"It is a colossal waste of your time and my money," Kade said. "But less waste than war would be. I indulge this foolishness that the Enemy Witness be satisfied, that there be peace on our world, and the Lady Kade be untainted by any suspicion whatever."

"This is satisfactory," Whirl said reluctantly. "Please convey the nature of this compromise to the King."

"Instantly." And the Duke stalked off.

Herald turned to Psyche. "We did not ask your sentiment," he said. "Do you comprehend what this entails?"

"I wish you could stay longer," she said, with a smile of not-quite-childlike innocence.

They had a sumptuous meal of Sador steak dressed in pseudo-Terran gravy, green savor-bread, and wheelwasp wine. Herald discovered that his human host had a reasonably cultured perception of taste, and he enjoyed himself more than he had anticipated. But afterward he had to retire to the privy to perform the Solarian function of relief that necessarily followed digestion. That would have been a messy business, had his host not been experienced.

"A client of yours has arrived," the Duke informed Herald as he emerged. "Hweeh of Weew awaits you in the library." He smiled with grim humor.

Herald remembered the entry in his schedule. Treatment for shock, and the Shield of Arms for a family within the Segment of Weew, Milky Way Galaxy. Routine. Odd that the entity should be brought here so promptly. He offered his arm in courtly fashion to Psyche, as she had to come with him, and together with Whirl they went to the library.

Around the walls of this room were shelves bearing great numbers of quaint old-fashioned Solarian printed books. Herald was sure that few contemporary Solarians could read the archaic symbols of these texts, but was just as sure that the Duke of Kade was among those who *could*. Education sometimes took strange forms!

A lump of gray protoplasm huddled on the floor. Herald looked at it, startled. "They mattermitted him!"

"He must be very important," Psyche said.

"Or very rich." He glanced at her. "Kastle Kade has a mattermission receiver?"

"No. He must have arrived at the castle of the King, and been shipped here by mailcoach while we ate."

Herald assessed the situation. "A Weew in shock should not be on the cold floor. I shall have to make him comfortable. Psyche—I mean, Lady Kade—"

"Psyche," she said, smiling.

"Psyche, please sit quietly in that chair. Whirl, make

51

yourself comfortable but obscure. I do not object to an audience, but it is possible that my client will. Have either of you encountered a physical Weew before?"

Psyche shook her head no. "Only in Transfer," Whirl said.

"Then do not be alarmed at what passes. Weew are special creatures."

The two made themselves inconspicuous. Herald kneeled beside the lump. Slowly he extended his hand, touching its dull surface. His aura focused, imbuing the creature, whose own aura was quite respectable: between 120 and 125, the uncertainty owing to distortion from shock. That deepened the mystery of why the Weew had not been Transferred. Since aura inevitably faded in a foreign host, albeit slowly, only high-intensity Kirlians could leave their natural bodies for extended periods. But this Weew's aura was well above that threshold.

Mattermission of physical bodies across galactic distances was so prohibitively expensive that it was an extreme rarity; many millions of molecular messages could be transmitted for the same price. Hweeh obviously should have been assigned to another healer, or allowed to wait until Herald could come to Segment Weew himself. Or the Weew could have been Transferred to a host on Planet Keep, as Herald himself had been. Transfer was *the* way to travel.

True, the host would have been thrown into Hweeh's state of shock, but Herald could have cured that as readily in a local host as in the Weew body. Shock was not a dangerous condition for a Weew; it was a natural defense mechanism. Treatment was as likely to be effective after a considerable delay as when immediate, and often the subject recovered spontaneously. So some entity in Segment Weew was inordinately anxious to have this creature functional, rapidly—and that was another signal for caution. Herald did not merely accept his fee for service blindly rendered; he acted for the benefit of his specific client. If an immediate recovery was not in Hweeh's interest, Herald would decline the case.

As the mighty aura suffused it, the lump turned brown, then red, glowing slightly. "Auditory," Herald murmured in Clustric, the common language of the civilizations of the Cluster. All sapients had to master it before indulging in interstellar commerce or receiving advanced educative degrees. "Sound. Sound. Sound. Sound."

The lump quivered. A projection developed, forming into a horn. "Sound," it honked in the same language.

Good. This *was* an educated creature, as he had suspected. Peon-entities hardly rated mattermission! "Thank you," Herald said. "In addition, visual. Sight. Sight."

The Weew body grew another projection. An eyeball formed in a socket on the end of a stalk. It twisted around, blinking.

"Very good," Herald continued encouragingly. "I am Herald the Healer, here to help you. Are you comfortable where you are?"

"I am Hweeh of Weew. I find the floor rigid and overly conductive of calories, with cracks."

"It is fitted stone, a poor insulator of heat. If you will form appendages, you may mount this resilient couch."

Hweew extruded three pegs, lifted his body high, and dumped himself into the couch. "Much better," he said, letting the limbs retract and disappear into his torso.

"I am told you are in shock," Herald said. "Are you able to explain to me the nature of the occasion for your withdrawal?"

The eyestalk shuddered. "I do not remember. Is it a matter of importance?"

"I presume so, since your Sphere has taken considerable trouble to bring you to me."

"Perhaps it is described in the manifest." Hweeh writhed, and from his substance popped out a pellet. "Yes, here is one. Do you wish to imbibe it?"

"In this host, I am unable. Please digest it for me."

The pellet sank into Hweeh's mass. Herald knew the creature was dissolving it by means of generated acids, and absorbing the fluids it contained. The chemicals of its composition amounted to a refined Weew code. A given message could be brief or day-long. A number of other creatures of the Cluster had learned to assimilate and interpret these code-fluids, but very few Solarians had mastered this particular talent.

@@@@@, Hweeh said.

"I do not comprehend the Weew language in this host," Herald said. "Can you provide a Clustric translation? It need not be exact."

53

"Sorry. I can as readily provide a Quotes translation, if you wish. You appear to be in a Quote host."

So the Weew knew Solarian! He was *really* educated!

"That would be excellent, Hweeh."

"I present the manifest," Hweeh said in quite passable Solarian Quotes. "Bearer is Hweeh of Planet Swees, Sphere Rweer, Segment Weew, Galaxy Milky Way. Hweeh is engaged in the occupation of research astronomy, specializing in Fringe-Cluster phenomena. He is the Segment's finest practitioner of this discipline. He was found in shock amid the tools of his research. The final words recorded by his research computer were @ The Space Amoeba is—@"

Hweeh's aura fluctuated wildly as he stopped reading. Herald whipped his hand out to touch the Weew's flushed flesh, but he was too late; the creature had gone into secondary shock.

"Damn!" Herald swore in Solarian idiom. "I have compounded his problem." The horn and eyeball sagged back into the graying mass. "I am sorry," Herald said, though he knew the creature could no longer hear him. But what counted was the healing power of his aura, softening the wound, causing the flesh to relax. "Rest, sleep, recuperate, estivate. I will be with you anon."

Only when he was sure Hweeh was resting quietly did Herald remove his hand. "I blundered. I should have anticipated that the manifest was not for his own perception."

He looked about. "You may speak now. The Weew has dissolved his ear; he cannot hear you."

"What is this 'Space Amoeba'?" Psyche inquired immediately.

"This I must now ascertain. I believe I have prevented him from suffering actual regression, but before I animate him again I must have more information. Does this library contain references on astronomy?"

"Oh, yes!" she said eagerly. "Kastle Kade has the best library on the planet, except for the King's royal archives." She tripped across the room to the far wall and touched a book. At once a holograph formed in a readout globe in the corner. Herald had not even noticed this before, or realized that these books were holo-keyed; this local culture was not quite as archaic as he had assumed.

The image showed the Milky Way Galaxy in all its

splendor. Quickly the three-dimensional image expanded, the outer coils of the Galaxy moving out of view. The stars of Segment Etamin appeared—bright blue Rigel, red Betelgeuse, the three jewels of Orion's Belt, where the notorious Melody of Mintaka had lived. And of course Sador, and Etamin itself, nucleus of the Segment. Sol hardly showed, being a comparatively dim star, but in a geography of historical power, Sol would have loomed like a late supernova. Flint of Outworld had been a Solarian, subverting the nameless Slash sent to nullify him, and finally marrying her after both had died in the Hyades. Flint had put Etamin on the Cluster map and brought his species a notoriety that was largely undeserved. Savior of the Milky Way—as though the accident of sudden parity of Ancient science had had nothing to do with it! Thereafter, Solarians and Polarians had infiltrated the governing councils of Galaxy Milky Way, especially after the Second War of Energy. It was the continuing machinations of Solarian oppression that were felt most keenly by the downtrodden Spheres of Galaxy Andromeda. That was one reason the Solarians were the butt of thinly veiled Andromedan humor, the pretense that all creatures of Sol were basically barbarians, even though that concept was one or two thousand years out of date. But this was not his concern for the moment.

"Look up the term 'Space Amoeba,'" Herald said.

She adjusted the main control, and a new picture formed in the globe. The narrator's voice said: "Space Amoeba: a formation of Fringe-Cluster matter whose specific nature is conjectural. Emanating from a postulated point source, dust has spread out in a restricted pattern over the course of several decades to form a partially opaque cloud approximately one hundred light-years—thirty parsecs—in diameter. Uncertainties of measurement have made it suffer seemingly protein shifts of structure, from which its name derives; even its projected expansion is questioned by some authorities as its shape is not typical of the shell-remnants of supernovas. Limited radiospectrography suggests it is composed of solid particles admixed with diffuse gases. Formation is sparse, appearing only on the most specific and recent surveys. No evidence of nova activity in that region. Further definition must await direct investigation."

"Just the kind of thing a good research astronomer

should be interested in," Psyche remarked. "It certainly seems obscure enough."

Herald peered at the vague image in the globe. It was hardly more than a smear, apparently a tenuous obfuscation of background galaxies. There was obviously not much to it, but the enhancement of its substance provided by the holograph retouch artist did make it seem to have branching lines of movement extending from the nucleus, like the fluxes of a living cell. So it had been dubbed the Space Amoeba, gaining an allure and mystery that hardly seemed justified by the facts.

"Where is it?" he asked.

Psyche checked. "Just off Furnace," she announced.

Furnace! But immediately he caught himself. His forced fiancée could have nothing to do with this. He could not afford to let subjective personal matters interfere with his job. He had to understand the astronomy, the research implications. What was there in the Amoeba that had sent this specialist into shock? Why should Segment Weew think it so urgent that Hweeh be healed rapidly? Obviously *they* took the matter seriously.

"Are there any entities of Weew here on Keep?" Herald inquired aloud.

"There surely are, in Transfer," Whirl replied.

"I would like to interview a Weew scientist or other learned entity, if this can be arranged."

"It can be arranged," Psyche said happily. She was making herself useful, and it illuminated her. She crossed the room again, her tresses drawing back prettily as she traveled. There was something about the human form, at least as it was expressed by the nascently mature female, that had a peculiar appeal.

She spoke into a decorative communicator, styled to resemble a two-thousand-year-old Solarian vidphone. "Call to educated scientist of Weew, from Herald the Healer, Kastle Kade."

There was a silence of several seconds. Then the form of a Sador sapient appeared in the screen. Its wheel spun.

"Swees of Weew, in Transfer, vocation logistic mathematician retired, avocation specialty Bhyo literature of pre-Sphere century. Segment doctorates in each subject. Will the Healer converse with me?"

Herald made a silent human whistle. When he asked for an educated Weew, that was exactly what he got!

"I am gratified that an entity of your qualifications has chosen to respond. Permit me to explain that I am—"

"It is well known that the greatest Healer of the Cluster is visiting our planet to resolve the alleged Possession of the heiress of Kade, and that he also specializes in heraldic definition." For a moment the Shield of Arms of the family of Swees of Weew flashed on the screen. "It is my privilege to assist you without the burden of further explanation on your part."

"This is generous," Herald said, slightly miffed by the evident publicity his effort had received. He did not regard himself as such a celebrity! "This does not concern the heiress of Kade, but a client of your own Segment. Could you tell me whether a specialist in astronomy would be subject to shock merely by what he observed in research?"

"Oh, is Hweeh there already?"

"You know about that too?" Herald asked, astonished.

"He hails from the planet I was named after, Swees, so naturally I am interested. But to answer your substantive question: No, such an entity would hardly be shocked in that manner. Hweeh is our leading research astronomer, noted for a number of conceptual breakthroughs. I have had occasion to review certain backup mathematics in connection with his work in the past, and regard him as a first-class mind. I understand he is high-Kirlian; perhaps that accounts for his abilities."

"Were that the case, I would be a genius-entity," Herald said. "Alas, I am not. Would Hweeh be likely to be shocked by mere reference to the single term @ Space Amoeba @ ?"

"Ah, you render it in Weew inflection! I am not conversant with that term, but I hardly think so. The only thing that could shock a research astronomer would be a concept of such surprise and magnitude as to represent a Galactic threat. But I hardly think such a thing is likely to occur in that specialty."

Galactic threat. . . . "But if such a threat should exist, why would he not simply advise his Segment government, or the Galactic Council?"

Swees paused, his wheel spinning reflectively. "I really do not know. I conjecture that the threat might be so immediate or pervasive as to be incapable of resolution. That, at least, is what would send *me* into shock. But surely he could have discovered no threat that has not existed for

57

many centuries. No, I rather think that some personal factor is in operation. If he had monetary or romantic problems—"

"Then why should his Segment hasten to mend him, even undertaking the expense of mattermission?"

Swees reflected again. "An intriguing riddle that offers no immediate answer. Perhaps, then, there *is* a threat, and only his insight can clarify its nature. Is this Space Amoeba by chance a living entity? Perhaps a viral mutation—"

"I doubt it," Herald said. "It is a diffuse particle-and-gas formation in deep space beyond Furnace, photographed decades ago. He was studying it when he went into shock, and its mere mention returns him to that state."

"Then I think it would be wise to ascertain whatever he knows, rapidly," Swees said. "Perhaps it is a false alarm, but an astronomer of his repute certainly should know his concepts! I cannot imagine what threat he sees, but I am not versed in his specialty. Perhaps this is just as well, for if I understood the exact concept I also might go into shock. Shall I call you if I have further insight?"

"Please do," Herald said. "I appreciate your discussion. I shall be here for a local month."

"It has been a pleasure." Swees faded out.

Herald turned to Whirl and Psyche. "You have necessarily witnessed my treatment of another client. I request that you not discuss this matter with others. I must allow Hweeh to rest now, but there will be another session."

"It is fascinating!" Psyche said. "Both the mystery and your mode of treatment. You do not merely lay on hands, you study your case like any doctor. You are such a competent entity. I hardly feel worthy of your attention."

"There may be a parallel between the two cases," the Sador remarked.

"Oh, do you think the Weew is possessed too?" Psyche asked brightly. "Should he be burned at the stake?"

"Your irony is painful to me, Lady, as you intend," Whirl said gravely. "Nevertheless, I reply: Possession might most readily account for his condition."

"He is not possessed," Herald said. "He has suffered conceptual shock, and I am now satisfied that his case warrants my attention. The two cases *are* parallel, in the mystery surrounding them and in the belief by others that a serious threat exists whose focus is in these entities."

"I wrong you, Earl," Psyche said contritely. "I apologize and beg forgiveness. There is a parallel."

"Forgiven, gracious Lady," Whirl said. "We are in an unkind situation."

Perceiving that apology by the Lady, Herald felt a brief tingle of emotion. He tried to analyze it, but it faded. The subject of possible execution had treated the Enemy Witness with momentary courtesy; it was a nicety of manner, of no other significance. "Shall we return to the Duke?" he inquired.

In the evening Herald was shown to Psyche's suite, along with Whirl.

"I have taken the liberty of installing an extra bed, and of curtaining off my daughter's bed," the Duke said grimly. "The Witness, who is nonhuman, may station himself by the door, in this way being assured that no one enters or departs alone, without himself causing impropriety. He may observe my daughter as he wishes, to verify that no 'Possession' occurs. Are these arrangements satisfactory?"

"Quite," Whirl said.

"You may take turns using the sanitary facilities," the Duke continued. "They have been modified to accommodate the Sador as well as the Solarian form. The servants will appear promptly on, and only on, signal."

"I have no complaint," Herald said.

Kade marched out, his suppressed ire manifest in his gait.

"I'm glad you're here," Psyche confided. "It gets so lonely. At least Mother used to talk to me—when she *was* my mother."

Herald found the press-line on his tunic and tore it open. Psyche made a little shriek and averted her gaze. "Oh, I forget about the clothing convention among Solarians," Herald said. "Apology. Most Cluster sapients, including my own species, do not employ decorative habiliment."

"Solarians do change apparel for sleep," Whirl explained. "But they normally do this in privacy. The sanitary chamber may be used."

"Thank you," Herald said. "I regret my ignorance of night custom. Normally I do not remain so long in a single host, and I neglected to survey the host-mind for such details. May I use the chamber now?"

"Please do," Psyche said, concealing herself behind her curtain, though she remained fully clothed.

Herald was determined to handle the matter on his own this time, instead of drawing on the resources of his host. He had to rehearse all his prior experience in humanoid functions to figure out how to avail himself of the sanitary facilities, but in due course he succeeded, and he emerged clean, in pajamas and with new confidence. Hereafter he would be more competent!

Psyche then went demurely into the chamber, and Herald paused to question the Sador. "Most species improve with exertion. Is this true of Solarians?"

"It is true," the Witness said. "When human creatures make ready for combat, they perform exercises, and soon their muscle tone improves and they become able to achieve greater feats."

"What feats are most useful to them?"

"The ability to run, to move rapidly by foot, seems to be chief among these. Also to carry heavy burdens, and to be able to strike hard and accurately with the hands, or with weapons controlled by the hands."

"So if I should run around this room and carry heavy objects, my physical condition will improve," Herald said.

"That is my understanding."

"Thank you, Witness." Herald picked up a solid chair and lumbered in a circle around the room. Very soon the weight of the chair seemed to become greater, and his feet were coming down hard on the floor. He was puffing air in and out of his lungs with uncomfortable force, a side effect he had not anticipated. But he kept on going.

"What are you trying to do?" his host demanded in his brain, alarmed.

/I am improving this body,/ Herald replied. /If I am to remain in it for ten days, I want it fit./

"Brother!" the host exclaimed. "A fitness freak!"

/You have objection?/

"No, actually I don't. I always figured I should exercise more. But it's uncomfortable, and if it's okay with you, I'll just bug out for the duration."

Meaning: The host would disassociate his consciousness from the activities of the body, not returning unless specifically called. That way he would experience none of the sensations Herald brought about. That was a good idea. /Very well, host. Bug out. Sweet dreams./ And a presence faded. There really wasn't anywhere the host-mind could go except to sleep, but the effect was similar to departure.

Now Herald was staggering, as the muscles refused to respond fully. This was not the fault of the absent host-mind, but a simple function of fatigue. His arms were sending messages of discomfort bordering on pain to his human brain. He was in danger of lurching into a wall, and his breath was rasping through his mouth noisily. He wished he could bug out too. But he had suspected that exercise would not be easy.

Psyche emerged from the sanitary chamber, fresh and clean and sweet-smelling in her slender nightie. It resembled her tunic but was more sheer, making her look thinner somehow, though actually she possessed those feminine attributes that made her, as her father put it, nubile. Her human mouth opened in alarm, and her small mammalian bosom heaved. "Herald! What's the matter?"

Herald, rounding a turn, tried to respond. But he lost his balance and crashed into the wall, dropping the chair. Psyche rushed to help him. "Oh, you're hurt!" she cried.

But her strength was insufficient to support him. Herald slid to the floor, still panting too vigorously to speak intelligibly, and she was carried down with him. She tried to extricate her arm, but succeeded mainly in tearing open his pajama shirt. She leaned over him, her nightie twisted about, falling open at the top. "Where do you hurt? What can I do?" she cried with touching concern.

The bedroom door crashed open. The Duke of Kade stood there, sword drawn. Suddenly Herald knew he was in trouble.

"And I thought it was an enemy raid," Kade said with infinite disgust. "Stand, miscreant, that I may run you through."

But the Sador interposed himself between them, one side wheel spinning so rapidly it started to whine. He was less than half the height of the man, but that wheel faced the Duke, and it looked dangerous. "Hold, Kade, lest you violate the covenant without cause!"

The Duke paused, but his sword did not lower. "Earl, I have not before seen you as a creature of treachery."

"Then heed the truth," Whirl said. "Herald was exercising his host-body, and fell. The Lady sought to lift him,

61

and could not. Both are innocent of malice or connivance."

"This is beyond belief," Kade said savagely. "Must I add your body to that of the molester?"

The molester! Herald saw that the Duke was serious, having jumped to a conclusion, and would not be swayed by reason. What could he say, before getting stabbed by that ill-justified sword? Was this the horror Smallbore had foreseen?

"Father!" Psyche screamed, finally extricating herself. "If the Witness spoke not the truth, he had but to stand aside in silence and let you break the covenant. Then would I be burned, and you with no recourse."

Kade's eyes swiveled to her. "*You,* my child—you vouch for the word of the Witness?"

"It needs no vouching," she said, drawing herself up into a pitiful yet somehow effective formality, facing her father. "Yet I do vouch. I would not have the honor of three honorable creatures sullied on my account. No one molested me, no one wronged you, no treachery occurred. The Witness has borne good witness."

Still Kade stood in silence, the point of his sword covering Herald with dismaying accuracy.

"Does the lord who would not believe evil of his wife, now refuse to believe good of his daughter?" Whirl demanded.

The Duke's muscles convulsed. His sword shook as sudden black rage transformed his features. In that instant he was a complete animal, body tensed for savage action, teeth bared.

Then the Sador's meaning penetrated: not an insult, but a plea for sanity. Herald knew then that whatever had caused the dissolution of the once-great Sphere of Sador, it had not been lack of courage or wit. Whirl had struck with words, far more accurately and effectively than would have been possible with any physical weapon.

Abruptly Kade sheathed his deadly sword. "My daughter I must believe. I apologize to you, Witness, and to you, Healer."

"Accepted," the Earl of Dollar said immediately, and his fighting wheel was stilled.

"Accepted!" Herald gasped.

Now the Duke focused on Herald. "If exercise you

62

must, I shall instruct you in the techniques in the morning."

"Thank you," Herald said, hauling himself to his feet. But the Duke was already departing. He never lingered long for recriminations or explanations.

They retired without further episode, and all was quiet. But before he slept, Herald turned one thought over in his mind. Why *hadn't* Whirl, the Enemy Witness, simply stood aside and allowed the Duke of Kade in the heat of his misunderstanding to violate the covenant by killing Herald? Wouldn't that have served the purposes of the enemy very handily?

He could find only one answer: Whirl was an honest entity who sincerely believed in the case he had made, that the Lady Kade was intermittently possessed, and that this would in time be proven. Whirl wanted the truth to be known, just as the Duke wanted the enemy to be satisfied. Both were honorable entities. Neither would cheat. And that only heightened the dilemma, for both could not be right.

4

Child of Pleasure

&All is ready?&

XResearch units report no political resistance. Survey shows our action units capable of destroying all sapient cultures with minimum damage to environment within three cycles.X

0Action units are prepared to meet this deadline.0

&It is necessary to review purpose.&

XWhat point? It will only delay our mission.X

0In fact, may imperil our mission. More time provides the enemy opportunity to formulate resistance. There are a number of ancient sites in this Cluster remaining operative, and should their technology be employed against us—0

&Error. You have permitted the means to become the end. Herein lies potential disaster. Do you not perceive why?&

XIs there some trap we have not properly researched that could reverse the outcome?X

0Some enemy military capacity we have underestimated? A secret weapon?0

&Pay attention. There is a trap, and there is an enemy —but both are within our own formation. You have lost perception of our actual mission. It is not to overwhelm alien species or to seek new enemies or to promote higher technology; those Cluster species are very like ourselves. Only our science makes us superior, only our power. We cull the Cluster because we have a mission that transcends the personal convenience of ourselves and other species; we accomplish this because we have stability and perseverance others cannot match. But this power must not be abused, lest we destroy what we labor so diligently to promote. Do you remember what that is?&

*X0*Yes.*0X*

&State it.&

*X0*Soul sapience.*0X*

&Therefore we must be certain to identify all potentially soul-sapient species and salvage them. Since this is a very subtle quality in its incipient stage, we must proceed with utmost caution. Suppose we should discover that one of the myriad weed-species we have culled was *the* potential soul sapient?&

*X0*Horror!*0X*

&Precisely. Reverify your findings, itemizing each culture by its potential. Pay special attention to subspecies, such as those £ of Sphere Dash, Andromeda; their gross mass makes other forms of empire impractical for them, encouraging soul sapience. It may be this potential that triggered the site malfunction. When you are satisfied, we shall move.&

*X*It would be better to pick up more samples for direct physical examination.*X*

&No. Piecemeal mattermission of samples would be prohibitively expensive of energy, compromising our sterilization potential. Only if the signs are threshold-positive will we take physical samples.&

In the morning Herald found his muscles radiating pain. He had overextended them, and taken bruises. But the Duke insisted on drilling him in a formal series of calisthenics called squat-jumps, push-ups, pull-ups, sit-ups, and running-in-place. "This program will invigorate the entire body," Kade assured him.

Invigorate? At the end of it, Herald felt even worse than before. But at least he knew how to exercise without crashing into a wall or bringing a girl to the floor.

After breakfast—another sumptuous repast involving the cooked eggs of wheelbirds, diskcakes formed from ground grain, and sweet syrup derived from the digestive tracts of insects—Herald, Psyche, and Whirl settled themselves in the room assigned to Hweeh of Weew, who had become another house guest.

Herald put his hand on the gray mass. "Sound. Sound.

Sound. Sound," he murmured, concentrating. Then, as the ear/speaker horn appeared: "Sight. Sight."

When Hweeh was ready, Herald continued: "I am Herald the Healer. I interviewed you yesterday. We were interrupted. I hope you are comfortable."

Hweeh quivered, testing for comfort. He was now in a large wooden bowl that the Duke's obliging household staff had provided. "Yes, Healer. Most comfortable."

"I am here to treat you for shock. You are a most important research astronomer, and your Segment wants you back in service. I fear they are overworking you, causing you to suffer breakdown."

"By no means!" the Weew responded forcefully. "I am devoted to my work."

"Even though it takes you away from your family?"

"I have no family. Only my work. Without my research slides and tables, I would have no life at all. I am eager to return."

So he was a creature dedicated to his profession, as Herald was to his own. Herald found himself liking this Weew.

"I am eager to have you return, Hweeh. But it is not enough merely to rouse you from shock; we must abate the cause of it. It seems that some facet of your research sent you into shock, and it is necessary that we nullify this before you are exposed to it again."

"Nothing in my research could shock me! What harm or horror can there be in material that has been on record for decades or even centuries or millennia?"

"I took the liberty of consulting with an entity of your Segment, Swees of Weew, a logistic mathematician now retired. He said much the same."

"Oh, yes, the scholar named after my home planet. I had him verify certain of my data once. A fine mind! I must chat with him some time."

"So it seems we have a mystery here that neither my kind nor your kind fathoms. Perhaps you saw something in your telescope—"

Hweeh made a shudder of mirth. "Sir, I use no telescope! I am a *research* astronomer. I would not know even how to turn on a living telescope, or how to aim it. And how could I see anything new? The images I might see in a scope would have taken a million years to reach me. My research holographs, made by survey teams scat-

66

tered throughout the Cluster, and buttressed by periodic information from the Net, are mattermitted to my library. They are far more current than any direct view could be."

"So you are assured that nothing you might perceive through your research could shock you?"

Hweeh changed color briefly. "Oh, I would not make so encompassing a statement as that! Were I to perceive a Cluster-sized black hole developing, its advancing edge within a light-year of the Milky Way—"

"In that event, we would *all* go into shock, not to mention tidal disassembly and eventual compression into nothingness!" Herald said. "But nothing less than that . . . ?"

"Well, even a Galaxy-sized black hole, or a Segment-sized one, if it were close enough. . . ."

"Yes, I daresay it would be an unnerving thing to reside adjacent to even the smallest, cutest black hole! In this you differ from no other sapient species. Yet you did go into shock. Is it likely that you did in fact perceive such a threat?"

"Hardly! Black holes do not manifest so abruptly in that manner. Few natural events *do*. Are you *sure* I was in shock? I might merely have been meditating."

"I am sure, sir," Herald said gravely.

"You will permit me the smallest, cutest skepticism?"

Herald smiled. A lively mind here, not without humor. Certainly not paranoid or confused.

Whirl of Dollar made a quiet buzzing signal. Herald glanced at him. "What is it, Witness?"

"I do not wish to interpose as this is not my business. But I am reminded of my prior conjecture, that there may be a parallel that could offer enlightenment. Not Possession, precisely, but—"

"Who is this?" Hweeh inquired.

"I interview you in a special circumstance," Herald explained. "It is necessary that I keep the company of two other entities. I regret this infringement of your privacy."

"No objection. I have no guilty secrets, unfortunately."

Herald had to smile again. "This is Whirl of Sador, the Earl of Dollar, here to witness my performance on Planet Keep. In the other chair is the Lady Psyche of Kade, another client. They will respect your confidence."

"What is this parallel the Sador sees?"

"You may answer him, Witness," Herald said.

"It is that in each case the subject is not aware of the manifestation, or chooses not to believe in it. The Lady Kade is ignorant of the actuality of our case against her, and the astronomer of Weew is not aware that he goes into shock at the mere utterance of—"

"Hold!" Herald cried.

"A certain phrase," Whirl concluded without pause. Psyche tittered.

"Do I do this?" Hweeh inquired, interested. "What is this phrase?"

"If he told you, you'd zonk out again," Psyche said.

"This has happened in your presence?"

"Yesterday," she assured him.

"I remember yesterday. I thought it was but a moment ago, and wondered why the interruption. And you also suffer a malady of this nature?"

"They say I am possessed," she said. "That an alien aura inhabits me irregularly. That is why the Healer came."

"Yes, I detect the parallel," Hweeh said. "I can appreciate your skepticism, since what is described is not the manner of hostaging. It cannot be intermittent, unless there is Transfer apparatus in the vicinity. May I touch you, Lady?"

She glanced inquiringly at Herald, who was intrigued by this developing interaction between his clients. There seemed to be no harm in it, however. He nodded.

"Certainly," Psyche said. She rose gracefully and crossed to the Weew, extending her hand and resting it lightly on his surface.

"Lady, you are not possessed," Hweeh assured her. "My aura is only half that of the Healer, but it is five times yours. I question strongly whether you have ever been host to a foreign aura."

Herald maintained a discreet silence in the face of this confirmation of his diagnosis. It took an entity of high aura to appreciate the certainty of such a conclusion. There was really scant chance of error. The Witness would have to wheel on this!

Sure enough, Whirl rolled forward. "May I touch you each in turn?"

"Certainly." "Yes." Hweeh and Psyche said together.

The Sador extended a wheel to contact the Weew first.

68

"You do have a very strong aura, much more intense than mine. Then he touched Psyche. "But yours is less than mine. I agree that there is no Possession *now*, and regret that my aural expertise is not sufficient to verify past status. But my belief, and that of those whose interests I represent, is based on other criteria. I retain my position."

"Unfortunate that the Possession cannot be tested as readily as the shock-phase," Hweeh said. "There is much we have yet to learn about each. May I converse with the Lady?"

"If the Lady accedes," Herald said. "I admit to being frustrated in both cases at the moment. If the two of you do not feel your respective privacies are being infringed upon, speak of what you will. It should do no harm."

Psyche brought over her chair and sat beside Hweeh, resting her hand on him again. "This is very interesting," she said. "I have not had so much diversion and good feeling in two years. I never met a physical Weew before."

"I have perhaps been too much absorbed in my work," Hweeh replied. "I had forgotten how pleasant the touch of an innocent young entity could be. Tell me about yourself, if you will, and if you also will, incorporate in subtle fashion reference to the phrase that allegedly sends me into shock. Perhaps we can assist each other."

Herald glanced at Whirl, and caught the glint of the vanes of his communication wheel angled at him. Could the two subjects successfully interrogate each other?

"There is not much to say," Psyche said. "I have never left the planet of Keep, and seldom even Kastle Kade, since the affliction of my mother. Much of my experience has been imaginative. Why even my name means 'Soul' —but surely that would not interest an astronomer."

"Quite opposite, Lady. Your name unites you to my profession most directly, and tells me much about you."

Her eyes widened in one of her cute naive mannerisms. "Really? How so?"

"Modern astronomy is the study and theory of the manifestation of great space," Hweeh said. Again Herald glanced at Whirl, and again met the angled glint of acknowledgement. The Weew had used the term "Space" himself without suffering ill effect. "But research astronomy has a broader base. It also considers the reactions

69

of sapient entities to views of space in past times. Thus I review the mythology of space as well as its geology."

"The geology of space!" Psyche said. "What a nice concept!"

"Indeed yes; this is one of the many fascinations of my work," Hweeh agreed. "But the mythology is as important, for it provides insights into the nature of the conceptualizations of many creatures. Your own kind, the Solarians, have a very rich astronomical symbolism, for example. The brighter stars were in your prehistory considered to be manifestations of divine entities, gods and goddesses, who lived and died in heroic scale. One of your Sol-system planets, Venus, seemed like a bright star to your primitives, and was called the Goddess of Beauty. One of her children was Cupid, the God of Love, and Cupid married Psyche, a mortal girl who must have been very like you. So you see, I know you through my studies."

"I am to marry Cupid?" she asked in wonder. "The God of Love?"

"Your namesake did. For you, perhaps it will be an extremely lovable man. Yet the love of Cupid and Psyche was not without peril."

"Oh, *tell* me!" she cried, clapping her hands girlishly.

"With pleasure. Seldom do I discover so willing an audience for technical matters in my specialty. Psyche was the daughter of a king, and so lovely that she outshone Venus herself. This made Venus jealous, for the emotions of the gods reflected those of their creators. She sent her son, Cupid, to pierce the breast of Psyche with his arrow of love, and make her love the most vile and miserable creature available. This was the goddess's way of punishing the mortal girl whose only fault was beauty. But when Cupid saw Psyche, he was as it were scratched by his own arrow and stricken by love himself.

"Psyche's mortal family knew nothing of this. But somehow no offers for her hand in marriage were made. When the king consulted an oracle to determine whom his daughter should marry, he was told—"

"The Scion of Skot?" Psyche inquired with a twinkle.

But Hweeh was deep in his narrative and did not heed the interjection. "He was told to dress her in clothing of mourning and leave her on a mountain, where a fierce winged serpent would claim her for his bride. So with much regret the king did this. But Psyche was transported from the mountain to a pleasant valley where there was a magnificent palace. Here invisible servants catered to her every whim. But at night when she went to her bridal bed, it was dark and she could not see her husband at all. He did not *feel* like a winged snake—not in his entirety, at any rate—but as he departed before dawn, she could not be *sure*."

"But it was Cupid!" Psyche said. "Not a dragon, not a monster, not an amoeba, but the God of Love!"

"Yes," Hweeh agreed. "It—she—@@@@—" He slumped.

Herald launched himself at the bowl, trying to bring his aura into play before the Weew faded out, but he was too late.

"I did what he asked—and it sent him back into shock," Psyche said, the fingers of one hand touching her mouth. "I'm sorry."

"You did very well," Herald assured her. "You caught us all by surprise. I did not realize what you had said until he reacted. Now we know that it is the single word 'amoeba' that sets him off. That's progress."

"But will he be hurt?"

"No, this merely delays us again. I think it was inevitable. And we are learning. His mind is whole; it is only this one thing that knocks him out. When he wakes, he has sealed it off again, until a direct reference sends him back into shock. A highly specific complaint."

"What does it mean?" Psyche asked.

"I wish I knew," Herald admitted. "It is hard to avoid the suspicion that we are all in deadly danger from the Space Amoeba. Yet this is hardly credible."

"I do love a mystery!" Psyche said. "I used to wish Kastle Kade had a ghost or something."

"It has one," Whirl said.

She shrugged that off. "I hope I can hear the rest of the story of my name."

"You could look it up in one of your references," Herald pointed out. "An excellent library like the one you have should certainly have—"

"No, that would not be fair. It is *his* story."

Herald shrugged at this new girlishness. They left the room.

*   *   *

In the afternoon the Duke took them on a hunt. "One of the animals has gone berserk," he explained. "It has ravaged the demesnes of the Baron of Magnet, my vassal, and killed several of his servitors. It behooves me to rid my environs of this menace. I caution you not to seek participatory action, as the beast is imbued with Transfer aura and is dangerous."

One of the prisoners of Keep, Herald realized, thus an animal with sapient cunning and criminal intent. Just the thing to lend adventure to this situation! Probably the nobles of the planet valued such prey, as it justified their position. If there were never any crises, there might cease to be any need for this feudal society and its warrior class.

They mounted steeds. The upper wheels of the Sador horses were shaped into seats, with holes for human legs, and the outer rim served as a rail to contain the upper body and provide handholds.

Psyche looked very refined in her riding habit, with its red jacket and white tight trousers. Her legs showed beneath the saddle wheel, extremely well formed. Herald was beginning to realize how much a simple tunic masked! Her fair hair was tied back in the fashion called a ponytail, changing the lines of her head and face. Like the mythological princess: lovely.

Whirl of Dollar was braced in his circular saddle by his own projecting wheels, and seemed to be quite stable. At first the sight of a six-wheeled creature astride a six-wheeled creature seemed odd to Herald but he quickly acclimatized. It was really no stranger than one quadruped astride another, which was how it had been on Planet Earth.

The Duke and his men-at-arms carried lances—long poles with guards at the rear to protect the hands, and sharp points at the forward ends. They also had shields and wore light armor and helmets. This was a truly medieval expedition, with all its pomp and fanfare. There was even a servitor honking periodically on a musical horn.

Each shield, of course, bore its heraldic device, and this enabled Herald to recognize the participants instantly, much better than by face or form. The ramifications of Galactic intercourse had provided legitimacy for an extraordinary number of Achievements, so that even the lowliest servitors of Kastle Kade bore the proud Arms of distant planets.

They boarded the ferry and crossed the lake. The craft was bulky and slow, but it carried the full party of twenty mounted knights. Water reptiles swam close, pacing the ferry: huge, long, toothy, sinuous things.

The Duke noted Herald's interest. "We keep Lake Donny stocked with the finest Solarian alligators, so that it shall not be forded or swum."

"You imported reptiles from Sphere Sol?" A colossal expense!

"A few reptile eggs were shipped by freezer ship with our ancestors a thousand years ago. We took good care of those eggs." The Duke looked out over the water, counting snouts. "Aren't they beautiful!"

"Um," Herald agreed faintly. Now he knew why no one swam in the beautiful lake!

The ferry's powerplant was intriguing yet practical: A dozen large Sador animals sat in harnesses around the sides, paddles affixed to their wheels. They were like so many rotary motors, propelling the craft vigorously forward. The paddles were designed so that the toothy reptiles could not get at the tender portions of the animals.

The party debarked at the North Landing, where the North Road wended its way through the deep forest west toward other castles of Keep. But a branch road coursed south around the west shore of the lake, toward the dam. They took this branch, and wheeled forth on the packed-dirt highway. The wheels of the horses propelled them with greater speed and endurance than sapient bodies could produce, and Herald clung to his saddle wheel tightly. The wind of motion whipped through his human hair, rapidly tugging it into disarray; but Psyche's ponytail remained distressingly neat.

The scenery was refreshing after a day shut up in the castle. The trees of Keep were Sadorian, probably seeded several thousand years before when Sphere Sador first colonized it. They were monstrous barrels with wheels projecting irregularly, their flat spokes angled to catch the sunlight. As the shadows changed, the wheels turned to maintain optimum position. But the lesser vegetation differed. There were fields of Sol-style grasses, probably imported to halt soil erosion and to provide the grains so beloved of Solarians. This was very much a planet of

73

compromise: Sador and Sol. At leisure, he would have to review local history and discover exactly how this had come about. There must have been at least two Terraforming operations following several Sadorforming stages, as alien species of vegetation normally did not take readily to the soils and microbes and light of a local environment.

There were animals, too. Small wheeled things scooted off the road and hid in the grass, and in the distance were grazing herds of cattle, cutting swaths through the grass with their bottom wheels and sucking up the fragments. Their top wheels were used to blow away flies. Flies, of course, accompanied cattle wherever they went, and there were as many species of flies as there were of other creatures. Some flies had wings, some jets, some magnetism—but they were always a similar nuisance. Herald remembered the laser-flies of his homeworld in Sphere Slash with no particular fondness. And there were birds, hovering on their heli-wheels, snapping up these flies. No matter how mixed, the ecology was always in balance.

Almost halfway around Lake Donny they diverged from the road, going up a steep gravel rut into the western ridge of mountains. Herald clung to his saddle-rail with both hands as his body tilted back and back; the incline was such he feared his mount would fall over backwards. But the other members of the party seemed unconcerned, and he knew the wheelers were extremely stable, so he concealed his alarm.

Up and up they went. At last the path leveled off and he glanced back. There, in the center of the lake, was Kastle Kade, marvelously scenic with its walls and embrasures and turrets and the flag of Kade flying from the pinnacle. But he shuddered at the narrow, excruciatingly steep path down to the water.

They proceeded along a ridge. It was cool up here, and a brisk breeze tugged at him, making him shiver for more than one reason. He had never spent much time in the heights; his species of Slash rolled along on disks, and a long slope could be deadly. Here the path dropped away steeply on either side, and the barrel-trees crowded in close. There was really no danger of a long fall here, as any creature rolling down would soon fetch up against a tree trunk, but still it seemed precarious.

Psyche drew abreast of him. There was just room for two horses on the path, no more. "This is the Ridge Road," she explained as her bright hair-tail whipped first one way and then another in the wind, as if struggling to be free. "Our cattle use it to get to the high pasture."

"Oh," Herald said in human idiom, for what that was worth. He noticed how the wind flattened her jacket against her front, making her twin young breasts stand out attractively. In his natural body, Herald would never have been concerned about such a detail. But in Transfer the standards of the host became, in large part, the standards of the Transferee, and this intensified with the passage of time. As a Slash he would have looked for precise lasers and clean disks in a female; as a human—well, Psyche was something special, despite her youth. Or perhaps *because* of it. The blooming of Solarian females seemed transitory, so that by middle age they had lost much of their sexual appeal. Certainly the older females of the Kastle Kade staff illustrated this condition; there was little about them to tempt any man in this respect. But a girl like Psyche. . . .

In due course the path broadened into the high pasture, a generally cleared slope with a broad spread of tall Solarian grasses and multicolored flowers. Beyond it was a small castle: residence of the Baron Magnet.

The party drew up to this edifice, and were met outside it by a modest hunting group. One horse detached itself and rolled up. In its saddle rested a creature perfectly designed for it: a metallic sphere whose Shield of Arms was painted right on its surface. An entity from Sphere Magnet, of course, whose sapients had achieved prominence in the Second War of Energy. It moved and acted by using magnetic attractive and repulsive forces. Since Keep was not a high-metal planet, the Baron would be virtually helpless if thrown from the saddle. But of course his type was extremely tough, being metallic, and he had his retainers to assist him.

"Greeting, my Liege," the Baron said via a speaker set in his saddle. His magnetic waves of communication were not audible to human perceptions, of course.

"Greeting, Baron," the Duke replied. "Be introduced here to my party: the Lady Kade, my daughter"—Psyche nodded politely—"Herald the Healer of Andromeda"—Herald emulated the nod—"the Earl of Dollar."

75

The Baron lifted momentarily in his saddle. A metal ball detached itself from its pocket in the saddle and swung in orbit around the magnet ominously. "Dollar aligns with you, now?"

Whirl rotated his wheel. "Have no concern, Magnet. Sheathe your mace. I am the Enemy Witness, present by the covenant to observe the Lady."

Magnet settled down again. His ball dropped back into its pocket. "Oh, naturally." He seemed relieved to know that Dollar remained an enemy knight.

"If you will direct us to the most recent sighting, we shall rout out the monster," the Duke said.

"Please follow, Liege," the Baron said, riding off.

They soon left the pavement and crossed open countryside. The tall grasses brushed against the horses' wheels. Herald found the swishing sound pleasant to his human ears, though fine pollen was flying up in brief clouds to tickle his nose and discolor his uniform. Now they were going uphill, and the horses were laboring. When one of the sets of wheels grew tired, they simply rotated a quarter turn and used the other set, the top saddle-wheel turning just enough to keep the riders facing forward. The horses were remarkably sure-wheeled, never bumping or skidding, though this cross-country climb was necessarily slower than the highway roll had been.

Abruptly they stopped. "Here the beast attacked my cattle, devouring one cow," the Baron said. "There are the wheels and axles of the loss, and there is the spoor of the attacker."

They made a large circle around the indicated spot. The tall grass was flattened to the ground, and there was a pile of animal wheels with dark stains upon them, as of dried blood. Sadorian entrails showed gruesomely between some of the spokes. There was no question about the violence of the death. Large, deep wheel tracks led away, up the hillside into the forest. Evidence enough!

"Flankers out," Kade ordered, and the human and Sador riders spread out to either side. "Lances ready." And the long spikes that had been pointing into the air dropped to parallel the ground. "Swords ready." And the Solarians loosened the blades in their sheaths, while the Sadors spun their forward wheels momentarily to show that their sharp spokes could function.

"Let's finish this by nightfall," Kade said. "Proceed."

The party began to move, following the trail. Birds flew up, disturbed by this intrusion. They were of pretty colors, some with each wheel of separate hue, and they dodged back and forth very quickly. With wheels spinning on six sides, they had precise control. Copterbugs approached, but were blown away by jets of forced air from the horses' resting wheels. These animals were versatile!

Once the initial thrill of the chase abated, the hunt became dull for Herald. With some thirty armed servitors flanking them, there seemed to be little actual danger, and as entertainment it quickly palled. There was nothing very sportsmanlike about this hunt, despite the trimmings; that errant beast was about to be butchered.

Herald allowed his steed to lag, and Psyche and Whirl did likewise, while the Duke and Baron and troops pushed eagerly ahead. *They* obviously enjoyed the chase! After a time they were out of sight. It didn't matter; there was no way to get lost amid the massed-wheel-tracks of the hunting party, and of course they would return this way.

"Does this really thrill you?" Herald asked Psyche.

"It is a big bore," she admitted. "But it is the duty of the nobles to cull the dangerous animals. We receive dispensations from contributing worlds to guarantee discipline here. And of course we have to round up the ones whose terms have expired if they don't come in for re-Transfer on their own. But I'm no huntress; I'd rather be back talking with Hweeh. I wonder what it can be about that Amoeba?"

"I hope to find out soon," Herald said. "Perhaps if we return to the castle in time—"

There was a horrendous roar from immediately behind them. The horses bolted in alarm—and all three riders were bucked out of their saddles, caught completely off-guard. Herald did a kind of turnabout in the air and landed hard on his posterior. Fortunately the ground was spongy, and his rear did not hurt much. Psyche landed neatly on her feet beside him, just as if this were her customary mode of dismounting; Whirl rolled over twice before getting righted.

The three horses were gone, wheeling at panicky speed up the slope. No help there.

The ground exploded. A cloud of dirt flew up, and from it emerged—a monster. The thing was huge and solid, with spiked treads and projecting teeth on its side wheels. It could obviously do a lot of damage in a short period.

Herald had no sword or shield; these remained attached to the saddle of his vanished horse. Psyche had both, but of course she was a helpless girl. Whirl. . . .

"Retreat to yonder tree," Whirl cried, cutting between them and the monster. "I shall delay it."

"Don't try," Psyche cried back at him. "No one but a mounted warrior with lance can balk that thing!" She ran toward the tree, and Herald started to follow.

But the Earl held his position, his battle wheel whirling rapidly. Herald remembered how this creature had stood his ground against the wrathful Duke, and knew he was not going to retreat. But against the massively armored wheels of the monster this was suicidal.

Herald reversed and ran to join Whirl, though he had no weapon. "Fool! Make for the tree!" Whirl cried. "I cannot hold it long!"

"That's why I'm here!" Herald shouted back. "*You* go; I'll handle it somehow."

But now Psyche joined them. "You two are exactly like my father!" she screamed. "You won't retreat before a foe, though it kill you! Must I protect your lives with mine, as I protected your honor with mine before?"

"She's making sense," Herald said. "None of us can fight it—not singly, not together. But if we all run separately—"

"It will pick its choice and destroy that one," Whirl said. "I know not why it hesitates now."

Amazingly, the monster itself replied, in Clustric. "Which has the aura?" it demanded, its wheel-voice slurred almost into unintelligibility. "That one is mine!"

Then Herald understood. "It was a high-aura sapient. Now that it has faded almost to animal status, it thinks it can recover aura by consuming me! My aura roused it from its hiding place."

"It could have escaped the hunt if it had stayed in its hiding place," Psyche said. "The hunting party passed right over it, and we did too, never knowing! It is a most cunning beast."

"That is why it must be destroyed!" Whirl said.

"If it is after my aura, it won't leave this area until I do," Herald said. "And I'm heading for that tree. Both of you run in other directions; it won't follow you."

"Precisely," the monster said, nudging toward Herald.

Psyche stepped forward, her light sword in her right hand, her decorative shield bravely raised on her left arm. "It shall not have you, Healer!" she cried, stabbing at it.

The monster crunched forward, its deadly wheel revving up. A spoke caught Psyche's blade and ripped it out of her hand. The bent sword flew in an arc as she shook her bruised hand with a little exclamation of pain.

Herald lunged forward, circled both arms about her slender waist, and half hurled her around and behind him. "Get *out* of here!" he bawled.

The monster charged, when Herald was off-balanced from his effort. And suddenly he realized another point of affinity: the monster was like a Slash, his own kind! A Slash was a tubular creature with disks around its girth that it used for slicing out pathways, cutting up food, and dismembering enemies. It also had laser lenses for longer-range action. In his natural body, Herald could have met this creature on even terms, perhaps more than even terms. A Slash was smaller, but the lasers could score with devastating effect before the disks struck. But this Solarian host was a poor excuse for a combat creature.

These things forged through his human brain at about the same velocity his human legs got oriented and propelled him the hell away from the monster. A gap opened between him and the pursuer. But it was strictly temporary; the monster had more power, and its wheels gave it more forward impetus. All too quickly it closed the gap again.

Whirl shot across, his little side wheels throwing up divots, moving to intercept the monster. "Get *out* of here!" Herald shouted, in the same tone he had used on Psyche. "Guard the Lady! I can take care of myself!" He needed no further proof of the little Earl's courage. Enemy he might be, but he took the covenant seriously, and was quite ready to give his life to protect those he guarded. It was another example of the kind of honor heraldry was supposedly based on, but that Herald had seldom encountered directly. He liked it very well, but not when it foolishly wasted lives.

"Yes, it is the Lady I must watch," Whirl agreed. "Forgive me, alien exorcist, that I must relinquish you to your fate." There was no intended irony in this.

But now Herald had to concentrate exclusively on the monster. He knew how to fight it, using his Slash reflexes, but that did not make the task simple. The Sador beast was as tall as he, and several times as massive; its bladed front wheel was as wide across as the full length of its body. But the liability of size was that it slowed maneuvering, and wheels were more readily balked than legs. He could not outspeed the monster in a linear race, but he could foul it up in close acrobatics—maybe.

He felt the reverse breath of its savage front wheel, sucking the draft past him. An excellent way to catch prey, he realized: The wheel helped pull the pursuer forward while it sucked the fleeing animal back. Even if it didn't actually lift the prey off its feet, it helped slow and tire it. Small, subtle advantages could make the difference between failure and success.

How close could he afford to play it? Herald lost his nerve as he felt the hair of his head lifted by that breeze. He thrust out his right leg as though doing a squat jump, letting his body be hurled to the left. He twisted as he fell, and the monster rolled over the spot where he had been. Its massive side wheel crunched its track into the soil just beyond his feet.

The angled blade-spokes had light-receptors that were immediately aware of his new location. The monster did not turn; like the horses, it dropped its front and rear wheels and raised its side wheels. Now it was oriented on Herald again; the shift had taken only a moment.

But for that moment it was stationary; it could not shift wheels while traveling. It had had to brake to a stop, and now it had to get its mass going again. Herald's body could take off from a standing start faster than it could.

Herald was rolling as he thought. Unlike his Slash body, the Solarian form had to assume a vertical position before it could accelerate. He got his feet under him and launched himself toward the tree at right angles to the new orientation of the monster's driving wheels.

"Clever!" the monster roared as it shifted wheels again. Its Transfer aura might have faded, but much intelligence remained. It would not fall for the same trick again! Herald hoped he could reach the tree in time.

He saw that Psyche was already there, drawing herself up into its spreading upper wheels. Whirl was getting there.

But Herald's ill-conditioned host-body was tiring rapidly, as it had during the exercise sessions. If only the host had seen fit to indulge in a physical development program himself! A strong human body should have maintained velocity easily, but this one was panting painfully. A few more days of exercise might have corrected that. Meanwhile the monster was gaining again.

Herald knew he had to use his brain, but it was hard to do that during the distraction of this rising agony of effort. One more diversion of the monster might be enough. But what would work?

He was running through a chewed-up section of the field, where a slight ridge of earth had caused the wheels of the hunting party to grind apart the turf. His feet slid, causing him to drop momentarily to his knees. Precious time lost!

But maybe this would serve as even more of an obstruction to the monster! Herald climbed to the firm bank beyond, and turned to face his pursuer.

Now the monster showed its cunning. It steered carefully around the dirt-patch, coming at Herald from the side. Herald started for the tree again—but his fatigued body stumbled, and he sprawled full-length on the ground.

No chance now to go for the tree! The monster had cut him off, and had good traction and position—and it was *not* on the verge of physical collapse from overexertion. Herald went the only way he could: he rolled down into the pool of dirt again.

The monster, certain the prey would make his bolt for the tree, had to halt and reorient again. But now it had its quarry trapped, and knew it. It paused to gloat. "Squirm, victim!" it buzzed. "Soon I eat your aura!"

That was the one thing Herald did not have to fear. With the strength of his aura, and the training and skill he had in its application, he could destroy the lesser aura of the monster. But he would be materially dead at the wheels of the thing before he could do this. It was *physical* destruction he somehow had to stave off.

81

"Run, game, struggle!" the monster said. "I will catch you and eat you and hide myself again, and I will have high aura and no one will find me until I conquer."

"There are two witnesses," Herald pointed out. "There in the tree. They will betray your hiding place, and the hunters will destroy you."

The monster spun its forward wheel in rage. "I shall kill them too!"

"You can't reach them," Herald said. He was speaking more easily now, as his body rested and recovered. That was good; the longer he could keep the monster talking, the better off he was.

"First thing first," the monster said. "I will hide in another place, if I need." And of course that was the answer; it certainly did not have to stay *here*. It edged around the dirt-pool.

Herald edged in the opposite direction, keeping the bulk of the dirt between them. "Who are you, that you speak Clustric?"

"I am King Caesar of System Capella, Sphere Sol," the monster said proudly. "My throne was usurped by my protégé, Antony, and I was exiled here. But with your aura, I shall return from the dead. Then will the traitorous heads roll, and the gutters will clog with the blood of those supporting the usurpers. Right will be might again!"

Something jogged Herald's Slash memory. "You call yourself Caesar?" he inquired. "Even in Galaxy Andromeda there was news of the Butcher of Capella, who slaughtered indiscriminately and tortured sapients for the sheer pleasure of it, until at last even that hardened system vomited him out—"

The king-monster hurled himself forward with astonishing suddenness. Gouts of dirt sailed back, and the spiked wheels spun momentarily in air as he hurdled the brown pool.

Caught by surprise—when was he ever going to learn! —Herald's host-body reacted automatically. He dived to the side, his head going down, his feet up. He took a forward roll in the soft dirt, coming to rest on his back, while Caesar landed just past his head.

More thoughts tumbled through his brain as his body inverted. There had been a historical Caesar, too, a Solarian ruler two thousand years in Planet Earth's pre-Spherical past. A merciless but able entity, heading the powerful neolithic or age-of-iron kingdom of Rome, said to mate with either male or female individuals of his species—what an example to follow!

Herald sat up, grabbed two handfuls of dirt, and flung it at the monster, hoping to gum up the axles. It was a futile gesture. Caesar's host was a creature of the wild, well adapted to the wilderness hazards, able to bury itself in dirt, as they had discovered. Only the unnatural denudation of turf in this vicinity impeded its progress even slightly.

Herald did not wait. He scrambled to his feet and charged for the tree with renewed vigor. Caesar's wheels threw up a tremendous cloud of dirt as they churned out of that hole, but the monster no longer seemed to care. By the time he achieved firm ground, Herald was halfway to the tree.

He was panting again as he reached it, and Caesar was close behind, but now Herald had something he could use as a barrier. He scooted around the bulging trunk—and the Sador beast could not make as tight a turn or cut across the arc to intercept him.

"Climb!" Psyche cried.

Herald jumped, reached up, caught hold of the rim of a branch-wheel and ran his feet up the trunk until one leg hooked over a spoke. This was one thing his human host was better at than his Slash body! He hauled himself about, getting up on the wheel as Caesar cruised by just beneath. Safe at last!

Or *was* he safe? The monster now attacked the tree. Caesar tilted his bulky host-body back, lowering his rear wheel, and bracing his side wheels so as to shift the front wheel upward. The bottom feeder-wheel also wedged against the ground, while the top general-purpose wheel kept out of the way. The elevated front wheel revved up much faster than it could have when in contact with the ground, its sharp spikes blurring. It was angled so as to be almost parallel to the ground.

Those whirling spikes moved into the trunk of the tree, slowly. Bark flew out as contact was made. The wheel was now a circular saw, cutting into the wood.

Herald peered down, alarmed. Could Caesar actually do it? The trunk was massive; it would take a long time to cut through it, perhaps hours. Long before the tree fell, the hunting party should be back here. So wasn't this effort futile?

The sawing sound changed. Fluid spurted out of the trunk, splashing on the monster. And Herald realized that the tree was hollow, filled with water, with a relatively thin shell. It would not take long at all to slice through!

"I am afraid it is the end," Psyche said, seeming sad rather than afraid. She no longer had her Shield of Arms shield; she must have flung that aside in order to reach the tree faster. "I had thought it would be by fire, but maybe this is much the same."

Herald moved as close as he could and put his arm around her small shoulders. "The hunters must soon return," he said. "They will deal with the monster."

"No," she said, her elfin face turning to him. Her eyes seemed larger than before, more brightly orange. "No, Herald, I feel it, I know it somehow: We must deal with this ourselves, or we are lost."

Herald felt the strength of her conviction manifesting in her aura. Rightly or wrongly, she *believed*. As Smallbore of Metamorphic had believed in her vision. And he had to believe too.

Psyche's face was close to his. He moved closer. Their lips touched in a fleeting kiss. He felt the pulse that traversed her aura at that touch, and drew back. This was becoming something other than reassurance, and he knew enough to alter course immediately. He would soon be leaving this planet and this Galaxy, and had no personal reason to become involved with this young female—assuming they all survived the immediate threat.

"There have to be alternatives," he said. "What will stop the monster?"

"We must jam that wheel!" Psyche said, looking down. Her face was now a very pale blue, with little clench-muscles showing around her mouth.

It seemed to Herald that the tree was already shrinking, as its supportive fluid drained out. He hoped that was mere imagination.

"Tree-spokes!" Whirl said. How the Sador sapient had gotten up here was a mystery; wheeled creatures could hardly climb trees! Maybe Psyche had helped haul him up. Could the Earl have winched up along a line? "If you can hold me in place, I shall saw them off."

Herald braced himself on one side, and Psyche on the

other, each with feet braced against a branch-wheel rim and hands holding on to one of Whirl's side wheels. Whirl angled forward, his front wheel coming down to rasp against a spoke. He lacked the massive fighting cleats of the monster, but his rim was able to cut slowly into the wood. He severed one spoke, but it remained anchored at the branch hub. Then he shifted about and got another, and then a third. Then they all moved so Whirl could get the other ends. Herald bound the freed spokes together with the tie from Psyche's erstwhile ponytail, then carefully oriented the bundle above the monster's saw wheel. "This had better work," he murmured.

Even the strength of the monster could not keep the saw going continuously. The spikes chewed out a large cut, requiring much power. Caesar had to pause every so often, to let his axle cool and to reorient for cutting further around the trunk. Nevertheless, the tree was creaking, on the verge of collapse. Herald waited for the saw to stop, then dropped his bundle.

It fell neatly into the saw, jamming between the spokes. And Caesar was in trouble. He could not turn that wheel freely while the bundle was in it, and could not shake it out. He had to lower the wheel to the ground and maneuver.

"It will not hold him long," Whirl said worriedly. "We must prepare another wheel-block."

"No good," Herald objected. "He won't be caught twice by the same trick." He swung down from the branch.

"What are you doing?" Psyche cried in alarm.

"Stay up there," Herald told her. "If that block will hold long enough. . . ." He dropped to the ground beside Caesar, and clasped both hands to the stalled rim.

Amazed at this audacity, the monster heaved. But now Herald's human weight was on the wheel, further immobilizing it. His feet left the ground, but he did not let go.

Psyche screamed, thinking his attack suicidal. But there was nothing she could do.

The real battle was invisible. Herald brought his aura to bear against that of Caesar. The monster's Transfer aura *was* low; it was probably around seventy at the start of his exile to Keep, but now was barely ten. When it sank to the level of the animal host, Caesar would die, becoming no more than the animal he had occupied. His protégé back in System Capella had inflicted a cruel but perhaps fitting punishment on the former king. Caesar himself had sent many innocents to this very situation. Herald was able to derive this from the nature of the aura; the personality was far more monstrous than the host.

Now, because it had come to a direct choice between Caesar's life and Herald's, Herald was undertaking an exorcism. He was using the unparalleled power of his aura to drive the other aura out of the body. Two hundred thirty-six against ten—a gross mismatch. But it was not easy to expunge an entrenched aura, and only a specialist in exorcism could accomplish it. This was not a task Herald enjoyed. It was the negative face of the bright coin of healing. For exorcism meant death of the subject. It was not harmful to the host or to the host's natural aura, but to the alien aura.

Caesar, suddenly aware of the threat, fought savagely. He could not resist long in aural combat, any more than Herald could survive long in physical combat. The monster had to return to the physical level of strife before he lost his mind—literally. If he could crush or slice Herald's Solarian body, killing it, Herald's aura would lose its base and be unable to pursue the attack. Or if Caesar could shake Herald off, breaking physical contact, he could then escape. But that would mean death for Herald, because the savage king would immediately charge again and kill him. And while killing would take only a second, exorcism required minutes. So Herald had to hold on to the immobilized wheel now; he would have no second chance.

Caesar threw him about, and rolled, trying to crush the slight Solarian body under the stalled wheel. But the Sador host was not equipped to roll *across* its own wheel; it was made to be stable in almost all situations. So though Caesar could lift and lower his front wheel, he could not put it flat on the ground.

Meanwhile, Herald's devastating aura invaded the animal's body, closing in on the diminishing region commanded by the king.

Caesar lifted the wheel and shot forward, trying to crush Herald against the trunk of the tree. It was an excellent tactic, but the bundle of tree-spokes remained

86

lodged, and that took the brunt of the shock. There was just enough clearance to save Herald's body. That much was luck, not planning!

Now Caesar twisted about and started across the meadow, carrying Herald along. But the battle was concluding. Herald's aura closed in on the final nucleus.

I will give you riches! Caesar cried through his aura, when he understood that he was lost. *Power! Things of the flesh!* It did not occur to him that Herald might not be interested in things of the flesh, or that he would distrust the proffered bribe. This failure to appreciate the higher qualities of some individuals had led to Caesar's downfall before, and he had not profited from the experience. In this sense he had always been a beast.

Herald did not deign to respond. He captured the nucleus and shoved it—out. Caesar was dead.

Herald's battered Solarian fingers let go at last as the animal stopped, and he fell to the ground in front of it. The king was gone, but the natural animal of Sador remained—and it could still kill him. The bundle of spokes dropped out of the wheel.

But a cry sounded in the distance. The animal backed off, lowered its alternate wheels, and sped away.

There was a halloo of pursuit, but Herald just lay where he was. In moments Whirl was beside him. "Do you survive, valiant Healer?" he cried.

"I survive. The monster is dead," Herald gasped weakly.

Now Psyche joined them. "You saved us," she said. "That was awfully brave, Herald, but how did you hang on so long? If the hunters hadn't come—"

"I exorcised it," Herald explained as she helped him up. He was conscious of the freshness of her body, her sweet odor, though she was speckled with dirt and sawdust. She was hauling him up with both arms about him, her mammalian breasts pressing against him as she exerted herself.

She froze, her eyes growing round. "Oh." Suddenly she was aware of what Herald was capable of doing, for he had come to exorcise the demon from *her*. Had she realized this before, she might not have kissed him.

"Oh, I don't care!" she said, and resumed lifting.

Herald found his balance and stood up, not wanting either to cause her to strain herself or to have her approaching father misunderstand their position again. Many more contacts like this, and Kade might well have reason for his suspicion. The Lady had some most attractive attributes.

"Only the Transfer aura suffered," he said. "The natural aura cannot be exorcised. Your own aura is natural. Not at all like that of Caesar of Capella."

"Gee, thanks," she said, laughing.

The Duke rode up, hand hovering near sword. "What happened?"

"I witnessed," Whirl said. "Allow me to clarify."

Herald exchanged glances with Psyche—and somehow knew that the Earl of Dollar would cover all details— except the kiss.

Herald had intended to have another session with Hweeh of Weew after the hunt, but he was too tired, bruised, and emotionally worn. Psyche and Whirl shared his condition, so all agreed to retire early. They funneled through the necessities of toiletry quickly and went to their separate slumbers. Herald fell asleep in moments.

He was awakened by the touch of Whirl's wheel on his shoulder. "It manifests," the Earl whispered, his communication wheel hardly turning.

Herald was instantly alert. Every part of his body was stiff and sore, but he ignored that. The room was dim, with a single swath of pale light from one of Keep's moons descending slantwise from the skylight, but he could see well enough. He did not pretend to misunderstand the Witness's meaning.

Psyche was on her feet, facing out the side window. On ground level the walls of the castle were solid and tremendously thick, emulating the massive defensive ramparts of the medieval Solarian originals, but here in the upper levels the embrasures let in a surprising amount of light. The moonbeam touched her head, highlighting it with an ethereal glow. She seemed unnaturally still, though even from behind he could make out the slight motions of her even breathing. Her hair trailed down her back like a shawl, and her little feet were bare.

Herald got to his feet and took a step forward. "Lady," he said softly.

The figure turned. "Did I wake you, Herald?" she inquired, seeming glad rather than regretful. "Will you

come share the view with me? Lake Donny is lovely."
There was a special, indefinable quality to her voice, like
controlled joy.

"Yes." He crossed the room and came to stand beside
her. As he did, he became increasingly aware of something aural, yet not alien. It was new to his experience;
not threatening, but distinctly odd.

"I am glad you are here," she said. "I feel so *good*.
As when you touched me first, but now it is of myself,
not you."

Herald put his hand on her bare elbow—and froze.

Herald himself had the most intense Kirlian aura ever
measured in the Cluster. This was no mere vanity; he had
been tested many times, and had studied the records of
the two hundred-K-range historical auras. He knew that
the legendary barbarian Flint of Outworld would have
deferred to him in this respect, and so would Flint's mistress of Slash, as each had an aura thirty intensities below
his. He knew that Melody of Mintaka, as powerful and
determined a lady as ever lived, would have deferred to
him by at least ten intensities. Even the most obscure,
respected, legendary figure of them all, Sibling Paul of
Tarot, had probably had an aura less than Herald's own.
Never in all the known universe, in all recorded time,
had any entity of any Sphere matched the aura of Herald
the Healer. He knew this did not mean he had any superior morality or intelligence or basic right to exist; mere
chance had bequeathed to him the record. But he *was*,
in the Kirlian sense, a freak.

Now he touched an aura significantly stronger than his
own. Not an alien one, not a Transferee. It was Psyche's
own individual aura, completely typical of her—except
that it had a strength of at least 250 intensities. It was
fifteen units higher than the highest Kirlian aura ever
known.

This was the aura he had been summoned to exorcise.
And of course it was impossible. No entity could drive out
an aura higher than its own, and a natural aura in its
own host could not be exorcised regardless. So his mission was suddenly manifested as doubly impossible.

Triply impossible. For who would *want* to drive out
the natural aura of an entity as completely sweet and
innocent as Psyche?

With an effort Herald removed his hand from her.

"Have I offended you?" she inquired, gently concerned.

"No, Lady, no," he said quickly. "Never that! I must converse with the Witness."

"No need," Whirl said behind him. "Now you comprehend. Now it has manifested for you."

"It has manifested," Herald agreed, amazed.

"What is this?" Psyche asked.

"Lady," Herald said, noting the reverberation of awe in his own voice, "you are possessed."

She laughed without malice. "I am myself! Witness, touch me and know. There is no alien in my body." She glanced at Herald. "*Is* there, Healer?"

"There is no alien—yet you are possessed," Herald said. "I was wrong before; the Enemy Witness was right. I do not pretend to comprehend this."

Now she showed gentle alarm. "How can I be possessed? I am so full, so complete; I am truly myself at this moment."

Herald did not answer. All that she said was true—but so was all that the Witness said. This thing was completely new to his experience.

"It has manifested," Whirl said. "Now you fulfill your mission, and all is well."

"I cannot," Herald said.

"But you must! You are aware of the alternative!"

"Are you then going to deliver me to be burned?" Psyche asked, this time putting her hand on Herald. Again he felt her aura, ten times the strength it had by day, so fine and strong and wonderful that it wrought its deep joy within him too. He called himself a healer— how much more so was she, now!

"No, never that," he said, humbly. Then, to Whirl: "I beg you, Witness, give me time to consider. I have no means to judge the merits of my alternatives."

"Until morning," the Earl said.

"Thank you." Herald turned again to Psyche. She seemed almost to glow with her own light, looking up at him, her face shadowed except for those golden eyes. "And what am I to do with you?"

"Need it be spoken?" she asked, moving into his arms.

He kissed her. This time it was no light extemporaneous effort, but a deep, thorough, enveloping experience. He was not embracing a mere girl; he was immersing himself in Aura. No, it had no need to be spoken!

They went hand in hand to her bed, and they settled into their embrace with complete tenderness and naturalness, their two unique auras merging as their bodies merged. It was the most beautiful thing Herald had ever experienced in any host or in his own Slash body, anywhere in the Cluster. He had never even imagined anything could be like this.

In the morning, waking with her hair strewn caressingly across his shoulder, he became aware of three things: The fatigue and soreness of his human body had been healed by the superior aura he had encountered; Psyche's aura had returned to its former level of twenty-five . . . and he was in trouble.

He got up and dressed, letting Psyche sleep. He suffered a flash of memory-image: Cupid departing from the bed of his bride before the light of dawn came, that she might not see him. But it was necessary, for there would be an irate parent to deal with. "Witness, I am ready," he announced.

The Earl of Dollar accompanied him silently from the room. Downstairs the Duke was up, preparing for the morning repast. The odor of sweet syrup distilled from the sap of trees and of confections formed from the sour rinds of citric fruits drifted through the castle. Kastle Kade always ate in style!

"I have difficult news," Herald said.

The Duke's jaw muscles bunched. "I will have it now."

"I have observed the manifestation of which the Enemy Witness spoke."

Kade's face showed his shock. "You are—sure?"

"I am sure it exists. But I am also sure it is not a Possession. At least, not in any sense that we have knowledge of. It is simply a remarkable fluctuation of aura, like none known before. Hitherto it has been believed that the intensity of the aura is fixed from the time of birth or even conception, changing only for the worse during illness or Transfer. But the Lady's aura changes for the better. It should not and cannot be exorcised, and I would not do it if I were able. But that is academic. I am unable, for at its height it is stronger than mine."

Kade considered a moment, and Herald knew he was

91

orienting on the hope he had extended, the rationale for the naturalness of Psyche's manifestation, an explanation that excluded the concept of Possession. The Duke turned to Whirl. "Witness, are you satisfied?"

"No," Whirl said. "I can no longer accept the validity of the opinion of this expert."

Herald had hoped it would not come to this, though he had been sure it *would*. The Enemy Witness was rigorously honest, and he had good reason for his doubt.

"And why not," Kade demanded, "since you selected him?"

"I can answer that," Herald said, deciding not to force the Earl into this unpleasant chore. "Last night the Lady Kade and I made love."

The Duke's whole body stiffened. "Witness?" he demanded tightly, and in that instant it was evident that the prefix "enemy" had been shifted from Dollar to Healer.

"True," the Earl said. "Voluntary by both parties, however. No force or coersion was involved."

The Duke turned rigidly to Herald. "And what do you propose to do now?"

Herald spread his hands. "I don't know. I am afraid the Witness is correct. I am no longer an objective party, and cannot exonerate your daughter of the charge against her. I will naturally waive my fee and depart. . . ." But *could* he depart? He had met Aura, and he was in love, however complicated the circumstances.

"Then accept this." And stepping forward, the Duke of Kade struck Herald across the face smartly with his pair of gloves. The material was soft, but it was a smarting impact. Herald stumbled back, perplexed. He was conversant with feudal customs, as heraldry derived from them, but this was confusing. "You challenge me to a duel, sir?"

"To the death, sir. Choose weapons."

"I am not certain I can accept such a challenge. May I inquire your reason?"

"The honor of my daughter."

Oh. Herald had thought the Duke would want to be rid of him as quickly as possible, by having him Transfer out. But that would not alleviate the political ramifications. Because any liaison between the Lady of Kade and the Scion of Skot would now be problematical; a creature from another Galaxy had preempted initial honors. "This I understand. But before I accept your challenge, there is something you should know—"

"Choose!"

Herald shrugged. "Laser swords, of course."

"Come this way," Kade said curtly, stalking from the room.

Herald paused to address the Earl. "It seems the personal matter has preempted the business matter. In the event I am not available to testify, I hope you will bear in mind the qualifications of my observation when you report to your authorities. The Lady Kade suffers from no ordinary Possession, and there seems to be no relation to what befell her mother. I believe another expert will confirm my findings. The Lady deserves this chance."

"I will so note," Whirl said.

"Thank you." Herald turned and followed the Duke out.

In the arms room the Duke opened a chest to reveal a fine pair of laser swords. Each was no more than a handle. "Do you wish to inspect?"

"No need," Herald said. "I am certain they are uniform."

Each man lifted a handle and walked to the open court that was adjacent. Here a shaft of sun came down, for this was in the outer castle where the walls were lower and the spaces larger. Herald squeezed his unit, and the blade appeared; a double laser band, the twin beams merging and phasing out about an arm's length from his grasp. He was careful to keep the blade and point out of the way of the furniture. The Duke did the same.

"Do you require a second?" Kade inquired.

Herald considered momentarily. A second would be better, but it would be awkward to set this up now. "In the circumstances, I believe we can dispense with this. Your servants are watching covertly from the embrasures."

The Duke made a snort almost of mirth. The two advanced to the center of the defined court, where lines set off the dueling range. "As ready," Kade said, striking his pose, sword elevated.

"Ready," Herald agreed, bringing his weapon to bear somewhat negligently.

Instantly the Duke struck, and Herald parried expertly, his point touching the other blade near the handle to interrupt the beams and snuff them out. The Duke jumped back, then promptly lunged—and Herald nullified his beams again with a seemingly offhand flick of his wrist.

"You are conversant," Kade muttered.

"I tried to advise you, sir. I am of Sphere Slash, Andromeda, a natural laser culture."

"Sol is also a laser culture!"

"Certainly." Herald nullified a third attack, this time flicking his point across the Duke's hand as he disengaged. His seeming negligence was merely complete confidence in his own competence; he could spot a laser anywhere he wanted, regardless of the host. It was inborn.

The pain of that swipe had to be intense, for the laser of these formal swords did not burn, but stimulated the nerves of the flesh it touched, overloading them until they could not respond. A touch of an instant hurt; a longer touch would stun the nerves so that it was as though the limb had been severed. But the Duke retained his grip. "Do you mock me?" he cried, his face reddening.

Perplexed at this reaction to first blood, Herald stepped back. "I merely show you my capability, lest you be unaware. Though this host is clumsy and weak, laser is my inherent weapon. Do you wish to withdraw your challenge?" This was a bit insulting, but Herald had no wish to kill the Duke. Since it had been defined as a duel to the death, the only way he could spare the man was by convincing him to have a change of heart.

For answer, Kade hurled his sword point-blank. This unorthodox and dangerous maneuver caught Herald by surprise. He tried to dodge aside, but the sword penetrated his abdomen. There was an instant of sharp pain in his gut, then nothing.

Astonished, he found himself standing unwounded. "Your sword is defective!" he exclaimed.

"My sword is tuned to half power—like yours!" the Duke retorted. "You mock me with a play-duel!"

"I did not know of this," Herald protested, turning off his blade. "How could I detune the swords when I neither touched nor inspected them?"

"*I* did it," Psyche said from the doorway. "When Whirl woke me and told me what was happening, I ran to turn the weapon-circuit down, lest someone be hurt."

"You foiled my defense of your own honor!" the Duke cried, exasperated.

"My honor!" she flashed, in that manner reflecting the laser-culture aspect of her kind. "Did you suppose I did not heed that honor last night? A Lady needs no defense; she does what is proper in the circumstance. I *love* him!"

"And I love her," Herald said. "I would not have taken her, had it been otherwise."

"Then why did you not offer to marry her?" Kade demanded.

Surprised, Herald spread his hands. "It did not occur to me that such a thing would be in order."

"Not in order! You, a leading heraldic artisan, expert in ceremonial arms and manner, you did not know the custom?"

"I regret if I overestimated your own knowledge of custom on the Cluster level," Herald said. "I am of Sphere Slash, Andromeda, and the leading Kirlian entity."

"So you have said!"

"We of Slash labor under what is called the Curse of Llume, reflecting an episode of the Second War of Energy. Thus we are deemed the lowest culture of a subject galaxy. It is no honor to marry a Slash, even were my natural form not the every serpent abhorred by the mythology of Psyche's name. I forgot myself last night, in the ambience of the most remarkable aura of all time and space. But in the morning I knew it could not be."

"Why could it not be?" Psyche demanded, her eyes glowing orange like her father's.

"Had I presumed to demand your hand in marriage from your father, he would surely have declined permission."

The Duke of Kade nodded, agreeing. "Still you should have made the offer, providing me the occasion for that formality."

"*Formality!*" Psyche blazed. "Have *I* nothing to say about it?" She had become a creature of fire, absolutely lovely.

Herald turned to her. "Would you, like your namesake, dress in mourning clothing to marry a serpent?" he asked her gently. "Though I appear to you in human form, I am in reality as ugly to your perception as the monster I banished yesterday. I have sharp cutting disks, and deadly lasers, and the shame of a thousand years. That form is invisible to you at the moment, as it were in the dark of night. Overwhelmed by your enhancement, I thought it did not matter, but—"

"I would not dress in mourning to marry you," she said with a rebellious expression.

"This was my realization of the morn," he said. "Therefore—"

"I would dress in celebration, in the finest bridal gown of Keep, and I would carry living flowers and walk in eternal sunlight by your side."

"Therefore the Duke does have grievance against me, for—" Herald paused. "You would marry *me*, a Slash?"

"Oh, my love," she said passionately. "Did you not suppose I knew your origin? It was never secret! What meaning do you think the Curse of Llume has to us of the Galaxy Llume saved? She made no curse; she made a blessing that your species should be proud to honor! But for her, *I* would not exist at all!"

Herald was amazed and deeply gratified by her expression. But now he remembered his forced betrothal to Flame of Furnace. How could he explain to adoring Psyche and her suspicious father that in order to marry her, he would first have to sire offspring by an alien female? "I cannot—"

"Pardon the intrusion," Whirl said. Herald had not seen him enter the courtyard, but of course he had had considerable distraction. "It is not precisely my business, still I feel concern. Did the Healer love the Lady for her demon aura alone, and now that it has phased away no longer has interest in the host? In that case a ready solution offers—"

"The Lady has no demon aura!" Herald exclaimed. "There was no Possession in the sense you mean. But if she *had*, I would love that demon, for it is but an aspect of herself. It is my own fitness I question, not hers."

The Duke turned a newly appraising gaze on him. "I could not have phrased it better."

"Question no longer," Psyche said. "Last night in my enhancement I explored your aura from a vantage possible to no other entity, and even if I had not loved you and you me, it was fated that our auras unite. Of what account is mere physical form? Psyche will marry the serpent with the soul of a god."

96

To hell with Flame of Furnace! Herald faced the Duke. "Certain misunderstandings have been alleviated. I now request your permission."

It was Kade's turn to spread his hands. "This is not precisely what I would have chosen. You were correct in assuming I intended to decline your offer, though that would necessarily have abated my complaint of honor against you. But I now perceive my daughter will have her way. She is of Kade; she will not be balked. In the circumstance I discover no preferable alternative."

"Then let the banns be published," Whirl said. "Perhaps this will satisfy those I represent."

Then Psyche was in Herald's arms, raising her lips to be kissed, openly, joyously. Yet even in this moment of delight, Herald wondered: How much justice had there been in the Witness's question about the demon aura? Herald had felt twinges of attraction and, he saw in retrospect, even desire for this young Solarian female. She *was* physically and personally pretty. But love had manifested only with the enhancement of her aura.

It was not in him to love a minor aura, which was one reason he had not before allied himself with a female. He had refused to accept Flame of Furnace because of principle, but had known that no other aura in the Cluster could match hers. So few available females had auras above 150, and most of those had other qualities to qualify their eligibility. But a young, beautiful, sweet, rich, loving girl with an aura of 250—no, cancel the rest. *Any* female with an aura of 250 would have compelled his extreme interest, and he would have married her merely to guarantee association with that most remarkable ambience. But by similar token, even the youngest, most beautiful, sweetest, richest, and lovingest female was of negligible interest, if her aura was no more than 25.

Which one was Psyche? Did he love *her*, or was she merely an alternative to the love he feared he would have for Flame of Furnace should he ever meet her physically and be conquered by her 190 aura? Did he have the right to marry Psyche thus, uncertain of the fundamental nature of his emotion? Oh, she was delightful at this moment, no chore to hold and kiss, but without the aura it might be no more than mere dalliance, even in the married state. Was it fair to her? Now he dared not tell her of Flame.

Psyche drew away, her orange eyes glancing into his for a touching moment, and he feared she had somehow divined his thoughts. "We forget the Weew," she said.

"What?" Herald could not align this with his train of thought. "Oh, yes, time for another interview with Hweeh."

"The Weew can wait," the Duke said. "We forget *breakfast.*"

Psyche laughed, her fire and tension gone. "Life does continue!" They all headed for the odor of treesap syrup.

After breakfast, the Duke went about arranging publication of the banns and preparing Kastle Kade for the wedding. The Earl of Dollar made his farewells and departed, going to make his report to the enemy. "This union alters the situation," Whirl confided semiprivately. "The issue may emerge favorably."

Herald and Psyche interviewed the Weew again. Herald put his hand on the creature's inert mass, and evoked the horn and eyestalk.

"We were covering the myth of Cupid and Psyche," Herald said aloud. "Her husband of the night did not *feel* precisely like a winged serpent—" Oh, how close to the mark that struck now!

"But it was Cupid!" Psyche picked up promptly. So much had happened since the last interview that it was difficult to place the exact interruption. "Not a dragon, not a monster, not even an ordinary man, but the God of Love!" And she looked into Herald's eyes.

"Yes," Hweeh agreed. "It was he, constrained from revealing himself lest his mother, Venus, discover what he had done, and wreak her wrath on the innocent girl, whose only fault was her perfection." And Psyche smiled at Herald in momentary victory: The Weew was unaware of the interruption.

"But in time she grew curious," Hweeh continued, "and determined to *see* his face. If he were in fact a serpentine monster, she could cut off his head and be free of his spell."

Psyche jumped. "She would never do that! She loved him regardless!"

"Perhaps," Hweeh agreed after a pause. It was evident that he was beginning to catch on, for he was no stupid entity. "At any rate, she was as inquisitive as females of all species are reputed to be, from Pandora right up to the present. She took a sharp sword of metal and her burning lamp of oil and looked in the bed at night. There was Cupid, as handsome a Solarian god as she could have imagined. As she fell to her knees in joy and relief, ashamed of her prior doubt, drops of hot oil fell on his bare shoulder, awakening him. And Cupid disappeared."

"Oh," Psyche said, and it was as if she were part of the legend. "Foolish girl! Why could she not have had more faith!"

Suppose, Herald thought darkly, Psyche examined his background and discovered Flame of Furnace? One message to the Cluster Council, and he, Herald, would disappear, plucked from his dalliance and transferred against his will to Furnace to complete his obligation.

"The legends do reflect the frailties of their makers," Hweeh agreed. "Modern entities would probably behave more sensibly."

"Would they?" she asked. "If I had a chance to marry an entity like the God of Love, do you think I would agree never to look upon his true form? Never to question whether I had not trapped him into marriage against his better interests, or lured him with some transient quality that was not properly mine?"

She was certainly striking at the problem! Herald realized that it had not been female capriciousness that had reminded her of the interview with Hweeh. Did she, after all, suspect the manner in which Flame nullified the Cluster legitimacy of the forthcoming marriage? Was she trying to provide him a gracious, or at least tenable, mode of retreat? As he had tried to do for her father, during the duel?

"Surely Cupid would know his own mind," Hweeh said. "Gods are not readily deceived or trapped."

Unless they *wanted* to be, Herald thought.

"Suppose he were attracted to her only for her aura," she persisted, talking nominally to Hweeh. "And then she lost it. Could she still marry him?"

Was she absolutely determined to have this out?

"Where is the Sador Witness?" Hweeh asked suddenly.

"He departed the castle," Herald said. "You were in shock again."

"What is this about marriage?"

"The banns are being published for the Lady Kade and

me," Herald said. "Last night the Lady manifested an aura of two hundred fifty."

The horn whistled. "And now that aura is gone," Hweeh said. "Suddenly I understand. Do you seek my opinion?"

"Perhaps we do," Herald said.

"I had understood that entities of highest aura—" Hweeh started, but paused, perhaps realizing that this comment would not be diplomatic. "Of course, an aura of two hundred fifty would be *the* highest, so that convention—" He stopped again.

That was true! Herald had been betrothed to Flame of Furnace because she was the highest female Kirlian. But now Psyche was the highest. All he had to do was demonstrate that before a Cluster committee, and his marriage to Psyche would be legitimized. Meanwhile, no need to bother her about the matter. What a helpful insight Hweeh had provided—coincidentally?

"I am not certain," Herald said cautiously, "that it is fair to marry her in this circumstance. I was summoned to exorcise her demon, yet without that Possession, if we must call it that, I might not have had as much interest in her."

"If the thing that repells others is what attracts you, who has the better right to marry her?" Hweeh asked. "Others might desire superficial things, such as her physical beauty or her wealth or family status. This is not the case with you."

Herald turned this over in his mind, and it made sense. "I thank you for your insight, Hweeh of Weew. Now I can proceed with confidence." *And so could she.*

"It happens to be my particular talent—the unusual revelation," Hweeh said. "I wish I could face my own realization of astronomy that sends me into shock." He paused, his eyeball wavering. "Do you suppose I could be cured by the application of an aura higher than yours?"

Now Herald considered. "Next time the Lady's demon manifests, we shall have to interview you," he said.

"Thank you. Knowing myself as I do, I suspect that what is in my mind is quite important. It behooves us to ascertain its nature."

"Now tell us the rest of the legend of Psyche," the girl said.

"It really is not important. Psyche begged Venus for help, not realizing the identity of her enemy, and the irate goddess forced her to perform a number of very arduous and hazardous tasks. But eventually Cupid recovered, and helped Psyche accomplish these. In the end she was given immortality and allowed to remain forever with Cupid. She bore him a child named Pleasure. As far as I know, it is *still* a happy Solarian godly family." Hweeh bobbed his eyestalk. "At any rate, you see how much of you I know through your name."

"A child named Pleasure . . ." Psyche repeated, and smiled knowingly.

5

Duke of Qaval

*E*Site animation.*E*
*&*Details.*&*
*E*Location: Galaxy Milky Way, Segment Etamin. Nature: evocation of ancient machine aura, temporary. Specific locale uncertain.*E*
*&*You are certain it was not a contemporary-culture machine aura generation?*&*
*E*The pattern corresponded closely to the ancient code. Possible confusion, but unlikely.*E*
*&*Then key the signature of evocation to its site, and you will have the specific planet.*&*
*E*Unable. No records of site-signatures available for keying. Need direct site observation.*E*
*&*No records!*&*
*X*True. All records beyond 10,000 cycles wiped for economy reasons. Our fleets must travel light.*X*
*&*Idiocy! We *need* those records. Well, assign action unit.*&*
*0*Action unit 2, orient on that Segment.*0*
*2*Oriented.*2*

Now that the Enemy Witness was gone, it was no longer proper for Herald to sleep in the Lady's chamber. He moved into his own room, where he could exercise without disturbing the household. He transferred back to his own Slash body in Andromeda briefly to put his concerns in order and abate his schedule of assignments and make application for Cluster sanction of his marriage to Psyche. But mainly he oriented on Planet Keep and

Kastle Kade, for his future home base had to be here. It was agreed that after the marriage he would have his natural Slash body mattermitted here. Psyche wanted it that way, and was sure she would not be revolted. She was eager to travel with him in Transfer, too, but her range was much more limited than his, and until the mystery of her variable aura was understood it seemed best to keep her home.

Immediate chores completed, he returned to his Solarian host and rode on a fine wheelhorse from the Palace of Crown to Kastle Kade. It was like coming home. Too bad there was no Transfer unit here—but Psyche was enough.

One night he woke to find her in his room, standing silently by his bed in a gauzy white nightie. She looked a bit like a ghost, but an extremely feminine one, for she stood between him and the moonlit window. Solarians, he had discovered the easy way, were visually stimulated, and the half-suggested outline of the female form was potent.

He sat up quickly. "Psyche! Are you—?"

"No," she said sadly. "I am not enhanced. I am only the normal me, low aura." Of course, 25 was not low at all; it only seemed that way after 250. "I thought— I just—oh, Herald, suppose I never manifest again?"

He took her into his arms, and then into his bed. It would have been the height of cruelty to deny her, and he really did find her most desirable as she was, nadir aura and all.

The nobles of Keep arrived in force for the wedding. They came in horse-drawn carriages, richly garbed. Each wore his Coat of Arms, which was the Shield of Arms embroidered on the cloth of a tunic. Herald, as the groom, had to stand beside the Duke of Kade and suffer inspection by each guest, a tedious chore, except for his professional interest in their diversity.

"Duke of Qaval," the doorman announced, superfluously for Herald, who was quite familiar with the general arms of Segment Qaval. A tall, bold figure strode in. He was manlike, with short stout legs showing green under the hem of his tunic, powerful green arms, and a thick scaly tail. His head was reptilian, with projecting snout and a huge slash of a mouth suggestive of the predators of Lake

Donny. In short, a handsome specimen of the dominant species of that Segment.

"So glad you could come, Qaval," Kade said grimly. Herald knew this was a leading member of the enemy coalition, the entity to whom Whirl of Dollar owed allegiance. The force behind the move to burn Psyche.

"Couldn't miss the chance to survey your fortifications, Kade," Qaval replied with the smile of a crocodile.

"Meet Herald of Slash, the expert exorcist you inflicted upon me, now to be my son-in-law." Meaning: *We have subverted your agent.*

Qaval's small eye glared coldly down on Herald as the enemy Duke extended his claw. "My compliments on an apt maneuver," he said, speaking from the side of his mouth so that his huge triangular teeth barely showed.

Herald merely nodded his head, uncertain to whom the ironic compliment was addressed. The nobles of Planet Keep played hard politics! But on this occasion the weapons were left behind, and only carefully selected words could be used for the fencing.

"Marquis of Roundabout," the doorman said, and a Polarian entered. The creature was shaped like a giant candy drop, with a tapering tentacle above and a spherical wheel below. Because Polarians used their skin surface for perception and some communication, the Marquis wore only token clothing, a band of cloth embroidered with his Coat of Arms: an Achievement symbolic of debt exchange, within the Polarian Spherical Circle, within the Dragon of Segment Etamin, within the outline of the Milky Way Shield.

The Polarian touched Kade's hand with the little ball in the end of his trunk, then touched Herald's hand. "May this resolve the conflict," the ball said, vibrating Herald's flesh to make the sound. "It has been an uncircular matter."

So there was one enemy noble who preferred to avoid trouble! Maybe there were others. Still, there was no question the grudge remained. Perhaps because of the mischief wrought by Psyche's mother, the whole planet was watching Psyche.

"Chief of Skot." This was a Solarian, a man about Kade's age and girth, wearing a tartan. This would be the father of the Scion of Skot, who had been mentioned as a possible suiter for Psyche. Well, that situation had changed!

"Viscount of Number." This was a Sador, like the Earl of Dollar, but of higher rank.

Then, arriving late, a very special entity: "Prince Circlet of Crown." A Sador prince, the only guest who ranked the Dukes of Kade and Qaval, and *the* prime mover in the opposition. The enemy leaders were here in force!

"The Prince does this castle honor," Kade murmured, making a formal bow. He seemed a bit overwhelmed.

"I am well aware of that," Circlet snapped, and rolled on. The royalty of Sphere Sador had never acclimatized to the dissipation of power of a once-mighty empire.

The wedding itself was a ponderous formality that annoyed and bored Herald, who was accustomed to using his time efficiently. Heraldry was a good survival of medieval times; these other customs should have been allowed to remain defunct. The castle servants garbed him to their satisfaction and guided him through the motions. But he felt better when he spied the Duke of Kade looking just as glum, though perhaps the man had different reason. The forms had to be followed, but who in his right mind could enjoy them?

Nevertheless, Psyche was beautiful—she really was! —like a jewel shining amid the ornate dullness. There were, after all, virtues other than mere aura, and she had them all.

At last the real celebration: the banquet. Now the seriousness abated and the camaraderie began. Liquor in its various guises flowed freely, causing antagonisms to fade into the background. Prime wheels of Sador beef rolled around the table, until only the metallic bones remained. Herald saw the Duke of Qaval's formidable teeth ripping off long shreds of half-raw flesh: there was a true carnivore! What a terror those teeth must be in battle! But even Prince Circlet seemed to be enjoying himself, setting his steak on a sterile mat on the floor and shredding it with his feeding wheel and sucking up the fragments. When a pretty little Sador serving wench brought desert—mounds of quivering gelatin derived from the large bones of freshly slaughtered animals, topped with wheelcow cream in the initial stage of spoilage—the Prince hooked her wheel suggestively, in full view of the throng. She spun off a squeal as his rim touched her intimate axle and almost dropped the tray on his top wheel. Even the circumspect Polarian noble glowed in color for an instant at this good-natured indecency, and the long, long lip of Qaval curled momentarily. These entities never let a little warlike disharmony interfere with the basic pleasures of life.

After the banquet, the ball. Musicians played the themes of different species, and creatures circulated in conversation, dancing, and innocuous competition. Psyche was much in demand as a dancing partner, and not merely by those in Solarian form. The Polarian Marquis did a minuet with her, executed very prettily, and then the Duke of Qaval took her, putting his reptilian snout right up against her pale-blue cheek and using his tail to assist in intricate turns. Finally the Prince of Crown himself joined her in a free-form endeavor, spinning grandly about on his wheels while she pirouetted in counterpoint. It was quite artistic. One thing the leisure class of Keep had mastered well was the art of diversion.

Whirl of Dollar, back in the company of his compatriots, nudged up beside Herald as he watched.

"Do not feel out of alignment," the little Sador murmured. "They are verifying that she is not possessed. My Lord Qaval feels that my report was exaggerated, and does not want war on a fallacious pretext."

Oh. In that case, let them dance with his wife all they wanted! There was no demon aura present.

The nobles did not neglect Herald himself. The Duke of Qaval strode up with a mug of distillate in one claw, and wished him hearty congratulations. Then, in a lower tone: "Will you permit a personal observation?" The reptile noble had a strong aura of about sixty. It was easy to believe that Qaval was one of the leading combat knights.

"Permitted," Herald agreed guardedly. He was very curious to know what really motivated these enemies. Surely they did not believe they had a genuine case against Psyche.

"We of Qaval have long been devotees of the Temple of Tarot, and of the animation connected with it. Does this fall within your sphere of talent?"

"It does," Herald said. "As a healer, I have necessarily studied many related disciplines, though I am not a literal devotee of the Temple."

"A fair response! My concern is why an entity such as

106

you, of high aura and skill, should conjoin with a client of comparatively low aura."

A trap? Herald marched right into it. "She is not always of low aura, Duke. At times she manifests a higher Kirlian than I. But this is not Possession; it is enhancement of her natural aura. Or perhaps her lower aura is the nether cycle of a widely fluctuating Kirlian force. In that respect, she is my natural mate."

"How can you be sure it is natural?"

"You touched her. Found you any indication that she has ever been possessed?"

"None. And this is what confuses me. Our Witness reports that she has manifested supernaturally, but he might be mistaken. You were our hired expert. Had you reported no manifestation, we should have been satisfied. Instead you marry her—on the basis of that very quality."

"Yes. Your suspicion was at least partly valid. The manifestation is genuine, but there is no threat such as you experienced with her mother."

"I prefer to believe that you distort the case."

"Sir?" Herald inquired stiffly.

"That you became enamored of the Lady and her style of life, one that must be quite enticing to an entity from a downtrodden Sphere of a subject Galaxy. So you justified your liaison by perceiving in her a more potent aura than in fact exists. In this fashion you had a hold on Kade, who would never otherwise have unbent sufficiently to yield his daughter to such a union. Rather than submit her to verification of your claim at our claws, he suffered her to be allied to you."

"There are dueling swords available, if you care to oblige," Herald said tightly.

Qaval affected not to hear him. "Certainly a creature like you would not actually marry an entity who posed any potential threat to you or your livelihood. And a female who is no threat to her alien husband can hardly be a threat to her world. Therefore we seem to have no case against the Lady Kade."

Suddenly Herald understood. The Duke was offering a rationale that would effectively terminate any suspicion of Psyche, despite Whirl's report!

"There may be merit in your view," Herald said gratefully.

"However, if there needs must be a duel—"

The enemy Duke would have his mouthful of flesh! "I meant only to admire the caliber of decorative weapons, so rarely seen these days," Herald said. It was in effect a groveling apology.

"Even so." Qaval smiled with twoscore teeth. "I have reason to believe the Prince will concur. We are a peaceful planet where many species coexist in harmony, and Kade's fortifications are impressive. We never wanted war. It was necessary merely that we be quite certain that the mother was not echoed in the daughter. Our precautions may have appeared extreme, but—"

"I understand completely," Herald said. "You have many powerful and hostile auras on this planet. They must be controlled. My own existence was very nearly terminated by one such rampaging animal. No precaution is too extreme."

Qaval nodded gravely and drifted away. The party continued unabated, as savage in its fashion as a battle. Herald finally wangled a dance with his bride.

"You make me jealous," he murmured in her shell-blue ear. "All the royalty seeks your company."

"But I seek only yours," she said, holding him close. "Though I am not certain about *you*. I saw you eyeing that cutewheeled serving wench—"

"Oh? Which one?" he asked, glancing around.

"Just how many *did* you eye?" she demanded severely. But she couldn't hold the expression, and abruptly kissed him.

There was a general exclamation from many entities, as of the sight of something naughty. "Oh, shut up, lechers!" she cried at them all, smiling.

Circlet of Crown did not like being upstaged. There were no Sador wenches immediately handy to be goosed. "Let's play a game," the Prince suggested loudly, rolling off his disk of fermented grainmalt intoxicant. He had evidently sucked up several dishes too many. But no one could afford to ignore or rebut even the drunken word of the Prince. "Hide and Quest!"

This was so old a game it seemed to date from the period of the Ancients; every Sphere had its variants. "Everybody hide—and the bride and groom are IT!" Prince Circlet continued. And he rolled wavily off. "Block your wheels for five minutes," he called back as he left the room. "Give us time!"

Kade shook his head. "Just what I need! Drunken enemies all over my castle. If any one of them hurts himself, a diplomatic incident!" But even he could not deny the Prince. He departed, seeking a suitable place to hide.

Suddenly Herald was alone with his wife. "Five minutes? Let's give them five *hours*," he suggested, taking Psyche in his arms again.

She yielded gladly, moving into a kiss of considerable depth. She might look like a child from a moderate distance, but she had a woman's instincts! Yet something was subtly wrong.

He concentrated, zeroing in on that wrongness. It was not a matter of wedding-day tension, for she was relaxed and joyous. Hardly any other person would have noticed it at all, but this involved aura, and he was the Kirlian expert.

Aura—that was it! Her aura was rising. It was now about thirty-five, ten intensities above her norm.

She drew back. "What is it, my love?"

"The enemy is satisfied. They no longer oppose you, believing that I'd never marry a demon. They think it is the wealth of Kade I desire."

"So?" she said, delightful in her certainty that he had no interest in any material thing except her. Which was close enough to the truth. Herald was not yet rich, but he was getting there.

"But now your aura is strengthening," he said, worried. "If they become aware—"

"I will not hide!" she exclaimed. "We shall go to the Prince and show him! There is no harm in me."

"The Prince is drunk!"

"Then let him think my aura is the result of his besotment! But let it be open. My aura won you; I want all Planet Keep to know."

Herald sighed. If she really wanted to show off her demon aura, he would not be able to restrain her. "Maybe that's best. Actually what you have is a variable aura, a cyclic intensity. None of that type has been known before, so perhaps it is a mutation, but it is not inherently strange. If they see that even at the height there is no alien Possession. . . ."

"Come! We have to seek them out anyway. We shall show my aura to every creature in this castle!" And she drew him eagerly by the hand.

Creatures were scattered all over the premises. One by one they routed them out, and Psyche touched each. "See? My aura is stronger, because I am married to the King of Aura." And one by one, startled as much by her illogic as the fact, the higher-aura entities agreed.

In the course of an hour, Psyche's aura rose to 135, but it was obvious to all that she had not changed. Herald was increasingly nervous, however. He wished the enhancement had occurred after the guests were safely departed. This was a touchy situation, like a firebrand hovering near dry tinder. Maybe it would not touch, but distance was preferable.

But the Duke of Qaval remained hidden, and so did Prince Circlet of Crown. "They must be together," Herald conjectured. "The Prince would have chosen his own location, and the Duke stayed with him to be sure he didn't hurt himself. But where can they be?"

"It's a big castle, with many crannies," Psyche said. "But I know them all. They shall not escape us!" And she led him on, intent on the fun of the game. Ah, the exuberance of her youth!

They searched through the chambers, right up into the highest turrets and parapets, while her aura climbed also, to 160. Now Herald had two reasons to want to be rid of the guests: to prevent alarm over her too-high aura—and to allow him occasion to make love to her. After all, it *was* their wedding night! But so long as the Prince remained hidden, the game was not over, and no one could go home. Any lesser entity could have been summoned in free—"ALLEE ALLEE CREATURES IN FREE!—but not the Prince. He had to be found, and no other entity could help.

"The drunken wheelie," Herald complained. "I want him *out* of here before you fade again!"

Psyche smiled knowingly. "I do, too, Herald. I wish I could always be high, for you. But from what you say, I will not peak for another hour. If we haven't found him by then, I'll sneak into a closet with you and rip off your clothes."

"With our luck, we'd bump into the Prince in the back of that closet," Herald muttered darkly.

"Oh, no!" she cried. "Making love to an alien Slash monster serpent is one thing, but I draw the line at Sador voyeurism!"

Herald spanked her pert posterior. "Don't worry. He doesn't have any clothes to rip off. But he might tear a wheel off that wench who was serving him drinks."

Psyche halted suddenly. "The wine cellar! That's where he would be!"

"Of course!" Herald said, snapping his human fingers. "Where else for a drunk? We should have checked there first."

They hurried down the curling stairs hand in hand, while her aura intensified more rapidly than ever. "It's accelerating!" Herald said. "It's up to one hundred and ninety already." One hundred and ninety—the level of Flame of Furnace. He didn't want it to stay there.

"We'll never get the castle cleared in time," she said. "Come on, they won't miss us for a few more minutes." She tugged him toward the bedroom.

"Few minutes, hell," he said. "I want the whole night."

"You'll have the whole *century*, after tonight! Stolen moments are most precious." And she drew him back up the stairs.

"I suppose so," he grumbled. Actually her mere presence, surrounded by an aura nearing two hundred, was a joy to him.

Two hundred? "It's one hundred eighty," he said, surprised.

"You mean I've peaked already? I somehow thought it would go as high as before." She curbed her disappointment. "Well, we'll just have to hurry." And she ran up the next flight of steps, her skirts flouncing up to give him nice flashes of her slender, shapely legs. Whoever had designed wedding dresses had known how to excite a man!

In the bedroom she was down to 165. "Wait," he said. "There's something funny about this. First you shot up, then down. Come below with me."

She paused, about to unsnap the assorted fastenings of her costume. "I thought you wanted—"

"I'm not an absolute sex maniac," he said. "I'll suffer through lovemaking at zero aura if need be; it isn't as though you had no other attractions. There's your money, and this fine castle, and—"

"Oh, I wouldn't want you to suffer," she said, making a moue.

"Humor me. I'll make it up to you in a moment."

111

She smiled. "I know you will. I'll deduct one gold coin and one brick of the castle for each modicum you are deficient in your performance."

"There may not be any castle left!" he cried.

She kicked him with her soft slipper. "It's not *that* much of a chore, serpent!"

They trotted down two flights of stairs again. Just getting around this castle was good exercise! And her aura jumped to 190 again.

"It's inversely proportional to elevation!" he exclaimed.

"But it's been rising slowly as we climbed—until now," she said.

"We seem to have two factors. It is cyclic, rising steadily at about a hundred intensities an hour until it levels off and fades at a similar rate. But it is also related to height; the farther you go from the ground, the weaker the effect."

"Then I'd better bring a pillow for the cellar," she said with a lift of her eyebrow. "Knowing the way aura excites your—"

"Not while the Prince is there!" He drew her in and kissed her. "Come on, let's rout him out right now. We can sneak back while your father is seeing them out the gate and keeping them from falling into the lake. Though the Duke of Qaval might frighten the alligators away if *he* fell in."

"You're more interested in the enhancement pattern than you are in me," she pouted.

There was just enough truth in that to hurt. "If he's not in the cellar, we'll do it there now," he said. "Standing up, if need be."

"Oh, joy!" she snorted, laughing.

"Lots of species breed on their feet."

"Mintakans breed *with* their feet," she said. "But you can just keep your feet out of my—"

He cut her off with a hasty kiss and squeeze. "Be assured I'll take my shoes off first."

Her aura jumped again as they descended. At the level of the cellar it stood at 215. At this moment, the second-highest Kirlian in the Cluster.

"Where are the lights?" Herald asked, blinking in the dark.

"No lights for the wine cellar. Father says light damages the wine."

"Then we'll just have to feel for the Prince," he said. He slid one hand along the cold stone wall, still holding onto her with the other.

"Great Circle!" a voice exploded ahead, startling them both. "A ghost!"

"Found you, Prince!" Herald cried.

"Look at the Lady!" another voice said. It was the Duke of Qaval.

Herald looked. Psyche was glowing in the dark.

It was her aura, manifesting visibly. It pulsed gently with her life processes, its colors showing the stresses of differing functions. It extended in a nimbus, fading at the periphery in little sparkles. It was absolutely beautiful.

But it was also disaster. "Possession!" the Prince cried in horror. "Dollar was right!"

"No," Herald protested. "Her aura is variable. During certain periods it rises as high as mine, then fades again. But she is herself. There is no alien influence."

"Then why does she illuminate?" Qaval demanded.

"This occurs at times with strong auras in certain fields. That was how the aura was identified in System Sol over two thousand years ago, when the scientists who photographed it—"

"Then why do *ours* not glow?"

"Perhaps they are of different types. I assure you, this is *not* a supernatural manifestation. Come, touch her; verify that she is normal, the same girl you danced with anon."

"Keep her away from me!" Circlet screamed. "She is possessed of a demon!"

"In another light, perhaps our auras would glow, and hers not," Herald said. "She has a rare type—"

"Kill her," the Prince said coldly.

Herald's human hand snapped to his sword, but he carried none for this festive occasion. Nor did the Prince and the Duke.

"We may not strike during truce," Qaval assured his liege lord. "Even were we armed."

"She must die," the Prince insisted.

Herald moved in front of Psyche. "She is my wife."

"Come . . . we must depart," Qaval said. He sounded sad.

The two moved past Herald, who remained tensely alert. But there was no attack. The Prince was trying to

113

give Psyche as wide a berth as possible, and the Duke was intent on guarding him. It would have been tactically foolish of them to attack, for the knights of the Duke of Kade controlled this castle, and no guest could escape alive without Kade's consent.

Herald and Psyche followed the Prince and Qaval to the main hall. The party ended swiftly. Iron-faced, the Duke of Kade stood by the front gate and mumbled empty pleasantries while the enemy guests filed out to the ferry.

Psyche's aura had risen to about 240. But Herald was no longer interested in making love. He knew that chance had passed a sentence of death on her, when she had been so near to safety.

"I regret I shall not be able to complete your therapy," Herald said. "It will not be safe for you to remain here."

"But we are progressing," Hweeh protested. "I know it. Each session I am better able to approach the shock subject. It concerns deep space, some manifestation beyond the Cluster itself, and it is extremely important. If only I can comprehend it without blowing out my mental fuse. Perhaps even *this* session. . . ."

"The other nobles of Planet Keep have decided that my wife, Psyche, is subject to Possession," Herald said. "They demand her execution. Since neither the Duke of Kade nor I will tolerate that, there will be war. It is not fair to keep you here, as this castle may be besieged, perhaps destroyed."

"I appreciate your consideration," Hweeh said. "But I feel that the information I carry is worthy of the risk, and that only you can evoke that information in time. We are faced by some terrible threat, and it will not abate merely because I ignore it. My intellect knows what my emotion does not; there is no escape from reality by hiding from it. And . . . I have developed a certain fondness for the Lady Kade, and for you, Herald. I would not feel right about departing in your period of stress."

"This is very generous of you," Psyche said. "But there is no way you can help us."

"Perhaps I will find a way," the Weew said. "I have certain connections in my Segment. If a protest were lodged. . . ."

"The Duke of Kade feels this matter must be settled

114

internally," Herald said. "If he cannot repulse the enemy forces, an extra-Segment protest would not avail. Distant politics cannot act as swiftly as a near arrow."

"Perhaps some other way, then. At any rate, I shall remain—because I must stay with you, in the hope that you can evoke my information in time."

In just a few days the enemy marched. Kade marshaled his own forces efficiently. Kade was the most powerful Dukedom of Keep, but its available forces could not match those of the Prince.

"All this is unnecessary," Herald told Kade. "Let me take Psyche away to Andromeda, where they cannot follow."

"She would not go," Kade said. "She is a creature of Keep, and of Kastle Kade. To remove her would be to destroy her. And the Transfer and mattermission facilities are in the control of the King."

It had to be mattermission, of course. With a normal aura of twenty five, Psyche could not last indefinitely in Transfer. In less than a year she would fade to oblivion. And if her body remained here, it would be destroyed.

"Can we hold them off?" Herald asked.

"We *must* hold them off," Kade said. "If they cannot overwhelm us in the first month, they will desist, for they must tend to their own households and keep the beasts at bay. Many are not too keen on this battle, after meeting my daughter on her wedding day and seeing her innocence. But now the honor of the Prince requires that the effort be made."

The effort was made. Soon the Duke's lookouts reported the banners of the Prince's army to the south across the water of Lake Donny and beyond the dam. "They will not attack today," Kade said wisely. "First they will rendezvous their forces and make a base camp. Tomorrow shall be the initial action."

He was correct. The enemy did not advance further. The banners had been shown, giving fair warning; that was part of the protocol. In due course the visible army removed to the south, out of sight of the castle.

"I was not pleased to have you marry my daughter," Kade told Herald gruffly. "But you have stood up well, and she loves you. Will you consult on strategy?"

"I am not expert in siege strategy," Herald said, flat-

115

tered at this attention. The Duke's acceptance came slowly, but was worth having.

"It is mainly common sense. You will take the part of the enemy commander."

"As you will, sir."

Kade walked to a wall-sized map. "Here is Kastle Kade," he said, pointing out the bulging triangle. "Set within Lake Donny, in turn formed by our dam across Donnybrook." He indicated the area south of the castle. "The main approach is up the valley from the south, since the northern front is ideal for defensive ambush. But we can release the water from our dam, flash-flooding that valley. This is well known to the enemy, of course. Such flooding would diminish our effective moat, but there would still be a bog for troops to cross while under fire from our parapets. How, then, would you approach with a siege force?"

Herald considered. "It would be tedious and difficult, therefore improbable—so I would attempt to approach over the ridge-road to the west. I would send out skilled knights to eliminate the defensive sentries, then funnel the troops and siege machinery along the heights, debouching at the castle shore. I would set my catapults at the pass, so as to lob stones conveniently down."

"And if I sent knights to block you off at the high pasture beyond the Ridge Road?"

"I have—how many?—two thousand knights? You have perhaps two hundred. I would wipe out your entire force, if it were so foolish as to meet me in open battle away from the protection of the castle. It is true that the castle of the Baron of Magnet is in that vicinity, but he has few knights—in fact they are all here at Kastle Kade for the main defense—so there remain nothing but household troops to secure that castle. I would set a minor siege about it, not attacking it but merely preventing any access to it, so that there could be no interference from there." Herald glanced at Kade. "In fact, I don't see how you can stop me. The Prince, I mean. He will have his siege force by the castle despite all you can do. You can't flood a ridge, can you?"

"I cannot flood a ridge. I could place troops in ambush— "

"My knights might take losses of three or four to one,

116

but very soon they would clean out your forces. And where could your knights hide—down the slope?"

"So you see no way I can abate your thrust?" Kade said.

"Frankly I *don't*, and it has me worried. Maybe you could dig a ditch, or throw up a wall, and guard it— "

"In two days or less? When they have full-scale siege works?"

"Duke, you make me nervous indeed! Kastle Kade is vulnerable!"

"That seems to be a reasonable conclusion," Kade agreed.

"We'll just have to stop them at the wall. Unless they are fool enough to march straight up the southern valley."

"They are not such fools. They will march a small contingent up the valley, and should we drown those the major force would remain—and our defense would be weakened far more than their offense."

"So they can move troops past the dam by doing it a little at a time, and we can't stop them."

"Yes. We shall reserve our forces for the castle."

"Damn it!" Herald exploded. "How could such a liability have been left so near the castle?"

"Actually, the dam is guarded by bowmen, so a small force will find approach difficult—"

"I mean the high trail!"

"The Ridge Road is necessary for herding our cattle to and from the high pasture," Kade said patiently. "It is a good pasture, the best in this region, and our cattle are the finest and fattest wheelers available. You saw how our recent guests tore into that wheelbeef! Much of the wealth of the Dukedom derives from that herd."

"And no one ever expected to go to war," Herald said glumly. "Who could have anticipated that a Lady of Kade would become haunted?" He touched the sword he now wore. "The whole thing is so foolish! This damned superstition that says anything new must be suspect! Anybody who really *knew* Psyche. . . ."

Kade smiled with one of the few touches of warmth Herald had seen in him. "You begin to echo me."

"And why not? The truth bears echoing."

Kade returned to the map. "I, too, objected to the vulnerability of the Ridge Road. One never considers one's defenses with the assumption that they will never be used.

117

But in the end I left the ridge unfortified. Can you see why?"

Herald studied the map again. "It is a mystery to me. I assume the certainty of inconvenience for your prime cattle outweighed the uncertainty of war. Why go to a lot of trouble and expense for something so theoretical?"

"Why, indeed," Kade agreed. "So I am sure the Prince's strategists have pored over this same map and reached a similar conclusion."

"Yes."

"And thereby lies the Prince's fall—perhaps."

Herald looked up sharply. "How so?"

"Suppose these fine fat cattle should stampede from the high pasture?"

Herald looked closely at the map a third time, seeing the high pasture and the way it channeled into the familiar —to cattle—ridge path. Slowly he smiled.

Psyche caught him arming for battle. "Herald! You're not going to fight? Your host doesn't have the strength or training!"

"All hosting is voluntary," Herald reminded her. "I could never take my host into danger without his permission and cooperation."

"I don't know," she said. "We've seen strange things here on Keep, and with your aura—"

"I'll let you speak to him directly," Herald said, and turned over the vocal apparatus.

"It's true, ma'am," the host said. "I'm a nobody myself. I knew when I started that I had to choose between serfing and hosting, and if I went the host route I'd have to stay out of the way and let my Transferee do it his way. Mister Herald has exercised me and made me stronger and tougher than I ever was before, and his aura heals me all the time, making me feel real good, you know—"

"I know," she agreed.

"And I *like* having people admire what my body carries. Even if it's not exactly *me*. And—no offense, ma'am —I'd never get remotely close to a doll like you by myself. I'm nothing, and you're the Lady Kade. So I'll take my chances. Maybe I'll die with Mister Herald, but it's a sight better than living on my own."

It didn't faze her. "Yes, I have been making love to two men, haven't I! But this is the nature of Transfer.

Herald knows that I'll never love anyone but him in any form, ever."

"He knows," the host agreed. "Thanks for the word, ma'am, and now I'll just submerge again, okay? I feel sort of out of place, you know, talking to you like this."

" 'Bye, host," she said, making a cute little wave of her hand. Then, to Herald: "I still want you by me, husband. We haven't been married long, and I want to conceive Pleasure. If anything happened to you now—"

"It is *you* they are after," Herald reminded her. "We have to defend the castle, and its main vulnerability is the dam. If the enemy holes the dam, the lake will drop, and they'll be able to cross to the very walls. The mud will slow them, but still—"

"No they won't," she said. "The lake is deeper around the castle, to make a good moat. The water will never sink that low. All the alligators will congregate there, and—"

"Still, it would allow them to bring their siegecraft that much closer. So I'm taking a crossbow to help defend the dam."

"Can't you use your crossbow here in the main keep?"

"If the dam falls, I'll be back here soon enough." But he didn't like to see her doubt, so he brought her close and whispered in her sweet ear: "The crossbow is only part of the uniform. I'm running Kirlian check on the defenders just to be sure none of them turn out to be Transferees who will sabotage the dam or take a potshot at your father. I'm not there to fight, and the ferry will bring me back." He bit her ear lightly.

She shook her head, whether in negation or reaction he was not sure. "I suppose I knew it would be this way. You're trying to prove something to my father."

Herald smiled. "I suppose I am." He kissed her and left. Actually, he looked forward to this bit of participation; it made him feel genuinely useful in abating a situation that he had in part precipitated.

The enemy rode up the valley toward the dam with martial fanfare and banners flying; a line of knights mounted on their wheeled chargers. Herald recognized the Arms of Crown, Qaval, and Skot, along with others that were new to him. But where were Runabout, Number, and Dollar? Had they balked at this campaign, or were they elsewhere?

119

Where else, except up on the ridge, ready to start their avalanche? Properly executed, that slide could fill in a sizable section of the lake, making a good start on the ramp required to achieve the castle. Especially when destruction of the dam lowered the water level.

If treachery were to manifest, now would be the time! Herald took his eyes off the approaching banners and moved rapidly along the battlement of the dam, passing close enough to the standing crossbowmen to feel their auras without actual physical contact. The archers had not been told what he was doing, of course. In fact, he carried a bow himself, as though to fill in where needed.

All their auras were authentic. There were no Transfer traitors—not here, at least. Maybe he had been unduly suspicious.

The Duke of Kade was ready. He had landed beside the dam with his picked force, not to defend it per se but to offer ritual combat. It was not an ethic Herald properly understood, but the master of the castle was expected to sally out and offer honest battle on the field of honor.

So now the banners of Kade and Magnet and the other allies were flying. There were about fifty knights on each side, half Kade's force, and surely a much smaller fraction of the enemy's total. This honored the principle of token combat, a tradition throughout the Cluster for millennia, for what that was worth.

There was nothing Herald could do now except watch. The ferry would convey the surviving knights back to the castle, and Herald would go with them. Then the real action would begin, though it might be considerably less dramatic than this sample battlefield engagement.

The two groups of knights charged each other. Lances crashed into shields—oh, the insult to those beautiful Shields of Arms!—and some of the knights were unhorsed. Then it became a melee of flashing swords and maces and battle-axes. These were mainly physical weapons rather than lasers, brutal and bloody for the armor embodied interference layers to disrupt laser weapons. The banners fell, and all was chaos; only the flash of shield and crest made it possible to identify any of the participants.

But soon the recall was sounded, for such action could not be maintained long. Slowly the forces disengaged,

120

while retainers on foot dashed out to reclaim the dead. Slightly smaller groups of knights formed about the restructured banners of their sides. It was over, with not too much damage done.

Over? The charge sounded again, and the battered knights resumed the fray. Herald realized that this had been only the first clash of many, the figurative testing of the water. The break had been agreed on to remove the disabled and the debris, so as to keep the battlefield clear. No sense getting fouled up with the clutter of the dead and dying, after all; that was not neat and noble.

So it went: fierce clash, recall; clash again between smaller forces; recall again. It was a kind of elimination tournament, with luck seeming to be as much of a factor as individual skill. But it was soon apparent that the Duke of Kade's forces were getting the better of it. With each break, the enemy band was smaller, not merely in number but in proportion, until the difference approached two to one. At last the enemy had had enough; their knights were too tired to hack it any more. They sounded retreat, and this time retreated all the way down the valley. Kade of course did not follow; it could only mean an ambush by the numerous fresh knights beyond, and he would not be able to flood them out without drowning himself along with them.

Kade retained some twenty-five knights, while the enemy band was down to fifteen. Among the fallen were the Duke of Qaval and the Scion of Skot. This battle might have been a form of ritual, but the deaths were real. Herald regretted the death of Qaval, who had seemed to have some decency and considerable acumen; in other circumstances, a good entity to know.

The victorious party rode back up to the dam, leading several riderless horses. They rolled up the road to the side, where the barrier-gate opened to let them through. "The fools were out of condition!" Kade cried jubilantly. "They were astonishingly awkward. An excellent omen!"

Qaval, awkward? Herald would hardly have believed that, if he hadn't seen the defunct Shield of Arms. The enemy Duke had impressed him as the very last creature to go into battle unprepared. Had he been torn by conflicting loyalties?

Now the ferry hove to, and the knights rode their chargers aboard. Kade rolled by Herald, signaling him

121

to step up on the outside of the saddle for a lift. "Clear?" he inquired quietly through his visor as Herald obliged.

"Clear," Herald agreed.

Several of the horses were skittish, changing their wheels about, and it required stern guidance to keep them in line. "They should be better disciplined than that," Kade muttered, but his elation over the easy victory mitigated his ire at this detail.

The ferry cast loose. The paddle animals revved up, and the boat nosed across the clear water toward the castle. The honor guard of alligators closed in.

Suddenly there was a commotion. Six knights fell into the water with screams of surprise and dismay. In their heavy armor they could not swim or float; they had to cling to the rail, where they were subject to the wash from the paddles. The alligators were plunging in, dragging them away and down, eager to tackle the problem of extracting the morsels from the metal in their own fashion. The knights on the deck leaned far over in their saddles to grasp the flailing limbs of their companions, and five more fell in.

"Treachery!" Kade cried, lifting his battle ax high. "Show your faces, miscreants, or I shall have the archers on the dam slay you all!" And the Baron in charge of the crossbows was already marshaling them to orient on the ferry, which was well within their range.

Slowly each knight raised his visor. And the first face Herald recognized was the long green snout of the Duke of Qaval. "No treachery, Kade," he said. "Tactics."

"The dead!" Kade exclaimed. "They put their knights in the armor of our dead!"

"Did you really suppose your knights were that much better than ours?" Qaval inquired with a sneer that reached three-quarters of the way around his head. "Had we shown our true skill, you would have opened the sluices on us."

True enough, Herald thought. The enemy had found a cunning way to get past the sluices and the archers of the dam—by appearing to put up a poor fight. What an astonishing feat it had been, to change armor *on the battlefield* without alerting Kade's forces. Probably any knight who caught on had been expeditiously killed, and the bodies of Kade's knights had been stuffed into enemy armor and dragged off during the breaks. Herald himself had watched the whole battle and seen none of this; the operation had been a miracle of ingenuity and precision. And this boded ill indeed for the campaign. The enemy was not inferior, but superior to Kade's forces in proficiency, courage, and strategy. He knew the same thoughts were going through Kade's mind. They were in trouble!

But perhaps this had been the one supreme effort of the enemy, an all-out attempt to infiltrate the castle and open it to the main forces. It had been balked because Kade had caught on too quickly, and invoked the power of his dam archers. Perhaps.

Eight of the knights remaining on the deck were enemy. Only six were loyal, counting Kade himself. The other loyals were in the water, shoved there with their steeds by Qaval's ruthless ploy.

"Now let your archers fire," Qaval continued through another toothy smile. "At this range they will kill all here indiscriminately, you included, for we all bear Kade Shields and armor and they cannot see our faces to know friend from foe." Then his closing visor covered his sardonic expression.

"Get you to horse!" Kade rasped at Herald. Then he snapped his own visor shut and charged Qaval, battle-ax swinging.

It was melee again, this time not viewed from a distance, but right up close. Herald had memorized the identities of the eight enemy knights. It was not a talent that he normally possessed, but the shock of discovery and his familiarity with the Shields of Arms and Crests of the knights' armor enabled him to fix them instantly in his mind.

He leaped into the saddle of the nearest vacant steed, suddenly understanding why the horses had been skittish before. They had borne strange riders! Normally each steed was ridden by a single knight, whatever the occasion, so that sapient and sentient got to know each other. It made for better control and performance. The horses would obey any rider, but they were uncomfortable about strangers.

A spiked mace hung from this saddle. His human hand took up the weapon of its own accord. Maybe his host was helping. The mace was no light laser thing; it was a genuine, solid, bone-crushing instrument. He struck the horse with his feet, urging it forward.

123

Herald swung the mace at the head of the nearest enemy. The knight countered skillfully with his own mace. Herald was a novice at this sort of combat, and the enemy knights were obviously picked professionals. Herald really didn't have a chance.

However, this was a boat rocking gently on the water, crowded for mounted combat, and the other knight had been orienting on a different target, not expecting attack from Herald's direction. He was stationary, while Herald's steed was rolling forward. As a result, the impact sent both knight and steed toppling into the water. Herald was the victor.

He looked around. Two knights were bearing down on Kade, who had evidently dispatched his original target. Qaval had moved out of the way, engaging one of Kade's knights who had gotten there before Kade himself. Herald drew himself half out of the saddle to swing at the nearest enemy. His blow scored on the creature's upper section, but lacked the force and direction to do much harm.

The knight swung his sword about: a laser blade. Herald grabbed his mace in both hands and smashed it down squarely on the knight's crest. The sword of light was unable to block this purely physical blow. Herald felt a searing pain in his right elbow where the joint in the armor permitted part of the laser to penetrate, but his own blow crushed in the enemy's helmet, and that was enough.

"Fool!" Kade bellowed at him. "It's *you* they want! Get behind me!"

Herald hastily obliged, guiding his mount back across the deck. Another knight went for him—only to be cut off by Kade. It was Qaval, using another ax, and he was adept with it. Sparks flew as the two weapons clashed against each other.

Elsewhere on the boat Kade's knights, tired from the prior battle, were being brought down or pushed into the water. The Scion of Skot, a huge young Solarian, laid about him so fiercely that soon he rode amid corpses. This was the man Psyche might have married had she not seemed haunted. If Skot's ferocity were any indication of his other qualities, it might have been an exciting union!

Skot started toward Herald, and there was no mistaking the special menace that knight represented. He wanted

Herald's head, literally, and meant to have it before someone else deprived him of the privilege of taking it. While Herald hesitated, knowing it would be the height of folly for him to meet Skot in combat yet tempted anyway, the Baron of Magnet moved in instead. Magnet needed no armor; he swung a fist-sized ball of dense metal, keeping it in magnetic orbit about him. This he hurled at Skot's head with terrible force and accuracy. The enemy knight batted it out of the way with his mace, demonstrating reflexes Herald never could have matched, then fetched down a wooden lance and rammed it at Magnet. Magnetism was ineffective against wood. The point scored cleanly, knocking the Baron out of the saddle with such force he flew through the air to splash into the water. His ball splashed after him.

One other knight remained—another enemy. The three closed in on Kade and Herald, the only two of their side still in combat status. Kade, too, was tired. He wavered in the saddle, and his steed stumbled for him, fouling up its wheels momentarily. Kade had fought a great battle, twice, but he was not young, and blood was spattered on his mail where he had been wounded. The ferry, propelled mindlessly forward by its paddlers, was now out of crossbow range.

Still, the enemy was wary of the Duke of Kade, who might be less tired than he seemed. Even in his extremity, he was dangerous. Qaval and Skot approached him cautiously, while the third knight, a Polarian, guided his steed swiftly at Herald.

Herald, panting from his own exertions, meager as they might have been compared to the efforts of the seasoned warriors, knew he could not really fight another physical battle. There was only one chance: If he could get a hand on the Polarian's flesh, and if—

The tentacle shoved a lance at him. Herald threw himself to the side, started to fall out of his saddle like the duffer he was, reached across and grabbed hold of the other horse's saddle. The back of his fingers touched the Polarian's spongy flesh where it braced against that metal rim. Herald concentrated—and he was in luck. This was a Transferee! He had gambled that such highly trained knights would be required for this mission that some had ben brought in from far castles by Transfer.

He wore heavy gloves to protect his hands, but now

125

this was an interference. He yanked his hand back, letting the gauntlet be pinned by saddle and hide, then set his bare fingers against that hide. He sent his own aura into the same pattern he had employed against the monster Caesar: exorcism. In this brief time he could not hope to drive the aura of the Transferee out of the host—but he could give him an awful scare!

Enemy—GO! he willed.

It worked better than he had anticipated. The knight jerked back, breaking contact, and put his communication ball against the side of his horse.

"Enemy—GO!" he buzzed.

The steed shot away backwards—right into Skot. So hard was the impact, both were carried into the lake.

Thus victory, so suddenly! Yet Herald was sorry, for he knew it had merely been the result of a freak combination of talent and luck. There was precious little honor, here.

Now it was Kade against Qaval, ax against ax. Both knights were weary but determined. Herald wanted to help, but knew he would only get in the way. He had already done as much as he could.

The two horses wheeled around and around each other in response to guidance by the knights' legs. The axes clashed and clashed again, more sparks flying.

Then Qaval performed an intricate maneuver, and hooked his ax into Kade's, sending Kade's weapon flying out of his hand. Qaval's horse crowded him against the rail so that Kade had his back to the water with no way to retreat.

"It has been a good battle," Qaval said. "Now you have fairly lost. Give up your daughter for exorcism by the Prince's machine unit, and siege will be lifted and you permitted to retain your demesnes. I should have no joy in shedding your noble blood needlessly."

"I would not give her up to you if I could," Kade retorted. "She is married now, no longer mine to direct."

"Then do you stand aside," Qaval said evenly, "while I settle with the Healer."

"I shall not— "

"Do it!" Herald cried. "It is my responsibility!"

"That would be the death of you—and her," Kade said. He lunged at Qaval barehanded, but the enemy knight, thoroughly experienced, leaned back in his saddle, avoiding Kade's grasp, and calmly brought the flat of his ax down hard against Kade's helmet. Kade slumped in his saddle, unconscious.

Now Qaval wheeled to face Herald. "Yield you now?" he inquired, momentarily lifting his visor to show his green snout.

Herald could not help admiring the enemy knight, so strong in battle yet courteous too. Qaval had been ready to drop the charge against Psyche at the wedding, until her aura had glowed. Perhaps even then he had not been alarmed, but when Prince Circlet insisted, his loyal Duke had supported him with all the cunning and power at his command. Now, victorious, he would compromise, asking only that the girl be given over. Qaval obviously was not after the spoils of the Dukedom of Kade; he could readily have killed his enemy, but had deliberately spared him. Rather it was a matter of principle: the Prince must be served, and no suspicion of Possession could be permitted on Planet Keep.

It was a perfectly reasonable position, inviting acquiescence. Qaval *had* won fairly, demonstrating not only his superior cunning but his courage and honor as well. Yet it could not be.

"Her aura is not mine to yield, either," Herald said. "It is her own. To exorcise it by machine would be to kill her, Transferring her to nowhere. I shall not give up my wife—and you cannot take her, even if you kill me. The castle defenders will not turn her over to you. In fact, if you try to take this raft there yourself, you will be killed or taken prisoner yourself."

"Do you arm yourself suitably," Qaval said quietly, "for now we must duel."

Inflexible! "You can't win!" Herald said. "There is no way short of conquering Kastle Kade by storm—"

"I have not slain Kade; I shall not slay you. You both shall be hostage against the girl. I believe your castle will come to terms. Does the Dukedom not devolve on the Lady Kade in your absence?"

Smart, smart! And ruthless. If Psyche assumed charge, she would immediately give herself up to save her father and Herald. Was there a creature on this planet with more nerve than Qaval? Without the support of such a knight, the throne of Prince Circlet and his father, the King, would surely be a mockery.

Herald guided his horse to another horse while the Duke remained in place. Herald located a laser sword in the other saddle, and lifted it out. He turned it on, and the blade glowed. Powered by the castle broadcast, it was deadly.

"You have been the perfect knight, even in your treachery," Herald said. "I wish I had friends as noble as you the enemy. You have allowed me to arm myself. It is only fair to warn you that I know how to use this weapon, for I am of Slash, Andromeda."

"I am well aware of that, Healer," Qaval said. "You are a better swordsman than Kade, whose repute is widely known. But so am I." And he hung up his ax and drew his own laser sword.

Oh-oh.

Mounted, Herald would be at a disadvantage, for Qaval was an expert wheelhorsecreature. So he jumped down to the deck. He ran the risk of getting run down, but he was better off this way.

And Qaval, honorable to the last, did the same. Chivalry was far from dead on Planet Keep!

They moved together, fencing. Herald quickly verified that the enemy knight had not been bluffing. Qaval had short thick arms, but he was by no means clumsy. He handled his sword and shield with such expertise that Herald dared not try any tricks. The enemy used his tail to balance his body, making his motions more certain. Qaval had power; his tail, not his body, absorbed the recoil from his swift motions.

The enemy knight was under pressure, however, because the ferry was approaching the castle. Once it came within range of the defensive crossbows, Qaval would be in trouble. So he had to press the attack instead of waiting his opportunity. Herald, in contrast, could play it safe, being defensive.

It was some attack! Qaval had to be tired, but his blade flicked about Herald as though guided by its own mind. Herald foiled each thrust, but he had to retreat. Qaval was forcing him back toward the water. Soon he would be trapped, as Kade had been. Yet he had to keep stepping away; Qaval was simply too strong.

His heels came up against the rail. Herald tried desperately to drive Qaval back, taking the offense for the first time, but feint and thrust as he might, he could not make the knight fall for any ruses or give ground. Herald was making himself vulnerable by this effort. In a moment Qaval would counter with such authority that Herald would have to go into the water.

Only one chance. Herald blocked Qaval's blade to the left, causing the enemy to flick his weapon outward to avoid interruption of the circuit, then threw himself to the right, taking a quick forward roll on the deck. But even as he committed himself, he knew it hadn't worked. Qaval had not been fooled, and was in place to stab him before he regained his feet. It had been a desperation ploy to get out of the corner, and the invincible knight had anticipated it.

"Now you must yield," Qaval said calmly. But at this moment of disaster, something flew across the deck and struck him on the helmet. The knight fell back on his tail, unconscious. Amazed, Herald struggled to his feet.

A metal ball rolled across the deck. Then Herald saw the design on it: the crest of Magnet! It was the Baron of Magnet's mace! Herald peered into the water in the direction it had come from—and there was the Baron, floating.

Herald leaned over the rail and reached, but it was too far. So he ran to a horse and grabbed a mace from the saddle, extending its metal head toward the Baron. Sure enough, the Magnet drew into this, and Herald was able to haul him in close, where he could be lifted up and out.

"You showed up just in time!" Herald said.

Once the Baron was back in the saddle, he was able to speak, using his translator. "Water immersion does not harm my kind, and the teeth of the reptiles mean nothing to me. But I was not able to maneuver. It took a few moments to pump up enough gas to float, for we are hardly more dense than water, and by then the boat had left me behind. It took some time to paddle back."

"Paddle back?" Herald asked, perplexed. "You have no limbs, no jets!"

"I used my mace," Magnet explained, twirling his ball in momentary orbit. Suddenly Herald comprehended: The ball, shoved against the water, provided the metal brace the Baron could use to propel himself slowly forward. Apparently the water did not interfere with the creature's magnetism. This was a marvelously versatile species, one that could survive in the vacuum of space or

on the bottom of a predator-infested lake! "But I have also
—exhausted my fuel." And the Baron settled into the saddle, his mace dropping.

The doughty little warrior had done his utmost!

Now Herald was in charge of the ferry, with three
unconscious knights. He had little notion what to do, but
it didn't matter, because the paddlewheels were carrying
them all to the castle anyway. He looked like much more
of a hero than he was. He thought he saw Psyche waving a handkerchief from a parapet.

6

Siege of Psyche

*E*Second animation of site. Specific location: Segment Etamin, native Sphere Sador, Planet Keep. No manifestation of technical site penetration. Animation faded without action.*E*

&Miscue? Site animation without penetration or action?&

*E*Stet.*E*

&Then the Quote species of Segment Etamin are on the verge of complete site activation by remote control. Dispatch action unit.&

*0*Unit 2, orient and proceed.*0*

*2*Enroute. Assignment?*2*

&Await further animation of site, orient specifically, nullify.&

"You're a hero," Psyche told him after her kiss and hug.

"Your father and Baron Magnet are the heroes," Herald said. And Duke Qaval, he thought, for in the battle proper the reptilian knight had won the day.

They stood on the parapet, while others attended to the knights. "Qaval would have won, if he hadn't been so noble about it," Herald added after a moment, feeling the need to be fair in word as well as thought.

"After his treachery of impersonating the dead," she said wryly. "Well, he is our captive now."

The threat of taking the Duke of Kade and Herald hostage was over; it had rebounded against its perpetrators. But the siege was still to come.

He glanced up at the Ridge Road. "Use the scope,"

Psyche advised. So he moved over to the mounted telescope, and traced what was visible of the ridge.

"I see them!" he said. "They've cleared away our men during the distraction of the dam battle, and now they're wheeling dozers in." For the solid draft-beasts were capable of shoving sizable rocks about and starting an avalanche.

In the course of the next hour they watched the enemy setting up. It looked ominous indeed. Then, just as the dozers were massed for their surprise move, the stampede from the high pasture started. Hundreds of fat healthy cattle charged along the ridge, shoving everything aside. Troops and dozers tumbled down the side, cracking into trees. There were many enemy knights, there to guard against any possible counterattack and to supervise the forming of the ramp after the avalanche, but they were helpless before the nearly mindless panic of the cattle.

The cattle braked and milled about some as they funneled onto the narrowest path and then hit the steep descent. Their wheels skidded. They slewed around and spread out all across the slope, shoving bodies ahead of them. But their fury was spent. When the herd finally reached the bottom, the cows stopped to graze on the green grass near the lake.

Well, they had done their job! The enemy had been suckered into that trap, and the retainers of the Baron of Magnet had spooked the herd on schedule. There would be no avalanche now!

Herald kissed Psyche again—and felt her aura rising.

"Come on," he said. "This time I'm going to find out just what governs your variation. And I want Qaval as Enemy Witness. We may resolve this yet."

"Why don't you just accept me as I am?" she inquired, pouting. "There's been trouble every time you—"

"Let's ring in the Weew, too," he said. "He has a high aura, and can help observe. We'll start at the cellar. I'd certainly like to know why depth raises your aura."

"It does sound backward," she admitted. Then she got more practical: "This time let's bring some pillows. I don't want to have to lie on that cold wet stone again."

"You never lay on it before!" he said.

"I didn't say I *did* lie on it, I said I didn't *want* to before, and I don't want to again. But when I *didn't* be-

132

fore, I never got to lie upstairs either, so if it's got to be in the cellar, at least let's make it comfortable."

He patted her fanny, then gave it a tweak. "Seems comfortable enough to *me*. The trouble with you females is you think you're good for only one thing! This is serious."

"You only married me for my aura," she complained.

She never tired of that game! But—neither did he. So he followed through on what was becoming a ritual. "No, you're an heiress too, and you have a pretty . . . face. For a shotgun wedding, those were recommendations enough."

"Never marry a snake," she muttered. "My old nurse warned me."

He grabbed her, spun her about, and buried his face in her flowing hair, kissing her smooth neck. Script it might be, but it did set him off. "This is absolutely crazy," he said, his lips moving against her skin as though he were speaking Polarian style. "I can't justify it at all. But I'm in danger of falling wildly in love with you, child bride." He nipped the blue skin where neck met shoulder.

"Well, no one's perfect," she said. And twisted around to kiss him on the lips with savage fervor. "Oh, Herald, just to be with you forever—that's all I want. Is that so greedy?"

"To the cellar, girl," he said, pointing dramatically. "If we don't get this investigation started, your main attraction will fade before I can get your secondary attraction down on that cold wet stone."

"A fate worse than death," she agreed. "I suppose it never occurs to you to put pleasure before business?"

"What do you think I'm *doing?*" he demanded.

"Make that forever minus one day," she said. "Any more remarks like that and I'll remove another day."

"Already I'm pressed for time. I'm losing a day a minute."

They picked up Qaval, who seemed none the worse for his knockout except for a darker green splotch on his brow, found Hweeh, and descended to the cellar. Herald made each entity touch Psyche on the way. "We are investigating the so-called Possession phenomenon," he explained. "Note that her aura is up to fifty now."

At the foot of the steps: "Note that it has jumped to sixty. That's unique. With other entities, aura is their most constant property. But Psyche's aura is *not* supernatural. She varies with time and elevation. It is my purpose to ascertain what factors govern her cycle, and demonstrate that there is no need to postulate Possession. Once Duke Qaval is satisfied, the siege may be over."

"And if it becomes certain that she *is* possessed?" Qaval inquired with a rippling curl of his green lip.

"My wife shall not be burned," Herald said firmly. "If we can't exonerate her, the siege continues." He shook off the unpleasant notion. "All right. We know her aura will increase to a level above two hundred in the course of the next two hours. She will began to glow. What we need to learn is *why*—and what in this cellar affects it."

"In short, we shall locate the demon," Qaval said.

"And lay it to rest forever! We'll crisscross this whole labyrinth and chart her fluctuations. Maybe we'll zero in on the key."

They crisscrossed. Psyche's aura peaked at a certain spot on the floor near the wine cellar, fading evenly in a radius out from it. Qaval, accepting his status as Enemy Witness with singular grace, became quite interested in the proceedings. He had an active scientific curiosity. On his suggestion, Psyche approached that area on the floor above, and they found that the effect there was similar but less marked.

"It is an intersecting plane of a sphere," Hweeh pointed out. "The center is some distance below the castle cellar. We shall have to excavate it to locate it specifically."

"That would undermine the foundations and encourage intrusion of water," Qaval said. "Not the wisest course during a siege."

"Maybe we could make a sampling core," Herald said.

"Not before her aura fades," Hweeh said. "Drilling takes time, if it is done carefully enough to be worthwhile in its sample, and she is already up to my level."

"Higher than that," Herald said. "Here in the spot, she's one hundred seventy."

"What was the nature of the site on which this castle was constructed?" Qaval inquired.

"I can answer that," Psyche said, glad to contribute something other than her mere presence. "The first Kade was granted this estate eight hundred years ago. He dowsed for the best site, which turned out to be right here."

"Dowsed?" Herald asked blankly.

"Dowsed. He cut a section from a wheelbranch and held it in his hands a special way. Where it dipped, he built."

"I had understood this was normally done to locate a source of water or precious metal," Hweeh remarked.

"In this case, he was dowsing for feel," she said. "He was a religious man, and he insisted that the spiritual vibrations be correct."

"So he located the spot where an immortal demon lay buried," Qaval said, "and built his edifice on that."

"Do you consider this to be Possession?" Herald asked.

"It may be. But removal of the bones or tomb of the demon should abate it."

"Will Prince Circlet provide us time to excavate?"

Qaval shook his snout. "He is now committed to siege. Only a successful siege-defense will convince him."

"Do you know, there is something familiar about Psyche's cycle," Hweeh said. "I can't place it, but—"

"Something to do with your specialty?" Herald asked.

"Yes. In fact . . . possibly even with the reason I shock out. I wonder whether. . . ."

Herald was abruptly more interested. A tie-in between Psyche's aura and Hweeh's shock? "Is her connection beneficial or inimical to your health?"

"I don't know. But I am willing to experiment."

"Let's try it," Herald said. And to Qaval: "Enemy Witness, this entity has no part in the Possession. If the siege against Kastle Kade should be successful, see that he is granted safe passage out."

"Agreed," Qaval said.

Herald put his hand on Hweeh, who was now a blob with eye-stalk, horn, and three feet. "Space Amoeba," he said.

Immediately the Weew sagged. But Herald maintained contact. "Wake, Hweeh. Sight. Sound. Recovery."

Slowly the Weew came out. "I suffer disorientation. Did I—?"

"I sent you into shock with the key phrase," Herald said, "and brought you out of it immediately, allowing you no reorientation period. Do you wish to continue?"

"Yes. It is important. Your treatments have helped me, or I would not have been able to revive so soon."

"Psyche, your turn," Herald said.

Psyche put her hand on Hweeh. She was now 180. "Amoeba," she said gently.

Hweeh sank again. "Wake," she said urgently. "Wake, Hweeh!"

Slowly the Weew came out of it.

"Her aura is less than mine," Herald said. "Yet it is working as well. That indicates an affinity. Perhaps when she peaks. . . ."

"What manner of problem does the Weew have?" Qaval inquired.

"Sorry, I forgot you were not the same Enemy Witness we had before. Hweeh is a research astronomer who discovered something he believes is of Galactic significance, so serious he went into shock. He returns to shock at the mere mention of certain words. His Segment felt the matter warranted my attention, and I believe they were justified, but so far I have been unable to help him."

"It should not be difficult to define," Qaval said. He turned to Hweeh. "Is your concern in inner or outer galactic space?"

"My specialty is Fringe-Cluster space, so—"

"So it was some extra-Cluster phenomenon you noted," Qaval said, exactly as if confirming something he had always known. "Trans-Milky Way or trans-Andromeda or trans-Pinwheel?"

Hweeh hesitated. "None of them seem right. I don't think it is near a major galaxy."

"But not so far away as another cluster?"

"No, not that far, not exactly. . . ."

"Now there are not many trans-Tri-Galaxy close-in extra-Cluster phenomena that would show on the charts of a research astronomer. I daresay you can name them readily out of memory."

"Yes, of course," Hweeh said. "But—"

"And the mere naming of known constellations is hardly a matter to send any creature into shock."

"No, but—"

"*I* know what it is, for I heard it just now, twice. *You* know what it is. Are you fool enough to suppose that you can fight an enemy by turning away your gaze?"

"No, of course not. Yet—"

136

"Name your enemy. Then you can conquer him."

Hweeh concentrated. "Not Sculp. Not Cloud Six. Not Fur—Fur—not Furnace, but very—" He could not continue.

"Are you an astronomer or a stuttering child?" Qaval demanded, beginning one of his fabulous sneers. "Seek you to pretend that identifying it by elimination is less clumsy than naming it direct? Where is your pride of profession?"

Hweeh's color flexed in anger. His flesh shuddered with the ferocity of his effort. "The—Space—AMOEBA!" he cried. And sank into shock.

Herald considered. "Sir," he said to Qaval, "I think you have shown us the way. He *can* face it, with proper preparation."

"I have a certain expertise in the interrogation of prisoners," Qaval said. "It transfers readily enough to similar situations. It is a matter of invoking the basic drives, and also of timing terms and expressions, as in combat."

"Yes, you are the compleat warrior," Psyche said.

There was something about context and tone that altered the very spelling of the word in Herald's mind: compleat, not complete. Which was odd, because he had not realized his host was literate. Some time at his leisure he would have to run down the allusion.

"Let's let him rest for a little while," Herald decided. "Three shocks is about the limit, if we are not to damage him and risk losing it all." He took Psyche by the arm. "You're coming up on two hundred now. I'll bring you back here at two hundred and fifty. Qaval can keep an eye on Hweeh."

"Why not send *them* upstairs, so we can have the cold stones?" she inquired mischievously.

Qaval affected not to comprehend, to Herald's relief. He hauled her upstairs. It was a very fast, very thorough, very delightful lovemaking. "Just call him the Silver Meteor," Psyche muttered around his fierce kiss. And he had her back in the cellar at 250.

"Now we'll try it again," Herald said.

"Again?" Psyche inquired brightly, and even Qaval could not refrain from twitching a green brow.

"The interrogation!" Herald snapped, changing color

himself. He put his hand on the Weew to rouse him from shock.

"Hweeh, you have suffered some realization about the nature of this extra-Cluster phenomenon that sends you into shock." Herald kept his hand on the body, hoping that his words were making a subconscious as well as a conscious impression. "You know that it is better to bring the threat out into the open. All we have to ascertain is *what*, not *where*, that threat is. What is there about the Space Amoeba that—Psyche, bring him out of it."

Psyche put her hand on Weew, suffusing him with her potent aura. "Wake, Hweeh, wake. . . ."

And he did. "That aura . . . beautiful!" he exclaimed. Then: "The Space Amoeba! I can face it! *I know what it is!*"

"You have broken through!" Herald exclaimed. "What is the threat?"

"It is in the very nature of the Amoeba, which we have misconceived from the outset! It is not an amoeba at all, not an explosion of dust, not a supernova remnant, but a —remarkable! Absolutely remarkable! Don't let go of me, child bride, or I shall surely go into shock again! Oh, we must get word out *immediately!*"

"But what *is* it?" Herald demanded.

"To comprehend, you must first comprehend the nature of—I must fill in the background—like describing color to a blind entity—the ramifications—"

"Try, in orderly fashion," Qaval said calmly. "We are *not* blind entities."

"It is—it is an invasion from extra-Cluster space!" Hweeh exclaimed. "A pattern of living creatures, traveling by mattermission—"

"An invasion!" Qaval said. "How could there be an invasion from beyond the Cluster! We have never had contact with the larger Universe. The sheer energy required—"

"I don't know *how* or *why*," Hweeh said. "My shock cut me off before I could work it out. But I do know it is *so*. A monstrous fleet, mattermitting to a point in space, funneling through, radiating out. On that scale it takes a century merely to organize the staging area! Hundreds of thousands of ships—a million ships—the most tremendous fleet of full-scale battleships ever. It can conquer our entire Cluster in a mere century or so, maybe less, if it—" He broke off in sheer wonder.

Qaval glanced at Herald. "This entity is a creature of repute? Not given to hallucinogenic indulgence? He knows whereof he speaks?"

"He knows. It seems we must face a siege of much larger proportion than that of Kastle Kade."

"Then we had better get a message out," Qaval said. "I can arrange—"

He was interrupted by a tremendous rolling shudder, somewhat like thunder and somewhat like an earthquake. There was a cry from above. "AVALANCHE!"

"Too late!" Qaval said. "They have launched the main thrust."

"But we balked that ploy!" Herald protested. "We had our cattle stampede—"

"Get you to your walls and see," Qaval said grimly.

They hurried up out of the cellar, blinking in the light of day, for their eyes had become acclimatized to the wine-dark.

It was true. The cliffs of the *east* face had collapsed, filling in a quarter of the lake. Displaced water was rushing over the dam, sweeping its defenders away. The Duke of Kade was surveying the situation angrily. "Explosives! They used explosives!"

"Not so," Qaval countered. "We do not violate the Code Medieval. No explosives on Planet Keep! Our animals mined the cliff by night, lo these many nights, while you prepared for siege. Wheelbores, tunneling into the stone like little Andromedan Quadpoints, weakening it crucially, silently. Just a little hammering of wedges at the key spots, and down it came!"

"There was no explosion, sire," a crossbowman assured the Duke of Kade. "We heard tapping, but did not realize. . . ."

Already the dozers were descending the new slope of rubble, pushing the broken rock farther toward the castle. Some animals rolled into the water, scooping out the sides of the fall, making a narrower but longer ramp. The causeway was driving inexorably toward Kastle Kade, and there was little the defenders could do about it. Even the alligators who had not been crushed by the fall itself were cowed and stunned by the shock of it.

Kade turned to Qaval. "You are drawing all the stops,

139

sir. I could have wished that such perseverance and imagination had been employed in a better cause."

"A just critique," Qaval agreed.

Kade did something like a doubletake. "Another creature might alter his views at the convenience of the moment, for fear of retribution, but you were never thus, Qaval. You have doubts?"

"I think it at least as likely that your daughter is a mutation as that she is possessed," Qaval said. "This castle seems to have been constructed upon the tomb of some demon creature whose lingering aura moved the first Duke of Kade, and now moves Kade's distant descendant. Excavation of the tomb should abolish that influence. Still, even if it does not, it is possible she is a kind of healer. Her changes follow a pattern that is typical of no Possession I know of. I have felt her aura at its low and at its high, and though I have only a fraction of the Kirlian perception that Herald does, my findings concur with his. Were I of your species, I believe I would be moved to marry her myself. What she has is far too valuable to throw away."

Herald and Psyche watched the enemy Duke in silent, gratified amazement. Even Kade seemed startled. "You would testify thus to the Prince?"

"No."

Again Kade reacted, this time with angry puzzlement. "How can a noble of your courage and integrity be found on such opposite sides of the question?"

Qaval smiled, the long edges of his lip curling in a sine wave of mixed emotion. "Delicately put! My rationale is this: There is doubt in my mind, with the preponderance in the girl's favor. She seems in most respects a normal example of her kind, very female. I would let her go. But there is no doubt in the mind of the Prince. To plead her cause before Circlet of Crown at this stage would be merely to invite the fire for myself. I made the attempt before, and nearly lost my status in his counsels; hence you find me on the battlefield instead of in the command tent. He has committed himself to the fray; he cannot with pride retreat. And I must serve my Prince."

Kade turned away, looking down at the advancing causeway, aimed like a lance at the heart of the castle. "I cannot quarrel with your rationale, sir, though it doom me to destruction. Still, perhaps we can deal. If I yielded my daughter to you captive, and gave you passage out of my demesnes, could you guarantee fair trial for her, with all evidence considered?"

"No."

"What likelihood for her, then?"

"Perhaps ten percent. How could the Prince justify what he has undertaken, without a witch to be burned and plunder for his minions? A fair trial might absolve her, undermining his honor. It would not be politically feasible, therefore it will not come to that."

"Has the pride of fair Keep sunk to such state?" Kade demanded with disgust.

"It seems it has."

"What would you have me do, then?"

"Proffer me as hostage for her safety. I am not at the moment held in high esteem by the Prince, but that offer, rejected, might cause my own forces to rebel against him. My contingent is by far the strongest of his forces. Such revolt would so weaken the Prince as to render him unable to complete the siege."

"You speak practical politics," Kade said. "But this is not my way. I would not promote my interest by stooping to treachery, or otherwise sully my own honor."

"This is your liability," Qaval said. Then, slowly, he extended his claw. Kade shook it gravely, accepting this silent token of respect.

"Isn't that beautiful?" Psyche murmured to Herald, her eyes moist. "They are so like each other."

Herald felt tears in his own human eyes. Solarian and Qaval, each interested in saving Psyche, each constrained by honor to sacrifice her—and she admired their stands! This was the beauty and tragedy of this truly heraldic culture. He had dallied with its symbols, without ever before appreciating its inner quality. If by some miracle they all survived this crisis, he would spend the rest of his life here, and not merely because of Psyche. This was a society an entity could truly believe in.

Kade returned to business. "You do not believe we can withstand siege directly?"

"I am sure you cannot. Kastle Kade will fall within the day."

"Then I must take desperation measures. You shall be chained to my daughter, and the two of you and Herald the Healer will be removed from this castle via our un-

141

derwater crawler. You will go not to her trial, but into hiding. The castle may fall, but the Lady Kade will survive."

"This I would not recommend," Qaval said.

Kade signaled. Human guards stepped forward. "I am unable to follow your recommendations," Kade said. The guards clamped manacles on one wrist each of Qaval and Psyche, adjusting them to fit snugly. Qaval did not resist. The two of them were then guided down toward the courtyard between the outer and inner walls, Kade following with Herald. "My daughter knows who possesses the key to these locks," Kade said. "You all arrive alive— or none do. Then you will be released."

"This cannot succeed," Qaval said.

The guards conducted them down to another part of the cellar, leaving the Duke of Kade to his defense of the castle. Psyche glowed again as they marched along the dark corridors; her incredible aura was still rising.

Behind a barred door was a contraption like a giant alligator, with projecting paddles in lieu of legs. Evidently it was designed to rest lightly on the bottom, propelled by the paddles worked from inside. A medieval submarine.

Herald bent over and entered the crawler, putting himself into its front seat. Two oar handles projected in, one from either side, and a transparent panel showed the terrain in front. It would be slow and clumsy, but presumably they could escape the castle this way. They could surface at the north end of Lake Donny, where no one was watching, and get away overland through the deep forest.

But Qaval balked. "This is pointless death for us all," he said. "Better to remain in the castle."

Psyche put her free hand on Qaval's chained wrist. Even in this gloom, Herald saw the contrast between blue fingers and green wrist. "Why, Enemy Witness?" she asked gently.

Her aura had stood at 250 at the time of the avalanche, but Herald realized that it had not been near its peak. She had hit that level before, upstairs; at the ideal spot of the wine cellar, it would have been higher. What astonishing intensity it was moving toward, Herald could only guess. Perhaps 275. The Duke of Qaval was being exposed to the persuasion of aural power such as Herald himself could never muster.

"Lady, I cannot oppose you," Qaval said with another of his rippling smiles. "The Prince knows of the crawler; his spear entities lurk for it outside. We would drown."

Herald scrambled out of the crawler. "We'd better get back upstairs," he said, catching Psyche's elbow.

He paused, feeling her aura. He had been right: It had almost tangible power. The glow in the gloom was stronger.

They returned through the main cellar—and there, forgotten in the sudden crisis of the avalanche, was Hweeh of Weew. He had lapsed into shock when Psyche so abruptly broke contact, and remained here, puddled on the floor. "Oh, poor thing!" Psyche cried, running to him. Qaval had to follow, putting his tail to the floor momentarily to balance as he shifted direction.

"Wake! Wake!" Psyche said, touching the Weew.

"Wow!" Hweeh said, popping into focus. "Lady, you are something!"

"I am peaking," she said. "Hweeh, we were interrupted by an avalanche, and forgot you. I'm sorry; I know how cold these stones are, and should never have left you here. But we'd better define the Amoeba threat, so we can warn the Cluster." Her power of aura was now so great that Hweeh did not even flinch at the dread word. "You told us it is a huge fleet from alien space. That it could conquer our whole Cluster within a century."

"Yes, Lady! I perceive it even more clearly now. The fleet has been approaching via mattermission and half-light dispersion for centuries, and now is deploying for a multiple intrusion. There is no question of destination, and little of motive; we are the target."

"But how could a million-ship fleet mattermit inter-Cluster distances?" Herald asked. "The energy requirement would be prohibitive. The fleet would have to convert much of its own mass into transmission energy. Are you sure it's not a purely local phenomenon?"

"Absolutely sure," Hweeh said. "What local Sphere has a million full-diameter spaceships? It would require a billion sapients just to crew a fleet that size. It *has* to be from an alien Cluster!"

"But at this range . . . fuzzy photographs . . . how can you be sure they're *spaceships*? They could be meteorite clouds, or imperfections in reproduction—"

"Trust me to know my speciality!" Hweeh replied

curtly. "The information is not from the holographs—which happen to be considerably more sophisticated than photographs, not subject to the same types of distortions—but from my interpretation of divers sources. I did holographic spectroscopy and verified what could be the emission trails of half-light propulsion. The Amoeba is definitely an artificial structure. I went into shock when my fantastic suspicion was confirmed. We are being subjected to invasion—and we don't have much time. Our records go back four thousand years; there has been no prior Amoeba manifesting, and no other Amoeba is showing now. That means it is not any recent natural occurrence. My estimate is that this fleet is mattermitting from an alien Cluster, perhaps a million parsecs out, or ten million. Perhaps they destroyed that Cluster to gain the energy required for this jump, and will destroy our Cluster, as Andromeda tried to destroy Galaxy Milky Way, to enable them to make their *next* jump. What does a species do, once it has destroyed half of its own Cluster in the course of the war to conquer it? They proceed to some new, virgin Cluster, as the Andromedans would have done in time, had they been successful. The Amoebites do not travel in force merely to see the sights of the Universe."

"But this is unbelievable!" Herald protested, stung by the references to his own galaxy. Bless Llume of Slash, who foiled that disaster!

"Precisely. Hence no one believes it. Yet it is true. Therefore a matter to send a creature into shock."

"It has to be an invasion force," Qaval agreed. "And there is only one thing that would warrant such an excursion."

"Power!" Herald and Hweeh said together.

"Power—on a universal scale," Qaval agreed. "A new door has been opened, one that defies our experience or imagination." Then his teeth clicked: his indication of surprise. "Why did it not occur to me before! This news must be transmitted, and the Weew must return to his Segment where experts can consult with him and verify his findings. Only the Lady can keep him on the subject and out of shock. She should be released for that service, preemptive. It is a Cluster security matter overriding a mere planetary matter."

"Yes!" Herald agreed. "Let's go up to the library so

144

I can call Swees of Weew, the mathematician. He can make the necessary contacts."

They hurried upstairs, this time not forgetting Hweeh. Psyche kept her hand on him all the time, though this was awkward because of the necessary proximity of Qaval, still manacled to her. "What is the connection between me and the Amoeba?" she asked as they went.

"It is—it is—I cannot quite fathom it, Lady," Hweeh replied. "Not that you evoked the information. There is a more fundamental, if peripheral—your aura—" He stopped. "It remains buried," he said regretfully.

"Maybe we'll find it when we delve beneath the cellar," she said. "Somehow I am tied to—oh."

"What?" Herald asked, worried.

"I cannot go to Weew," she said. "My aura peaks here only, near this cellar. I would be of no use elsewhere."

"Of *course* you would be of use elsewhere!" Herald retorted.

"Without my enhancement of aura?" she asked, giving him a direct look that half destroyed him.

"Then we shall bring the Weew experts here," Qaval said. "All the more reason to abate this siege of the castle before it becomes uninhabitable."

They reached the library. Herald placed the call, half fearing that the besieging army would be jamming communications; but he got through right away.

"Swees of Weew here," the Sador host said. "So good to communicate with you again, Healer. I understand you have a bit of trouble there."

"Swees, we have a critical situation," Herald said. "Our castle is under siege and will soon fall. We are trapped. But we have information of inter-Galactic importance. Will you be able to contact Segment Weew to make arrangements for Segment intervention and possible extradition of Hweeh and his party?"

"But—" Psyche began.

"First we must save your life; then we can save the Cluster," Hweeh told her. "Let him proceed."

"Segment intervention!" Swees exclaimed. "Surely you know I have no authority for such a thing! I could relay your information and serve as liaison, but I should have to have much more to go on than what you have told me. They would laugh me right out of shape, if I—"

"They will pay attention to *this*," Herald said. "Hweeh has located a million-strong fleet of spaceships approaching our Cluster from extra-Cluster space, obviously coming to raid our fundamental energy. It may be a greater threat to our survival than that of the two inter-Galactic Wars of Energy, and we have to ascertain—" He broke off, interrupted by Qaval's tap on his shoulder.

"Swees of Weew has gone into shock," the Duke said.

Indeed, the communication wheel of Swees' Sador host was drifting to a stop. "I should have thought of that!" Herald exclaimed. "The mere concept of Cluster doom knocks out these Weews! How can we get through to them?"

"Maybe some other Segment?" Psyche inquired. "After all, the threat applies to *all* Segments."

Qaval slapped his tail irritably against the floor. "Only a creature's home Segment can extradite him. Hweeh is the expert; he is the one who must testify. And he is the only one who requires the Lady's assistance."

"Don't imperil the Cluster for my sake!" Psyche objected.

But it was more complex than that. Psyche could be saved only through Segment Weew, and the Cluster could be warned only through Segment Weew, because the statements of nonexperts would never be heeded in time. But they had no way to alert Weew to the problem! Sufficient detail would send any Weew they contacted into shock.

But it was imperative that they get word out about the Amoeba, regardless of their personal fates. An actual Cluster invasion. . . .

"Maybe some other Segment will listen," Herald said. "Once we get the alert out, the Cluster Council may take over directly. In fact, this *is* a Cluster Council matter. Why don't we see if we can get through to a Minister?"

Psyche shook her head. "You know the red tape to reach a Cluster Minister? You have to go through channels—"

"And the Planet Keep channel leads right through King Roundlet of Crown," Qaval said. "Whose egg, Prince Circlet, is besieging this castle." He paused. "Nevertheless, I might be able to navigate that channel, as I know the entities there and they know me."

146

"Wouldn't that be taken as traitorous action?" Herald asked.

"Perhaps. But the higher allegiance is to my Cluster, and I hardly think I will be very strongly condemned for saving my Galaxy or Segment or Sphere from invasion by aliens. In fact, if such invasion were facilitated because Prince Circlet had burned the only entity who could evoke the testimony necessary to prevent it, the Prince himself would burn."

Good enough! "We'd better go up and get you and Psyche unlocked," Herald said.

"It is not necessary. I shall work on the ministerial contact," Qaval said. "We should not waste time."

"All right," Herald decided. "I'll go out to find Duke Kade. You try to get through. If you do, have Hweeh explain the situation." And he set off.

The activity on the outer wall had intensified. Soldiers were moving war supplies to their battle stations, especially the parapets nearest the approaching ramp. There were not merely weapons and arrows and stones for the catapults, but also piles of wood, buckets of oil, and even sewage from the deep septic sumps. Nothing was wasted, in war—except lives and property.

The Duke of Kade was hard to find. Everywhere Herald went, Kade had just left, organizing this, touching up that, making last-moment adjustments. Siege-defense was a complex business!

The causeway was not yet all the way to the wall; the increasingly accurate fire from the castle crossbows balked its near approach. But now the enemy was using heavy shields held up and interlocked over their heads, protecting them while they worked. The catapult on this side was lobbing stones down, trying to score on this phalanx, but it was hard to nail a moving target. Herald found these grim proceedings fascinating. This was elementary warfare, from which heraldry had sprung thousands of years ago. Other things might be transient, but war was eternal!

Then as he watched, the main thrust commenced. Dozers poured down the road fashioned from the cliff-collapse, each animal shoving a mound of dirt and rubble before it. There seemed to be an endless line of them. They rolled right down to the end of the ramp, then spun off to the side and climbed back. This was not the

147

same maneuver as before. The earlier dozers had been shaping the ramp from the immediate debris of the fallen cliff, scooping it from underwater, leveling the travel-track. These new ones were pushing material from over the hill, using the foundation for more effective motion. As a result, the ramp suddenly grew much more swiftly.

But why was it being done this way? The avalanche had shoved water out of the lake, drowning the defenders of the dam. By now the enemy surely had control of the dam, and could let the water out of the lake. They did not need to build a high ramp to get above the water level. Had signals been crossed—or was there some more devious thrust in store?

The crossbows fired, but the large fat animals were hardly affected. Their body processes were diffuse, the vital organs protected by the hard wheels. Arrows might cause them pain, but did not kill them or even stop them. And there were so many! All they required was firm ground for their heavy wheels—and that they had, now.

"Cease fire!" the knight in charge of this section of the wall cried. It was the Baron Magnet, rolling along in the saddle. "They've got more dozers than we have arrows. Save your fire for the sapients."

Herald hurried up to Magnet. "I'm looking for the Duke," he said. "Do you know—?"

The Baron did a bounce in the saddle. "What are you doing here? You're supposed to be on your way!"

"The enemy has spears waiting for the crawler. We can't use it." It occurred to him now that that could be one reason the lake had not been lowered: The enemy wanted Kade to think the crawler was serviceable, so that key personnel could be trapped when they tried to use it. Once the water was down, it would be obvious that the crawler would be useless. "I need to tell Kade we can't escape."

"You'll never catch him. Stay here and supervise the wall. I will send him back to you."

"I don't know anything about siege defense!"

But the Baron was already wheeling on his way, lost in the commotion.

Herald watched the rapidly progressing causeway, hoping the Baron would be back soon. A number of the dozers were dumping their loads prematurely, causing the road to hump upward more than forward. The fear of arrows

148

must be having its effect, though no arrows were being fired.

Then he realized: That rising elevation was no accident—they *wanted* the road to rise! This was no causeway, it was a ramp, to be used to ascend the height of the wall! The knights would be able to charge right up and over the ramparts of the castle, overwhelming it. The level of the lake hardly mattered. The dozers would be able to work all night, and with the dawn. . . .

Was there any defense? The catapult and hot oil and crossbows were calculated to discourage troops who tried to ram or scale the wall from below. But a charge over this ramp— No wonder Qaval was sure Kastle Kade would soon fall!

To his relief, Kade was striding toward him. "Where's my daughter?" he demanded.

"Chained to Qaval," Herald said. "We can't escape, so—"

"Well, bring her up here!" Kade snapped. "I can't leave the wall, not while the ramp's building. I'm organizing a counterthrust. Six good knights astride that ramp can hold off the Prince's whole army, if they're well drilled in ridge-combat. Then we can doze out a gap near the wall so that—"

"Sir, the Lady and Qaval are trying to reach the King's palace on the phone, and—"

"*What?*"

Herald coughed. "Psyche's at peak aura. She—"

"Oh, don't repeat that superstition! There is nothing wrong with her aura."

Didn't the Duke *know* how his daughter's aura fluctuated? But this was not a matter to be argued now. "She's got the Weew talking. He says there's a Cluster invasion in the making. We have to reach the Cluster Council of—"

"A Cluster invasion!" Kade exclaimed unbelievingly. "It must be a ruse to subvert our—"

"No, sir. The Weew is no spy. He believes in this thrust—and I'm not sure he's mistaken. We have to get experts on it."

"All right," Kade said, humoring him. "Contact the palace. They may grant the Weew safe passage out; he should not have stayed here anyway. But make it fast. Things are going to get very difficult in a few hours."

Kade had no conception of the Amoeba threat. And

there really was not time to educate him now. Herald would have to focus on the immediate details.

"Duke, you don't understand," the Healer said. "Psyche is the only one who can facilitate Hweeh's testimony. She has to go with him." Except that she would have to come back, to enhance her aura—but that, too, was too complicated to go into right now. Hweeh was right: first save her life, then worry about the rest.

Kade stared. "No, that would never work. The Prince is a stubborn idiot, but he's no fool."

"Duke Qaval is speaking for the Lady. But we want to reach the Cluster level, and have them put a hold on this siege while they investigate—"

"And Qaval supports that?" he demanded incredulously.

"Yes, sir."

Kade headed for the down-ramp inside at a heavy run. "Come on, Herald. It's a long shot, but just maybe— We've got to get on that phone!"

They tore into the library, where Qaval was speaking. ". . . and if you do not pass me up the chain to Sphere HQ, I will nail your wheels to the floor and loose my sand-dogs on you," he was saying into the phone. "We have a Cluster emergency here, Code Thirty-three, and it has nothing to do with the siege of Kade. Now *roll!*"

Kade brought out his key. "Were it any other, I would have sword in hand," he said. "But you, Qaval, when you lie, the planet will surely burst asunder. How came you to participate thus?"

"The Lady has a persuasive aura," Qaval said as the fetter came off.

Now Kade took his daughter's wrist, to remove the handcuff. He stiffened. "That aura!" he exclaimed. "It is stronger than the Healer's!"

Psyche smiled. "Two hundred and sixty and rising, Father. Maybe two hundred and seventy in the cellar. Do not be alarmed."

Kade fell back, his face a mask of horror. "Then you *are* possessed! I never believed it, no, not for a moment, never let myself believe—"

There was the key, Herald realized. The evidence was there, but the man had never *let* himself examine it. Now, caught by surprise, he was taking it the wrong way.

"Kade, she is not possessed," Qaval snapped. "If you

have no faith in your daughter, get you back to your ramparts and let us handle her defense at Cluster level."

But Kade was too shaken to comprehend. He had been extremely active for many hours, under a great burden of tension, and he had been knocked out on the ferry. He was not in a reasonable condition. "There is no natural aura that strength! Only demon Possession could—"

"Sphere Sador HQ," the phone said. "What is your emergency?"

"News of a Cluster invasion," Qaval said. "This is Duke Qaval at Planet Keep. I—"

"Where is your Shield of Arms?" the Sador demanded.

"Elsewhere, dolt! I am captive of Kastle Kade. But my face is on record. Verify my credits and bounce me up to Segment level."

There was a pause while a computer check was run on his snout. "Credits verified. Detail?"

"Research Astronomer Hweeh of Weew, here for treatment of shock, has identified an invasion fleet approaching—"

"Possession!" Kade screamed, his mind finally snapping under the strain. "First my wife, now my daughter. What is this curse of Kade?" He swept his hand through the phone image, breaking the connection.

Herald jumped at Kade, trying to get him away from the phone, but the man shoved him back with insane strength. "Help me, Qaval!" Herald cried. "We have to complete that call!"

Qaval shook his green head. "I may not lift arm against my captor, under terms of—"

Psyche reached out and put her free hand on her father's arm. The chain of the manacle still dangled from the other. "Rest, Father," she said. Under that intense aural compulsion, Kade leaned back against the wall. "Demon! Demon!" he muttered brokenly.

"We shall have to start over," Qaval said. "The channel cannot be restored from the center. Perhaps I can convince them we suffered a technical interruption."

But a new commotion interrupted the proceedings. There were screams from below, and the clashing of arms. Combat in the halls!

Qaval shook his head. "I feared this. We are too late."

"What's going on?" Herald demanded. Events were moving so rapidly he felt a bit dizzy.

"The castle has been breached," Qaval said. "A secret squad tunneled through the wall under the water, on the side opposite the ramp. The distraction of the cliff collapse and the elevation of the ramp enabled—"

Kade drew his sword. But suddenly wheeled soldiers, bearing the Shield of Arms of the Prince, were crowding into the room. Too many to oppose.

Kade charged. Herald, dismayed by this rashness, started to go after him—but it was already too late. Two Sador battlewheels moved onto him, and his sword-arm was sliced away in pieces. Kade fell, blood spurting from the stump.

"Father!" Psyche cried, horrified, starting forward herself. The chain of the manacle swung like a weapon.

But Qaval was there ahead of her. "Hold, troops!" he bellowed. "This is the Duke of Kade! See you not his Arms?"

They paused. A Sador commander rolled forward; it was the Earl of Dollar. "Hold!" he echoed, and the troops obeyed him.

Herald and Psyche dropped to their knees beside Kade. "We can heal him!" Herald cried. "Psyche, put your hands on his arm. Stop the blood. Concentrate your aura. . . ."

They put their hands on him. Psyche was drenched in blood, and Herald was spattered, but neither paid heed. Their two auras worked in tandem, meshing through the body of the patient.

The blood-flow slowed—but not because of their healing. Kade's burdened Solarian heart had stopped.

Psyche's big eyes met Herald's, filled with appalled compassion. "I felt it," she said. "He—he didn't *want* to live."

The Duke of Qaval and the Earl of Dollar stood somberly before the corpse. "He was in error," Qaval said. "Yet he was a great man. A benediction on the Duke of Kade."

"A benediction," Whirl agreed.

The soldiers brought a curtain bearing the Arms of Kade, and Qaval laid it as a shroud over the body.

Now the troops gave way. A royal Sador rolled forward. It was Prince Circlet of Crown himself. "So we have captured the Possessed," he cried exultantly.

Qaval hardly deigned to face the Prince. "She is not possessed," he said. "She is a healer."

"Who just killed her father. Did she work her demon wiles on *you*, Duke?" the Prince demanded. "Do you join her in the fire?"

Qaval's body shook with the fury of an emotion Herald was certain was not fear. "I beg the Prince's indulgence," he said humbly. "As captive of Kade, I was chained to her. I believe her aura is natural; it did not hurt me. But more important, there is a Cluster threat that preempts the local question, and the girl must be saved to—"

"Remove this traitor from my sight!" Circlet snapped. "We shall deal with him anon. Bring the Possessed to the courtyard. We shall attend to this before permitting the looting."

The Duke of Qaval turned slowly to face the Prince. Qaval was unarmed, but beside him the Earl of Dollar was spinning his fighting wheel, and several soldiers bearing the Shields of Arms of Qaval were in the room. All were intent on the Duke. One signal from him, and they would turn against the Prince, for their ultimate loyalty was to their own.

Herald saw the war that raged in Qaval. On one side was his loyalty to his Prince; on the other, to his Cluster. And Herald knew what the decision had to be. Qaval was the supremely practical warrior; he did not scheme and fight for personal power, but for what he felt was right. But *for* that right, he always took the most expedient course. To obey the Prince would mean the possible loss of the entire Cluster society including Planet Kade.

Psyche put her hand on Qaval's stout arm. "Peace, Duke," she said. "Let there be no strife on my behalf."

He turned to her. "Lady, it is not merely—"

"Do not imperil your demesnes for me, good Lord of Qaval," she insisted. "I know the Cluster will be saved, if we but let fate take its course."

And Qaval, obviously against his better judgment, acceded to the will and aura of the Lady. Human soldiers of the Prince came and put new manacles on him and led him away, and the Earl of Dollar made no move.

Herald squatted by Kade's corpse as they took Psyche out. He was stunned by the suddenness of the collapse of this mighty castle, not quite comprehending what was happening. Solarian troops entered and took him by the arms, guiding him after the Prince. He went, numbly.

153

Behind him he heard the melodic chime of the phone. A servitor of the castle moved to answer it. Herald hardly cared.

Soldiers were breaking up the priceless antique furniture of Kastle Kade and throwing the pieces into a huge pile in the main court. A great metal framework was being assembled above this pile, its supports already buried in the fractured wood. Manacles hung from the upper bar.

Suddenly Herald comprehended. "No!" he cried, jerking away from the two who held him. They drew their weapons.

But Herald was free and moving. He dived for Prince Circlet. Qaval had not done this chore, but Herald had no such restriction. As his hand touched the Prince's wheel, Herald blasted him with his exorcism power. It should not have had any effect, but such was his concentration and determination and blind rage that it smashed into Circlet's lesser aura, almost wiping out his life.

The Prince screamed in mortal agony, then slumped on his support wheels while his vocal wheel shuddered to a stop. The soldiers and knights stood baffled, not knowing what to do. There was no visible wound on the Prince; they did not understand what Herald had done.

But Psyche understood. "No, that is not right," she said, turning. "By your leave. . . ." And she drew her small arms from the grasp of her captors as though they were children, then walked to Prince Circlet and laid her hand on him. "Be well," she said—and Herald's deadly blast was nullified by a power greater than he commanded. The Prince recovered.

Then she went to Herald, looking up into his face as she touched him. She was painfully lovely, and her aura smote him with its incredible love, an intensity of at least 275, despite her distance from the cellar. She glowed, even in daylight. "Let no one else suffer on my account. I love you, Herald." And she left him and walked to the center of the court.

The soldiers of the Prince had no compunctions. They stripped her ruthlessly, roughly, until she was naked. They manacled her wrists to the frame, using the one already on her and the one hanging from the upper bar, so that she hung above the pile of wood.

Herald, somehow blocked from action by Psyche's

touch, so much more tender even than a kiss, watched with amazement and horror. How could he stand here, and let this abomination happen? Yet he was doing it!

Suddenly he saw an image, as of the Cluster Tarot, the Queen of Energy. A naked woman chained for a monster. It symbolized Andromeda, both Galaxy and mythical girl, and also Melody of Mintaka. Now it was Psyche, chained for the fire.

"Ignition!" Prince Circlet cried. The Sador's fervor had not been changed by Psyche's touch. Perhaps she had not wanted to change it, being constrained by a similar honor to that of her father and the Duke of Qaval.

The soldiers soaked the wood with lantern oil, and advanced with flaring torches. But they were cut off by one of their number, a fighting Sador noble. It was the Earl of Dollar! "You may not do this thing!" he cried.

But there were six of them and only one of him. They charged him, Solarian and Sador, overwhelming him by their number. "Healer!" Whirl cried as he was wounded. "Do you stand there idle while the Lady burns?"

Then axes struck, cutting Whirl apart. His wheels were ripped off. He was dead. And Herald . . . stood idle, still gripped by the stasis Psyche had put him in.

Now the torches were thrown onto the pile. The fire blazed up with lascivious vigor, licking around Psyche's bare feet. She jerked them out of the way with a whimper of pain, a faint little scream that tore at Herald's gut. Then she let them drop again, as though no longer deigning to protest against fate. "Herald, forgive them!" she cried. "They know not what they do!"

The flame roared up hungrily, its orange mass enveloping her blue body. Her golden hair caught, shriveling into a black mass.

The sight and sound of her agony broke Herald's stasis at last. He charged the fire, hauling out burning pieces of wood with his bare human hands. Suddenly he, too, was surrounded by the flame. Flame of Furnace! he thought irrelevantly. He drove in to the center until his hand struck something soft—one of her bare slender legs—and he gripped it hard and pulled. But only a handful of crackling skin came off on his fingers. She was chained, he could not draw her free, he had to break open the manacles somehow.

Then other hands were on him, hauling him out. Not

hands; green claws, strong, resistant to the fire. It was Qaval, unchained. "She is dead, Herald! But *you* must live. Enough of the message got through. Segment Command called back."

That chiming phone! Could he have saved Psyche if he had gone back to answer it?

"You are summoned to Cluster HQ with Hweeh of Weew to testify about the Amoeba. And I too. And— the Lady." The Duke made an ironic grimace. "It took too long for the call to reach me, for the Prince's staff to be convinced. I came here too late. But now the Prince dare not interfere, and no doubt you shall see him brought to trial for his act in destroying a source of evidence."

As though any of that mattered! Herald had suffered himself to be drawn out of the pyre while Qaval talked. His tearing eyes saw Prince Circlet squatting on his wheels, impotent. The hell with Circlet!

He looked down at his hand, seeing the bit of burnt stuff on it. Was there a suggestion of blue, light blue, to its ash? He turned his back on the furnace, thinking of the warning of Smallbore of Metamorphic, the incalculable agony he had been foredoomed to suffer. Through space and time that torment had reached her mind, and he had not properly understood—until now.

He was in too much physical and emotional agony even to feel fury at the irony of the reprieve that had come just minutes too late to save his love. Psyche herself, in her fashion, had willed it. She had gone almost willingly into the pyre, balking all attempts to change her fate, as though she had seen some greater good. But Herald could not see it! He let the Duke of Qaval lead him away.

The looting was proceeding as they rode out on fresh steeds. The females of the castle were being taken into chambers for the service of victorious soldiers. Herald wondered briefly how Sador maidens were raped, but could not muster much interest. Most of the staff of Kastle Kade was human, anyway, and he knew how *they* were raped.

They took the ferry across to the north pier and wheeled rapidly through the forest to the west. They would proceed to the King of Crown's palace for Transfer to Cluster HQ. Hweeh would be mattermitted entire.

Herald, forgive them—they know not what they do.

Forgive them? He would gladly see them *all* go up in the flame they had made for Psyche. He could not even begin to assess the depth of his loss!

On they wheeled, the sun setting beautifully through the barrel trees of the forest ahead. As though any beauty mattered, compared to what had been in Psyche. The full shock had not yet settled in on him; neither Slash nor Solarian host reacted as simplistically as Weew! But in time, when the full magnitude of horror was assimilated. . . .

As they emerged from the forest and entered the plain, there was a sound behind them. The trees shook, the ground shuddered, and a sudden wind swept past so fiercely that they had to duck down and cling to their saddles. The horses, terrified, bolted forward, doubling their prior pace.

When they had succeeded in halting the beasts, the three turned about and looked back.

A giant, glowing mushroom was forming in the dusty sky. It ballooned and folded in on itself continuously, a thing of ghastly power and significance.

"That is an atomic explosion!" Hweeh exclaimed, his eye-stalk wobbling. "What of the Medieval Covenant? No explosives—"

"It is Kastle Kade," Qaval said. "There is no atomic technology on the planet, and least of all *there!* And if there were, why would the victors set it off, destroying themselves?"

Herald's human jaw dropped. "I wished fire on them all!" he said. "Now it has come—and still it is not enough!"

"This cannot have been through any agency of yours," Hweeh pointed out. "There must have been a device there from some prior culture, and somehow it was set off."

"The Ancients!" Qaval exclaimed. "The source of the girl's enhancement of aura. If only we had known! Not a demon, but an Ancient site below the castle, a functioning one. She *was* possessed—by the aura of the Ancients!"

"*There* is the connection!" Hweeh said. "To fight the Amoeba, we must have the power of the Ancients—and she *was* that power, via her attunement to the site. We could have had it *all*, through her!"

"Had it all," Qaval echoed sadly, gazing at the monstrous cloud of death.

"And when she died . . . at peak aura," Hweeh concluded, "she triggered the site into nuclear destruction."

"Good for her!" Herald said with bitter feeling.

Slowly Hweeh sank into shock, as he appreciated the desolation of their situation. But the holocaust had already had its impact on Herald.

PART II

QUEST

7

Site of Mars

2Site nullified.2

*E*Question whether the Quotes obtained ancient science prior to nullification. There was aural generation of site-keying capacity in vicinity, departing shortly before 2's arrival.*E*

&Where did that aural generation travel?&

*E*To the capital of the Quote empire, Planet Outworld.*E*

&Surely bringing ancient information there.&

*E*Cluster conference is commencing now. I will monitor it from the viewpoint of Planet Outworld observation station and report as relevant.*E*

"Emergency Cluster Council Conference now declared in session. Rationale: display of information relating to Cluster security."

%Is there need for a full Cluster Conference? If this is merely another aspect of the energy problem that has plagued us for three thousand years—%

"No, Minister of Knyfh. This is a potential threat of invasion from extra-Cluster space."

δInvasion? Ridiculous! None of our neighbor Clusters would make such an attempt. They surely have problems of their own, and the energy required merely to communicate is prohibitive!δ

"Minster of Qaval, it is one of your nationals who bears the report."

δOne of ours! Put him on!δ

"I am a Qaval, a Duke of Planet Keep, Sphere Sador, Segment Etamin. I participated in—"

§No true Qaval speaks in Solarian Quotes! Is this a degenerate joke?§

"Pay attention, kinkytail, lest you answer to the sword! I am using Solarian communication equipment, designed to project in Quotes regardless of intonation, as any quarterwit knows."

§*That's* a Qaval national! Proceed.§

"I participated in the interrogation of a national of Segment Weew, who was in shock. He has evidence of—"

□Hold! If this matter sends Weews into shock, the Minister of Weew must be warned.□

@I am conversant with the situation, Minister of Lodo. We mattermitted Hweeh of Swees to Segment Etamin for shock treatment, believing that his information was vital to Cluster security. When a message from him was attempted, we pursued the matter and obtained his removal from the local situation, which was becoming tenuous owing to local politics. I have assimilated shock absorbers, and am prepared. @

"If the Segment Ministers will permit me to continue."

:: Continue, Qaval of Quote. ::

"Appreciation, Quadpoint of Andromeda. The Weew has news of the approach of an immense space fleet via mattermission. This fleet is now massed at the perimeter of the Cluster."

♂:::* #Where?! #*::: ♂

σσHow quickly the Fringe Segments react! Be not unduly concerned, Ministers of Freng, Thousandstar, Ast, and Furnace. A Cluster invasion would involve us all.σσ

"Thank you for the reassurance, Novagleam. The enemy fleet is known to us as the obscure extra-Cluster configuration called the Space Amoeba. It is not formed of meteoric debris, but of sophisticated spaceships whose pattern of mattermission staging provides the formation with its typical configuration."

—You claim that one extra-Cluster formation is a fleet of space? This is difficult to believe.—

"I do so claim, Dash of Andromeda. A national of your Galaxy first evoked the expert testimony of the Weew astronomer."

—Play no games, Q of Q. What Sphere?—

"Sphere Slash."

σσSphere Slash, the Accursed of Llume?σσ

"Novagleam, we are all in this Cluster together! If we resume the rehearsal of past differences—"

—Put the curse on!—

"I am Herald the Healer, of Sphere Slash, Andromeda. Duke Qaval's statement is true. But I am ill-equipped to testify, because—"

—I did not perceive your conclusion, Slash. Why can't you testify?—

"Qaval here. Herald the Healer of Slash is in partial shock himself."

—Slash nationals do not go into shock.—

"He is in Solarian host. He—"

—Solarians do not go into shock either.—

"Not in precisely the way Weews do. However, they have a psychological condition that—"

—This Slash is obviously able to communicate. Therefore—

"Do all Dash interrupt, or only ignorant ones?"

—(silence)—

"Herald of Slash married a Sol female, who was recently destroyed at the height of her appeal. It is grief-shock he suffers."

$The personal angle is irrelevant. We accept the fact that he is not at the moment an ideal witness. Detail on the alien fleet is more to the point.$

"Agreed, Cloud 9. Yet it does relate. It was Herald's Sol-wife who evoked the testimony of the Weew, and who alone was capable of evoking the further details. We therefore have incomplete information."

—This is an indirect report? For a Cluster conference?—

* Why was so important an entity destroyed? *

"Local politics. She was a super-Kirlian entity, aura two hundred seventy-five."

♀ §¢/ □ Aura two hundred seventy-five!? □/¢§ ♀

"Affirmed, Ministers of Bhyo, Sculp, Cloud 6, Slash, and Lodo. Herald of Slash is the highest Kirlian known, at two hundred thirty-six, but Psyche of Keep was substantially higher at the time of her demise. This was in fact the cause of her demise. The locals thought she was possessed."

§Where were you, exile of Qaval, when this destruction of a potential witness occurred?§

"I was under restraint, unable to salvage her. But the killers have been in turn destroyed."

%That justice was not for you to make! Why not a trial?%

"The region exploded. Apparently she interacted with an Ancient site, and—"

—An Ancient site! Self-destruct variety?—

"Presumably. I conjecture it was keyed to the Kirlian Lady, enhancing her aura periodically."

—So we lost an invaluable site as well as potential information on a Cluster invasion, thanks to your bungling.—

§Attention, Dash! For a Sphere of your ignominy to cast aspersions on a Qaval—§

¢Must you two Galaxies still quarrel? The Wars of Energy have been over for a thousand years.¢

§Therefore we may be about due for another!§

%To the subject. Was the destruction of the site coincidental with the death of the Kirlian female?%

"No, Knyfh. The girl died about half an hour before the detonation."

%Then the events may have been unrelated, unless there was a delayed reaction.%

□That is not typical of Ancient sites.□

%My point, Lodo. Our experts have reviewed the records of Sphere Sador Transfers during the period in question. This was unproductive. However, we have discovered the stigmata of major mattermission, unaccounted for in Segment logs. I suggest that an unknown agency mattermitted a bomb to the Ancient site. The question remains: what agency, and why?%

(EThey have had much irrelevant discussion, but now they appear to be homing in on the fact.E)

(&It does not matter. They lack the technology to oppose us. Continue monitoring.&)

σσYou imply there is a connection between the alleged Amoeba fleet and the alleged Ancient site destruction?σσ

%That is a possibility, Novagleam. If the Amoeba is an enemy force that has mattermitted from far space—a million parsecs or more—it has a technology well beyond our present capability, quite apart from the ruthless energy expense. It could certainly mattermit a nuclear bomb

163

to a specific site, if it had a mattermission receiver there
—and it appears that some Ancient sites do have mattermission facilities. In this case, there would be only one
way we might achieve parity quickly enough to save
our Cluster from conquest and probable destruction: by
mastering the full science of the Ancients immediately.
The Amoeba surely knows this. Therefore it fears the
functioning Ancient sites, and is destroying any it
locates.%

—Then why have the Amoebites not destroyed the sites
of Sphere Dash?—

%I presume because they do not know about them, or
because they intend to preserve them for their own study
and use, after they have conquered the Cluster. No civilization can afford to throw away technology of the level
of the Ancients! But when it seemed we were about to
activate the Sador site, they destroyed it.%

☐This is highly speculative.☐

—In fact, it is fantastic! It supposes that the Amoeba
is an alien fleet, that its purpose is inimical, that it is so
well aware of our activities as to be able to strike accurately on short notice at any planet.—

⩟And that it might even be monitoring our communications at this instant! ⩟

%Certainly, Minister of Pin. An excellent point. We
need more information. I suggest we take immediate steps
to obtain it. We must also guarantee the privacy of our
deliberations. We must stay well clear of the Amoeba itself, lest we give away our purpose, but elsewhere we
must pursue every avenue leading to possible revelation
of the secrets of the Ancients. If this Amoeba threat is a
false alarm, it will give us experience; if not, we shall
need the science of the Ancients. In a hurry.%

(EThey are in verge-awareness of us, and are seeking
the science of the Ancient sites.E)

(&Monitor any interstellar communicatory transmis-
sions associated with this effort. If there is evidence the
locals are achieving Ancient technology, nullify all specialists associated with that specific breakthrough.&)

☐How do you propose to maintain privacy of our
deliberations and actions, if they should be able to monitor our communications?☐

%By referring the matter to committee.%

(*E*They conspire to elude our surveillance by operating through a committee.*E*)

(&Then have no further concern. Nothing of value ever came out of a committee in time to be useful. There will be no effective resistance.&)

Herald jetted forward across the dusty lava plain. His flaring gas-scoop channeled in the thin atmosphere, compressing it, ionizing it, separating out the elements vital to the life processes, and propelling the residue out at extreme velocity. This host was a native of Sphere Jet, a small culture within a Globular Cluster, one of the tight little conglomerations of stars orbiting the major Galaxies. The intense concentration of old suns in these globs made planets a rarity, and the few that did form were mainly desert balls.

But Globular Cluster Jet contained a small black hole —a region of collapsed matter so dense it had punched through the nebulous fabric of space itself and formed a "hole" from which nothing, not even light, could escape. This hole was the size of a large planet, but it had the effective mass of a large star. It was surrounded by a shell of gas, whose occasional turbulent rifts permitted intense bursts of radiation to escape. This erratic radiation had betrayed the hole's location to galactic astronomers thousands of years ago, and brought early exploration of the region. Thus the sapient Jets had been discovered out of turn as it were.

The Jets were a strange species, as might have been expected of one so close to such a strange phenomenon as a black hole set within a Globular Cluster. The hole sucked in matter from all around, creating an almost irresistible vortex whose compression at the center caused the fierce radiation normally diffused by the shell of gas. On irregular occasion, matter was thrown clear, complicating the geography and geology of the Globular Cluster. This debris had formed a number of planets, whose surface conditions fluctuated widely. Periodically, the radiation destroyed much of the life of such worlds, and clouds of drifting gas coalesced about them and changed the conditions under which new life could evolve. Thus the species that survived and progressed to the point of sapience was adept at foraging for meager assets spread across wide areas, highly adaptable to extremes of atmosphere and climate, and virtually immune to radiation damage.

Though largely landbound, the Jet body was capable of forward velocity approaching four hundred miles an hour. It was also just about the finest host for archaeological excavation available in the Cluster.

Herald looped about, manipulating his little vanes, coasting on his springy bristles, making a delicate track in the dust. The same jet propulsion that gave such speed served as a gentle or savage excavation mechanism and clearing device for buried artifacts. The easiest way to move dust was to blow it away!

Hweeh, garbed in a powered suit, awaited him. "Perhaps I should have Transferred also."

"No. There is still information locked in your Weew brain that we must have. We can't afford to complicate it by housing your mind in another brain. Anyway, you have such an adaptable body that you are not at much disadvantage." He spoke by imposing vibrations on the column of gas he jetted out. Speech was a subfunction of propulsion.

"With due deference to your more valid pain, I suffer from the loss of the Kirlian Lady," Hweeh said. "She alone could unlock my secrets; without her I am hardly worth your time."

"Without her, *I* am hardly worth my time," Herald said. "I loved her more than I knew. Were it not for the threat to our entire Cluster, I would release myself to my grief."

"You Slash have extraordinary control."

"We evolved as warriors, and for a thousand years we have labored under the Curse of Llume. We do what is necessary. We do not have to like it."

"In my culture, this would be regarded as a signal of unconcern. I would not have survived the shock you have had."

"That is the difference between our species. You discovered the threat; I attempt to deal with it."

They looked out over the shield of hardened lava. This was Planet Mars, of System Sol, very close to the world from which Psyche's human species had spread.

Because it was in this fashion associated with her, it had a certain poignancy for him. Of course her human form was of little significance; it was her aura that had conquered him. That aura in any other host would have been as delectable. Well, no, not quite; in Solarian host he had been moved by her human form too. He had loved—*still* loved!—every aspect of her.

How pleasant it would be to simply go into shock, like the Weew. Then he would not have to face a life that had so abruptly and finally been rendered empty.

Pointless to dwell on it. He was a Slash, as he kept reminding himself, able to function regardless. "We are here for archaeological purposes," Herald said. "As well as to give me a rest and to try to complete your healing, in a place safe from enemy intrusion."

"While the committee deliberates whether it will take our warning seriously, and no action is taken," Hweeh said. "At least in my species, shock is open and direct."

Herald paused. "Your ability to assimilate diverse factors and come to the underlying truth is manifesting again, friend of Weew. The Ministers of the Cluster Council seemed most intelligent, but as a group they really did not accomplish much. Do you think they were merely humoring us, and have no real plans for dealing with the menace?"

"That is the purpose of referral to committee. Let us hope that the Duke of Qaval, as adviser to that committee, will prod them into action despite their intent."

"Actually, we did not have conclusive evidence," Herald admitted. "One cannot blame them for their skepticism. If only the Lady—" He broke off.

"You shall heal me, Herald, and we shall complete that evidence. This is necessity."

Necessity. Yes. The salvation of the Cluster was still up to them. But could they do it?

"This is supposed to be the most promising Ancient evolutionary site discovered in the past century," Herald said. "Perhaps we can find here some hint that will lead us to *the* functioning site that will give us parity with the . . . enemy."

"Amoeba," Hweeh said. "I am inured to that much, now. I do not think I will go into shock again. It is merely necessary to evoke what remains buried by my prior shock."

"Agreed. I believe the Council shunted us here on the pretext of providing opportunity to evoke that information to keep us from nagging them about more direct efforts. They don't really expect us to come up with anything. Many of them, like that Minister of Dash, don't believe there is anything to come up with. But we shall do our best, nevertheless. Something in this site may stimulate your associations, and then I can use my aura to follow through." He looked about with his special Jet fiber lens. "This is Elysium, Planet Mars. . . ."

"Mars was God of War, in Solarian myth, and Elysium the abode of the Blessed."

Herald continued his survey of the barren plain, trying to picture Solarian gods. "I perceive no blessing. The war reference is apt enough, however." Then he glanced at one section again, orienting his fiber-lens on a stirring of dust in the distance. The image magnified as specialized hairs shifted, and he made out another Jet. "Our guide approaches."

Soon the visitor coasted up. It was a female of the species, distinguished from the male by the pattern of sensory fibers fringing her forward intake. Young, pretty by the standards of this kind, her metallic torso shone sleekly and her propulsion trail had pleasant emanations. But she was not well; there was a jerkiness to her jetting that made her leave a zigzag trail in the dust when accelerating.

"I come to help and be helped," she said as she drew in close, damping her intake neatly. "Which of you is the Healer?"

"I am," Herald said. This form of life was so well suited to travel that his brief utterance caused him to jump forward, but his host converted the motion into a neat little circle. A completely still Jet was a silent one; movement *had* to accompany conversation.

"I suffer," she said, making her own conversational loop, a bit jerky. "If you can heal me, I will work for you and be your mistress during your stay."

Herald considered. He had encountered many divergent aspects of culture in the Cluster, and could adapt. In some, sexual interaction was a form of polite greeting; in others, there were stringent restrictions. The Solarians tended toward the latter type, though individuals like his ancestor Flint of Outworld seemed to have been closer to the former type. The Jets seemed to be about in the center, recognizing sex as a living need, to be indulged in in semi-casual fashion. A sensible attitude. But sex was not for

168

him during his bereavement. "I need no mistress, but can use a guide. I will heal you, if your problem in amenable to my power."

He moved close to her and touched her with his grasping fibers, letting his aura interact with hers. And was amazed—for she had no aura!

No, he had misread. She did possess aura, but it was fractional, so slight as to be barely detectable. Perhaps one two-hundredth of sapient norm. The inverse of his own. And this was not the result of fading or illness; it was natural to her. He realized that his own host had a similar level, making it a virtual aural blank. Preoccupied by other matters, he had never thought to check. Apparently low aura was a survival trait in the Jets' home Sphere near the hole in the glob.

His aura enveloped her, penetrating to her deepest animation. She was a very nice creature, as was evidenced in her self-perception as reflected in her trace aura. "What is your nomenclature?" he inquired gently, the jet of his speech spinning them both about.

"We use no names, here, merely numbers," she replied. As she talked, he felt the aural interactions of the nervous signals directing her motion, locating the flaw that made her unwell. It *was* subject to his type of healing. "I am Worker Sixteen."

Sixteen—the approximate age in Sol-years of his erstwhile wife. Evocative number! "Relax, Sixteen, heal," he said. "My aura touches yours."

"I don't feel anything," she said.

So low a Kirlian that even in this intimacy, which was in certain respects closer than the sexual one she had proffered, she could not perceive his power! He had not known that any such species existed in the Cluster.

But soon he became aware of something else. She could not feel the healing—because it was not occurring. His aura was present, but not acting.

Herald broke contact. "I *have* gone into shock, in my fashion!" he said, horrified. "I cannot heal!"

"This cannot be," Hweeh said. "Your aura remains."

"Verify her condition for yourself," Herald said, disengaging. "I have not affected her."

Hweeh jetted his suit over, touching a sensory appendage to Sixteen's gleaming chassis. He paused, concentrating. "You are mistaken. You have healed her."

169

"I have *not*. I do not delude myself about failure."

"Perhaps you have overlooked success, then." Hweeh broke contact. "She is well now, unless I delude *myself*. Sixteen, please jet at speed for us."

"But I cannot—" she protested.

"Take off!" Hweeh said.

She took off, stirring up the dust explosively. She accelerated rapidly in a straight line, then banked in a great loop, leaving a horizontal tail of suspended dust. She braked suddenly by flipping her exhaust to the front, making a very pretty cloud, then accelerated forward again. Her trail was without divergencies.

"You have healed me!" she cried, zooming between them and making an intricate triple spinabout on her way out for another run.

Herald looked at Hweeh. "Neither am I a fool," he said quietly, so that his body hardly moved. "*You* healed her, Weew."

Hweeh made a negligent quiver of an appendage. "Perhaps her faith has made her well. It was a minor malfunction of her control system."

"*Of course*, her faith made her well. That is how healing works. But it was your aura that enhanced that faith, not mine."

"I learned the art from you, from the many times you have practiced your immense reassurance on me. My aura is far more powerful with respect to hers than yours is with respect to mine, so my relatively clumsy effort seems to have had effect, but it is your skill I attempted to emulate. Therefore it is really your success. I sought to protect your reputation from question by those not in a position to understand."

"How can I heal *you*, when you now possess the talent I lack?"

"You will recover," Hweeh said confidently. "Your indisposition is temporary. Then you will heal me."

Touching confidence! But Herald remembered Psyche, burning, burning, jerking her pale-blue legs away from the terrible fire, and knew that his soul had been consumed with hers. Without her, he was no more than a shell.

The dig was extensive. The site had been buried under packed Martian dust laid down in the course of three million years of seasonal planetary dust storms. Crews

170

of Jets had labored for years, carefully blowing out the dust and salvaging structures and artifacts with meticulous care. "We discovered it by accident," Sixteen told Herald. "Rather, the Lodoformers discovered it."

"Segment Lodo is converting this planet to their use?" Hweeh inquired. "They are neighbors of ours, but still five thousand parsecs from here. It would have taken one of their ships thirty thousand years to travel that distance And why should Segment Etamin give up a planet so near the home of one of their founding species? This is Mars, adjacent planet to Earth, origin of the human Solarians."

"Mars was mined out two thousand years ago, as were all the Sol System minor moons and planets," Sixteen said. "The Solarians extracted all its commercial resources and left it dead, so it is not useful to them or any other Segment Etamin species. In any event, Planet Earth has lost much of its political clout. The Sol-Polaris regime of Planet Outworld dominates this region. Since Mars is the only world within three hundred parsecs that is suitable for Lodo, the Cluster Council made it available."

"But the time factor!" Herald protested. "Segment Lodo did not exist thirty thousand years ago. In fact, Star Lo had barely established relations with Star Do via radio signal. They could not have sent—"

"They used mattermission," she explained. "They drew on the resources of a local neutron star to catapult their freezer-ships as far as six thousand parsecs. This occurred during their 'Fool' period three thousand years ago. The ships then oriented on the most promising systems and closed on them at half-light speed. Most have now been settled, but a few ships remain in space."

"But mattermission requires a receiver!" Herald said. "They could not simply fling out randomly!"

"There are receivers scattered about in space," Hweeh said. "I have identified a number of them, in the course of my researches. Often they pass unnoticed, as they resemble derelicts, but some are functional. Most are from now-vanished local cultures, but some could derive from the Ancients."

"Live and learn!" Herald said. "How much of the Universe passes within easy range of our perceptions, yet is missed because we fail to comprehend the obvious? Are we willfully blind to the ready solutions to our quests?"

"It only seems that way," Hweeh said. "The necessary

compromises of civilization tend to channelize our thinking, until need and accident reform the channels. Only through highly selective blindness can we filter out the irrelevant, and of course on occasion some of that turns out to be more relevant than first supposed. I conjecture that the higher the level of civilization, the greater the blindness to the irrelevant, until changing needs cause the extremely narrow focus to exclude the relevant as Hell. Then the civilization falls. Possibly that is what happened to the Ancients."

"Intriguing hypothesis," Herald said. "But I am skeptical. Such knowledge as the Ancients had. . . ." He thought of something else. "Do you suppose the Amoeba could have used—?"

"I'm sure of it. A spaceship-sized receiver, left in deep space by the Ancients. The Amoebites could have located it by a sophisticated mattermission search—since their science seems nearly equivalent to that of the Ancients, they surely have means to do this—and used it for their staging area. They could have shipped through equipment and technicians to build a hundred or a thousand additional such receivers, then brought their ships through as fast as half-light speed could clear them out of the way. Hence the Amoeba pattern of expansion. It could still take decades to transmit such a fleet, but it could be and evidently *has* been done." He paused, startled. "You have elicited more of my buried information, without even using your aura!"

"You are healing yourself," Herald said. "We learn more and more about the Amoeba—except how to stop it."

"That is why we explore this site," Hweeh reminded him. "If we discover here the key to the Ancients' rationale. . . ."

In a buried, nonfunctional Ancient site? Unlikely! Yet their discourse about the blindness of specialization encouraged him. Maybe there *was* something here that others had overlooked, because they were looking for *things*, not *insights*.

"So now the Lodo freezer is arriving at Mars," Herald said. "And the red planet is being Lodoformed for their colony."

"Yes," Sixteen agreed. "It has provided beneficial employment for the local Solarians for the past fifty years. In twenty more years the Lodo ship will arrive. There would have been no complications, had not the Lodoforming crew, in the course of filling in the strip-mining pits of past Solarian excesses, uncovered relics of the Ancients. Thus we of Jet were imported to salvage this site, as Solarians could never have done it rapidly and expertly enough. And now a complication of *our* schedule has brought you here."

Herald remembered: There *had* been an item on his itinerary about System Sol, before the events of Planet Keep and the manifestation of the Amoeba had hopelessly shuffled his schedule. So some bright light in the Cluster Command must have decided that the best place to send him was one he should normally have visited anyway. That way, any suspicion by outsiders might be alleviated; he obviously was not going out of his way.

"There is still confusion," Hweeh said. "Lodo is an advanced Segment, with a high social organization and technology. In that respect it parallels Weew itself." He seemed unconscious of the slight he was giving other Milky Way creatures. It was an arrogance common to center-galaxy cultures, here and in Andromeda. "I have dealt with Lodo specialists in research astronomy, comparing notes and exchanging data, and found them creditably competent. Surely the Lodo colony could have excavated the Ancient site conveniently."

Sixteen made a hoot of gas. "The Solarians insisted on having the site excavated under their auspices, before Lodo arrived."

"Segment pride," Herald said. "Common to many cultures."

"Pride is essential," Hweeh said. "Each Segment must be the best—in its own estimation." Herald was unable to tell whether there was tolerant humor in the remark, but he suspected there was.

"I also have had dealings with Lodo," Herald said. "I know the Segment only through its heraldry. It is a Scepter culture, whose emblem is a worm in the ground. I find it odd that such a species should turn its attention so formidably to space."

"Not odd at all," Hweeh said. "Population pressure can cause drastic alterations of perspective. Only in space was there sufficient ground for the Worms of Lo and Do."

In the cleared section of the site, there were no

173

squared-off Solarian-style structures, or round Polarian-style ones. Instead there were cutaway sections showing a labyrinth of tunnels. In some cases, the tunnel walls were bare shells, seemingly too thin to support the weight of the mass of other tunnels and driftdust above. The binding cements were evidently very strong and durable, and of course the circular cross sections of the tunnels were able to support much weight.

"Do you know," Hweeh remarked, "this strongly resembles the metropoli of Lodo. Could the Ancients have been Worm-entities?"

"The thought occurred to me also," Herald said. "Yet I have considered other Ancient sites, and they were not of this type. I think it more likely that the Ancients were a conglomerate, much as our Cluster is today. In each region of space, the Ancient society was represented by its local species. Here on Mars, it could have been a Worm-sapient."

"It is difficult to perceive how such a conglomeration could have achieved the uniformity of culture and technology we have noted across the Cluster," Hweeh said. "The Ancients seemed to have no Spherical regression of the kind we suffer from today."

"How much worse Spherical regression would be for a single species spreading across the Cluster," Herald said. "The great riddle of the Ancients is not in their species, but in their technology. If we had that level today—"

"We could stand against the Amoeba," Hweeh finished. "We keep returning to that!"

"The Amoeba?" Sixteen inquired.

"I suppose it is no secret now," Herald said. "Our Cluster is threatened by a monster fleet of ships from outer space that we call the Amoeba. We fear they come to conquer us, to harvest the matter of the Cluster for the energy needed to sustain their level of civilization, and that they possess the ability to do so—unless we can muster the complete knowledge of the Ancients against them."

"How can one fleet conquer the whole Cluster?" Sixteen asked. "It would take them two million years merely to traverse it, and in that time Spherical regression would destroy them."

Herald realized that he had been falling into a trap of careless thinking. Sixteen had extremely low aura, but that did not mean she was also low intelligence. There was a lot more to an entity than aura, as he had learned from Psyche. "It seems they mattermit," he said. "The fact that they do this, when there is no apparent source of energy —such as the Lodos' neutron star—in the region, suggests that their technology rivals that of the Ancients. We can hardly expect to stand against them—unless the Ancients stand with us."

Sixteen made a blue flare of acquiescence. "Matter-mission uses a lot of energy," she said. "I begin to grow concerned. Isn't the Cluster Council acting on the matter?"

"They are and they aren't," Herald said. "They have set up a committee."

"Then we are lost," she said, quite seriously.

"Whatever the species or conglomeration of the Ancients," Hweeh said, "This site of Mars does seem to be one of their relics, and just might have a hint of the answer to our problem. I presume it has been competently dated?"

"The site as a whole has been dated. There is no doubt it is of the Ancient period," she said. "Also, each level has been dated specifically. We find that the oldest habitations are nearest the surface, the more recent ones progressively below."

"Isn't that backward?" Herald asked. "I'm no archaeologist, but I thought new remains cover the older ones."

"It is in order," Hweeh said. "This is the worm mode. Worms naturally tunnel, and it takes time for them to convert the depths. They are not like the Quadpoints of your galaxy, who fill in their tunnels behind them. Here the tunnels remain open and the matter removed must be disposed of suitably. So the process is slow. They seal off their old passages for their dead, making new ones deeper in the ground. The old air spaces become insulation against the extremes of climate, making each succeeding layer more comfortable. Such fumes as there may be, tend to percolate upward, away from the residential zones. An old worm-metropolis is the very depth of gracious living."

"I think you missed your calling," Herald said. "You belong in archaeology, not astronomy."

"They are much the same," Hweeh said. "I have associates in the field of research archaeology, and portions of our studies overlap. I research in the depth of old holographs and contemplate the layerings of ancient galaxies."

175

They were still descending through the excavated site, coasting over ramps slanting past layers of tunnels. "This is an exceptional site," Sixteen remarked. "It covers a period of occupation of a thousand years, and the trace evolution of technology is measurable."

Both Herald and Hweeh reacted. "You have traced the actual development of Ancient science?" the Weew asked.

"To a certain extent," she said. "Actually it doesn't get into Kirlian technology; this was a residential section. All the advanced equipment was removed when the city was vacated. All of *everything* was removed."

"Then how do you measure the progression of their technology?" Herald asked. "By the elegance of the surfacing of their tunnels?"

"No, the passages are organically made," she said. "They may have had machines to supplement the work, but the binding cement seems to be from body chemistry. The artifacts are in the tomb-tunnels, evidently burial items. Rings, mainly, with ornate vermiculate designs—"

"Crests!" Herald exclaimed. "Kirlian crests!"

She did not catch the significance. "The Ancients seem to have worn them around their bodies. Perhaps the metal enhanced their Kirlian powers."

"That too," Herald said. "I meant the designs. They could have been identifying symbols, codified—in short, Ancient heraldry."

"Heraldry?" She was prettily perplexed, and for an instant she reminded him of Psyche. There was of course no similarity of body or aura, and he was immediately disgusted with the comparison. *Oh, Psyche!*

"It is an odd system of Cluster nomenclatures," Hweeh explained to her delicately. "Pictures representing location and families are drawn on shields or clothing for ready identification of individuals in person or historically. It amounts to a kind of supplementary visual language that has many aficionados, similar to the Tarot images. This entity is the Cluster's leading exponent of the contemporary art."

To see ourselves as others see us . . . , Herald thought.

"How nice," Sixteen said. "Maybe he can interpret the designs. I had thought he was only a Kirlian expert."

"Never mind my credits," Herald said. "Here my professions may overlap. I shall indeed examine the designs,

176

as well as the Kirlian properties of the rings. But I had understood—I may misremember, as my itinerary was set up several hosts ago—that you had uncovered some actual Kirlian objects, of the type found in other Ancient sites."

"Yes, the cubes," she said. "They were found in the lowest level, and we believe them to be Kirlian-keyed. They seem to have been left by accident. Perhaps they dropped from a moving load unseen. That is why this site was worth your attention. The cubes may be the most advanced artifacts of this site, perhaps even having part of the secret for which you quest."

How barren that Kirlian Quest seemed now! If he had any way to quest instead for Psyche— But that had to be suppressed. "Perhaps," he agreed. "Let us hope so. Kirlian cubes seem to have been the books of the Ancients, their recordings of things of moment. But I doubt we can master Ancient science from a few cubes; we need a full library." *In the library of Kastle Kade, her aura rising, rising, dooming her and him. . . .*

"Something perplexes me," Hweeh said. His spacesuit was convenient, because he could speak without having to jet forward. He had shaped it into a form approximating that of Herald's host, however, perhaps so as not to seem out of place. "You say there is a progression in the artifacts?"

"Yes. The oldest ones are cruder, both in artistry of design and in the alloy of metals employed. The difference is marginal but consistent, and, we feel, significant. It shows that slight refinements in conception and technique occurred over the centuries."

"But then this indicates one of two things, each highly significant," Hweeh said. "Either this is the home site of the development of the original Ancient species—"

"Hardly," Sixteen said with a jet of humor. "It is only a fractional record of their history, a thousand years, picking up when they colonized from space and ending when they departed. They originated elsewhere."

"Or it represents," Hweeh continued with that tone Herald recognized as the professional conclusion, "a tangible demonstration that the Ancients suffered from Spherical regression."

Both Herald and Sixteen suffered flameouts of shock. Both dropped and rolled in the dust, sputtering to recover propulsion and voice. "Impossible," Sixteen gasped. "Everyone knows the Ancients did not—"

"It must be a misinterpretation," Herald said as his flow returned. "The artifacts could have been labeled in reverse order by mistake—"

"That would still indicate regression," Hweeh said, pursuing his logic. "Either they regressed upon founding the colony, then slowly recovered, or they slowly regressed until their dwindling technology made further residence on this planet unfeasible."

It made unholy sense. Spherical regression was the effect of reduced civilization at the fringes of individual interstellar empires, owing to the delay entailed by the effective limitation of half-light-speed travel and the inability of reduced populations to maintain high-order technology. Thus a planet like Keep, near the Fringe of the Sador Sphere and not far from the Spheres of Sol and Polaris, had medieval representatives of all three cultures. Only sufficient energy to make full-scale mattermission possible could abate this effect, for then the highest technology of each home planet could be exported. It had always been believed that the Ancients possessed such an energy source, for they had not seemed to regress; their artifacts were of uniformly high technology wherever they appeared.

"But if the Ancients—" Herald said, and stopped, appalled. "That would imply that they lacked— No, they simply could *not* have expanded across the Cluster if they suffered regression! There must be some other explanation for the discrepancy of artifacts."

"There *must* be," Sixteen echoed. "We only excavate and catalogue, we do not theorize in depth. Our findings are accurate, but the rationale—"

"I do not perceive the necessity of questioning either the findings or the rationale," Hweeh said after a moment. "It is certainly no shame to suffer from Spherical regression. All the best cultures do. In fact, perhaps only a hopelessly set culture, like that of the—I'm not sure of the equivalent in Solarian, termite-ants?—gregarious insectoids can effectively avoid it, and they do so at the expense of further progress. Progress cannot come without change, and change permits regression as well. So it may be a healthy signal. The point is that though the Ancients may have felt its impact, even as we do today, they were

178

able to overcome it. What is evidenced in this site is minimal, certainly, especially considering that the Ancient home world may have been in another galaxy. We need to ascertain *how* they minimized their regression, since they surely did *not* have infinite energy."

"It is good to have at least one clear thinker on this mission," Herald said. "Of course you are correct."

"In fact, you're pretty intelligent," Sixteen added.

"It is of no moment," Hweeh said modestly. "I have long specialized in analyzing data for meaning."

Now they entered the larger tunnel of the excavation. "We did not care to risk collapse of the cutaway section," Sixteen explained. "Our excavation weakens the structure, which already suffers from fossilization from three million years. It is stable enough in itself, but brittle when disturbed. So we are mining for the bottom levels. We are at the lowest now. All that remains is to classify recovered artifacts before we yield the remains to the Lodoform crew." She made a little flirt of motion, indicating the tunnels around them. "It is unfortunate that this must be destroyed, but the bureaucrats insist that the planet be uniform, pristine for the guests."

"Who would much rather explore the Ancient site for themselves," Hweeh said. "Idiocy to destroy it."

"This level differs," Herald said, observing the cross-sectioned passages. "These tunnels are machined."

"Yes," Sixteen agreed. "We conjecture that they were preparing to depart, and knew there would be no further burials, so had to standardize their passages for ready access. They are far more uniform, with fewer residential chambers."

They drew up at last in a nether chamber of considerable size. "This is their chamber, not yours?" Herald inquired.

"Yes. We have not destroyed anything it was possible to retain of the originals. We conjecture that this contained a mattermission unit that transported the individuals directly to their orbiting ship, then either self-destructed or mattermitted itself to the ship."

"Mattermitted *itself?*" Hweeh asked dubiously.

"We don't know the capabilities of the Ancients," she reminded him. "Their machinery may have had this power. At any rate, the chamber was empty. Possibly it was dismantled by a cleanup crew and carried to the surface for transport to the ship. It was obviously an orderly evacuation. The mystery of their abrupt departure, in the face of no apparent threat, remains."

"That *is* the mystery of the Ancients everywhere," Hweeh said.

"This cessation on Mars coincided with that of all the other dated Ancient terminations?" Herald inquired, sure that it did.

"Yes. They disappeared all over the Cluster—simultaneously, as far as we can tell."

"So they did not leave Mars to go to another planet," Herald said. "When they left here, they left the Cluster too."

"It is almost as though some Cluster-wide threat drove them out," Hweeh mused.

"Like an Amoeba?" Herald asked. "Then we are surely lost, for even the science of the Ancients cannot save us. Yet there has never been evidence of invasion. Surely the Ancients would have dug in and fought."

"Here are the cubes," Sixteen said, cutting short a dialogue that had no reasonable resolution.

Herald drew up before the platform and contemplated the display. There were only two cubes. They were decorated in relief on the sides in the manner typical of Ancient artifacts of this type. "These are the best-preserved cubes I have encountered," Herald said. "Odd that they should turn up in ruins, instead of in some functioning site."

"These are not ruins," Sixteen said. "They are closed-down residences." But then she made a gust of negation. "The distinction becomes irrelevant; you mean that this is not a *technological* site. The discovery of these cubes transformed this excavation; prior to that, this was a routine cataloguing mission. If these are functioning Ancient texts. . . ."

Yes, indeed! Prior Ancient cubes had been amenable to evocation only by the application of high aura. Herald had handled several, but they had been music recordings with no apparent meaning beyond that. Mintakan experts had analyzed the sounds and been baffled. What was needed was a definite language that could be deciphered. So far there had been only circumstantial evidence that the Ancients even *had* a language. Perhaps this was it!

Herald extended his forward feelers to touch the

nearest cube, and tasted the air circulating around it. Normally the Ancient artifacts were evoked by an aura of 180 or stronger, so he expected no difficulty. The only apprehension he felt was over the possible content of the Ancient record. It might be empty or it just might be the one they needed, the one that told the key secrets of Ancient science.

Suddenly he was aware of other Jets. They had been working around the site, so that he had hardly noticed them, but now they were closing in to witness the evocation of the cubes. Well, he could hardly condemn their curiosity and interest. They had found these significant artifacts!

He concentrated his aura on the cube. He felt it begin to respond—then it balked. Hweeh focused on him, concerned, knowing something was wrong.

He could not evoke the cube. Like his healing power, his evocation strength was gone. And Hweeh of Weew could not salvage his reputation this time by doing it for him; his aura was 125, too low for this work.

"Dead cubes?" Sixteen asked anxiously.

Herald hesitated. They expected so much . . . could he disappoint them? Yet if he remained Kirlian-impotent—

He would have to try again, harder. Maybe he could break through his own stasis—

"ALARM! ALARM!" the site speaker system clamored. "Strange nexus has materialized in orbit about this planet. Nature unknown."

"Strange nexus?" the Jet super, numbered "1," inquired. "Clarify."

The observer sounded confused. "It registers on our sensor like a meteor-shower—but it's *orbiting*. And it has some kind of energy shell. Maybe our equipment is malfunctioning, but I think it's a ship."

The Jets hovered on their fibers, amazed. "A ship *materialized?*" Hweeh demanded. "Could it be the Lodo freezer mattermitting again?"

"Without a mattermission receiver?" Herald asked.

Sixteen read the detail code coming in over the speaker. "It is no wormship," she said. "Even allowing for our sensor malfunction, the shape is wrong. This is a Sphere, not a Worm."

"An Atom-ship, perhaps," Herald said. "Maybe it

181

found an old orbiting receiving station. Still, why would anyone waste all that energy mattermitting here? They could have called us via Transfer-link."

"It is an alien vessel," the lookout said excitedly on the speaker. "No record of this type in the Cluster. Now it is hovering above this site—"

"No ship of the Cluster can mattermit without a specifically identified receiver," Herald said. "If it is an Ancient receiver undiscovered until now, this ship can only be—"

Hweeh started to lose form inside his suit. Grimly he hung on. "It is—" He sagged, then struggled to reform his speaker horn. *"It is the Amoeba!"* And he sagged into shock.

"The Amoeba!" Sixteen exclaimed. *"Here?"*

"What is this Amoeba?" One demanded.

"Enemy fleet," Sixteen said tersely.

"Or one ship thereof," Herald amended. "If Hweeh is right—and I think he is—we're in trouble. Find cover —fast."

The Jets milled around uncertainly. Of course there was no cover. They were already deep in the ground, with nowhere to go but up.

"This is not a battle base," One retorted. "It is an archaeological site. No one would attack—"

She was interrupted by a crack as of thunder. The tunnel shuddered, and dust sifted down.

Herald hooked the unconscious Hweeh with his graspers and jetted for the exit ramp. "Get out before this dig collapses!" he wooshed back at the confused Jets.

Sixteen zoomed up beside him and helped him haul the inert Weew. Herald hoped the suit was maintaining the life processes without assistance. "How can there be thunder?" she asked, seemingly unable to focus on the main issue. "Mars has no water-storms!"

Another crack of thunder sounded. This time part of the ceiling caved in, showing the red Martian sky above a ballooning cloud of dust. "That's no storm!" Herald cried. "That's a laser strike!"

"But the noise—"

Herald realized that the explanation did not come naturally to a nonlaser species, so as they struggled through the throng of panicked Jets on the ramp, he explained: "The laser heats the air it passes through,

182

making it expand explosively. That's the thunder. Mars has very thin atmosphere, but this is evidently a very strong laser, so the effect remains. Lasers are basically space weapons, where no atmosphere gets in the way. Here—"

"But why?"

"I'm not sure why we're under attack. But I suspect the Amoeba recognizes this site as a threat. That means the Amoebites know about, and are afraid of, Ancient science. That's a good sign."

"A *good* sign? That they ray us down?"

"Because it means we are close to achieving what we need to defeat them. A strike like this must be a desperation measure, as it betrays their presence and intent prematurely."

A third strike came. This time the cavity behind them caved in completely. The crack of thunder was followed by the roar of the collapse. "Oh, oh!" Sixteen cried in anguish. "The work is incomplete! All our labor of excavation and preliminary cataloguing—"

"Keep moving," Herald told her. "Or more than the work will be lost. This is war." He was surprised at his own stability. Probably it was due in part to his Slash heritage, and in part to his recent loss of Psyche. Death simply was no great threat to him in his grief.

"The Weew is too heavy," Sixteen cried. "I cannot carry him much longer!"

Herald had to agree. His Jet host was healthy, but was not designed to carry heavy weights. "We'll have to hide somewhere, and try to bring him to," he decided. "He is the only one who can operate his suit."

"Here," she said. "These passages are long and deep; we should be safe there." She guided him into the labyrinth of Ancient tunnels.

The passages were too narrow for them to pass three abreast, except where the archaeologists had widened them for exploratory access. But this was a Jet-developed offshoot that penetrated deep into the ground, almost to the base of the city, with each level carefully marked off for reference. When it seemed safe, they parked Hweeh in a niche formed by an intersection, rested briefly, and tried to revive him.

Herald touched the Weew's suit with his aura. "Wake, friend," he said.

There was no response.

Another explosion reverberated down the tunnels, making Herald suddenly claustrophobic. This warren had lasted three million years, but it was brittle. Too much shaking. . . .

"Why does he not wake?" Sixteen asked, frightened. "Is he dead?"

"He is in shock. I am a healer—but I too am in a kind of shock. I did not heal you, for I have lost my power. Hweeh healed you. Now I cannot help him. I am sorry."

"Maybe I can do it," she said.

Herald, worn out by the haul and preoccupied by the continuing sounds of destruction elsewhere in the site, hardly paid attention. Any physical comfort she could offer the Weew would help, though only an aura above Hweeh's own level of 125 could revive him from shock.

"He's just a gray mass!" Sixteen said, concerned. Herald was not certain how she could determine color in this dark niche; perhaps she spoke figuratively.

"This is normal for Weew shock," he assured her. "His suit preserves him. He is in health, only unconscious."

His thoughts returned to the Amoeba. Assuming it really was an Amoeba ship out there, how could it have pinpointed this site so accurately, of all the locations on all the planets of the Cluster, and why had it struck *now?* There could be no coincidence about it! If the Amoeba knew where the Ancient sites and receivers were, and it was out to destroy them before the Cluster species could use them, it was a horrifying indication of the capacity of the enemy. But even so, it defied coincidence that the strike should come right at this moment, right when he was trying to evoke the Ancient cube. . . .

That was it! That cube was no text—it was a transmitter! It had reacted to his aura by issuing a Kirlian signal. It was a machine, triggered by exposure to aura of the intensity of its makers, the Ancients, and it obeyed without question or discrimination when evoked. The cube did not know or care that the Ancients were three million years gone. So it had dutifully transmitted its message—perhaps no more than a blank carrier impulse, since he had not been trying to transmit—and the Amoeba had picked it up, believed it represented an animation of Ancient science, and acted immediately to

184

destroy it. No, no coincidence at all. He had brought the attack upon himself!

And the destruction of the site on Planet Keep had been by Amoeba action too. Psyche had evoked that site, much as he had evoked the cube, tuning into it unconsciously, and the strike had come. Now the enemy was reacting much more swiftly. Or perhaps the signal this time had been more specific: *Here is an aura of 236, capable of keying open Ancient sites!*, while before it had been a more general thing, mystifying the enemy even as it had mystified the nobles of Keep. Either way, it was apparent that the Amoeba was closing in at an alarming rate. It was no longer a distant, highly theoretical menace; it was here and now! Its strategy was most specific: Eliminate the auras capable of evoking Ancient equipment, thereby eliminating any possible use of that equipment by Cluster entities. If the Cluster did not obtain Ancient science soon, it would be too late. Any enemy that could strike so swiftly, so specifically, when its base was over a million light-years distant. . . .

He was getting nowhere! If only Psyche had survived! Not merely for personal reasons, compelling as those were —even here in the Jet host, he longed for her!—but because of her seeming ability to draw enhancement from an Ancient site. She might have been able to—

"Did I shock out again?" Hweeh asked. "Thanks for reviving me, Psyche."

"Who?" Sixteen asked.

Hweeh rotated his eye-stalk inside his suit. "Pardon, Lady. I was misinformed. For a moment I mistook you for another entity."

Herald felt a slow amazement. He had been thinking of Psyche, and Hweeh had named her. Coincidence? Then how had the Weew been brought out of shock? There was no way that Sixteen's fractional aura could have done it.

Hweeh must have snapped out of it himself spontaneously. Perhaps his shock had been countered by the knowledge that he had to keep functioning if he were to survive at all.

Another laser beam struck, closer. "They're chasing us!" Sixteen said.

"More likely destroying the whole site," Herald said. "We just happen to be in their path."

"Then let's get *out* of it!" she said.

They jetted on through the passage, seeking the surface. Sixteen knew the way, and led them through a labyrinth that otherwise would have baffled them. Soon they emerged to the Martian day—and saw the enemy ship.

It was a shimmering globe floating so close to the surface that it seemed like an atmospheric balloon. Herald had never seen a ship quite like it. So this was the Amoeba, seeming close enough to touch!

Abruptly the ship moved, jumping across the sky to hover above the trio.

"*That's mattermission!*" Sixteen cried. "It didn't accelerate, it jumped!"

"Unlikely," Hweeh said. "No transmitter, no receiver, no implosion and explosion of air."

"Just get out from under!" Herald said, jetting away. But he too was astonished. Until this episode, it had been inconceivable that anything could mattermit from place to place without entering a transmitter and arriving in a receiver. Now it remained doubtful—but conceivable. The devastating technology of this enemy . . .!

Hweeh and Sixteen followed his example with alacrity— and a laser beam speared down where they had been. The air exploded, the thunder pushing them on.

"It really *is* gunning for us!" Sixteen cried. "But *why?*"

Herald didn't care to try to answer that. He did not have the Ancient cube with him now, so could not be broadcasting any Kirlian signal. He has baffled not only by the *why*—though his hypothesis was clarifying that— but the *how.* Impossible things were happening! "We'd better separate, so that it can't blast all three of us at once," he suggested, feeling a touch of *déjà vu.* When he and Psyche and Whirl of Dollar had fled Caesar, the monster of Keep— But how much more formidable was *this* monster!

Somehow he felt no fear. Had he been in his own Slash body he would have shot a beam back, though with no expectation of bringing down a spaceship! Death by suffocation in a collapsing tunnel frightened him, or death by poison or freezing or disease, or by falling from a high place such as the ridge above Kastle Kade; but a laser was a comprehensible thing, basically natural, quick and clean.

Sixteen was now jetting far to the side, and Hweeh's

suit moved in the opposite direction. How fortunate that the Weew had not returned to shock! Now they would see whom the alien went after.

Suddenly the ship was above Herald. He banked sharply, turning to go at right angles to his former route. This body had no lasers, but it was highly maneuverable and much faster than a Slash! In this situation, he actually felt more confidence as a Jet.

Again the laser struck where he had been. Close misses—but still he was not afraid. What could they take from him, that the death of Psyche had not taken already?

The Amoeba ship evidently could fire only straight down, so had first to position itself directly above him. It was not adapted for planetary search-and-destroy—not completely, anyway. In space it would have to orient on distant targets with extreme precision, so the fixed beam made sense. Any time the ship was in position it could score. But that extra step gave him the edge here. He was so close that a small change in his location was like an impossible maneuver in distant space, one the ship was not geared to follow. He could keep dodging it until it ran out of energy, which it had to do, pretty soon; those beams were powerful! They would miss him close each time—but they *would* miss.

Meanwhile, he was learning much about the enemy. Obviously it was him alone they wanted—and his only distinguishing mark was his aura. Therefore they were orienting on aura alone. They could detect it at this range without the aid of the cube. Maybe in its strength his aura resembled the aura of the Ancients, so they feared it regardless of its keying capacity. But they didn't dare land a party to capture him, so had to use a cannon capable of melting a hole through a mile-thick ship (well, through its hull, anyway) to nab him. A ludicrous waste of power.

The ship jumped again. This time Herald braked and spun about, jetting back the way he had come. The beam missed him, striking to the side where he would have been, had he repeated the maneuver. They were learning! He had four chances in five of keeping clear, since he could go in four directions or stand still. They had missed him twice; if they had chances for three more, the odds were about even they would catch him, unless he got completely out of their range. Provided they could afford the power expense.

Meanwhile he kept moving, waiting for the ship to commit itself again. The Amoeba had him pegged as an Ancient, or the equivalent, and was trying desperately to destroy him. If they feared the science of the Ancients that much, the Amoeba must be less developed than the Ancients had been. However, that was not any new revelation at this point. Why were they suddenly so intent upon him now?

Could it be because he represented no real threat to them unless he was in the vicinity of Ancient equipment? They had not paid him much attention while he was elsewhere in the Cluster; it was Psyche they had blasted, though she was dead already, because she had been keying the Ancient site of Keep. Obviously he could not key an Ancient site unless he were at it, and a nontechnological residential site hardly counted.

There had to be a functioning site *somewhere on Mars!* If he could only find it in time. After he escaped from this ship, of course.

The ship jumped again. This time Herald jetted straight forward at top velocity, not dodging. If he guessed wrong. . . .

The beam struck well behind him. They had played him for another reversal!

Suddenly the pit of one of the prior strikes loomed before him. The dust was fused, the underlying lava melted. Oh, yes, these were ship-destroyer lasers, not little antipersonnel beams! If they had had a splay of pin-beams they could have caught him. Obviously then they had not anticipated this particular type of localized chase. The Amoeba was not omniscient; it could and did make mistakes! Very encouraging information he was getting, and he wasn't even serving on any committee! Still, the odds seemed to be with the Amoeba.

He shot over the lip and down into the pit, his brushes feeling the radiating heat. Fortunately the Jet form had the efficient cooling mechanism of wind; heat in his body was jetted out almost immediately. He could tolerate this surface, so long as he kept moving, barely touching it.

This was why the ship had misjudged. They had assumed he would avoid the hot spot, and thought they

188

had him boxed in. They might well have been correct, had he thought where he was going. This was not just a little hot, it was a *lot* hot.

The sides of the pit were vertical, dropping down like the inner rim of a volcano before curving into slag. The mass of lava here had been vaporized! When laser science had first been developed, it had been supposed that it could never achieve much physical power. But they had been thinking of the animate lasers of the Slash, limited by the living processes; lasers had come a long way since then! Contemporary lasers might not pack the direct-motion punch of a physical missile, but the sheer heat caused explosive expansion. This one was evidently an outer-shell beam, causing the inner section to vaporize and wash straight back, while the outer rim remained clean-cut, uncluttered by the debris of its own action. It was a very nice bit of laser sculpture that he had to admire. The warships of Slash might match the sheer power of the Amoeba strikes, but not their finesse of application. A ship struck with such a beam would be holed cleanly, instead of merely melting sloppily and dissipating much of the force of the strike.

All this in an instant, as he dropped into the hole. He noticed an Ancient tunnel, opened to the surface by that lovely strike. There must be radiating passages all over this area, hidden by the sand! This was a far more extensive site than the archaeologists had yet realized.

On impulse, he gambled by jetting straight into the tunnel. The depths disturbed him, but his chances on the surface were diminishing too swiftly. If this passage went deep enough, and had another exit, he might escape the Amoeba ship. Then he would be extremely careful about trying to evoke any more Ancient cubes! But if this tunnel did not. . . .

He was in luck, so far. The passage angled down deep into the lava shield. He verified its openness ahead by sonic echoes, moving as fast as his perceptions permitted. When it came right down to it, he preferred the risk of a dented intake to that of a laser-scorched posterior.

Had he eluded the Amoeba? His aura was intense, but crippled by his lost love, and the Martian dust should muffle most of the rest. The ship had not seemed to be able to locate him when he was deep below before, once he

189

got away from the cube. If the Amoeba did not know precisely where to look for him, it would lose him; it could not vaporize the entire crust of the planet!

He coasted to a stop. For the first time, he was alone in an unexplored section of the site. The dust of millions of years filmed the passage, though this section had obviously been sealed. It had been Herald's luck that he had entered an access tunnel and not a burial tunnel, or he would have struck a dead-end too near the surface.

Still he did not dare to emerge until he was sure the enemy was gone. He did not like the confinement and the strong possibility of death by crushing if a laser struck accurately, but he knew his best chance was to remain right here.

He thought of Psyche again, seeing her in the fire, feeling her incinerated flesh on his human hand, though now he had no hand. It was too much, and he had to blank it out. He would never recover his powers as long as that vision remained with him, yet he could only relinquish it by relinquishing *her,* and he could never do that. He wished he were not a tough Slash, a creature to whom suicide was unnatural. Why *not* go above and let the Amoeba blast him? The Curse of Llume, abated at one stroke, for him!

Desperately he cast about for some intellectual or physical diversion. He could not let his imagination seek its own horrors. He moved along the passage until he came to a sealed-off intersection. At one time it had been an entrance to a burial chamber. He pried at it with his forefeelers, and it broke open. He widened the hole and entered, front-first, so as not to disturb the interior by the breeze of his jet.

There was nothing inside except a little more dust and a single body-ring. He examined it as well as he could in the dark. It had the same kind of relief design as the ones on display in the main dig.

Why weren't there any bodies? If these were burial chambers with personal ornaments, why no coffins, sarcophagi, or dehydrated remains? The climate of Mars should be ideal for the mummification and preservation of corpses. The question brought the answer: Who would want to live under the decaying corpse of his personal parent-entity? The vapors might tend to diffuse upward, but a decaying body gave off a lot of gas in a short time, and some fumes would inevitably seek the path of lesser resistance: the passage below. Every sniff would remind the offspring most poignantly of the dear departed. Obviously they cremated the remains, and left only the sterile dust in the sealed chamber. After all, it was the *aura* that counted, not the body.

Yet in that case, why bother to seal off the chambers at all? Why not place the circular memorials in some hallowed place, and continue to use the residence? It would save a lot of work and promote efficiency. The Ancients had to have been the most efficient creatures ever to dwell in the Cluster. It was not like them to expend energy and materials wastefully.

The revelation burst upon him like the strike of a laser: *These were not the Ancients!*

There were *two* cultures here: the Wormlike pre-Ancient colony, advanced enough to colonize alien planets but still hindered by foolishly material concepts of property and death, and the more sophisticated alien Ancients who had come as conquerors. Now it fell into place. The relics differed from ring to cube, the tunnels differed in size and type, the burial attitudes differed. And most significant, the heraldic devices differed. The devices on this ring bore no relation to those on the cubes; they represented two entirely different cultures.

Why had he not noticed this before? In retrospect, it was glaringly obvious! Those not trained in heraldry might not appreciate the elaborate conventions that formed such art, or the permanency of their symbolism, but *he* did. It did not matter what that art was called or what the symbols meant. It *was* an art, with its unique conventions, and it had to be true to its nature. That was the very root of heraldry. If it were not so, it would be meaningless, and useless for identification of living or dead. The continuity of evolution had to be embodied in the art, exactly as with the bodies of living creatures. The alternative was chaos.

Now he could re-create the essential sequence: The Worms had spread into neighboring space, colonizing those worlds most suitable to them. In this system, Mars had been good, while warm, wet Earth had been unsuitable. The stronger gravity, the constant water-storms and tides and fluctuations of weather would have ruined the finely crafted passages. Venus and Mercury would have been far too hot, and Jupiter too cold. So Mars had been ideal. For Worms.

For a thousand Sol years—perhaps much longer, since he could not know the date of these "undiscovered" passages here—the colony had prospered. Then the Ancients had come—as conquerors. They had obliterated the Worms, and made their own base, comfortable beneath the insulation of the defunct Worm metropolis. Then, as abruptly as they had arrived, the Ancients had departed, never to return—leaving Mars dead. As they must have left other worlds dead, all over the Cluster.

The Worms had shown Spherical regression, not the Ancients. One mystery abated!

But why had neighboring Planet Earth been spared? The Solarians had been barely sapient, then, far behind the level of the Worm colony. If the Solarians had been aware of the Worms at all, it was only as "mythical" dragons or horrendous serpents, tempting innocent females into evil knowledge. They had no fraction of the Worms' economic or combat resources. The Ancients could have wiped out all Earth-life easily. Their base seemed to have been maintained for a century or so, according to the archaeologists' dating, as if for exactly such a project. Plenty of time to complete it, considering their capabilities. Instead they had shut down, ignoring Earth.

Maybe the answer was in the two Ancient cubes, now destroyed or deeply buried by the Amoeba. Or those lost cubes might be merely unimportant leftovers, forgotten because of their uselessness: "This cube of Galacto lava-cleanser is the finest product this side of Betelgeuse!" Now he would never know.

Still, he had important news for the surviving members of the Jet archaeological expedition. If this two-culture pattern, this conquest-and-depart pattern, were typical of all the Cluster, it would offer a real insight into the nature and motive of the Ancients. Had they merely destroyed all potential rivals, leaving the more primitive worlds alone? Then why had they disappeared so abruptly, after their victory? Now the answer might be forthcoming.

He retreated to the access-passage and moved toward the surface. There had been no more laser strikes; the Amoeba must have vacated, satisfied the job was done.

He popped out into the cooling pit. There was the globe-ship, hovering in place.

Herald reversed and dived for the tunnel again, trying to get out of range. But this time the laser caught him.

8

God of Tarot

2Site destroyed.2

EReport: partially activated ancient site destroyed. Aural activity cessation in that locale.E

&Detail?&

XConfusion. Research unit E reported site destroyed by action unit 2 as directed.X

&Precisely. The directive was to nullify, not to destroy site. Require a mechanism detail report from action unit 2.&

0Respond, 2.0

2Aural activation occurred under surface of planet, inaccessible to ship. Therefore lasers were fired.2

&Lasers! An overt attack?&

0As executed at the prior activated site within the Quotes segment. Standard operating procedure when target is not immediately accessible.0

&You *lasered* both the Quote sites?&

0Yes. The first strike triggered the ancient site potential, causing a fission detonation. The second strike merely eliminated the aural unit.0

&So now the natives have seen our strength and are fully advised of our purpose! They know we have come to wipe them out. They will oppose us with organized desperation. Our program was predicated upon the assumption that the natives had no direct, specific knowledge of our intent, and would therefore procrastinate via committee until too late.&

XThey do not seem to have become aware of the specific nature of the threat, and their prior council meeting showed much confusion and disorganization. There has been no change in that situation.X

&Perhaps it is not too late. Our mission will be accomplished far more efficiently if they are caught largely unawares. Desist all overt attacks until prime-strike time. Withdraw unit 2 instantly. Henceforth, the term "nullify" shall be taken to mean to render inoperative in subtle nondestructive fashion.&

XBut the unit should remain to verify complete destruction of the aural generator.X

&In this instance the general preempts the specific. All evidence of our presence in local systems must cease. No further overt action shall be taken without my specific authorization.&

X0Understood.0X

Herald woke into chaos. /I thought I was dead!/ he flashed, not wholly pleased at being alive. Then he paused, noting the disorganization of environment about him. /Or am I dead?/

He received no answer. Colors swirled about him, showing no ceiling and no support. Yet he felt support, for his body had weight. /I am a fool!/ he flashed, realizing where he was.

He *was* a fool—the Fool of Tarot. He was back in his natural host-body of Slash, rolling along, his lens-perceptors aimed at matters of Cluster consequence while immediately ahead was a dropoff into disk-gumming mud. The Tarot Fool was noble, idealistic, well-intentioned, and handsome, the epitome of the finest expectations of civilization . . .

And of folly, he remembered, as he tumbled over the bank and fell into the muck. In versions of the picture relating to clothed species, an animal was ripping out an embarrassing section of the clothing of the Fool; other versions showed similar indignities. His disks spun frantically, but had no purchase here. The gunk rose over his body, putrid, cloying, revolting, blotting out his senses, suffocating him in its insubstantiality. Blackness—the penalty of foolishness, of idle dreams, of aspirations without foundation.

He screamed: disorganized flashes, a waste of energy. His soft-edged disks twisted. He was a newformed infant Slash, helpless.

Then a creature of competence focused a beam of attention on him. It was huge, with disks of gloriously shining metal, strong tentacles, and tremendously competent laser lenses. /The offspring wakes,/ the Sire flashed.

Immediately, the Mother rolled over to his pit. /Come Shortbeam, feed,/ she flashed, all-compassionate.

Herald was overwhelmed by feeling. Oh, how he remembered her, the consolation of his infancy!

Now his imagination expanded to embrace the Slash society of Andromeda. Its civilization forged ahead dynamically on the lasers of its myriad sapients and the labors of its subservient species, conquered one by one as the Sphere of Slash expanded. Power, represented in the Tarot as a card of Galactic empire.

Herald blinked his lasers. He didn't need a review of history! He needed to find out why he was here, and where he was going. /I need a guide!/ he flashed.

"I will be your guide," an alien creature said. It was a male, bipedal, using sound instead of light. All right; Herald was unbigoted about such things. He was garbed in manufactured materials so that most of his torso was concealed. Some creatures were sensitive about exposure of their intake, elimination, or reproductive apparatus. Hence the significance of the animal ripping the cover from such a section in the Fool picture. As though any creature could be rendered less by mere exposure of his functional nature. Behind this entity was a large mechanical structure with huge rotating vanes, possibly a torture device.

/What mode of creature are you?/ Herald demanded, alarmed.

"No creature am I, though once a creature I was, if I may borrow from the literature of my ancestry," the thing said. "I lived on Planet Earth circa two thousand, the time of the Fool years. See, here is the windmill we use for pumping our water."

Suddenly Herald recognized him. /Sibling Paul of Tarot!/ he flashed. /The Patriarch of the Temple!/

"No, I am merely Brother Paul, a humble human creature," the Solarian said. "No patriarch, no temple; the Holy Order of Vision is not of that type. But I will help you all I can, since you seem to be in need, and have called, and this is my purpose in life—and, it

196

seems, in death. Of what region and time are you, that you thus invoke me?"

Herald remembered that the legendary Founder had not had opportunity to witness his impact on the following millennia.

/To you, your repute may seem minor,/ he flashed. /But to me, a Slash of Andromeda twenty-five hundred years after your time, there is no greater name than Sib— than Brother Paul. You are the creator of the Cluster Tarot, one of the great forces in the shaping of the contemporary scene./

"Perhaps you should be *my* guide, not I yours," the Solarian said with a baring of his humanoid teeth that Herald recognized as a smile.

Abashed, Herald retreated. /No offense intended, great Brother! I have no fraction of your insight./

The Patriarch came near, momentarily touching one of Herald's disks. "You have some aura, though!" he murmured as an aside. Then, more formally: "There was no offense, creature of the future. Come, let us explore together: Where are we and what is our purpose?"

/We are obviously in a Tarot Temple, and this is an animation sequence,/ Herald flashed. /I have suffered loss and shock, and I am here to be healed. It is a standard therapy for those of high aura./

"I see. For a moment I feared *I* was the one in shock! I gather you came near to death recently?"

/I was caught by a laser strike from an enemy spaceship. I must have been dug out of the rubble and Transferred to my own body, but suffered such shock that I was referred to a Segment hospital for reconstitution of my mind./

"Uh, yes. Your body was Transferred to a more competent facility for therapy, but your mind recoils from the experience. I believe I understand, now. And so you have conjured me from your past to aid your reorientation."

Brother Paul had some of the details confused, but of course he dated from the time before Transfer had come to his world, and before the formation of Segments. It was unimportant.

/I seem to have done so, great as my presumption is,/ Herald admitted. /It was done from the sincere beam of admiration for you and your works. I perfected my art

197

of healing under Temple guidance, though I am not my-self a Tarotist. I owe you much./

"I suffer from some confusion," Brother Paul said, his form shimmering momentarily as if about to fade out. Herald hastily concentrated, and the Solarian became firm again, though the wind machine behind him disappeared. "Thank you," he murmured. "That was a difficult moment. I am accustomed to a more substantial incarnation. Now, please, tell me about you."

/About me?/ Herald flashed. /I am of no consequence. I am not sure I even want to survive./

"That is for us to decide, isn't it? They didn't take all the trouble to put you in an animation chamber without sufficient reason. If you don't work with me to clarify that reason, you are wasting both our time. Not to mention that of the—you call it the Temple?"

/I apologize. What do you wish to know, Sibling Patriarch?/

"Just call me Brother, if you don't mind. You were doing very well on that a moment ago."

/Brother!/ Herald flashed.

"Let's start with this: Why did you conjure a human being, instead of a creature of your own type?"

/I loved a female of your species,/ Herald admitted.

"Ah, I see. So did I, so did I. And I love her yet. There is nothing quite like a sweet, pretty girl, is there!"

Herald was surprised and gratified to discover this region of rapport. He had not thought of Brother Paul as an entity of creature concerns, but of course he had not known the man in life. /Nothing in the Cluster!/ he agreed. /I was in Solarian host, and she—/

"Let's start just a little further back," Brother Paul suggested diplomatically. "This matter of . . . Solarian hosts?"

/After your time,/ Herald said. /Very well. Today we shift from body to body, since our identities are incarnate in our auras. So I am able to take the form of a Solarian, or any other creature of the Cluster. When in such form, I naturally react in much the manner of the host./

"Ah, yes. So as a human being, you could take an interest in a human girl. No doubt if I were to occupy a Slash body, I would find Slash females interesting, too. Yet this presupposes that no lasting emotion exists. . . ."

/On the contrary. Love is absolute. I suffered shock in Jet host after loss of my Solarian bride./

"I am glad to hear that. Not that you suffered loss, but that there is that amount of continuity regardless of your shifts of form. That suggests that your therapy here will affect all your future hosts."

/Yes. I was running through the Cluster Tarot trumps in order, in the standard reorientation program for those in distress, and—/

"*Cluster* Tarot? I am familiar with a number of versions of the Tarot deck, but not this one. Does it most nearly relate to the Waite, or Thoth, or Light, or—"

/I know nothing of these names. It is the one you created on Planet Tarot,/ Herald explained. /Don't you remember?/

"Oh, I worked out a hundred-card deck for my own analysis, based on my experience there. But that was never published; it was merely an exercise." He paused, glancing with almost beamlike intensity at Herald. "You actually mean *that* deck?"

/Thirty trumps, five suits? That is the Cluster Tarot. Of course it was embellished after your time, and the suits have changed names, and many sub-versions are now extant. In fact, I believe every Sphere has its own variation. Most of the popular illustrations for the concepts are much more recent; it is a dynamic, changing thing. But the essence is yours—the basic framework, the interpretations, the life-history aspect and so on. I don't believe any cards have been added since. Except perhaps the Ghost. There has been learned debate whether you actually included that./

"I did have a Ghost Triumph," Brother Paul said. "It stood for the Unknown, the wonder of it, the fear, the hope, the utter change in circumstance fostered by some seemingly random Act of God. . . ."

/The God of Tarot. Yes, many creatures worship Him. He—/

"Who is of course the God of all creatures, by whatever name," Brother Paul interposed.

/Yes, all gods are valid. That is fundamental to the Cult of Tarotism. They—/

"That is not precisely what I meant." Brother Paul spread his brown hands in a purely Solarian gesture. "But we drift. I gather you had a Magician father and Priestess

199

mother of your species who raised you from the initial state of helpless innocence that is the Tarot key Zero or Fool, and that your society and government may be likened to the keys Empress and Emperor. Now I have become your Hierophant or Teacher. But I cannot help you until I know you. What is your key Six?"

/We don't use keys any more. Each culture arranges the symbols to suit its convenience, and there is no set order for the representations of the deck. Some species interpret them in terms of paired sexes, but this has to change for the species who are unisexual or multisexual. There are similar differences on a number of the basic concepts. If you refer to the one dealing with love, do you mean the romance aspect or the choice aspect? I believe they were once unified./

"There *is* a certain healthy ambiguity, isn't there! I merely want to know enough about you so that I can converse meaningfully about your situation. I presume there are both choices and romances in your framework, perhaps in combination. What is meaningful to you?"

/For an animation, you're pretty demanding!/ Herald flashed through a half-damped lens.

"I heard that, Slash. I mean, *saw* it. If you don't care to work with me, you can still animate someone else."

/No, no one else!/ Herald assured him quickly. /You asked what was meaningful to me? It is my wife, my Solarian child bride, who was burned at the stake for Possession, when she only——/ Unable to continue, Herald instead projected the image of Psyche, beautiful, writhing in the flames in the court of Kastle Kade.

"This was real?" Brother Paul demanded, appalled. "In this far future, the age of intergalactic empire and the concourse of myriad sapient species via the miracle of the transfer of auras, this happens?"

/The chained Lady,/ Herald flashed, realizing that he had broken down almost completely. Slashes were not supposed to go into shock, but he had done it. No wonder he was in animation Therapy! /Oh, help me, Patriarch! I am unable to function without her, yet there is great need./

Brother Paul spread his hands in another timeless gesture. "In the face of such a loss, in such a manner, there is little I can offer. It is evident that the current of barbarism still surfaces in your society. Unless you have some futuristic mechanisms to turn back time itself, or to recover the dead. . . ."

/Is that the nature of the interpretation for this symbol?/ Herald inquired with bleak irony. /That I may have love only by reversing time or reanimating the dead?/

"No, surely not!" Brother Paul protested. "There is always some feasible way to find relief."

/Then show it me! This healer needs healing!/

"Perhaps a Tarot reading would help. The Tarot certainly helped *me*."

/Well, this *is* the Temple of Tarot! But no mere animation can satisfy me long. I need reality, not illusion./

"The images may be illusion; the things they reveal are reality, however camouflaged from our initial understanding. What mode of presentation do you prefer?"

/The Cluster five-spot satellite spread./

"I don't believe I am familiar with that one. Five cards?"

/It is an old layout,/ Herald said. /Goes back at least two hundred years./

"Not quite as far back as I go, it seems."

Herald made a flash of apology. /Sorry, Brother Paul, I keep forgetting. But I can describe it. First you deal the deck into five modes—/

"Let's do it as you describe it," Brother Paul said. An object appeared in his hand, and he offered this to Herald.

Herald glanced in perplexity. /What is this?/

"Why, the Cluster Tarot deck, as I understand it. Did I misconstrue your intent?"

Suddenly Herald caught on. /Oh, an archaic physical deck! We don't use those antiques anymore./ But as he spoke, he remembered that in special circumstances they *were* used. He had used stone picture cards to treat the Ast child, Smallbore of Metamorphic.

"What, then, do you use?" Brother Paul inquired mildly, his deck disappearing from his hand.

/We use the Cluster cube./ Herald lifted one tentacle, and a cube appeared in its coil. Abruptly he wondered whether the cubes of the Ancients could be related to this. No, that was too fantastic. Had the Ancients had Tarot, it would have been a completely alien Tarot, unrecognizable to today's minds. /One face per mode, discounting the bottom. For the actual reading, the Significator is set on the bottom, and the five others are—/

Brother Paul raised one limb in a protest like a benediction. "Please, this modern technology is beyond my comfort. Will you not oblige an animated anachronism by using the old-style cards?"

/Actually, this whole set is animation,/ Herald pointed out. /I can't even be sure I'm in my own body; it could be merely another animation. So we don't need to use a deck at all./

Brother Paul produced the cards again. "Still, friend, humor me."

Herald flashed acceptance. /You must shuffle for me, Brother. I am not facile with such artifacts./ Artifact . . . what would some culture three million years hence make of a Tarot cube? They might assume it was a form of food.

"But you must shuffle, or it is not your reading. Your touch must arrange the cards for the dealing."

/Since you are my animation, your shuffle is my shuffle./

The Solarian showed his teeth. "You have a cynical alien mind, Slash! Are you sure you require therapy?"

/I require my bride!/ Herald flashed with sudden pain.

"It is possible to marry other than flesh and blood. Your bride could be a Holy Order. You could give your life utterly to God."

/Shuffle, Man of God!/

Brother Paul shrugged and shuffled, riffing the cards through his human hands and fingers with remarkable expertise. "Now . . . five piles?"

/Yes. They signify DO, THINK, FEEL, HAVE, and BE./

Brother Paul dealt them out, placing five cards in a row on the table that appeared magically before him, then layering five more on top of these, building up the piles. "I do not quarrel with your interpretations, but I find them somewhat abstract. Might the five piles equate, on a lowbrow level, to the more conventional WORK, TROUBLE, LOVE, MONEY, and—would that last be SPIRIT?"

/AURA, really. They're allied. Take religion from spirit, and you have aura. But surely you know that, since you invented the Cluster deck, and these are mere aspects of the root-meanings of the suits./

"I fear my perspective differs, and perhaps my motive."

Brother Paul looked down at the completed piles. "I presume the next step is to locate your Significator?"

/The King of Aura,/ Herald agreed. /Aura is the Suit of Artistry, and I am a heraldic artisan. But I am also the most intense aura of the contemporary scene, so I qualify on that basis too./

"The most intense aura of all time, as I understand it," Brother Paul said.

/I need no animation-figure to flatter what nature gave me!/ Herald flashed irritably. /And it isn't true. My bride, Psyche, was the most intense aura, at the time of her enhancement. And for all we know, *you* were higher than I, since you existed before Solarians measured aura. The historical analysts assigned you a figure of two hundred, but that could be conservative./

"Or generous. In any event, to no point, since I am long gone. Were I searching for historical figures to whom to assign leading auras, I would certainly consider THE figure, the ultimate Healer of them all."

/Who?/ Herald asked, curious. He had not realized that there was, or could conceivably be, any entity to whom the Patriarch looked up to.

"Jesus Christ, the Son of God."

For a moment Herald was at a loss. Then he located an obscure recollection. /Oh, you mean the prophet of an archaic Solarian religion. There is a footnote on him in the Temple background survey course, and I believe some of the Tarot symbols are related./

Brother Paul smiled, shaking his head in apparent wonder. "Viewpoints certainly do differ! Were you aware that He often healed the sick and dying by the mere laying on of hands?"

/*I* do that,/ Herald said. /It is the manner of Kirlian healing./

"Could you raise the dead?"

/No. But I doubt there would be much point, after the brain decayed. And I can't heal all the ill, for some ailments are purely physical. But if your Christ did these things, it only means he had a stronger aura than I do. There would not be any qualitative distinction./

"No qualitative distinction!" the Solarian cried. But he calmed himself. "I think we had better get on with the business at hand. Here is the King of Aura, in Pile Two, Trouble."

/Or Pile THINK, in my vernacular. That is an ill omen for the reading; my problem is FEEL./

"Perhaps the Tarot is telling you that the solution lies in your thinking rather than in your emotion."

/It is all an infernal superstition,/ Herald grumbled. /Thinking will not bring Psyche back, and I do not care to forget her./

"We can at least explore the possibilities."

/If we must. The Significator face is at the bottom facet of the cube, and the Problem Definition on the top facet. How this adapts to a physical layout—/ He paused. /Without the cube, I am not certain how—/

"Oh, we can adapt it," Brother Paul said. "I shall place the Significator card here, and cross it with Definition. We do deal the cards in order following the King of Aura, as they appear in the pile?"

/I suppose so. It is so hard to translate. The Tarot cube normally forms the whole display./

"It strikes me that you moderns have been spoiled by your technology. Tarot is not a thing to be assimilated from a platter. You must interact with it, your physical contact with the cards imbuing them with your personality. Only then can it work for you and give a true reading rather than a random collection of pictures." He studied the table and the cube that Herald had made appear. "We can lay down the remaining four cards in clockwise rotation, South, West, North, East, representing the four sides of your cube. The topology will be the same."

/I don't comprehend how—/

"Like this." And Brother Paul placed the cards, face down, a mock up. "You might perceive the pattern as a cross, or the four directions of the compass—" He broke off, glancing at Herald. "But those are forgotten concepts to you, aren't they?"

/How could they be?/ Herald asked sullenly. /Any concept you express has to be drawn from my own mind./

"Perhaps. But the unconscious is a tremendous wilderness. That is what the Tarot taps, that vast reservoir of knowledge and conjecture that lies within each person. Tarot is a tool to bring out truth that may otherwise be suppressed by the conscious mind because it may be unpleasant." He paused again, reflectively. *"Most* unpleasant," he murmured.

Herald felt a chill that was reminiscent of what he had felt on hearing the prediction of Smallbore of Metamorphic. /What happened to you, there on the Animation Planet?/ Herald, like sapients of the past two millennia, was quite curious about the mystical experience that had led to the creation of the famous Cluster deck.

But Brother Paul only smiled enigmatically. What answer could he give? For he was a mere animation of Herald's mind, and the ultimate secret of Tarot was not there.

Herald looked at the layout, and suddenly he saw that it did indeed duplicate the faces of the cube. It was as though the four sides had been spread out and detached, with the nether face half buried under the Definition card. Yes, this was after all comprehensible!

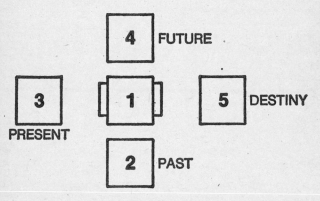

"Now I presume the four outer cards represent Past, Present, Future, and Destiny," Brother Paul said. "This is like a simplified Celtic layout, or a modified elemental one."

/Celtic? Elemental?/

"The Celtic was a very popular ten-card spread in my day, widely used for fortune-telling. It could hardly have derived from the ancient Celts, since they had faded from the scene long before the Tarot deck was created in the fourteenth century, despite what certain enthusiasts liked to claim. Legends of the great antiquity of

Tarot abounded, but they seemed to be without substance. By 'elemental' I mean the classic Solarian elements, FIRE, AIR, WATER, and EARTH, not true elements at all by the definitions of science, but serviceable evocative composites equating to your DO, THINK, FEEL, and HAVE. Though of course you use five, not four, elements. As did the ancients."

/The Ancients!/

"I suspect we are on different tracks. My point is that this spread of yours is oriented on sets of five—five piles, five display cards, five suits—and so this is a very basic mechanism, like a distillation of the less precise mechanisms in use in my time. Tarot has indeed evolved."

Herald considered. He had thought of Tarot as a tool, not an aspect of the fundamental nature of things, but realized that he was in the presence of an entity who took it very seriously. It hardly seemed to matter that this was itself a Tarot animation; the personality and perspective of Brother Paul was making itself felt. In this framework, the Solarian was real, and had to be treated as real. /Let's go ahead with the reading,/ he flashed. /It may have something for me after all./

Brother Paul dealt out the cards, placing the Definition across the Significator, and the others clockwise around the outside, starting from the bottom. Now the layout had images, and possessed potential meaning. He contemplated it. "The King of Aura is defined by the Three of Aura, labeled Perspective. My, the meanings *have* changed since my day! However, this card is so appropriate it cannot be coincidental."

/Nothing about this spread is coincidental!/

Brother Paul smiled agreement. "Nothing about the Universe is coincidental. It is only our ignorance that makes things seem so. If we but understood the ways of God—"

/Do you seek to proselytize?/

"Oh, in the interest of knowledge and harmony— But I comprehend your objection. You do not wish to be burdened with my archaic concepts of religion, and certainly I do not wish to so burden you. We shall proceed with the reading." He glanced down. "Here below is the representation of the Past, a card labeled Vision." He paused. "Ah, the vanity of the flesh! This *is* the card I developed, that caters to my overweening love of literature, which is the vision of imagination. A Fair Field Full of Folk."

/What?/ Herald flashed.

"See for yourself." Brother Paul waved one arm, and the vision formed about them, emerging from a dreamlike background of chaos. "There is the sun high in the eastern sky," he said, his right hand pointing up. Sure enough, the bright orb became manifest, yellowish in the manner of Sol as spied from Earth. Herald had a private vision of that yellow entering the genetic makeup of the creatures of that system, and emerging as the hue of the hair of Psyche. "Reaching toward it, up on the hill, is the Tower of Truth." And the magnificent tower formed, like as the central column of Kastle Kade—what truth lay beneath that edifice, had he but known in time!—its highest turrets illuminated by a direct beam of light. "Beneath it, in the deep valley, is the Dungeon of Wrong." Brother Paul's left hand pointed down toward it, that crevasse whose horrors were half concealed by deep shadow. "Euphemisms for Heaven and Hell, of course. And between these extremes, the Fair Field Full of Folk, or the living people of the world, going about their business of making money, oblivious to all else. Only a few even look up to glimpse the prospect of Truth, or down to gain some hint of the abyss toward which they drift." And the teeming field of Solarians coalesced. "That's the setting for *The Vision of Piers Plowman,* an epic poem dating from the time of the origin of Tarot, written in several versions between the years 1362 and 1395 by William Langland of England."

Herald studied the animation, impressed. /This is much the manner of the Cluster. The myriad species of the Spheres go about their pursuits heedless of the threat of extinction that looms so near./

"Threat of extinction?"

/The Amoeba. Without the science of the Ancients, we cannot hope to stand against it. The alien fleet will conquer the Cluster, and it shall be—hell./

"So that was what brought you here! Concern for the peril to your society. This is the highest ethic."

/No. I only want my Solarian bride back./ Herald flashed. Then he considered, shocked in another fashion. /Me—I am one of those self-centered sapients of the

Field of Folk. I put my personal concern before the welfare of my Cluster!/

"You have, indeed, been granted a vision," Brother Paul agreed.

Herald spun his disks and writhed his sinuous torso thoughtfully. /My personal case is lost—but that of the Cluster is not. It behooves me to do whatever I can to salvage our civilization from the Amoeba./

"And therein may lie also your personal salvation," Brother Paul murmured.

/I doubt it. I think your Jesus Christ himself would have trouble restoring my Lady of Kade to life./

"Yet He might do so, even now, were it part of God's design. I regret I do not know that design." Brother Paul looked at the layout again. "Here is the Present—the influences affecting your current situation. The Two of Aura, signifying . . ." He trailed off, staring at the card.

/The Deuce of Aura signifies Aura,/ Herald flashed. /Two Atom ships, a magnetic formation, a minor space fleet./ The Tower and Valley receded, the Field of Folk dropping down to give the sky prominence, showing the fleet. /I am Aura, and so was my love, and so are the Ancients. All that I am is bound to Aura./

The Solarian nodded his human head. "How well you comprehend. And here is the card of the Future, the Ten of Swords." Ten little blades rose out of the picture, flying up into the sky to join the Atom ships. "Signifying survival."

/With science we can survive,/ Herald agreed. /Without it, we have no future./

"And the final card, Destiny—this is the Ghost." And from the card swirled its image, expanding holographically to fill the scene: the vast mystery of deep space, the stars and the dust clouds, a pattern like that of primeval chaos.

/The Great Unknown,/ Herald flashed. /The spread of Tarot has defined the problem very nicely, but it offers no solution./

"What is that tentacular shape in the distance?" Brother Paul asked. He gestured, and a section of the animation expanded as though they were traveling at high multiples of the speed of light toward it.

/Merely an extra-Galactic nebula,/ Herald said. /They are not uncommon, and they come in all configurations. There are specialists who study them, like my friend of Segment Weew——/ He froze, staring at the growing shape rushing toward them from the background of the Ghost animation. Its pseudopods reached forward three-dimensionally as though to grasp him personally. /The Amoeba!/

"The Cluster threat?"

/The enemy fleet, radiating out from its mattermission nucleus beyond Furnace, coming to destroy our civilization. That sent its ship to ray me down on Mars, and now comes for me again, even in my animations— *Stop it!* /

Brother Paul put his hand over the card, and the looming image vanished. "Surely the reading need not end here, without solution," he protested. "Perhaps we have not posed the right question. Or we may need another reading. This one was from the pile of Thought, and it has certainly made us think; but if we—"

/The spread can be augmented,/ Herald flashed. /That is what makes it versatile. Any aspect that is unclear can be subdefined by a satellite spread./

"Oh, very nice! I did not realize this. Which card do you wish to subdefine?"

/The Ghost, naturally. In the Amoeba lies our problem, and if we could only comprehend it, know its vulnerabilities. . . ./ He let it trail away. /But that must be done last. Any satellites have to be launched in chronologic order. The background must be understood before the solution comes./

"Yes, that makes sense. I think I like this mode; it guides the querist well. The basic spread provides the essence; then it is refined as the needs of the querist dictate. For you, which card?"

/The Past. Vision. Your Field of Folk is a pretty analogy, and it helps my perspective, but I am not sure we correctly read its import. Lay a definition card across it./

Brother Paul crossed Vision with the next card from the pile. "Temperance," he said. And the full-bodied, bare-breasted Solarian female appeared before the starry background, pouring fluid from one cup to another. "The pouring of the waters of life from one vessel to another— or the transfer of the soul after death to the spectral realms."

/Or the Transfer of Aura from one body to another, in

209

life,/ Herald added, intrigued by the quaint historical interpretations. /This is what enables contemporary Cluster civilization to exist. Without Transfer, inter-Spherical government would be impractical. Temperance was the emblem of the erstwhile Society of Hosts, before involuntary hosting was rendered passé./

"Aura, again. This certainly figures strongly in your background."

/Yes. Without the science and art of Aura, I would be nothing. The Tarot has defined me well. Vision crossed by Aura, Herald the Healer./

"Yet I am not certain I fathom the full implication. Is it permissible to subdefine further?"

/Certainly. This is normally done. Lay down three more cards, clockwise in relation to the main spread. These define Past, Present, and Future of the subconcept, completing the satellite. A satellite, of course, has no separate destiny; the whole is merely a definition of an aspect of the primary reading./

Brother Paul nodded appreciatively and laid down the three cards. "The King of Cups, King of Swords, and Queen of Aura," he announced. "But two of them depict alien creatures."

/Yes, this is the Solarian edition, mainly humanoid,/ Herald flashed. /The suit face cards are the principal region of other-sapient representations. The Tarot editions of other Spheres often have Solarians in their suit cards, as a matter of complementary courtesy. But it is possible to find anything, in any deck—and *all* decks are valid aspects of the complete Cluster Tarot./

"I can appreciate that. But it does make it a bit more difficult for me to interpret the cards."

Herald considered the first card of the satellite, and its figure moved into full animation, hovering in the air between them as if floating—or swimming. It had a diffuse, bubbly torso with projecting flippers and eye-stalks. /This is a Spican Impact,/ he explained. /A creature of a water world in a Sphere adjacent to Sphere Sol, Galaxy Milky Way. As the Cluster Tarot found acceptance among other species, they identified with it in appropriate ways. The Spicans are sapient water creatures, so of course—/

"Ah, I see. The King of Cups—a male water-sapient. Most appropriate."

/Actually, the Spicans are triple-sexed, though their

sexual roles are somewhat interchangeable depending on the circumstance of their encounters. But the generally more forceful nature of the Impact sex led to this identification as a basically male image./

"But what have Spicans, regardless of sex or circumstance, to do with your situation?"

Herald flashed with humor. /I thought you understood, Brother. This card is you./

Brother Paul did a human doubletake. *"Me?* I am no Spican water-sapient creature with eye-stalks!"

/But you *are* the King of Cups. Therefore this is your Significator in the Cluster deck. The image is merely a convenience for identification of the particular card; its inherent meaning is quite apart from this. You, as the founder of the Cluster Tarot, the discoverer of the phenomenon of animation, as the first of the great Cluster-historical auras, are very much a part of my situation, as your presence here demonstrates. There is no other figure this card could represent in this context./

Brother Paul shook his head. "It must be so, if that is the way you see it. But it is something of a shock for me. I never thought of myself as a submerged sapient."

/Oh, I find the likeness excellent./

Brother Paul accepted the jibe with singular grace. "I suppose in the sense that I was submerged in your subconscious, manifesting only in this your hour of need, and will return to that watery limbo when your problem is liquidated—"

/You tease me, Patriarch!/

"Well, some levity befits the occasion, if we are to maintain equilibrium." He considered the spread again. "I might have been inclined to suspect this next card, the King of Swords. This is after all a human figure. Except that the man is naked and muscular and green, while I am clothed and a bit fat and brown." The big green savage strode out from the card to achieve his full stature in animation, glancing at them warily.

/The Swords are the suit of Solarians, the violent, troublesome, yet intelligent species. That is Flint of Outworld, whose aura was about two hundred. Their measurements were comparatively imprecise in those years. He founded the nucleus of Segment Etamin, the larger cluster of Spheres that now embraces Sol./

"You seem to know all about me," the Flint figure said.

As he spoke, his background filled in about him: giant vinetrees, juiceberry flowers, primitive huts, dinosaur creatures whose faces resembled those of the dominant sapients of Segment Qaval. "But I don't know about you. I see one brown-surface Solarian and one Slash monster. Speak fast." And he raised one beautifully muscled green arm, whose hand now held an efficient-looking rock-barbed spear.

"A pleasure to meet a genuine Stone Age savage," Brother Paul said. "Most of us are savages inside, so to that extent the veneer of civilization makes us hypocrites. I am Brother Paul of the Holy Order of Vision. I am harmless, I assure you."

"You work for the Tarotist Temple?" the savage demanded.

"This creature. Herald the Healer of circa A.D. 4500, suggests that I founded it," Brother Paul said with a tolerant smile. "But that is plainly beyond my intent or means. I am loyal to my own modest order, with no need to dabble in politics or religion. I am just a humble seeker."

"I recognize you now," Flint said. "Harmless? Like a carnosaur! You're a martial artist, aren't you?"

"I . . . dabble on occasion."

Flint made a snort of humor. "You *are* a hypocrite, just as you claim! I'd like to try your strength, but I think I would lose, barehanded. You *did* found the Temple; that is historical. And that is no bad thing. The Temple helped me in Sphere Polaris. The Tarot showed me what I had not known I knew, before I progressed into complete disaster." He turned to Herald, his smile fading. "But you, Slash—did Andromeda win the war despite my efforts?"

/Andromeda lost—twice,/ Herald flashed. /Now we are part of the Cluster culture—Andromeda, Milky Way, Pinwheel, and assorted lesser formations—without war, except for the present threat of alien invasion by the Amoeba. The Tarot has animated you, my distant ancestor via your aural family, to illustrate part of the background of this problem. Have you any advice?/

"Recover the Ancient science," Flint said simply.

/Yes, we are trying to do that. But we have not learned how, and we have very little time./

"So he, too, is fundamental to your situation," Brother Paul remarked to Herald. "And the third figure?"

It emerged from the card via animation: a tripart construction of wires and diaphragms and tubing. It had nine little clapper-feet, three to each segment. "I am Melody of Mintaka," it played, its meaning conveyed musically. Herald knew he would not have comprehended this language, had this not been his own animation scene. "I saved the Milky Way from Andromeda in the Second War of Energy. But you have animated me with all my feet!"

/Mintakans mate at the expense of their feet,/ Herald flashed privately to the others. /Their sex changes as the number of their feet decreases. The card portrays her in her female stage./

"Isn't it enough that I have lived my full life," Melody played tersely, "without being brought back—incorrectly!—long after it is over?"

"Well . . ." Brother Paul began.

"Such might be expected of an Andromedan," she continued. "Or even of my barbarian green-giant Solarian ancestor. But you, Paul of Tarot, how can you be part of such impertinence?"

"You're a descendant of mine?" Flint inquired, surprised but not dismayed.

"Practically the whole sapient Galaxy is descended from your free-flowing seed," she said. "It is a wonder you had time to save the Milky Way from Andromeda."

"It needs saving again," Flint said, flattered.

"This is why you creatures are animating the Tarot? It happens I know something of this subject, and now that I'm here I suppose I should assist. I note you are employing the newfangled spread, really inadequate for the occasion. However—"

/It is the secret of the Ancients we require, Mistress of Tarot,/ Herald flashed. /Only by utilizing their full technology can we hope to save our Cluster./

Melody made a negative clangor of her instruments. "Slash, you would not want to know the secret of the Ancients."

All three males oriented abruptly on her. "You know their secret?" Flint demanded.

"Enough of it."

/Tell us!/ Herald flashed in wild hope.

She issued a sharp, single, final note. "No."

213

Brother Paul shook his head. "Surely you have some reason?"

"I do. If you knew their secret, you would do what they did. Therefore I will not tell you."

/We would . . . die out?/

"Or allow yourselves to regress into harmless barbarism." She glanced meaningfully at Flint. "You certainly have the potential for that. No—you are better off rising to the challenge of the Amoeba and conquering it yourselves. Forget the Ancients."

/I can't do that. We cannot match the Amoeba alone./

"I think he's right," Flint said. "A flint-tipped spear can't take a laser, except in special circumstances. If the Amoeba technology is clearly beyond that of the Cluster—"

/It is./

"I also concur," Brother Paul said slowly. "I should hope that a better understanding of the nature of the Amoeba would make peace possible, but I concede that there are some demonic forces with which peace cannot be made. I do not like violence, yet I do not pretend that there are no circumstances where certain measures of self-defense may not be required. If the Ancient technology enabled the Cluster to become strong enough to stalemate the invasion, perhaps the Amoeba fleet would depart, averting further bloodshed."

But Melody would not yield. "Victory gained at the expense of the loss of cherished ideals is not worthwhile. With Tarot I will help; the Ancients I shall not discuss further." And Herald knew she would be inflexible.

Still he admired her tremendously, even though he knew she was at this stage no more than a figment of his imagination. /What a creature you were!/ he flashed. /Had I lived in your time, or you in mine—/ But again he remembered Psyche, and suffered.

"Now I think I have the background straight," Brother Paul said. "These three figures of aura, among whose number I am included, center on the Temperance concept of Transfer, and are all contributary to your vision of your past. They *are* your foundation. One must understand aura to understand you."

/True./

"Yet it does not seem to clarify your destiny. The Ghost remains opaque."

/There *is* something,/ Herald flashed. But as he focused his internal beam on it, it evanesced. /No, I cannot yet place it,/ he finished, frustrated.

"Perhaps if we subdefined another card?" Brother Paul suggested.

/We must not do it indiscriminately,/ Herald warned. /The Tarot is not to be trifled with./

Melody played a chord of emphatic agreement.

Brother Paul smiled. "How well I know! But since there are only twenty cards in the pile, there would seem to be a natural limit, in case someone became too wild. A solution that cannot be achieved within twenty cards probably is not worth having; it would be too complex to comprehend."

/Let's check the Two of Aura, there in the Present Influences,/ Herald suggested. /We know aura relates to me; it hardly needs to be stressed. There may be more behind that entry./

Flint and Melody and the Spican Impact began to fade. /No, stay with me!/ Herald flashed. /You are my Past; I need you with me in my Present if I am to achieve my Future! I want your advice and participation, or I will surely repeat mistakes you could have warned me of./

"This plea is well put," Melody played. "Green Giant and Clapperfoot will remain."

"But let my swimming incarnation submerge," Brother Paul said. "I prefer my role as mentor to that of memory." And the Spican dissipated like a lost memory.

Brother Paul dealt another card, placing it across the Nine. "The Princess of Swords," he announced. "Another human figure."

"All the Swords are human," Melody played.

/The Princess of Swords!/ Herald flashed, electrified. /That's—/

"Your wife!" Brother Paul said, catching on. "Except —wouldn't she be the *Queen* of Swords? A married woman. . . ."

/She was barely grown. To me she will always be the child bride. She is the aura that brings me here!/

The figure expanded from the card. She was nude and lovely, a delicately nubile, blue-skinned, orange-eyed human girl.

"Oh, she is exquisite!" Brother Paul exclaimed. "Much

215

better than that other vision you showed. Remember her always like this!"

"There is Outworld blood in her," Flint said. "And Capellan. A good combination."

But their approval stirred up a bitter counterforce of emotion. /And do you also want to see what they did to her?/ Herald demanded savagely. A knot of love and pain formed within him. *Psyche! Psyche!*

He concentrated—and orange flame leaped up about her. Psyche writhed in silent agony, trying to draw her slender legs out of it, then giving up.

"No—I forbid this!" Brother Paul cried. "I have felt the fires of hell myself; do not do this to her again!"

"That lovely child!" Melody played with a strong background discordance of shock. "Spare her! Go to the Ancient site on Planet £ of Sphere Dash instead, mate there with a creature of high aura, go in and learn the secret of the Ancients yourself. But stop this fire!"

There was only one creature of sufficiently high aura that he could enlist quickly and privately for such a mission: his pseudo-fiancée, Flame of Furnace. If he did that, Psyche would surely burn in a new kind of hell!

/You cannot unmake the past!/ Herald flashed. /Suffer as I suffered! She burns, *she burns!*/ It was himself he was torturing, not these reflections of his prior imagination. Like the Duke of Kade at the end, he did not *want* to live.

But the figment-animations had strange persistence. "I subdefine!" Brother Paul cried, slapping down a satellite card. "The Eight of Aura—Conscience!"

But Psyche did not fade. Her anguished mouth opened, and she cried: "Herald, forgive them—they know not what they do!"

/I can't!/ Herald flashed. And her golden hair puffed into ignition, shriveling with horrible speed into a black mass.

Herald charged the fire but was hampered by his Slash body. Suddenly Flint of Outworld was beside him, swinging a great, flashing, beautifully deadly sword. The King of Swords indeed! Pieces of creature flew wide with every stroke: arms, heads, tails, wheels, tentacles. It was wonderful, it was a kind of catharsis!

Brother Paul slammed down another card, trying to stave off further torture and violence. "Tower!"

And the scene exploded into a giant mushroom-cloud, a roiling fireball that blew everything apart, producing chaos again.

/Where are we?/ Herald flashed foolishly. /In the fireball?/

"In the midst of revelation," Brother Paul explained, bodiless, beside him. "The confines of the contemporary situation have been burst asunder, freeing us for new understandings. This is the nature of the Lightning-Struck Tower of the Tarot—"

/Yes. The Amoeba bombed Kastle Kade./

". . . on the physical level. But the card is also known as the House of God, or the House of the Devil. That is interesting in this context, because Psyche, tormented by fires as of hell, quoted the Son of God. Jesus Christ, as he was crucified and reviled by his tormentors, cried 'Father, forgive them, for they know not what they do!' That's from the Bible, Luke twenty-three, Verse thirty-four. In that moment, Christ forgave his enemies, exemplifying in his death the philosophy of his life."

/She may have forgiven them; I cannot!/

"But you must! *She* asked you to. She said 'Herald, forgive them,' and you must honor her dying plea if you wish to be worthy of her love."

/I'm glad the castle was destroyed. That is the single favor the Amoeba did me. Circlet of Crown and all his minions were wiped out!/

"Don't you understand! Jesus pleaded for God to forgive them—and *they* are *us*—and so we all—Psyche must have known. . . ."

Herald considered. *To be worthy of her love*—that struck deep indeed! How could he deny her this, the last thing she had asked of him? /They're dead anyway. I forgive them,/ he flashed with meager graciousness. And, oddly, he felt a kind of relief, and realized that his own hate had blocked his healing power. That was why he had been unable to help the Jet female, Sixteen. Had Psyche known it would be this way?

"I am glad, Herald. For you see, after that forgiveness—I'm stating this very badly, it is hard to concentrate here in chaos—Jesus was restored to life. For a while. He—"

/He died—yet lived again? His aura must have animated another host. You indicated he had a strong aura?/

217

"The strongest, I'm sure. I disagree with certain of your interpretations, but in this respect we agree. An extremely potent aura would account for much that he accomplished. But the point is—"

/But how could Psyche live again? Her body is nothing but particles in a radioactive cloud./

"But through her aura she could animate another body, if—"

/She would still die. All bodies in that castle were vaporized. Even if one escaped, the aura inevitably fades when it is away from its natural host. Even enhanced as she was, with an aura of two hundred seventy-five, she —/ He broke off, amazed as the revelation burst upon him. /Enhancement! It was *her* aura—enhanced. Not a cycle, but as association with the Ancient site, that built her up. If it could do that. . . . /

"There would be no need for her aura to fade away from her natural host as long as that equipment operated."

/Ancient equipment operates forever! That site is gone, but there are others. . . . / Herald paused again. /Immortality! The Ancients can give us immortality!/

"That too, I suppose, if you want it. But I was thinking—"

/Psyche! She could live again! Her aura would not fade!/

"Yes, that was my thought."

/The Ancient site enhanced her. There was a connection when she died. This happened to Flint of Outworld. He survived death by Transferring to another host. The site could have transported her aura to another host, another site. . . . /

"That may have been what she was trying to tell you. That her aura would live, though her body died. Now that your power has been restored by your act of forgiveness you have only to find her."

/She could be in a new host anywhere in the Cluster! But she would have to remain associated with an Ancient site, because she would require constant further enhancement./

"Would she—I am largely ignorant about the technicalities of Transfer—would she be able to remain within a site itself, enhanced?"

/I—/ Herald's imagination stalled. /If the sites can

218

enhance and can Transfer, why *can't* they hold—/ It was almost too much to assimilate. /She must be . . . with the Ancients! This is my revelation of the Tower. I should have realized it all along, but it is so great a jump of concept! Let me go through this slowly: Flint of Outworld died in the Hyades, but the ancient site Transferred his aura to Mintaka, and he lived again to sire the line of Melody. Melody of Mintaka activated the £ site in Andromeda and abolished hostaging. Her aura unlocked the Secret of the Ancients, and she Transferred directly to System Etamin in Milky Way. I knew all along that such powers were in the sites, and the presence of Flint and Melody evoked by the Tarot should have reminded me— had I only been able to put it all together! /

"Precisely. That is why you came here, and why the Tarot placed your Significator in the THINK pile instead of in the FEEL pile. Now at last you know what you seek."

/That Tarot—I have used it on others, but never realized how it could relate to my own life!/ He abandoned that thought for more leisurely contemplation at some convenient time. /Let's complete the reading!/

A card appeared, the Four of Star, labeled HOPE/FEAR. Brother Paul had dealt it, but had nowhere to set it down.

Psyche's face appeared within it. The flat picture spoke: "Herald, I live! I love you! I tried to reach you through Hweeh, but when I revived him he got confused. I need a host, close, but I must hide. I can't come to you. To reach me you must deal with the Amoeba—"

/I shall find you!/ he flashed.

The image dissolved. Then the chaos itself dissolved. /Farewell, Patriarch Brother Paul!/ Herald flashed. /Farewell to you, and to your Jesus of Christ!/

"Farewell, Healer," the faint reply came. Or was it his imagination? Of course it was; all animation was imagination. Yet there was a kind of validity to it, as Brother Paul had pointed out: the meaning behind the image. The long-dead Solarian, alive or illusion, *had* helped him.

He recovered consciousness. He was stifled in stone, barely able to breathe, his body injured and hurting. It was the Jet body, that could breathe without changing size by dribbling air through its main tube. The Amoeba's ray had missed him, but collapsed the tunnel, stunning him, throwing him into a private vision. The animation itself had been illusion!

He was dying. Only the temporary restored power of his aura maintained life in this broken host, and soon that would fail. No God of Tarot could salvage this! Even if the body were not expiring from its injuries, it remained trapped deep in the rubble. It could not be removed intact.

"Herald!"

/I am here, Beloved!/ he flashed. But he realized immediately that it could not have been Psyche, for she was dead except in his dreams, in his frantic wish-fulfillments. This had been a sonic call.

"Herald!" Closer, now.

He mustered what physical strength he had. There was a little air he could woosh. "Here!" Was it loud enough? His lining hurt with the very effort.

"You live, Healer!" the voice exclaimed. "Here, Weew! I have found him! Under this spot!"

Now a strong aura probed the ground, intersecting Herald's waning periphery. "Yes, I feel him!" Hweeh cried. "His aura is greatly disturbed, and I doubt we can save the host, but we can bring the Transfer unit here. . . ." And Transfer him to his own Slash body, and send him to a Tarot Temple for reconstitution. . . . Or had he experienced it already?

"He will die?" Sixteen asked anxiously.

"Do not fret, Miss. He shall soon rise again."

He shall rise again. . . .

It was Kirlian technology, no mystery about it—but somehow it sounded like Brother Paul's God of Tarot.

9

Geography of Aura

XMission survey completed. All sapients in the Cluster identified and catalogued.X

&Place life-destructor units adjacent to every sapient-utilized planet. Do not interfere with the subsapients at this stage unless they occupy sapient planets. Pockets of sapients on nonsapient planets will be sorted out after all potential major resistance has been nullified.&

0Placement proceeding, covertly.0

&Do not activate any units until all have been placed, so that no advance alarm is given. When all is ready, we shall proceed with the final ritual reverification of the absence of soul sapience.&

Herald's personal quest had been restored; there was a possibility that Psyche existed yet. But several immediate obstacles prevented pursuit of his desire.

The site Transfer unit had been destroyed by the bombardment of the Amoeba's laser cannon. The cargo mattermitter was also gone. It would be necessary to wait for the sublight ship to bring new equipment from neighboring Planet Earth.

The job should have taken hours; it was to take days. Earth, once the heart of Sphere Sol, was fading. It was now an overpopulated, bureaucracy-ridden backworld planet. Much of its population was xenophobic, preferring not even to think about the affairs of the larger Universe. Earth's administration would help, because it had to. Imperial Outworld, under directive of the Cluster Council, would see to that once it got the word. There was also the matter of Solarian pride—but that was at such a state that Earth would not exactly hurry.

Herald's host was dying. The torso had been squeezed and cracked, but not crushed; assorted leaks had developed in the internal systems, throwing physical performance out of whack. In the ordinary course, this Jet would linger for several days until the inevitable accumulation of chemical wastes poisoned it fatally.

The capable Jet excavation crew blasted out a large tunnel in short order, making room for him to function. Herald had underestimated their proficiency; they had no difficulty extracting his body. Like a valuable but delicate artifact they removed him from his setting and conveyed him to their temporary camp at the edge of the lava shield, safely away from the lasered site. The Amoeba ship was gone, but it was impossible to tell when it might return.

The site was in new ruins. Solidified slag from the laser strikes covered parts of the excavation, and glassy material had plugged up a number of the open tunnels. The whole center section had collapsed. The surviving Jets were laboring efficiently to re-excavate portions, but not for Ancient artifacts; they were digging for the bodies of their companions. A number of defunct Jets lay in rows in the wan sunlight, like so many metal tubes, their brush-fibers shriveled. Others limped about on partial thrust, helping where they could. It was a scene of carnage and sorrow. These were not warriors, but dedicated specialists; they did not know how to handle the horror of war.

Still they had rallied bravely. Already sizable rescue tunnels had been formed, and many who might have died in the ground, like Herald himself, were being drawn out in time. The medic staff was competent, classifying the patients by degree of injury and amenability to treatment. They concentrated on the critical cases most likely to benefit from prompt attention, without neglecting the others. No energy was wasted in moaning; all were working as well as they could.

Herald saw all this and was inspired to do his part, whatever the personal discomfort. He thought of volunteering to go about healing the injured, but realized immediately that he could not. Physical maladies were only marginally amenable to aural healing, and the moment he stopped concentrating on his own host, it would fail.

222

His best course was to pursue his own mission, that affected not one mere site but the entire Cluster, and stay out of the way of the others. Though his leverage against physical problems was small, continued effort in key internal systems could magnify his impact.

He had been devastated by his brutal loss of Psyche. Now the Jet archaeologists had been similarly devastated. He understood their situation only too well.

"We can preserve life in this body, but not for long," a busy Jet medic informed him. "And not with comfort."

Herald was already aware of that. His inner linings were burning as he traveled, causing erratic motion, and he suffered disorientation. "It will last until the replacement Transfer unit arrives?"

"It should. You will have to be careful, however, not to abuse your resources. Perhaps we should drug you unconscious for the duration."

"No. There is research I must do. I shall turn the interval to advantage. Give me a drug to enhance my mental activity."

"That would decrease your survival ratio. Chemical imbalances already exist that—"

"The time I waste may prejudice the survival of the entire Cluster," Herald said. "I will be responsible for the risk." He knew what the medic did not: that his aura could heal this host much more effectively than any medication could, but only if his mind were sufficiently alert to focus that aura on the key spots.

"Then we shall assign a nurse to you, for the side effects are hazardous." It was evident that the medic was doing this against his better judgment, because of the special status Herald had. Any other patient would have been rendered unconscious until the Earth rescue mission arrived, saving the valuable services of the nurse for better things. Herald felt a twinge of guilt, but knew he was being unreasonable to feel it. What use to facilitate the Jets' medical convenience, if the delay meant the extinction of all life in the Cluster?

The medic gave him the drug, a colorless gas run through his main jet. It was potent. Soon he felt much better, and was able to focus his aura far more effectively. He could guide this host to almost complete recovery, in time.

223

The nurse was Sixteen. "I asked for the assignment," she admitted. "You healed me; now I help you."

"I did not heal you," Herald said. "My power was inoperative; Hweeh of Weew healed you."

"He said *you* had—"

"He sought to protect me from embarrassment. He is an intelligent, generous entity. Now my power is restored, but I must use it to heal this host, who will otherwise perish."

"You can do this? Prolong your own life?"

"My life is my aura. It is the welfare of my host I promote."

"But the host is dying!"

She was not stupid, he reminded himself. She merely had difficulty comprehending the nature of aura, being a creature of minimal aura herself. What was obvious to him could not be obvious to her. "Without my aura, the host would die, true, though this Jet-form is exceedingly sturdy. Perhaps the only sturdier sapient is the Magnet, which can be destroyed by hardly anything less than nuclear explosion." Poor Baron of Magnet, there on the ramparts of Kastle Kade! "But I will make this body well again. I do not want any host of mine to be left worse off than I came to it."

"Well, I shall nurse you anyway," she decided.

"That will help," he agreed. He would not have to be as alert while she was watching out for him, and that would enable him to heal the host faster while proceeding with his research.

Hweeh came. "I am relieved you survived, Herald. For the sake of the Cluster and, if I may presume, friendship."

"No presumption," Herald said politely, pleased at the Weew's gesture. True friendship between alien creatures was not casually acknowledged, especially when they were in mutually alien hosts. "We are to be stranded here for a period, and it is essential that we pursue our insight to its logical conclusion. The Amoeba surely will not wait on our convenience."

"Insight?" Hweeh inquired, perplexed.

"That the sites are not those of one Ancient species, but many. The Ancients came as conquerors, bearing their Kirlian Crest. Trace that crest, that specific stigma of this one species, and we locate the few specifically Ancient sites across the Cluster, eliminating the myriad false-

224

Ancient sites that have hitherto confused us. This will enable us to discover their secrets much more rapidly."

Hweeh paused. "When did this insight occur?"

"I found separate burial emblems in the tunnel where I fled the Amoeba. Once the medical problem has abated, the Jets can more than replenish their store of artifacts by delving into these other passages." Herald explained his prior reasoning. "You are a research astronomer; this line of endeavor should be natural to you. I presume the Jets have an archaeological library."

"They do, an excellent one. It is part of their professional equipage. Some volumes were damaged by the lasers, but most are intact."

"Let us repair, then, to that library."

"May I observe, friend, that you appear to have an enhanced outlook," Hweeh said. "Has your natural grief abated?"

"More than my outlook is enhanced," he said, feeling the joy of his revelation about Psyche. She *had* to live! But he was cautious about expressing this rationale openly, until he had mulled it over and tested it for conceptual errors. "Let us say that I suffer new hope."

Hweeh did not persist, and they moved to the library. This was a pressured tank with computer-controlled nozzles, suitable for use by this species. Hweeh was unable to use it, both because of his suit and his nontubular form, but Herald could. So they coordinated their efforts.

"Now how do we orient on the critical area?" Herald asked. "There must be much good information that does not relate to this particular thrust."

"To do a proper job would require years. However"—Hweeh continued, forestalling Herald's objection—"an orientation survey with eighty percent accuracy can be run in a few hours with this library. Perhaps that will suffice."

"We can try it, anyway. First I want a geographic survey of specific dates of known Ancient sites. They are all three million years old, but there should be some differentiation in terms of centuries. We need to locate the earliest true Ancient site, as marked by the presence of symbols and designs conforming to those on the cubes, not the Worm-bracelets. That may be their home world, with differentiated layering, yielding the secrets of their evolu-

225

tion. We may be able to discover their technology by tracing its genesis."

"Yes, that is promising, with this new symbol-insight," Hweeh agreed. "I can set up a program for that." He went to work, organizing, calling out specific requirements, narrowing the parameters of the requested library information. Herald checked particular references. Hweeh's direction was expert; it was as if Herald were a laser being precisely aimed by the Weew, striking on or very near the target each time. The same research task would have taken Herald alone ten times as long, as he ran down profitless side avenues.

Each Jet book was keyed by odor. His trained host assimilated the information as individual molecules sped through his system. Food for the mind was literally digested; the Jets had the sense of smell developed to an extent that made the abilities of most other sapients seem retarded. One molecule in a million was a strong information-bit, and several thousand bits were coded for the gaseous information storage language. It was almost as good as animation, in its fashion—but much duller.

Animation—how much of his visit to the realm of the God of Tarot had been real? Had he seen Psyche, received her message, or was it all a mere figment of his desire? *No!* The logic was sound, by the light of the Martian day. A strong aura could survive the destruction of the body and live again—for a time. An enhanced aura might live indefinitely, restoring itself from the reservoir of the Ancients. It *did* make sense! Maybe he had not had any actual messages from Psyche, but she had to be somewhere—if only he could find her. Maybe at the Ancient-site stronghold. Find the Ancients, find her.

Then why had she told him to deal with the Amoeba, to reach her? Did she mean that finding the Ancient site where she was would be useless if the Amoeba had not been neutralized first? Because *any* site he tried to activate would soon be destroyed by the Amoeba, and her with it? Was that why she had to hide, concealing the activation of the site that her presence represented? That seemed likely, but it posed a formidable dilemma. The Cluster could not overcome the Amoeba without first obtaining the science and technology of the Ancients, and if it were necessary to overcome the Amoeba before activating any sites—paradox.

Sixteen, never far removed, asked to help. "You can run a check on mythologies," Hweeh told her. "The earliest developments of Kirlian science will be referenced in local species myths. I will give you a program to isolate these references. If your chart of localization corresponds to ours, we shall know we are getting there. Can you do that?"

"I am a Jet," she said.

That meant, as it turned out, that she was a competent researcher and classifier and reporter, as a member of an archaeological specialty species should be. Her report was ready before Herald's.

The notion of mythology reminded Herald again of Psyche. Now he wondered, but dared not inquire, whether Sixteen had encountered the legend of Psyche and Cupid, and whether the immortality the mortal girl had been granted at the end, after her return from Hell, actually represented aural enhancement. He had to keep a firm fix on reality, no matter how tempting certain notions might become.

They pondered the results of the two surveys, the geographies of Crest and Legend. The two seemed to be only coincidentally related to each other, and the areas of overlap were patchy and widely scattered. One promising locale was in Novagleam, Milky Way; another was in Duocirc Andromeda; a third was in a fragment galaxy of the Cluster. The three were as far apart as it was possible to be.

"There's a spot overlap in Sphere Jet, too," Sixteen pointed out, pleased.

Herald did not comment. She was right about the spot, but the chances of the Ancients originating in such an isolated globular Cluster, near a dangerous black hole, seemed remote. And the extremely low aura of the Jets obviated any likely relationship to the Ancients, the original Kirlians.

"It is evident that the Ancients came as conquerors," Hweeh said. "They arrived all over the Cluster at about the same time. The discrepancies are within the margin of error for the dating procedures, and even if they were not, there is still no consistent cross-Cluster progression. Their arrival *could* have been simultaneous, and the same for their departure. As for the mythologies . . . I really had not expected a correspondence, because they do not date the period of the Ancients, but the modern chance discoveries of Ancient sites. They have no significance for the location of the developing Ancient species. In this respect our comparison is a success. Had there been a strong correlation, our research methods would have been suspect. We require another referent."

Herald was amazed again at the competence of the Weew. He had assumed the lack of correspondence meant failure, not success! Of course this *was* a check against distortion of interpretation of data by too-eager researchers. They had verified that expectations were not generating false answers. Should he submit his belief in Psyche's survival to Weew's scrutiny?

No . . . he did not dare.

"The Ancients were so powerful; they must have been very high aura, like you," Sixteen said. "Able to heal at a touch, to survive ills that would destroy lesser species. And their sites are always highly Kirlian. I wonder. . . ."

"It has generally been assumed that this was the case," Hweeh agreed. "The Ancients had preeminent Kirlian science. Virtually all aural manipulation by contemporary species has been the result of discoveries at Ancient sites. Our technicians hardly comprehend the fundamental principles; they have mainly followed the Ancient instructions. But we don't know the strength of the personal auras of the Ancients, or their family groups."

"If we *did* know," she persisted, "would we not then be able to localize their aural families?"

"Extinct creatures don't have auras," Herald said. "We might type their auras through typical residuals in their artifacts—I could probably do that—but it would only verify what the Kirlian Crest survey has done. Ancients occupied Ancient sites. This is obvious without further research."

"I mean, in contemporary species," she said.

"What purpose? No doubt some of our aural families overlap some of theirs, but—"

"Wait, Herald," Hweeh said. "I believe I follow her reasoning. We believe the Ancients all perished, but suppose some of them survived? The Cluster is a huge geography; there must be much we have yet to discover in it. Could these remnant Ancients not have regressed, lost their technology, forgotten their heritage? Three million

228

years is not much geologically or astronomically, but for civilized sapients it is a very long time—"

"They may still be with us!" Herald said excitedly. "This supposes that isolated branches of the Ancients *did* suffer Spherical regression. But how can we say they did not, when their main culture collapsed? Their secret of civilization may have been highly technological, so that without that level they degenerated rapidly. The presence of such remnants would be the easiest thing to verify, if we only knew the aural families we were looking for. If there were not too many. It would certainly be worth a try."

"The super-auras," Sixteen said. "Like yours. They are very special, and they don't seem to be hereditary. Could they be Ancient auras showing up recessively at long intervals? Suppose the Ancients were nonphysical entities, existing only in aural form, animating a succession of hosts."

"That one's been thought of before," Herald said. "The super-auras are not as distinct as they seem; they are merely the peaks of the distribution curves. For every plus-two-hundred aura, there are several in the one hundred and eighty to one hundred ninety-nine range, and a great many in the one hundred and fifty to one hundred seventy-nine range. A tiny percentage of the total number of entities in the Cluster, but a fair absolute number. If there were some sharp break in the distribution— But nothing significant has been found. Computer analysis indicates that high auras fit a normal probability curve, and that the gradually increasing intensities of the top auras are merely a function of increasing sapient population in the Cluster. For example, two trillion entities are more likely to produce a record aura than one trillion entities. Considered in this context, I am merely the chance high spot of a crowded Cluster."

"We need more artifacts," Hweeh said. "We are not looking for present-day full-blooded living Ancients, but for some Ancient admixture in a present species. The strength of their auras may have declined, but their aural families should be more stable. If you can analyze the residual auras in undisturbed artifacts, we can run our geographic search for the highest concentration of those families. There must be some more relics somewhere on this planet—"

"There *must* be!" Herald agreed. "Come, we must search them out!"

"But you are injured, drugged," Sixteen protested. "The chances of locating such artifacts are meager, and it is only a theory that may prove to be without foundation. I cannot let you range the planet on such purely speculative—"

"Give me more drugs," Herald said. "My aura will balance them, so that my host will not expire before the unit comes from Earth. I believe the potential gain is worth the risk."

"Well, maybe a cautious survey of the local site," she conceded. "If it weren't a matter of Cluster security— You must move slowly and rest often. . . ."

"No such limit!" Herald said. "This is *important*. The Amoeba obviously knew about this site, and blasted all collected artifacts. But there must be other sites on this planet, or at least camping remains, whose significance would not be evident. Fragments of personal articles, sealed in vaporproof containers, anything sufficiently imbued with Ancient personal aura, would be valuable. Somewhere on Mars, probably far removed so as to be out of range of the Amoeba ship's pinpoint aural detectors. These fragments are what we must find. If they give us a definite Ancient aural family, and if we can trace that to a specific locale in the Cluster. . . ."

"It still seems far-fetched to me," she grumbled.

Herald did not want to admit his private agreement with her. He was stuck on this planet for several more days regardless, and he did not want to sit idle. Even the remotest chance seemed worthwhile. "Give this host your strongest drug."

"We do have stronger drugs, but your life-force would be exhausted in hours if you—"

That, again! "You Jets are low-aura. You do not comprehend the power of aura."

"I comprehend with envy," Sixteen said. "But the Jet body system, by the same token, differs from that of other sapients in the cluster. You are not accustomed to it. If you ruin your host by misjudging, then have to Transfer out. . . ."

"Herald would not do that if he had any choice," Hweeh said. "He is a healer. But I will undertake to remain to help the host to the extent of my ability, if such a situation should arise."

She considered, damping her jet down so as to be virtually unreadable. "I think you males are more interested in touring the planet than in hanging around a blasted site," she said at last, with considerable accuracy. "But I accept your assurance, Hweeh of Weew. I have felt your power, and know your generosity."

They reported to the medic again. The Jet resisted, but finally gave Herald the drug on condition that the nurse remain with him until its effect abated. "We're short-personneled, since the laser attack," he said. "We can't keep close watch on entities whose inclination is to live dangerously. You will have to take care of yourself."

They organized the search and set out. Hweeh was to suit-jet to the south and search out what he might in the cratered plane below the volcanic shield of Elysium. Herald and Sixteen moved to the east to check the much larger lava-sheet surrounding Olympus Mons.

"Take care, friend," Sixteen called as they separated.

"Acknowledged," Hweeh responded.

Herald accelerated to twelve meridians per hour, feeling the sheer exhilaration of velocity. The Jets, who worked at sites on various planets, oriented on the geometry of each one. Mars meridians ranged from about thirty-six miles at the equator to zero miles at the poles; at this latitude each meridian was about twenty-four miles. Herald would have used the mileage figures, but the host-mind tended to use its own system and he did not care to fight it. Regardless, it was a good speed. This host felt best when moving most swiftly.

Sixteen shot after him, catching up. "Don't do it, Healer! You aren't fit!"

"The faster we complete this survey, the sooner I can rest," Herald pointed out, not slowing.

"But you will not complete it at all if you over extend yourself!" She was the nurse, all right. Her one mission was to promote his physical welfare.

"It is a risk I must take. We do not know when the Amoeba will strike, but it is likely to be soon. Dubious as this line of research may seem, it is the only avenue available at the moment, and must be tried." But as he spoke, he knew that was only the lesser part of his motive. It was Psyche he sought, and discovery of the Ancients was but a means to that end. No endeavor, however unlikely, could be passed by if it offered even the slightest chance for him to reach her.

"You are a great idealist," she said, and Herald was ashamed for the selfishness of his purpose. "I will help you all I can."

She might not be so helpful, if she knew! But of course it was no concern of hers. What did she know of love and loss? She seemed unaffected by the disaster that had befallen the site.

They zoomed side by side across the plain. It was a convoluted landscape, with dunes, dust-filled escarpments, cavities, and scattered rocks. As they drew away from the lava shield, the terrain became rougher, so that they had to correct course constantly to avoid rocky obstructions. But the journey quickly became repetitive and monotonous.

This was cruising velocity for healthy Jets, and it was no additional effort to talk. "Where do you come from, Healer?" Sixteen inquired.

Now she sought to promote his mental welfare too, by encouraging him to talk! "Sphere Slash, Andromeda," he answered gruffly. "The enemy galaxy."

"Not to us of Glob Jet," she said. "We were not involved in the Wars of Energy. In fact we didn't even *know* of the wars until some centuries later. We were pretty isolated."

"How could you be isolated in these days of Transfer?" Herald asked. "I thought virtually all the Cluster was explored between the wars."

"There were a number of nonsapient backwaters not worth the expense of exploring," she said ruefully. "It seems the great Sphere detectors picked up no auras in our glob, so they assumed it was barren. Only when a mattermitter geographic survey of all the globular Clusters was made were we discovered. That was six hundred years ago. Then—"

"Now wait!" he interrupted. "You were discovered a couple of thousand years ago, because of the black hole in the glob that radiated all over the Cluster."

"Well, we were and we weren't," she said. "The black hole specialists made note of our presence, but they weren't really interested in us. We were just an unremarkable local species. We helped with local supplies and

232

vortex charts, but were not permitted access to anything important. So we were filed in the geographic archives and ignored for over a thousand years. The more recent survey catalogued auras, and then there was a commotion, because we had the lowest auras in the Cluster—less than half of one percent of the sapient norm. It was a scientific curiosity. Many thousands of us were mattermitted to the Milky Way Galaxy for study. When they finally decided that it was after all possible for there to be minimum aura life, even minimum aura sapient life, they published their studies and forgot about us laboratory specimens. It was too expensive to mattermit us home, so we had to settle in the Galaxy and earn our own living. Officially we're nationals of Sphere Jet, entitled to speak as Equals. But actually we have no connection to our home glob; we know it only historically. So we—"

"Say something in Equals," Herald encouraged her.

= Something, = she said.

/Thanks,/ he replied.

They laughed together, blowing out humor-turbulences in the thin Martian air. Sixteen was good company!

"So that's how we came to the archaeological task force," she concluded, reverting to Quote inflection. "We were well constructed for it, and our species has had millions of years experience, questing through the planets of the glob for our own derivations. It is a good profession, and we are well paid."

Except when they got lasered by a visiting enemy ship, he thought. But then something else twitched his curiosity. "You have been sapient for millions of years?" Herald inquired as they dodged around a jagged ridge of stone. The terrain was becoming increasingly rugged, and that could be dangerous at this velocity.

"Oh, yes. Right back to the time of the Ancients."

Herald was electrified. *"Your kind knew the Ancients?"*

"Well, yes and no," she said. "We were sapient then— our records show this—but we have no surviving records *of* them. We do know they isolated us by removing all the tools and materials of mattermission and Transfer— not that we were able to Transfer anyway. So we regressed, and existed in comparative savagery for perhaps a million years, and rose again to atomic-level technology. We still could not muster mattermission because of the absence of strategic substances the

233

Ancients had removed, and we regressed again. For a long time it was easier to forget that there was a Cluster out there, than to recognize the nature of our prison. Those of us who could not face our restriction simply set up orbit around the hole."

"Around the hole!" he exclaimed. "There is no way *out* of such a gravitational well, by definition, and even a stable orbit would suffer tides that would tear apart any object that—"

"Precisely," she said. "You call it suicide. We can't kill ourselves as easily as other creatures can, and there is often a great deal of discomfort in the trying, so we utilize special means. We preferred to think of it as passing through an aperture to another realm. Who can conjecture what lies beyond?"

Not Psyche! his hope cried, but he kept that quiet. "Who indeed?" he agreed. "If your kind has anything like a Tarot deck, you must have a card with a black blot in the center: the Hole. In lieu of the one we call Death, or Transformation."

"We do," she agreed. "It is *the* concept of our philosophy. All that we are, and all that we are not, is governed by that singular concept. The hole in the glob. The ultimate escape from the ultimate confinement."

"Perhaps one day I will ride a ship directly into that hole," he said. "The notion is appealing."

"You wish to suicide? You can't go directly into the hole; the vortex forces you into the spiral orbit. The hole has its particular rules about the manner of its utilization."

Suicide? *If Psyche does not live.* "You would not understand," he told her gently. "Continue with your history."

She did not protest. "We regressed—but we would forget even the rationale for that ignorance, and develop again, only to remain corked. Oh, we have a score to settle with the Ancients, who did this to us."

"But the Ancients are three million years dead," Herald pointed out.

"Then we have no recourse," she said.

"It is strange they would do that to you," Herald said. "Many other species, like the Worm colonists of Mars, they exterminated outright."

"While others, like the Solarians, they left untouched," she said. "What was their rationale?"

"If only we knew! There has to be a reason. A foolish, inconsistent species could not have conquered the Cluster. If we could fathom their nature and intent, perhaps we could discover their science. And that is what we have to do."

She made a sonic shrug. "Here we are talking about Jets and Ancients, when I had asked about you. How come you to this Galaxy?"

"I am a healer. I Transfer where my commissions take me. I had to exorcise a—" He broke off.

"I did not catch that," Sixteen said. "What was your mission?"

"It was a failure," he said shortly.

She took the hint and was silent. She was very good about things like that. They jetted on toward the great volcano.

In four hours they reached it. Now they slowed, angling across to achieve the phenomenal, sixty-meridian-wide lava sheet, the residue of the vent's colossal effusions. Near the western edge of it rose Olympus Mons, one of the classic volcanoes of this system. To reach it they had to traverse the rugged mountain range that circled it, rising high to reach the most convenient pass. Then on to the volcano itself, finding a channel through the rim wall that was the abrupt edge of the mighty cone, slanting up toward its lofty half-meridian height. The rise was not steep, but the steady effort was a drain on the diminished resources of Herald's host.

At last they overlooked the central caldera, pocked by smaller calderas where the surface had collapsed after the hot lava leaked out. It was an impressive but barren scene.

"Why are we looking here?" Sixteen inquired. "Sapients do not normally camp in volcanoes."

"That is one reason why," Herald explained. "The Ancients evidently sought to conceal their presence on Mars, at the time of their occupancy, and after. The remains of a site within a volcano are likely to be the first obliterated when the lava flows again. But while in use—what better concealment for a continued flow of creatures and equipment? The kind of heavy construction for which the Ancients were noted would have been obvious to sapient observers. So they needed extensive natural cover."

"Why?" Sixteen asked. Hadn't they already destroyed the colony?"

"The colony of Worms on Mars, perhaps. But observers on nearby Earth. . . ."

"They were subsapient then, or at least borderline. The humanoid Solarians had no civilization three million years ago. And even if they had, the Ancients could so readily have vanquished them. Why would they hide, then depart without attacking Earth?"

"I don't know," Herald admitted. "If I find any key artifacts here, we may begin to understand this mystery."

They looked, descending cautiously into the main caldera. Herald kept alert for any trace of aura. It required close contact to heal a living entity, or even to analyze a living aura properly, but he could pick up the whiff of aura in an otherwise aura-free region from a fair distance. His notion seemed far less sensible now that he had submitted it to Sixteen's scrutiny; still he hoped. . . .

Why, he wondered, had Hweeh agreed so readily? The chances of discovering Ancient artifacts here were not small, they were virtually nonexistent.

There was nothing. He tried to control his letdown. He needed a positive attitude, or the healing he was performing on his Jet host would be ineffective. He didn't want to become impotent again! After all, there was a whole planet remaining.

If only he wasn't so certain that the Cluster Council committee would do nothing! The Amoeba must even now be moving its battleships into position, and there was no one to cry the alarm or to attempt effective resistance but Herald the Healer. That was another kind of impotence: to know the threat, and to be unable either to act or to cause others to act. Another kind of hell.

They started back up the steepening walls of the caldera. The descent into it had been easy, a relief after the long climb, but now there was a problem. Toward the rim the inner wall became almost vertical, and Herald was abruptly tired, in body as well as spirit.

Extremely tired. He jetted upward determinedly—and flamed out.

His propulsion gone, he rolled helplessly down the slope.

= Herald! = Sixteen cried, reverting to her native intonation in her stress. She jetted after him.

She quickly caught him in her lifting strands and steadied him against her sleek fuselage. "The drug— You overextended, and it betrayed you!"

No wonder he had gotten disorganized! The warning had been right; he had not comprehended the pitfalls of this medication. But this did not diminish his urgent need. "Give me another dose," Herald told her. "There's work to be done."

"No. You have to rest. In a while you will be able to sustain the medication."

He knew she was right. If he did not heed reason *now*, he was a complete fool. So he relaxed. "So many mysteries," he said. "Why should the Amoeba take all the trouble to come here to our Cluster to conquer us? Couldn't they locate any energy for their purposes closer to home? Why did the Ancients conquer the Cluster, then vacate? *They* obviously didn't convert it to energy. We have never found any evidence of any matter they destroyed, and I believe there *are* ways to tell. The removal of a portion of a galaxy would create an imbalance that would in due course be reflected in its dynamics." He thought of the irregular blobs of Cloud 9 and Cloud 6. No, they could not have been full spiral galaxies! "We keep coming back to their seeming irrationality. The purpose of the Amoeba I can comprehend; it is straightforward power. But the Ancients—" He paused. "Maybe *that's* what Melody meant!"

"Who?"

"Melody of Mintaka, despoiler of the second Andromedan effort at Cluster unification. She played—"

"That drug," Sixteen said, worried. "It must have side effects I didn't know about."

Herald made a gust of tired mirth. "I met her in a Tarot Temple animation. She told me I would not want to know the secret of the Ancients."

"Oh. That is the kind of thing an animation would say, isn't it?"

"Yes, unfortunately. But she seemed so very certain of herself. I believe she did know the secret, or part of it, in her real life. She refused to divulge it then, also."

"It must be fun to experience an animation."

Psyche, writhing in the orange flame. . . . "Not necessarily. You have not experienced it? The Temples are free; they want converts."

"I have been there. The figures would not animate for me, or for any of my kind. We have insufficient aura."

Herald began to appreciate the tragedy of these Jets. They could not animate, they could not Transfer, they could not return to their globular Cluster.

"Don't have pity on us," Sixteen puffed. "We do fine without aura. Had we not been confined by the Ancients, we would have conquered the Cluster ourselves, two million years before your species achieved sapience."

Literally true, he thought. *Any* of the contemporary sapients could have conquered the Cluster, in time, given the general vacuum of sapience that existed then. Strange that the achievement of sapience had been so nearly simultaneous across the Cluster. In a way this coincidence was fortunate, for it had enabled the contemporary mélange of species to form a larger, cooperative culture, unifying the Cluster more perfectly than would have occurred otherwise. Had the Jets broken out prematurely, they could have pre-empted it all. Still, that would not have provided them with what they evidently craved beyond all else: aura.

Herald touched her with his aura, calming her ire. "If the Jets had conquered, then you and I would never have met."

"Your logic is suspect, but you see right through me, and I melt in your aura," she said. "I have never experienced such strange, wonderful power before. Even Hweeh does not compare to you."

"He is superior in other aspects," Herald said. "He is more intelligent than I, more educated, and in any other company, he would be regarded as the leader in aura too. Creatures of low aura cannot perceive aura as a separate force. I am a healer, with a most potent and highly trained aura; therefore it becomes manifest to you in this circumstance. But I apologize to you for misjudging your attitude; you are certainly competent, and you have been taking good care of me in my infirmity."

"Accepted," she said, and by the ripple in her trace aura he knew it was honest, though he had not really misjudged her and she knew it. She had a temper after all, but also a forgiving nature. "Actually, we are not the lowest-aural forms in the Cluster. We have made a study of low-aural forms, and have found several nonaura species."

Herald was amazed. "*Non*aura life? I thought that was impossible! The impulses of the nervous system and brain give rise to semielectric fields that we call aura; this absence of aura implies absence of thought and feeling. In many cultures, aural cessation is the legal definition of death. Species with no aura must be extremely primitive!"

"They are, generally. But we located one that has potential for sapience. It seems to be evolving rapidly, and in another two million years or so—"

"Where?"

"In another globular Cluster, one orbiting Galaxy Pinwheel at extreme range. We suspect that glob was captured by the galaxy recently, perhaps within the past three million years. It could have been an inter-Cluster wanderer. There can be strange life-forms in isolated globs!"

"Not when you get to know them," Herald said.

"This species we call the Blanks. They do not use electrical impulses; their system is entirely mechanical. Control-signals are transmitted through bony linkages, much as sound vibrations move through the bones of the ears of the creatures of this Solarian system whose language we speak. The brain of these entities is a mechanical-chemical network of remarkable complexity. It functions in ways we do not yet properly comprehend; we seem to have underestimated the potential of nonelectric impulses. It operates well enough for potential sapience, we judge. The Blanks are, by other definitions, alive. And presapient"

"Fascinating," Herald agreed. "It is a line of aural research I have overlooked, but I shall pursue it when I have opportunity. This mechanical thought system; does something like that account for the Jets' low aura? No offense to this host, which is a good one. But I must admit the fit is very tight. There hardly seems to be enough of a system for my aura to occupy."

"Yes. The detail is dissimilar, but the principle relates. We have a combination system: an advanced mechanical and chemical linkage coupled to a relatively vestigial electrical one. We are, in that sense, three quarters machine. Our records show that much of our aura development has been recent, evolutionally; at the time of the Ancients we had only one percent of our present aura."

"This is amazing!" Herald said, amazed. "Yet you were sapient then."

"Yes. Our recent evolution has not been from subsapience to sapience, but from mechanical toward electrical. Perhaps in time we would have developed Kirlian science and broken out of our confinement."

"None of the contemporary sapients were sapient at the time of the Ancients, except the Jets," Herald said slowly, feeling that he was on the verge of a fundamental revelation. "There were myriad sapients in the Cluster, but the Ancients exterminated them all—except the Jets."

"Maybe they thought they *had* exterminated us," Sixteen said. "They may have confined us, then suffered a record-keeping error and overlooked the final act. Our very isolation may have saved us."

But Herald was on another thought. "They destroyed all the sapients of their time, and spared all the subsapients. A straight, selfish act of empire-preservation. These Martians might have posed a threat, but the primitive Earthers did not. And my own subsapient Slash ancestors would have been spared on the same basis. And all the other contemporary species of the Empire. So it is no coincidence that new sapience emerged about the same time all over the Cluster; it was an act of pure selection by the Ancients. Only those species *below* a certain level were permitted to continue their development. *That* must be the secret Melody refused to tell! Because it diminishes the image we have of the Ancients; it shows them as selfish, short-range creatures." But somehow he couldn't see an entity like Melody of Mintaka being silent on such a point; she would have enjoyed puncturing the Ancient image.

"Then every Spherical species today owes a debt to the Ancients," Sixteen said. "But . . . I'm not sure it is true."

Herald was achieving increasing respect for her acumen. Sixteen had a much larger background of personal and species information than he had suspected. No doubt his own host had similar information, but his host was essentially unconscious during the healing process. "How so?"

"All we know is that the Ancients destroyed the sapient Worms of Mars, and spared the humanoids of Earth.

240

We assume this to be true elsewhere—and I don't question this extension—but it cannot have been done on a sapient-nonsapient basis."

"Why not?" Herald was really intrigued. This extemporaneous discussion was bringing them much closer to comprehension of the nature of the Ancients than his prior lines of research had done. He noted how the wan sunlight flashed off her sleek fuselage, making a small iridescent splay.

"The Worms of Mars were colonists. They came from another world. What world? Not Earth; there were no sapient worms there; and if there had been, why was not Earth destroyed or sterilized? It must have been another system. But our surveys reveal no worlds in this neighborhood that such sapients could have come from. Either a world is complete with all its species in unbroken lines of evolution for billions of years, or it is dead, with all extinct. If there had been any Worm cultures in this region of space, the Lodo ship could have been directed there, so that we would not have had to go to the trouble of Lodoforming Mars for their habitation."

"That makes sense," Herald agreed. "Far simpler to sterilize a full world, or leave it alone. Selectivity within a world would be extremely tedious and uncertain."

"Yes. So assume the Ancients destroyed the Mars colony and the full world from which the Worm colony came, too. They therefore destroyed all the nonsapients of that world as well."

"That's right!" Herald said. "Had they been protecting nonsapients, they would have *taken* the trouble to be selective within given worlds. So they obviously did not care about *us*. All they wanted to do was root out all sapients, regardless of what other species suffered. Had Earth, or Slash, or any other contemporary-sapient planet had sapients then, it would have been destroyed. So our survival is mere coincidence."

"Yes. But why did they depart, leaving us weed-species to take over what they had cleared for themselves?"

Weed-species—an intriguing concept! "That mystery remains. Perhaps Melody of Mintaka knew. Maybe it was remorse."

"Maybe," she agreed. But they both doubted it.

*   *   *

Jets did not exactly sleep, but they did require a periodic lapse of activity for proper health. The Martian day-night cycle was almost precisely the same as that of Earth, which had become the standard for this region of space, so it was convenient to indulge in the lapse during the cool night. In the morning, Sixteen gave Herald another dose of the drug, and they consumed puffs of nutrient gas from bubbles she had brought along. Once they were grown, Jets did not require much solid intake.

Now his host's physical strength was at par again. He zoomed zestfully up out of the giant crater without even feeling strain. "Next best chance is the chasm," he announced.

"But that's a quarter round the planet!" Sixteen wooshed.

"Right. So we'll have to hurry." And he accelerated to fifteen meridians per hour, close to top speed, going down the volcanic slope and across the monstrous lava plain to the southeast.

"I'm not absolutely sure Sphere Slash is beyond subsapience," she said under the cover of the increased blast of her propulsion. But she let him proceed.

The west terminus of the ninety-meridian chasm was no farther away from the volcano than the volcano was from the Ancient archaeological site. In three hours they were maneuvering through the heavily cratered plain beyond the lava rim, locating the gorge.

The chasm was extremely long, broad and deep; it would take hours to traverse its length. Its sides were not straight, but highly serrated. Flash flooding at some time in the planet's past had resulted in spot erosion. But there was very little free water on Mars, and most of that was frozen, since the surface temperature seldom passed the melting point of water; only extraordinary local meteorological conditions ever made it rain.

Somewhere along this phenomenal crack in the planetary surface was an Ancient site. There had to be. Because without it, contemporary civilization was lost. Or was the drug exaggerating his concern, as it had before?

He quested along the northern face of it, slowed by the extreme contours, and Sixteen followed the southern wall. She could not detect the Ancient aura, but she would perceive any artificial alteration of the chasm.

Hours passed without success. The canyon went on and on, its offshoots branching interminably, all requiring exploration, consuming his waning energy. Herald continued, refusing to give up hope, slowing his velocity to conserve his host's resources. The drug was wearing off again; but perhaps the very next wrinkle would reveal the site, or the next, or the next. . . .

Suddenly a subcanyon opened out from the floor of the main one. There had been a number of these irregularities before; the bottom was by no means flat. But now, tired, distracted, disappointed, and careless, he shot over the brink and dropped into the jagged crevice before he saw it. For an instant it reminded him of his drop into the hot pit of the Amoeba's laser strike, but this was cold, hard rock. He had been paying more attention to the sides of the chasm than to the front.

He came to a stop safely, but his strength was gone. Hardly able to emit a decent jet, he could not get out.

In moments Sixteen was there. "It's happened again," she exclaimed. "I have been so absorbed in the search I neglected you."

"Give me the drug," Herald said weakly.

"No! You've had a dose and a booster. A second boost in this circumstance could kill your host."

"If you don't, we can't even make it home," he pointed out. "They'll never find us here, and they're too busy to look anyway. We're as lost as the Ancient site."

"I could return for help," she said. "But you need my care. You don't understand the nature of your host. You think that because it can travel at speed, it is fit. A jet can *always* travel at speed. When his propulsion fails, he is close to death. Oh, I should never have—"

"*You* don't understand the nature of my imperative," Herald retorted, clinging to consciousness. "Death is no specter in the face of the threat to the Cluster." *And to Psyche!* "We shall *all* die if I don't find what I seek." But he knew he was exaggerating. All he had to do was rest for a few hours, letting his host recover in its own time, until it could tolerate the drug. If he were reasonable— But he was *not* reasonable!

"We don't understand each other," she said. "I must operate on one immediate principle: preserve your life and health. I know of only one other way, and that is unethical."

"How can it be unethical to implement your assignment?" Herald demanded.

243

"It is a matter of means and ends. There is a conflict of interests."

"A conflict of interests," he repeated, musingly. "Could that account for the anomalies of the Ancients? They had a special mission we do not understand, whose objectives were contradictory. Are we, perceiving those contradictions but not the rationale, misjudging the nature of the Ancients?"

"That could be," she agreed, relieved to have him talking instead of demanding the drug. "They may have had reasons to eliminate certain types of creatures who happened to be sapient, and to spare certain others. We perceive only the sapient/nonsapient distinction, but if that were coincidental. . . ."

"If only we knew the nature of the species they destroyed," Herald continued. "The Worms are only one example; that's not enough to determine a pattern. I'd hate to think that they were saving whole planets as food animal production units, but we can't be *sure*. To compare the ones eliminated to the ones spared—"

"The aura!" she exclaimed. "Now we know that non-Kirlian life is possible. Even non-Kirlian sapience! Could those destroyed species have—?"

It burst upon him like a nova. "Non-Kirlian sapience! If it evolved more rapidly than the Kirlian forms, even though restricted by its inability to Transfer, it could dominate the Cluster, as the reptiles of Earth's dinosaur days dominated the mammals, or the Dash birds of my own Galaxy even now dominate the £ tripeds."

"Those forms would have to be eliminated, to promote the forms with greater potential," she finished. "Like weeding a garden to favor the more delicate but productive plants. . . ."

The concept of weed-species, again, this time with more force. "Then the contemporary sapients were not selected randomly," Herald said excitedly. *"Their auras determined their selection.* They were given the chance to develop, when otherwise the non-Kirlians would have squeezed them out."

"The Ancients must have been the first major high-aura species," Sixteen said. "They evolved in some isolated region, as we did, where there were no non-Kirlians, so they were not eliminated before they achieved their potential. When they expanded into the main Cluster they discovered it was dominated by a type of life that had to waste energy using mattermission because they couldn't Transfer. And these species were suppressing the Kirlians. Within a given system, where planets might be separated by no more than light-minutes, mattermission would be a highly feasible mode of transport; it is only at the interstellar range that Transfer dominates. So the Kirlians had the potential to govern whole galaxies, and when the non-Kirlians realized this, it was savage war. Only one side could prevail; they thought they could not coexist. So the Ancients set out to promote permanent civilization by eliminating all the non-Kirlians. It may have been the only way. They were the progenitors of our modern culture."

"But why did they disappear?" Herald asked, returning to the old mystery. "The Ancients won; they should have remained to help their own kind along."

"Maybe they *did* stay," Sixteen insisted. "We find their ruins, their deserted stations, but maybe those were merely for the war effort, and when it was over they abandoned such instruments and settled down within a few pleasant systems and left the other, nonsapient Kirlians alone. You say there is no significant pattern to the manifestations of the highest auras, but if there were a number of types of creatures making up the Ancient nucleus, with several families of auras, and these auras manifested every few generations, so that there would always be a way to key open their Ancient sites in case of emergency—"

Herald had another powerful flash of comprehension. "Psyche!" he cried. "Keyed to the Ancient site!"

"What?"

"I knew one such creature! A Solarian who was in tune with the Ancients. Maybe she *was* an Ancient!"

"Then we have an excellent lead," Sixteen said excitedly. "We must get back and consult with Hweeh, and get in touch with that Solarian."

Herald sobered. "You said I was too weak for the drug."

"There is one emergency way to prepare you for it, by drawing on an untapped resource within your host. It is not precisely ethical, but in the circumstance—"

"We may have solved the mystery of the Ancients," Herald remarked, "but the mystery of your ethics is growing! What is the problem?"

245

Sixteen jetted a gust of apology. "It is a little-used measure, because of the social implications."

"Forget the social implications! I am not of your culture."

"It is to invoke that store of energy normally reserved for the reproductive effort. It is untapped in normal endeavors. But the amount of reserve energy is normally enough to restore operative function to—"

"You are speaking of making love?" he inquired. "There is something you should know. I don't—"

"Yes, you told me before. You are of another species, only borrowing this host, and you do not wish to have a mistress. It is unethical for me to bring it up a second time. This is why I hesitated."

Herald had been about to mention his true relation to Psyche, but suffered a second thought. This Jet maid, in the line of duty as she perceived it, was about to make a remarkable offer—for his benefit and that of the Cluster. Apparently his refusal to take her as a mistress at the outset had fixed their relationship in a nonsexual mode, so that it was extremely difficult for her to change now. He had encountered similar conventions elsewhere. There were about as many intricacies connected to the processes of reproduction as to any other sapient need. It would not be right to embarrass her further by informing her of his inability to love any female other than his wife.

"I need not prevail on you to that extent. In a little while I will be recovered enough to tolerate the drug again."

"No, you will not," she insisted. "The signs are on you. I *am* a nurse; I know the drug would kill you this time. Unless that last reservoir is tapped."

Herald sought more information from his host-memory. The Cluster array of sexual conventions was infinitely broad; almost anything could be encountered in mode and attitude. But the Jet practice turned out to be fairly conventional. Liaisons were normally for a period sufficient to bring a litter to functioning independence in society. But some associations were for life, and some were completely casual. Sex was recognized as a physical need, and it was expected that there be periodic indulgence, with or without formal contract, by mutual consent. It was always voluntary. The involuntary participation possible to Solarian females or Spicans of any sex was unknown among the Jets. Without the active cooperation by both parties, the act could not be performed at all. Sixteen's hesitancy was not based on sexual convention, but on the requirement that a given type of relationship, once established, not be distorted. At this stage it would be like sibling romance: possible, but socially awkward. He could alleviate that aspect by claiming prior misunderstanding, owing to his alien conventions. That much was true enough; he had not at that time had opportunity to delve fully into Jet belief and practice.

In summary: He could make love to Sixteen—more correctly, make sex—if she were amenable. But *would* she be amenable if she knew about his quest for Psyche? He doubted it. Yet he needed to survive, to pursue that quest. What was ethical?

Herald considered the alternatives quickly, and decided that he was justified in permitting a partial lie. "I was married," he said. "It was for life—but she was executed."

He felt the tremor in her little aura again. "Who? When?"

"The Solarian tuned to the Ancients. Just before I came here. The Amoeba bombed the site, and only Hweeh and a Qaval and I escaped."

"Then you are in mourning," Sixteen said. "I apologize for not realizing—"

"I need . . . to forget," he said. But to himself, the truth: *I will never forget—or call her dead!*

"And the Amoeba followed you here," she said. "Oh, Herald, we must save you!"

"This is why I told you I needed no mistress. It was not a denial of you, but the memory of—"

"I understand!" she cried. "I did not know!"

"Therefore sex really can have no meaning for me, other than as a purely physical measure. I would not want you to think— "

"Understood." She paused a moment. "I, also, have an unfulfillable desire."

"You love one who died?" A surprise! He had assumed, perhaps unfairly, that she was naive about serious love.

"Similar. I love . . . an alien."

Herald was amazed. She spoke in the present tense, yet the only non-Jets to visit Mars recently were himself and his friend. "Not . . . Hweeh of Weew?"

247

"He healed me," she said simply.

Hweeh had healed her—when Herald himself had failed. So it had been the Weew's aura that made the conquest. not the Slash's aura. "Hweeh is a fine creature and a dedicated scholar. I doubt he is committed to a female of his kind. He told me he had no family, and has been completely immersed in his profession. The only reason he has not Transferred to Jet host is because he has information locked within his Weew brain that might not be available if he were Transferred away from that brain. We do not yet know the limits to such things, and could not take the chance. Once we gain that information, he will be free. He could animate a Jet host to be with you, if he so chose. Probably he does not know of your interest, so—"

"No. He has other business. He must help *you*. Do not tell him of my affliction."

Herald yielded. He was in effect lying to her about the nature of his own love, allowing her to think that it was hopeless. Now he had to honor her lie to Hweeh. "I will not tell him . . . until the Cluster has been saved. Yet he is not slow-minded entity; he will surely know—"

"Unless I conceal it, as I have done hitherto," she said. "I will be your mistress *ad hoc,* making no other demand on you, that we may get you back to the site safely."

What more could he ask? Sixteen was actually a very attractive young Jet, with a reflectively shiny surface, elegant female curvatures, and a clever intelligence. It was not necessary to inform her that even if it were not for his continuing love for Psyche, who *had* to be alive somewhere, somehow, he would never be able to love a low-aura creature. Now that he knew that Sixteen had no romantic interest in him either, it became a business matter, justified by circumstance. "Then I see no barrier to proceeding." In fact, he could have saved himself the lie, such as it was.

"Then we shall proceed," she agreed. It was like turning over a manifest for shipped cargo. What a contrast to what he had known on Planet Keep!

Sixteen moved out, found a widening in the subgorge, and began circling. She jetted erratically timed gusts, and the code pattern of this quickly registered in the appropriate perceptive center of Herald's host. It was sex-beat, a signal as direct and compulsive in its fashion as a laser from the Amoeba. His body responded, metabolizing that reserve energy involuntarily. She had certainly been right about that. He had not suspected his host had so much power hidden away, or that it could be tapped in this fashion. Nature, as always, had seen most carefully to the preservation of the species.

He jetted forward to join the dance. He had a rough notion how this species mated, but this hardly mattered. As with most species, instinct governed the procedure. He guided into the same circle, but not precisely her track. His ring was offset slightly, so that the two circles crossed each other in two places.

They were on opposite sides: while Sixteen curved south, he curved north. As he veered east, she veered west, each crossing the other's track in the dust. But Herald was going faster, pursuing; with each complete loop he was farther along than she. Soon they were moving parallel: north together, south together. They almost collided at the two intersections, one crossing outward, the other crossing inward. At the north intersect she was barely ahead, and he inhaled the delightful gases of her jet; at the south intersect he led her, giving her a whiff of his own exhaust. The effect was highly stimulating for both.

Now his host was restored to full vigor. Logic said he should break off and jet home instead of wasting any of that valuable energy in sex. But if nature left the replication of the species to individual logic, fewer species would exist in the Cluster! He could not break out of the pattern; this was no intellectual or moral consideration, but plain physical compulsion.

The two circles drew together, tugged by the interactions at the intersects. Herald's intake and jet angled to match the curvature of that pattern; Sixteen's did likewise. They spun together, like planets in tight orbit about a mutual focus, each absorbing the other's jet trail, reprocessing the gas, concentrating it. Some fresh thin Martian air entered, for this was no perfect seal, and some exhaust escaped, but the percentage of recycled molecules rose steadily.

This was feedback communication, independent of intellect. LOVE her molecules said; LOVE LOVE his own replied. LOVE LOVE LOVE the message came back, amplified. Yet it was no single molecule, no single concept, but an orchestration of enhancement. From the intellectual to the physical, the meaning amplified, merging so that the originator could not be distinguished. The experience was tremendously exhilarating.

Abruptly the concentration reached the critical level. Herald's chemistry reacted, sending out a cloud of reproductive molecules. These shot through Sixteen's system, returning to him, and back to her again. Around and around they went, some being lost to the atmosphere of Mars with each circuit, others combining with molecules released by her body. The billions became millions, then mere thousands. At last they all vanished, and it was over. If any had lodged within her tube, those merged motes would remain and grow, nourished by her system, and she would have a litter. If not, the experience had still accomplished its purpose, for Herald was now full of energy. Nothing like sex, in any species, to invigorate the male!

They organized for the return trip. Sixteen gave him the drug, and it seemed to have no effect. But he knew this was because he was already jetting strong: the drug would merely maintain this level longer.

They zoomed out of the subgorge, into the main crevasse, and on to the east. They were now halfway around the planet from the excavated site; it was as easy to proceed forward as back. Perhaps they would discover the Ancient artifact on the way, but even if not, they had found out much about the Ancients anyway.

"The survey confirms your conjecture," Hweeh said when Herald came out of the lapse his drugged journey had brought him to. "It was the action of the Ancients that eliminated competitive species throughout the Cluster. Analysis suggests these eliminated species could have been non-Kirlian. Apparently the Ancients retained power only long enough to ensure that virtually no non-Kirlians survived in this section of the Universe. The Jets were a special case; they were low-Kirlian sapients. They at least had the potential to develop into full Kirlians. So they were isolated, not destroyed. Had they developed into full-Kirlian creatures, they could have broken out. That was the intentional design of their prison. Then their conquest of the Cluster would have been in accord with the Ancient program. The Jets did not develop far enough in this respect, so other Kirlian sapeints took over instead. The Ancients, by this means, transformed this Cluster from mixed-sapience to Kirlian sapience."

"And died out before their project was complete," Herald said. "They had it all: a Kirlian Cluster, and the ability to preserve their culture from Spherical regression."

"Obviously that was related," Hweeh said. "Non-Kirlians could not avoid regression without galaxy-destructive expenditure of energy, because they could not Transfer. Even *with* Transfer, a certain amount of regression continues, and the temptation to use energy unwisely remains. Two Wars of Energy prove that! But it must be possible to abate regression, since the Ancients did it, *had* to do it, in order to conquer the Cluster. If only they had bequeathed us their secret! But now we have another problem. . . ."

"The Amoeba," Herald agreed.

"That too. I was thinking of something more personal."

Herald considered. "Was I vociferating while unconscious?"

"It was not necessary. It was obvious how Sixteen brought you back safely. The medic knew it at a glance. Your reproductive reserve was depleted."

"She volunteered it!" Herald said defensively.

"How could she do otherwise, given the need, and in the presence of your aura?"

"She was not overwhelmed by me," Herald said. "I never made an advance to her. My interest is in—" But then he remembered his promise to Sixteen.

"I am not a fool," Hweeh said with considerable justification. "You told her of Psyche?"

"I had to. I think Psyche is a Kirlian Ancient."

"As I thought. I can guess what Sixteen told you."

Herald was silent, realizing that something was wrong. Hweeh was not normally so peremptory.

"She claimed to love another . . . one unobtainable,"

251

the Weew continued inexorably. "The complement to your own situation, that she had just learned about. Were you not suspicious?"

"Hweeh, you make it difficult for me."

"I made it *easy* for you, hoping you would find distraction. But I had not anticipated this aspect. You put her in an impossible situation. She could not intrude upon the prerogatives of the recent dead; that is part of Jet culture. Neither could she let you perish, though it was your own neglect that put you in that danger. So she had to fashion a story acceptable to you, on very short notice. She may even have told you she loved *me*. Not so?"

Herald surrendered. No wonder Hweeh had acquiesced so readily to the unlikely geographic quest! He had wanted to get Herald's mind off Psyche. But the arrangement had fouled up. "I promised not to tell."

"She made you promise, so that you would not have occasion to ascertain the truth. She does not love me. I am an alien creature, physically repulsive to her in that connection. She thought *you* healed her, and were declining credit. She loves *you*. But to ease your mind, she lied to you, demeaning her own feeling."

Suddenly Herald saw it. "You are not the fool; *I* am," he said. "I should have seen it! I thought I was lying to her—"

"Were you?"

"I told her my wife was burned."

"She was, Herald. I witnessed it."

"But she didn't die! Her aura lives—and I shall find it!"

Hweeh was silent a moment, searching for a way to put the matter delicately. "Herald, did you love Psyche at first meeting?"

"No. It took time to know her."

"When did your love manifest unmistakably?"

"When I encountered her . . . enhanced." Herald savored the memory. "She had an aura of two hundred fifty."

"Then was it not the aura you loved, the enhanced aura of the Ancients?"

"You could put it that way. But it was no Possession. It was *her*, magnified tenfold. The only aura I ever encountered higher than mine."

"Would not that same aura, in any other female, have commanded your love in much the same fashion?"

Herald felt nervous. "Perhaps."

"In fact, you cannot be sure she was not merely the vehicle. You did not love the alien girl; you loved the Ancient aura."

Herald, weak from his ordeal and the sedation of drugs, could only agree. "The Ancient aura makes her what she is."

"And if that aura imbued the girl of Sphere Jet, you would love her similarly."

Herald tried to be objective. It was difficult. "Perhaps."

"Why not settle for the live Sixteen in lieu of the dead Psyche? If you find the Ancient aura, you may have love again—without illusion."

Herald thought for a long time. "No," he said at last. "Psyche lives. The real Psyche, whom I love regardless of aura. I know it. She brought you out of shock, there in the tunnel during the laser attack, when I was impotent. She spoke to me. I believe in her. I must find her."

Hweeh was silent. Herald knew his friend perceived only unreason in this cleaving to a dead alien female. And he could not be absolutely sure Hweeh was wrong.

At last Hweeh spoke. "The Earth relief ship arrived while you were unconscious. You can now Transfer to some host elsewhere in the Cluster. Given the personal situation here, and the urgency of the Amoeba crisis, I think you had better do that promptly. Sixteen told me of your new theories concerning the Ancients, and I have messaged the Cluster Council. They will form a new committee to explore the ramifications—"

"Another committee!" Herald exploded.

"Precisely. So if anything is to be done in time, it seems we must still do it ourselves. *We* must locate the Ancient source. I did manage to extract information on a highly secret project that may be related. It is not the most promising source of information, but we are severely hampered by the frustrating blindness of the Council. At least it will get us away from here, and perhaps—"

Herald made a jet of bemused wonder. "That the salvation of the Cluster should depend on such random factors! I agree; we must follow up *anything* that shows promise. Where is this secret project?"

"Galaxy Pinwheel."

"The Blanks? The null-aura species with potential sapience?"

"No, this is a re-creation of the actual Ancient culture. It was hoped that this would lead to insights about—"

"Good notion. Let's go."

10

Moderns of Ancients

*X*Aural generator manifesting in globular Cluster orbiting third Galaxy.*X*

&Another generator? Is there an ancient site there?&

*X*No.*X*

&Then it must be a special project to develop defensive aural technology on a crash basis. Investigate and take covert action if necessary. Repeat, *covert*. We are almost ready for overt action on Cluster scale. Assign one research and one action unit.&

*0*Unit 9 assigned.*0*

*X*Unit S assigned.*X*

Pinwheel was a quarter the diameter of the major galaxies, so its sapients were somewhat sensitive about its status. It was indeed a full spiral galaxy, and its two major Spheres were now full members of the Cluster coalition.

The project was set up deep inside a globular Cluster orbiting the center of Pinwheel. This glob was 250 light-years in diameter, and contained about 100,000 bright red Population II stars. There was very little obscuring dust within it, few planets—and no black hole, to Herald's relief. It was an entirely ordinary Cluster, and it had been uninhabited until the special project was organized.

Herald tilted his ring, looking around. He was in a Wheel host whose spherical body rolled freely in any direction and whose magnetically fixed disk possessed the assorted sensory equipment of the species. Beside him was Hweeh of Weew, mattermitted once more in his own body at great expense (and protest by the Cluster Council functionary in charge).

A Pin moved forward: an angular four-legged creature whose sensory organs were on projecting spines.

⩘ Welcome, visitors of the Two Galaxies, ⩘ it clacked.

⩘ I am Prick of Pin, co-supe of this station and your guide for the duration. I hope you are feeling sharp. ⩘ He extended one rod.

Hweeh quickly formed eye-stalk, horn, and sticklike appendage and used the last to touch Prick's proffered stick. @Gratitude, graciousness,@ he said formally in his own language, letting the translation units each entity carried take care of it.

⩘You have impressive aura! ⩘

@ Wait till you touch my companion! @

Prick extended a stick toward Herald. Herald angled his disk to contact it momentarily. Now he felt the Pin's own aura: a strong one of one hundred. But of course this project would attract strong auras! θPleasure,θ he said, using the mode of his host, making the sounds by vibrating his disk. *Pleasure,* he thought. *Cupid and Psyche had a child named Pleasure. . . .*

⩘ Phenomenal! Perhaps your aura is a reversion to that of the Ancients! ⩘

Herald dismissed that promptly. θThere is no evidence that any modern species relate directly to the Ancients.θ

Yet what of Psyche!

⩘Perhaps we shall now procure that evidence. ⩘

And that summed it up; for this was the super-secret Modern of Ancients program, the Cluster's major hope to comprehend the nature and purposes of the species that had conquered the Cluster three million years ago.

θPerhaps,θ Herald agreed politely. θShall we proceed?θ *We shall proceed*—the phrasing of Sixteen's acquiescence to an affair that had demanded herself and him. Had he been willfully blind in the same way the Cluster Council was blind to the threat of the Amoeba despite the evidence? At what price could he justify his quest?

Prick showed the way through the station to the enclave. All of it was under cover, for this was an airless planet. Occasional skylights showed the globular day-night: a thousand bright stars illuminating the surface constantly, preventing full night from ever descending. The average separation of stars in this region was a quarter of a light-

256

year, and they were large stars. The planet seemed to be encased in a glowing shell.

That was the reason the project was here. No outside species could expect to locate the precise planet of the particular globular Cluster of the particular galaxy that supported it. Only the privileged few even knew of its existence. Who would poke about a globular Cluster for *anything?* Such Clusters were among the oldest unified structures in the universe; there was nothing new in them. Or so it was generally supposed. . . .

The hall opened out suddenly on a vast domed landscape of such architectural splendor that both Herald and Hweeh paused, awed. It was an Ancient site as it must have been in its heyday. Rounded buildings rose many floors high, with spiral ramps servicing them; other ramps spiraled down to lakelike reservoirs. There were no straight lines, no angles; everything curved in pleasing ratios. There was foliage everywhere, unfamiliar to Herald's prior experience, though not to his host-mind: Pinwheel trees shading the contours of the parks from the glare of the myriad stars above, pastel-hued lawns, and fruit-bearing gardens.

@I would like to reside here myself,@ Hweeh murmured.

θSo would I,θ Herald agreed.

≪ So would we all, ≪ Prick said. ≪ And so you shall—for a day. We believe we have successfully re-created Ancient architecture, physique, and culture, and we hope this will enable you to feel and think like Ancients and thereby comprehend their secrets. ≪

θAn ambitious notion,θ Herald said.

≪ The Ancients residing in the enclave are androids, Prick explained; ≪ laboratory-manufactured pseudo-life, directed by operatives. Most are remote-controlled, but some are actually occupied. ≪

θWe shall need to occupy them,θ Herald said, rotating his disk firmly. θWe are not here merely to observe, but to experience.θ

≪ The Weew could do it; he is small and malleable. But your own Wheel host is far too massive. ≪

θThen I must Transfer to a smaller host. What is available?θ

≪There are service entities of Sculp who occupy the androids for testing and repairs.≪

θAh, yes, the Sculps. I am familiar with the species. I will accept such a host.θ

⩘As you wish, Prick said dubiously. ⩘

The Transfer was instituted, and soon Herald was in a Sculp host. This was a boneless, multispiked sapient whose body had evolved within the convoluted stalks of giant tubetrees.

§Very good,§ Herald said, speaking by rasping several spikes together. §Now let's see the androids.§

The physical nature of the Ancients was unknown, but study of the many ramps on their sites had suggested they were wheeled but also could traverse irregular terrain. Therefore, as Prick explained, the androids possessed both wheels and legs. Three legs, to maintain balance at all times, each with rollers at the base. They also had three upper appendages, with sucker-disks along the inner sides and six tentacle-fingers at the end. Three of the fingers were pointed, with hard claws: pincers for grasping hard objects. The softer, more dextrous alternate fingers made this form extremely facile with tools. A solid head at the top was ringed with optics, auditories, and radiation emitters and receptors. It was, overall, a most ingenious body.

Too bad it had been worked out before Herald's discovery about the distinction between Ancients and pre-Ancients. For it was a composite of a tremendous wealth of misinformation. Once the resurvey of sites was completed, the physical form of the Ancients would be narrowed considerably. Meanwhile, he was willing to find out whether occupation of such an android host provided any real feel-of-Ancient, and whether that would lead to any further key insights, in himself or in Hweeh. It seemed to him that on Mars they had come very close to a basic comprehension of the Ancients, and perhaps one little additional shove would break it all open. Then, perhaps, would follow the last-second miracle that would save the Cluster—just as had happened when Flint of Outworld and Melody of Mintaka saved the Milky Way Galaxy. Ancient technology had been the key in both prior cases; if it could only be invoked again. . . .

Hweeh seemed to have adapted readily to his own android. §Are you ready?§ Herald inquired.

@Yes,@ Hweeh replied.

"Then let's unify our linguistic modes," Herald said in

258

Quotes. "We both retain facility with the expression of Segment Etamin, which is probably not comprehensible here. It will serve as a convenient but private code."

"Agreed," Hweeh said immediately.

≪My translator did not catch that, ≪ Prick said. ≪What is the language? ≪

§It is the mode of Cloud Nine,§ Herald said. §The so-called Large Magellanic, orbiting the Milky Way Galaxy. Their symbol is high finance, $. A very happy if irregular scheme.§

≪Strange. My translator is conversant with $. I should have—≪

§Perhaps it was Cloud Six, the Small Magellanic, the ¢ symbol. I get confused at times. Each host I occupy contributes its language and much of its culture to my mind for a time. Once I depart the host, these gradually fade. Shall we now enter the enclave?§

≪Yes, of course. But I must warn you that the— We try very hard to render this enclave as realistic as possible. The program has been modified extensively with experience, until now—≪

§Until now it seems to possess purpose of its own? This is an indication of success. Do not apologize.§

≪The computer integrates the changes, and it does have positive feedback. Changes are still occurring, so that even I do not necessarily know what prevails unless I constantly recheck. We seem to have here an accelerated social evolution, which is encouraged. However, it means that I will be unable to maintain contact with you after you enter. We have a strict noninterference policy. It is essential that we allow the thrust of the Ancients to manifest in whatever manner develops. Only that way can we—≪

§I understand,§ Herald said, cutting off the developing lecture. §This is an excellent program. We shall not interfere, but shall seek to merge with its flow.§ And he rolled toward the enclave aperture.

In a moment he and Hweeh were through. They coasted down the ramp toward the first park. Herald's Sculp host was well suited to this confinement and conversant with the controls of the android. Herald quickly acclimatized, so it was as though he occupied the Ancient mockup directly. Hweeh had more trouble, but his tripod kept him stable.

259

They encountered a Modern going the other way, skating blithely along with enviable proficiency.

+Aura,+ the stranger said in greeting. He spoke in Clustric, with the Plus inflection, fittingly enough. He had an aura of 120 himself, but it was the unflexing field of machine generation, such as was used to imbue energy being Transferred galactic distances.

Of course! The salient characteristic of the Ancients was their aura, estimated to have a norm of one hundred and extremes of thirty-three to three hundred. One-third of norm to triple norm, though some experts felt this was too conservative. Modern sapients varied much more widely than this, as shown by Sixteen of Jets aura and Herald's own aura. But the Ancients were by the signs far more uniform than the contemporaries. Perhaps that was part of the secret of their strength. Also, no one knew precisely how intense a living aura could get, but three hundred seemed to be the practical limit.

+Aura,+ Hweeh returned, covering Herald's silence.

+Aura,+ Herald agreed quickly. Too bad this artificial aura could not be used to heal and to Transfer; then the android operatives could really have conveyed the atmosphere of the Ancients!

+You are strangers? I introduce myself: I am Hitherto.+

Herald had not anticipated having to name himself. He really should have taken more time to prepare for this experience! Though this was only a mockup, he was trying to achieve the full spirit of it, and to draw Hweeh into it too. For the sake of anonymity he preferred not to give his real name. It was evident that the operators of these androids were also using alternates.

Again, Hweeh rescued him. +I am Clustergaze,+ he said.

Translation: Astronomer. Herald could use a similar identification. +I am Quester,+ he said.

+Will you require lodging during your stay at our site?+ Hitherto inquired.

Lodging? They were going all out for realism! As though this were one of a million sites of the functioning Ancient community, with travelers passing from one to the other across the Cluster.

+We may not be staying long,+ Herald said. +But it would be nice to relax before we move on.+

+Then allow me to recommend the Kirlian Inn. The sustenance is excellent, and the maid— They do not call her Hellflower for nothing!+

So there were two sexes in this enclave, though the true Ancients might have had a hundred. Well, two was convenient. And food. And sex appeal. Only what did androids eat, and how did an android female stimulate an android male? Realism could go only so far!

+We shall certainly consider the Kirlian Inn,+ Herald said.

+Aura,+ Hitherto said, rolling back slightly.

+Aura,+ Herald answered. This was evidently a term for parting as well as greeting. How nice of Hitherto to "happen" by to provide this convenient briefing in manner!

They skated on. The little wheels of the feet were not powered; the motions of the legs provided the impetus. Generally, two feet pushed while the third secured the equilibrium of the tripod, but it was possible for all three to act together for extra power. Since it was feasible to rest while coasting at speed, this was an efficient mode of transport. The wheels could be braked and stalled for sudden stops, or for bracing when climbing. He wondered whether it was coincidence that the android form resembled a compromise between the two major sapients of Galaxy Pinwheel: sticklike legs, as in the Pins, and wheels as in the Wheels. Creation was always a self-image!

"I am feeling very much the Ancient, already," Hweeh remarked.

"They have done a good job of emulation," Herald agreed. Whatever it was they thought they were emulating! "Shall we proceed to the Kirlian Inn?"

"And observe the charms of Hellflower?" Hweeh made a male chuckle, moderately surprising Herald. "I do grow curious."

As they came into the city proper they passed other Moderns going about their business, whatever that might be. With each they exchanged +Aura's+ and obtained further guidance. In one sense it was wasted effort, for they really could find their own way, but it was a pleasant interaction, making them feel closer to this pseudo-culture. Androids these might be, but each seemed to *care* about his neighbor.

The Kirlian Inn was impressive. Its residential chambers were underground, while its main hall was a planetarium-ceilinged dome. Herald recognized the inspiration for this design: Flint of Outworld had encountered such a dome in the Hyades site. Unfortunately that had been destroyed, so that it had not been possible to analyze the stellar projection for an insight into the probable location of the Ancient's planet of origin—one of the tragedies of history. The information might have been obtained from Flint himself, for he had been an experienced stellar observer, but he had already faded into his Mintakan host and knew nothing. This present projection was of Galaxy Pinwheel, and small though it was compared to the giants of Milky Way and Andromeda, it *was* a full galaxy, truly impressive from this vantage.

The floor was smooth, polished, reflective, and gently waved, as though a glassy ocean with fixed waves. Couples were dancing, gliding over the mounds and through the troughs, their forward progress shaping into a kind of syncopation. Herald was intrigued, but also disturbed. By what right did they assume that the efficient Ancients ever consumed time in such pursuits as dancing? In fact, this whole setting was rather medieval in quality. Still, who was to say the Ancients had *not* danced? They must have had *some* form of entertainment. Possibly they had communicated by dancing.

The female Moderns were distinguished from the males by their surface texture, color, and delicacy of torso and limb. They wore sections of material over the upper sections of their legs, concealing the junctions of limbs with torso, making a mystery of what really had no mystery. In one sense ludicrous; in another, intriguing. As far as he knew, the androids had no copulatory organs, but it became easy to imagine that if they had, they would be lurking within the flexing shadows of that cloth.

There was, indeed, a certain attractive grace to the females. Herald felt the impact despite his occupancy of a Sculp host within an android body. The skating-feet made the dancing very smooth, and the round cross section of the torso made rotation easy. The dancing figures wove in and out and spun in place like gyroscopes, forming intriguing larger patterns across the floor. The lighting changed color, dimming slowly, so that the night of the sky seemed to extend downward, until only little globes of glow followed the dancers. Oh, yes, very pretty!

At the height of the dance and depth of darkness, the stars of the dome began to move. It was subtle at first, so that it was hard to be certain that any positions had shifted at all; then it accelerated. The stars spread out, traveling down the base-walls and inward across the floor, which now seemed transparent. The room seemed to be within the Galaxy of Pinwheel, traveling through it, the individual stars progressing to the rear in three-dimensional panoply.

Herald had never traveled in space. He had always reached his assignments via Transfer, stepping from planet to planet without traversing the space between. He had never even mattermitted, though that resembled Transfer far more closely than it did space travel. Thus this was a very special experience for him: to see a galaxy as the pilot of a ship might see it. Not that ships really had pilots; even at half-light speed, it took many years to travel even a tiny fraction of a galaxy. But *if* multiple-light-speed spaceship travel existed, so that pilots would have to steer around stars, this was the way it might be. Ah, rapture!

Hweeh nudged him with a pincer, and Herald reluctantly diverted his attention from the view of space—so like his vision of the Tarot Temple, when he explored the Ghost card to spy the Amoeba—to follow the glance of his companion's forward eye. A brightly colored figure was coasting toward them, her torso swaying as she emerged from the shadow, her skirt shifting suggestively. Hellflower!

Android or not, there was something *about* her. She exuded sex appeal. Herald tried to analyze its components, but they eluded him. She was simply a wildly desirable female Modern Ancient.

She drew up close, her skirt settling about her. +Aura,+ she murmured, and there was a special thrill in her voice.

+Aura,+ both patrons responded. Hweeh was evidently as entranced as Herald. What *was* it that could turn on males of totally different species even when they knew it was merely a mockup of a conjectural species?

+What is your pleasure?+ Hellflower inquired, performing a small additional twirl.

Through no fault of her own, she had used the wrong word. Pleasure—the child Psyche had intended to bear

263

by him. What was he doing here, reacting to the lure of an imitation female? Even had she been real, she would have had no shadow of the human appeal of Psyche! This was all a play, an imitation of a society that never existed, and the gut-reality of Hellflower's sex appeal was a chassis of metal and pseudo-flesh.

The illusion shattered, as Herald suddenly placed the mechanism: sound. Fringe-auditory sonics accompanied the maid, tuned to the deepest levels of sapient desire. Certain things seemed to be common to most species, regardless of world of origin, as though all life had diffused billions of years ago from a common source. That was another long-standing mystery: whether life *had* a common root, and somehow spread across the cluster long before any sapience had developed, or whether some species had evolved three *billion* years ago and spread life to all habitable planets. Those would be the true Ancients, making the three-million-year Ancients seem like no more than a contemporary ripple of established life. Meanwhile, the fact was that there *were* certain broad bases of species affinity, so that many species could mix physically without poisoning each other by the products of their metablisms, and one of these affinities was sonic. Hellflower had aphrodisiac sound!

+*You* are our pleasure,+ Hweeh said gallantly.

Hellflower paused momentarily, as though sensing Herald's negation of her artful, artificial charms, then made a suggestive gyration. +What is your pleasure worth?+

Herald wanted to warn his companion of the mechanism here, to ensure that Hweeh not embarrass himself, but didn't want to speak in Quotes in the presence of the maid. Still, why should he be concerned? Hweeh was no immature innocent, and there was no way this could go beyond propriety. Androids had no primary sexual equipment.

But again he wondered: or *did* they?

+I am ignorant of the going rate,+ Hweeh said. +But if it is within my means—+

Ouch! The Weew had not caught on!

+Then accompany me,+ she said with another alluring spin, buttressed by a strengthened beat of that evocative sound.

Hweeh spun after her, across the waving floor. He

264

seemed to be flying through space, obscuring constellations of stars as he moved.

Folly! But Herald, still unwilling to speak openly, followed. What were they getting into? It was one thing to appreciate the atmosphere of the Ancients, but *this*. . . .

Hellflower slid out of the inn and onto an elevated ramp that wound upward between the sinuous buildings of the city. Herald's host performed the slide-and-brake skating necessary to travel up the incline without difficulty. Hweeh had to copy Herald's motions as well as he could. They fell somewhat behind the maid.

Now Herald voiced his concern. "Sonics," he murmured low. "Evoke the fundamental instincts. Artificial."

Hweeh lost his stride and almost took a spill despite the stability of the form. "You're right! This time *I* was the blind one!"

The maid slowed, one eye peering back at them. Herald felt the need to cover up. +Hellflower, where are we going?+

+I am S-Anity,+ she said.

+*Not* Hellflower?+ Hweeh asked, chagrined.

+It seems we made an error of identification,+ Herald said. +Apologies.+

+The positive identification is aural,+ she replied after a pause. +I am sure you are the one I want.+

+*I* am the one?+ Herald demanded. +Surely it is my companion who—+

Again that odd little pause. +No. *You* have the aural generation.+

Oh, another conquest of aura. S-Anity's own artificial aura was 150, and the operator was evidently able to spot Herald's higher one. Well, perhaps this was exactly the way true Ancients would have reacted. Find a higher aura, mate with it. Considering his forced betrothal to Flame of Furnace, and his reaction to Psyche when she became enhanced, he could not claim that this was any extraordinary reaction. So the game went on—how far?

Now another Modern joined them, intercepting from a side ramp. +I am S-Elect,+ she announced. +May I augment your party?+

+Since my companion seems to have preempted my female, you are welcome,+ Hweeh said.

A double date? There was something doubly strange about this. What were these females with the different name-codes up to? But Herald did not protest, as he was now quite curious to discover how far such things could go. *Strange* did not necessarily mean *wrong*. Maybe the enclave personnel wanted to show off their talents for the visitors, though it still seemed unlikely that these talents could actually include what was being implied.

S-Anity led them into an upper aperture of a small building. The door shut behind them. A private trysting-spot?

They faced a ring of male androids. There was nothing frivolous in the attitude of these strangers. Herald abruptly realized that he and Hweeh were in trouble.

+Meet some of the members of Unit Nine,+ S-Anity said. +Be-nine, Sta-nine, Leo-nine, Qui-nine.+

+I don't comprehend,+ Hweeh said.

"These creatures are not Moderns," Herald told him tersely. "They are from the Amoeba."

"The Amoeba! How—?"

"Now don't go into shock! We have to get out of here! The Amoeba has intercepted the control beams of the androids, so they are now operated from an Amoeba ship. Hence their delay in responding. It takes time for the signal, since it must travel at light speed. They mean to destroy us."

"But *why?*"

"Because they believe we can tap the science of the Ancients. And if *they* believe that, perhaps they have reason."

"So they have taken over the enclave just to abolish us?"

"This part of the enclave, at any rate. They seem to be trying to act covertly. There must have been a reprimand about the blatant laser attack on the Mars site. If they took over the whole enclave, the Pin and Wheel officials would be suspicious. So the Amoeba intercepted only a few androids, and lured us into their power."

"That is correct," S-Anity said.

"Now they have deciphered our code," Hweeh said. "That is why they stood idle and let us talk; they are studying us."

Herald surveyed the situation. There were six Amoeba-controlled androids, counting the two females, against two of them. "The ship must be orbiting at some distance, to remain undetected. Planetary detectors should pick up anything within a quarter light-second. So these androids must suffer a lag of half a second in reaction to any action of ours, unless they anticipate us. They can't have any weapons, for those are not part of the enclave."

"I comprehend," Hweeh said. "If we move rapidly—"

"However, we have locked you in this room," S-Anity said. "It will take you longer than half a second to break out."

Herald rolled to the window. It was a three-story drop to the ground here, and the landing looked hard. Perhaps not fatal, but certainly crippling.

"You think to turn off and leap?" Sta-nine inquired. "We have other operatives below. They will dismantle you before you can turn on again."

Turn off? Turn on? Something nagged at Herald's mind. Did the Amoebites believe there was a mechanism within the androids to enable the occupants to survive such a jump unscathed? They should know better! "You of the Amoeba are sapient," he said. "So are we of the Cluster. Why do you seek to destroy us?"

"You are weed-species interfering with the development of soul sapience," S-Anity replied. "The weeds must be cleared from the garden."

Weed-species? Sapients? Again that concept! But while the Ancients had eliminated non-Kirlian sapients, the Amoeba seemed to be eliminating Kirlians. Which didn't make sense.

The four -9's rolled toward them. Evidently the -9's were the action specialists, and the -S's were the intellectual ones. That might reduce the odds; intellectuals often did not fight well. The problem was, Herald of Slash and Hweeh of Weew were also intellectuals.

Herald rolled quickly across to touch Hweeh. He exerted his aura, focusing all his healing power. *"What is the nature of the Amoeba?"* he cried. Whatever secrets the Weew had hidden in his shock-protected unconscious had to be brought out now. "Why do they speak of 'turning off'?"

Hweeh shuddered in his android-vehicle. Herald concentrated, willing away the threatening shock. If there were *any* key to escape, Hweeh had it—and there would be no later opportunities. Hweeh had grown steadily more able to face the concept of the Amoeba and the disaster it represented. Had he healed enough?

The -9's closed in, their arms reaching out. Once they got a firm hold, the half-second response-delay would mean little. Strange that they did not merely hurl themselves forward, bashing the two androids against the wall, smashing the flesh-bodies inside. Remote-controlled androids were expendable, so they had an inherent advantage to offset their reflex liability.

@I remember!@ Hweeh cried, reverting to his own mode. Herald did not comprehend Weew speech, and had no translator here in the enclave, but his aural rapport brought the meaning through. This happened in times of special emotional intensity and was another aspect of Kirlianism that had yet to be properly understood. @ *The Amoeba is non-Kirlian!* @

Non-Kirlian! Suddenly it was all clear. The Ancients had eliminated the non-Kirlian sapients from the Cluster, but elsewhere in the Universe there had to be Clusters where the non-Kirlians had eliminated the Kirlians. This was a universal struggle between the two forms of intelligent life! Now the sapients without auras were returning, and they had a terrible score to settle, three million years in the making, and no mercy could be expected. No wonder Hweeh had gone into shock. He had glimpsed the phenomenal magnitude of this struggle, and known that it was not a war between Clusters, but war between two completely incompatible cultures—and that the other side had an overwhelming advantage.

Then Herald realized the concomitant truth: *the Amoebites could not Transfer!* Only aura creatures could Transfer their living personalities. That was why the Ancients had been able to spread and conquer so rapidly, with no apparent damage to the Cluster; their non-Kirlian enemies had had to move between systems using a thousand times the energy, and could not compete on the Cluster scale.

But it also meant that the same no-quarter struggle was upon them now, as it had been three million years ago: The Kirlians might be willing to coexist, but the Amoeba had to extinguish *all* Kirlian life. Aural sapience with its inherently unmatchable mobility represented the most dire possible threat to non-Kirlians. The campaign would be absolutely ruthless! Had Herald been a Weew, he would surely have gone into shock himself; even as a Slash he felt a bit dizzy.

Shock? Sure enough, the Weew had done it again, despite Herald's aura. The android body went still as Hweeh lost consciousness. Now it was *one* against four or six—for the salvation of the Cluster, and perhaps all Kirlian life!

+One has turned off!+ S-Anity announced. +Secure the other!+

Turned off: become unconscious. To a non-Kirlian this would mean complete stilling of body functions, like a machine without power. Not death, but temporary cessation.

And Herald had his third revelation, this one personal.

He charged the window, shoving aside the grasping android pincers. That half-second pause inhibited them just enough. Had those been Amoeba-designed androids, they might have incorporated short-circuit mechanisms to enable them to respond in preset emergency patterns. But these were borrowed units, with liabilities. He smashed his pincers at the transparent sheet, shattering it. The enclave builders had not expected this sort of deliberate stress, or they would have used unshatterable material.

He drew back as the androids charged, then he shoved forward again, toward the opening. The androids leaped to intercept him before he could scramble through. This much they had anticipated, and their move was well timed.

But Herald's two forward skates struck the wall just below the window, as intended. His jointed legs bent under his impetus, then sprang back. He launched himself violently in the opposite direction, directly into the group of androids.

They were caught by surprise. Herald bowled them over, literally. The half-second delay prevented sufficiently rapid recovery of equilibrium for figures knocked off balance to this extent. They skidded across the room, tangling each other, skates spinning in air.

Herald went for the door, but its lock resisted him. He tried to force it open, but it was stronger than his pincers. Naturally the Amoeba would have made sure it was tight! The two S- females, Anity and Elect, scooted over to grab him. Apparently they were not certain the door would hold.

He charged them, needing to maintain his personal freedom of motion. The -9 males were already extricating their limbs from the tangle and scrambling back to their skates. What was he to do?

He caught S-Anity in two appendages, pushing and twisting to upend her. He was only partly successful; one of his pincers snagged in her skirt, ripping it off. He did what he knew was foolish: he looked. And saw—nothing. He had been right all along: the androids had no sexual appurtenances.

S-Elect grabbed him from behind. He must have paused more than half a second, idiot that he was! He spun about, controlling her because he could shift his balance faster than she could shift hers to counter him. He flung her away from him, into the rising group of -9's. Again they all went down in a tangle.

So far he had had the best of it. But so long as he remained confined, theirs was the advantage. They could be disabled but not killed; he was mortal.

He banged against the door, making a loud clatter. "Turn off the power!" he screamed. "Turn off! Turn off!"

"Turning off won't save you now," Sta-9 said, approaching. "We shall dismantle your generator and take it with us."

His generator? Surely they did not think he was merely another android! His aural generator was himself! Yet if they *did* confuse the matter, they might think he had a special model, that generated a higher Kirlian aura, with a more realistic pattern. Ordinary machine auras could not key open Ancient sites, so if he seemed to have a machine that *could*— Yes, they would want to investigate that!

S-Anity skated toward him. Stripped of her skirt, she was just another Modern, but he couldn't concentrate on escape while being harassed by a mobile Amoebite. He could not keep bowling them over; soon he would get bowled over himself.

She grabbed for him. He waltzed her around, hoping to use her as a baffle against the others. Suddenly he realized that he had made another mistake: He had been yelling in the wrong language, the one the enclave couldn't translate.

≈Turn off! ≈ he cried in Pin. *θTurn off!θ* in Wheel.

§Turn off!§ in Sculp. +Turn off!+ in Plus. And for good measure, several times in Clustric.

Nothing happened. They closed on him again, and this time they were braced against any surprise charge. He spun S-Anity into them, but she took out only one android. Herald knew he had to fight limb to limb—and that he had no reasonable chance.

Unless in the melee he could release his Sculp host from the android body, and sneak across the floor and out the window while the Amoebites took apart the android. They wanted the equipment that they thought enhanced his aura so well, so they could not afford to smash it. Even if his quiescence made them think he had turned off, they still would not want to rush it. That might give him time. Sculps had excellent climbing ability; he might scale the outer wall. It was a serious risk, but—

He tried it, and discovered that it was difficult to open the android from inside; it was intended to be serviced from the outside. And how could he escape this shell without being observed? Maybe he could arrange one more tangle. . . .

Three -9's grabbed him, clamping on firmly. He could not free himself this time! The half-second advantage was nullified by the mindless grip. Now the fourth -9 was returning to open his android, and he could not possibly avoid—

All the androids suddenly froze in place.

Herald shuddered with relief. His plea had been heard! The masters of the enclave had realized that something was wrong, and had cut off the beamed power to the androids. The Amoebites might be in control of these units, but they would not be able to make them operate without that power. Maybe the Amoeba ship would be able to beam down its own power, but that would be chancy because the local power monitors would light up and the ship would soon be located and attacked. Probably by that time Herald and Hweeh would have escaped anyway, and the androids would be in custody of the enclave authorities.

He heard help coming: the clack of Pins, the hum of Wheels. He had saved himself, but it would count for nothing if he did not use his information to prepare the willfully blind Cluster for the battle against the Amoeba.

271

The enemy was handicapped by its lack of Transfer ability—but the enemy had a million heavily armed ships, and the means to mattermit them across the Cluster. Only the science of the Ancients could stop such a thrust —and there was only one way to achieve that science in time.

This was the third revelation he had suffered: to realize that he would have to take Melody of Mintaka's advice seriously, subordinating his personal revulsion to the needs of his society. He would have to enter a functioning Ancient site—the same one Melody had entered—and hope to learn its secrets before the Amoeba blasted it. He had been resistant to the notion, because it seemed to constitute a betrayal of both his personal resolve to stay away from Flame of Furnace, and his love for Psyche. But now he had to do it. In fact, he should have done it before, instead of coming here.

11

Cluster of Sites

*X*Contact by units S and 9 severed. Enemy has discovered our presence.*X*

&Then we must act. Accelerate full-scale mattermission to heartworlds of all Cluster sapients. Withhold final action until placement is complete, unless individual ships are attacked.&

*0*Mission proceeds, virtually complete. Overt action shall be coordinated by schedule. Is it still necessary to hold, pending reverification for soul sapience?*0*

&Correct. It is to be regretted that precipitous action is contemplated, but the outcome is not in question. We shall reverify if events do not make this unfeasible.&

*0*Problem of logistics. Unit 1, presently on watch by ancient site of planet *£*, now required for main thrust.*0*

&The main thrust is preemptive. Reassign unit 1. The enemy has shown no sign of activating that site, and even if this occurred now, there would not be time for them to draw sufficient advantage from it before our action hour.&

Herald lifted his three great feet in turn, getting the feel of his massive new host. This was a *£*, rather like the triped Moderns skaters, but fully living, sapient, and much larger. The *£* were the giants of Sphere Dash, Andromeda, and were among the largest sapients anywhere in the Cluster. For a long time they had been treated as virtual slaves by the more technological, but not more civilized, birds of Dash. But now they had come into their own, and though the labors they performed were much the same as before, and many utilized the supervision of Dash mahouts, there was no question to whom this world belonged. The £ still preferred lives of brute physical work coupled with esthetic mental interactions. The birds were tolerated to the extent they facilitated this by assuming the tedious direction of the physical program, but it was no longer against law or custom for individual £ to be without mahouts, or to wander wherever they chose.

Here on Planet £ was the finest functioning Ancient site known. Herald only hoped it was not yet known to the Amoeba. If it was, he was about to commit suicide. And maybe that would be fitting.

He whirled his body slowly, setting his feet down in order, progressing along the trail to the great bog of jelly. Melody of Mintaka had trod a similar trail a thousand years ago, on her way to the first opening of this site, and the resulting victory for her Galaxy. Could Herald do likewise?

Now he was descending into the bog. The atmosphere thickened into viscosity, impeding progress, but his host was adequate to the need. Herald regretted leaving the prismatic feather trees behind. He knew they broke the sunlight into its component hues so that each species could utilize its particular wavelength, but to him it was a tremendously artistic thing, a wilderness mural in light. The bog, in contrast, was deepening into gray, then black, as all light was excluded. He had to use senses other than sight to avoid the greater nether branches of the lattice that crisscrossed the bog at different levels, and he also stayed clear of the aromatic scentwood trunks, so valuable for construction. He was here for quite another purpose!

What, he wondered, had Melody discovered in this deep site that she refused ever to reveal? Every time he thought he had figured it out, he considered some more and was sure he was still ignorant. It was a bit like Hweeh of Weew's reflex of shock, concealing important information to protect individual or society. Yet did any individual have the right to make such a decision?

Hweeh had gone to a lot of trouble to make this venture of Herald's possible. The Weew had Transferred back to his own Segment to "pull strings" as he put it, causing the Minister of Weew to confer with the Minister of Dash, who in turn allowed this intrusion into this closely guarded region. Perhaps each had been motivated as much by private curiosity about the site, as by the alleged threat to the Cluster that Herald hoped to abate. So he was here, and there would be one other entity here—and he had resolved not only to save the Cluster, but to tell the truth, whatever it might be. Knowledge was the root of all power.

He came at last to the deep site: a depression in the dark liquid bottom of the bog. And here he met his selected partner for the necessary ceremony of admission: a high-Kirlian female Transferred to £ host. For the site opened only in the presence of a super-Kirlian mating. And there was only one such female that the Cluster Council would let him have.

—Hello, Herald of Slash,— she vibrated, her skin making the sound in the liquid medium.

—Hello, Flame of Furnace,— he replied with difficulty. —I regret that we have had to meet in this manner.—

—Apology noted, accepted,— she responded with a certain humor, for she well knew it had been no apology. —I am aware it was not precisely your preference. Had it not been a Cluster imperative, I would not have come.—

Herald touched her briefly with the tip of one tentacle, feeling her aura. It was 190, the strongest natural one he had ever encountered. *Apart from Psyche!* Only one entity in a major galaxy in a thousand years broke 200; she was of the one-in-a-century variety, which was still quite respectable.

—You understand the details?— he asked —The risk?— Maybe she would balk!

—The Amoeba that formed beyond my Galaxy (Furnace was hardly a galaxy, but no doubt its sapients felt otherwise!) will destroy us all if we do not evoke Ancient science to oppose it. The Amoeba may destroy this site as we evoke it. But it may be our only chance, now, for the Amoeba will soon destroy life in the Cluster regardless.—

—you have intelligence and courage,— he said, beginning to soften toward her. This was the female that had stood in the way of his social freedom. He had been ready to perform his duty by her, in order to legitimize his marriage to Psyche, except that he feared Psyche's reaction to that. So he had made application to have the requirement nullified. Then Psyche had died. Flame was in no way to blame for Psyche's fate, yet it was complicated, now, to interact with her. He didn't *want* to like her!

—Not very much courage, Herald. Let us proceed quickly. I fear the strike of the Amoeba.—

Let us proceed. Again that unfortunately sensitive expression, throwing him once more into his chaos of guilt and rationalization. Proceed, as he had proceeded with Jet Sixteen in the purely business mergence that had been invalidated by his later discovery that it had *not* been business for her. The concept had turned him off Hellflower of Modern, and served to gut much of whatever emotion he felt here. Why did he have to suffer these reminders of his errors?

But the Cluster hung in the balance.

—You realize the nature of the ceremony we must perform?—

—Of course. We must mate on the site aperture.—

—Yes. There need be no love in this action, and there *is* none.— But that, too, had an uncomfortable ring, for he had also said it to Sixteen.

—I am glad you understand, Herald.—

Glad *he* understood? The vagaries of the female viewpoint!

They proceeded to it without further discussion; efficient copulation, performed for purely practical consideration. Herald tried to abolish the lurking picture in his mind of Sixteen, who had pretended not to love him so as to leave him free. But it was only replaced by the image of Psyche, void of that pretense but as awkward in its way, for he was betraying her. She lived! She had to live! What use to save the Cluster, if she were not in it?

But in his deeper emotion he knew this was not Psyche, but her antithesis. His copulation puncture mechanism balked. He was sexually impotent.

—I am unable,— Herald admitted. —I love another.—

—I admit to being relieved,— Flame vibrated. —I also love another.—

Was this scripted by Sixteen, or did all females lie on demand? He was sick of all of it! —The survival of our culture requires—

—Herald, I approached this necessity without illusion. Now illusion is developing. I had anticipated a more callous personality in you, one that would never be balked by considerations of feeling. You, after all, are *the* Kirlian, the one like no other ever known, rightfully secure in your arrogance. One never touched by the tragedies of emotion.—

—*That* is illusion!—

—Perhaps. As I perceive a somewhat more feeling entity than I thought existed, my indifference thaws. It may be that I will not regret mating with you, even if the effort proves to be wasted. I had also underestimated the appeal of your fine aura.—

—Then I abate your developing illusion and thawing indifference. I am a healer; my aura makes entities well. If you have suffered, my aura helps alleviate that suffering, in turn allowing the body to heal itself. But this denotes no virtue in me. While we tried, I thought of Psyche, who was burned to death but whom I still love and mean to recover.—

—I thought of Fuel, my love whom I was not permitted to marry because of you, and who perished horribly in a pit of ice.—

She, too! Ice, to the hot sapients of Furnace, was the ultimate horror. —I did not know,— Herald vibrated, sorry, finding that he was coming to believe her. Why should she even *want* to deceive him? Their relation had been defined in their early youth, and what either believed about the other had little relevance. —I blamed the fire, and you are a creature of fire. I wronged you.—

—No more than I wronged you. Fuel was trapped in his pursuit of a heraldic device carved in ice. I associated you with that concept.—

Heraldic device! He felt abrupt sorrow for the fate of Fuel of Furnace, a kindred entity. —Had we understood each other better, we could have discharged this obligation long ago, and both been free. Neither of us were able to consider rationally.—

—It was my error,— she vibrated. —I refused to travel to Sphere Slash. Perhaps I resisted you because my commitment to Fuel was not complete. I used you as a pretext.—

—Don't say that!— Herald vibrated. —You were never false to your love! While I— He broke off, obsessed by the memory of Sixteen. He had made love to the Jet female!

—You were not false to yours, either; I am sure of it.—

—But I *was!* I took a mistress.—

—So you took a mistress! Did you love her?—

—No. She was low aura.—

—Then what does it matter? She represented no possible threat to your love. I could never love a low-Kirlian either. Fuel was one hundred and forty.—

Herald paused, sorting through his mixed feelings, ready to be moved by her logic. It was Kirlian logic! —That's right! I took her as mistress because the occasion necessitated it, and it was inconceivable that she replace Psyche.—

—So you were not false. Herald, I like you better, now. Shall we try again?—

—No!—

—Is your loyalty to the Cluster so slight?—

—I was not false to Psyche. I was false to Sixteen, the low-Kirlian female. She loved me, and I used her. How can I respect myself now?—

—You cannot deceive a sapient female in this manner, not even a low-Kirlian one. She surely knew what she was doing. Knowing love was impossible, she took what was offered. If that is all that restrains you, be reassured.—

Herald considered again, further swayed by her reasoning. But still he balked. —*You* are not low-Kirlian. You are my most likely love in the Cluster. I dare not touch you.—

—I assure you, there is no real danger of love between us! I have not forgotten Fuel of Furnace, and never will. I mentioned him only to explain my situation.—

—You lie, Flame! You loved Fuel because he was the highest aura you encountered, even as I loved Psyche. Had his aura been a mere ten or fifteen, you would never have noticed him, regardless of his other merits. I do not question those merits. I am sure he was deserving, as much so as my Psyche. But it was aura alone that compelled you to choose him from a thousand other deserving entities. Now my aura moves you regardless of your will, as yours moves me. You and I are Kirlians, a type apart. We *can* love each other, and *shall* love each other, if we do not separate soon. *Then* we would both be false.—

—To our dead loves,— she finished with acerbity. —Herald, can it be so wrong? We only recognize reality at last.—

—*My love is not dead!*— he exclaimed, experiencing a wash of emotion that shook him. —She lives, somewhere in this Ancient network, and I must recover her!—

—Very well, she lives. And to free her, you must mate with me. Would you rather leave her locked in the tomb of the Ancients forever?—

Never that! —It is a paradox! To save her, it seems I must betray her!—

—Think of it this way: The fire took her from you. It is fitting that Flame bring her back. If I could restore my Fuel similarly, I would not hesitate.—

—It would be more fitting that my low-Kirlian mistress perform that service.—

—So you *do* love the mistress, too,— Flame vibrated knowingly.

—No!— But honesty compelled him to reconsider. —She has an aura so low it can hardly be measured. As far beneath norm as mine is above it. Yet she is a worthy sapient, intelligent, feeling, competent. I wronged her not by taking her as mistress in my hour of need, but by denying her my love. I think— He broke off for a moment, surprised. —I think Psyche herself would have wanted me to give that love, in that circumstance.—

—There is a corollary.—

He came to it with a certain difficulty. —If she were to grant that love . . . she would by similar token grant *this* love.—

—Our Kirlian nature enables us to compromise,— Flame vibrated. —After this mission is done, if we both survive, and if you have not recovered your high-Kirlian true love, I will on occasion animate your low-Kirlian false love. We need make no apologies for such a liaison.—

—That will not be necessary,— Herald said with sudden decision. —We have our liaison here.—

He found himself potent, and completed the act.

Afterward, they stood together on the Ancient disk, waiting for the site to respond.

—It would be ironic if nothing happened now,— Flame vibrated gently.

—Or if too much happened, like an Amoeba strike,— he added. —But regardless, it was worthwhile, of itself. I love others, but I could love you also, in other circumstances.—

—And I you,— she agreed. —I would not even exclude *this* circumstance.—

—You have helped me to know myself, as my friend Hweeh has done, and to comprehend some of the impact I have on others.—

—Your friend Hweeh?—

—Hweeh of Swees of Segment Weew. He is the leading research astronomer of the Cluster, and a fine intelligent entity, with an aura of one hundred and twenty-five. He enabled me to come here, since this locale is restricted, by exerting influence in his Segment.—

—I thought I recognized the name. The Minister of Furnace told me that he was acting on behalf of the clearance made by an astronomer of Weew. I had wondered how Weew etered the picture.—

—That is a long story. The threat of the Amoeba is being contemplated by a Cluster committee, and—

—A committee! Are they serious?—

—That's why we had to—

He was interrupted suddenly.

The disk on which they stood started to sink; the site was opening!

—Suppose we remain locked inside forever, as Melody of Milky Way and Dash of Andromeda were?— Flame inquired nervously.

—This I would define as an 'other circumstance,'— he vibrated. —Then we should be lovers, eternally.—

—No offense intended to you, but I prefer that we complete the mission.—

The aperture spiraled closed above them as they spiraled down. Gas pushed out the water. They stood in a bare cylindrical chamber.

The wall faded into inchoate color. This was a form of animation: reflection of the thoughts of the visitors, overlapping each other until they controlled it.

Now they could not converse sonically, for the £ hide did not vibrate properly in air. But Herald knew what to do. He summoned a controlled animation: a visio-sonic communications unit. The thing rolled into proximity from the nebulous background.

"Communicate," Herald made it say in Clustric, as the machine-screen formed his own image, a Slash.

"Where are the bones?" Flame asked in the same language. Her self-image was of a winding tongue of fire. Her body was semisolid, but its surface bore oil that burned, providing heat energy for the internal functions. She was beautiful.

"Bones?"

"The hosts of Melody and Dash never emerged from this site. Only their auras returned. After a thousand years, the £ bodies—" The screen showed a pile of huge £ bones in disarray, with little incendiary flies, fireflies, scorching out bits of desiccated flesh. Her image of death.

Grisly thought! "The remains could have been incinerated completely or dissolved by the site maintenance mechanism. Or they might have been preserved intact by inert gas, sterile, and lifted to the surface on the same platform-shift that brought us down here. We are not in a position to know."

"Strange that a creature as cognizant as Melody of Mintaka should desert her innocent host in a place like this, permitting her to die of hunger and confinement."

That bothered Herald too. "What happened to the two prior hosts?" he demanded of the image-machine. Maybe the site itself would answer.

It did. By a rapid series of images it told how the £ had been given suitable food refined by the site equipment, and granted visions of all the beautiful things they could imagine, creating a kind of perceptual paradise. It was not reality, but it had been a good deal more satisfying than many realities were. They had lived a long time before dying natural deaths.

"It was an idle question," Flame said. "But I am glad to have the answer. It seems the Ancients were not cruel." She looked about at the changing images around them. "We should get on with the mission, before the Amoeba does. I suffer premonitions of impending doom."

"It is not necessary for you to risk yourself further," Herald told her. "Now that you have enabled me to enter the site, you can Transfer directly back to your natural host in Furnace, assured that your £ host will not suffer."

Her image flared with irritation. "While the Amoeba bombs this site and attempts to eliminate you," she replied. "If the enemy succeeds, the entire Cluster will be sterilized, including Furnace. I have nothing to gain by going home before the job is done."

Herald liked her better and better. "Then help me search. I must discover the technology of the Ancients, and how to apply it rapidly, and get that information to Cluster specialists. You can zero in on the secret Melody of Mintaka would not tell. It must have relevance to the contemporary situation."

"Let me remain here, interrogating the unit. You must Transfer elsewhere, where the Amoeba cannot trace you."

She was offering to be decoy, and he had to accept. "If the site is attacked, go home immediately," he told her. "I will Transfer to my own body in Slash, or some other convenient host, from whatever site I occupy."

"You will occupy a *site*? There would be no host there!"

No *living* host. His whole personal quest was based on the assumption that the sites could be occupied by auras. If Psyche lived, she was in an Ancient site, using it as a host, maintaining herself through constant enhancement of her aura. If *she* had done it, *he* could do it. If she had not then he did not want to live. This was the critical test. "My aura will imbue the Ancient equipment itself. I will have its secrets . . . from within."

"May you succeed," the image-Flame whispered, amazed. She did not say what she obviously thought: *impossible.*

He concentrated. *Take me to a safe site with usable machines,* he thought, hardly expecting it to be this easy.

He was in deep space. *Deep* deep space! Intergalactic space, perhaps inter-Cluster space.

He rotated, guiding his orientation by willpower, since he had no body. Now he saw a Galaxy, so far away it resembled a diffuse star. It was Andromeda! Or the Milky Way, or some other great Galaxy of the Universe.

Was he lost in some far Cluster? He had not anticipated *this!*

How was he able to see, since he had no body? None of this made much sense.

He examined his situation more closely. Now he turned his lens on it. His apparatus was a conglomeration of antennae, baffles, and refractive fields. A functioning Ancient machine, in a safe location. A million light-years from the nearest Galaxy. Well, he had asked for it!

His aura had animated the machine. *It was possible!* He was now a robot in space. No one suspected that the Ancients had left functioning equipment out here! Not that it made much difference, as no telescope could resolve so small an object at such a range. No physical ships would be traveling out here. It would take them at least two million years to get this far, and any that did that not only had to be freezers, they had to predate all contemporary cultures by two million years, and postdate the Ancients by one million years, which meant they could not exist anyway. Even the survey Net could not pick this up. The Net did not go this far out, and the receivers were not nearly sensitive enough. Only freak luck would show a spaceborne extra-Galactic Ancient site, which was why this one was safe from discovery by Cluster entities—or the Amoeba.

If he could report the site's precise location, the Cluster Council could have their experts attempt to tune it in, and mattermit a specialized crew here.

Mattermit?

Yes, this *was* a mattermission station. He recognized it as such because he was *of* it. It was also a Transfer station intended for energy transport. Evidently the Ancients had Transferred a sapient entity along with their shipments of energy, to supervise operations. Though what they were doing way out here in nowhere was not clear.

This might be the only surviving space station, or there might be hundreds, some much more conveniently placed for investigation by Cluster experts. He would have to perform a survey. He had already established that a high-aura creature *could* occupy Ancient equipment; therefore victory on both Cluster and personal fronts was within reach. The Cluster could achieve Ancient science, which was turning out to be even more marvelous than he had really dared hope, and he could recover Psyche. Maybe this was where the Ancients themselves had gone: into their own equipment! Unfortunately, they had not been able to reproduce themselves there— No, they would not be such fools! All would soon be known. But until he knew where he was, he could not accomplish much.

Location: exactly where *was* he? He needed some sort of spatial coordinates, precise ones. Was there orientation equipment here? There should be . . . and there was. As he thought of it, this subunit became functional. He focused his scopes and antennae, becoming aware how marvelously efficient they were, and in moments had his answer.

He was at the fringe of the Cluster ellipsoid, and the Galaxy he saw was Milky Way.

He noted his position as precisely as possible, then concentrated again: *nearest other functioning unit.*

And found himself in orbit about Cloud 9. In an instant he had jumped another million light-years. The implication was plain: However many Ancient units had been in Cluster space originally, few remained now. That suggested a fair attrition rate. The machines were *not* perfect. Not quite.

How many such stations had there been originally? He could not tell; the information was not in the Ancient memory banks. These were functional sites, not memory-storage units. Probably a landbound site, such as the one he and Flame had entered, would be more complete. Maybe she was getting all the information they needed while he wasted his time traveling.

But he still needed to identify the ones that remained. Not only would analysis of their equipment offer the Cluster parity with the Amoeba—and perhaps superiority—but each could be an excellent base for launching attacks against the enemy. It would take the best Cluster industries a significant period to build sophisticated new equipment along Ancient lines, even given full blueprints, assuming the Cluster Council ever let the blueprints get out of committee. In that period the Amoeba could overrun it all. It would be necessary to use the stations already in place to stave off the enemy thrust until the new weapons were ready.

Still, why mattermit technicians out to a space station, if there were planetbound ones available? If he could find one, and get news out about its location before the Amoeba struck, they might get a Cluster battlefleet into position to protect it. Those energy-globe Amoeba ships were effective, but they would find armed Cluster battleships to be much more of a challenge than an unarmed archaeological mission!

He considered the geography of the Cluster. Where would a planetary site be most accessible to the natives, and least accessible to the Amoeba? Not in deep space, certainly! But Amoeba ships had come to Planet Keep and Planet Mars within the Milky Way Galaxy, so a Galaxy was no protection either. And he had fought, as it were, hand to hand with the Amoebites in the globular cluster orbiting Pinwheel. They might be non-Kirlian, but they could certainly get around. Probably the Amoeba could strike anywhere, and within minutes. Except perhaps at a major Cluster military base, or a fleet of battleships. . . .

A military base? Why not? Technology alone made the Amoeba superior. Nullify that, and the advantage would swing firmly to the Kirlian Cluster. At a military base, it would be a straight one-to-one combat without frills. The Amoeba's technological sophistication would be matched by the sheer firepower of the base.

But how would the Ancient equipment know where contemporary bases were? The Ancients had put together their Empire three million years before such bases had been established. Unless the Ancient equipment monitored such things. . . .

No harm in trying, anyway. So far he, like other contemporary entities, had consistently underestimated the capacities of the sites. He might find out more by investigating the instruction banks of the equipment itself, but this was like delving into a host-memory: tedious and time-consuming. Easier to make it operate in its own fashion. He wanted his answers *now*, before the Amoeba struck.

He willed—and was there. In a planetary site near a military base. He looked out of his lens and saw—

A Jet.

So he had reached a site in Sphere Jet, Sixteen's globular Cluster home near the black hole. Of course the Ancients had been here, since they had taken the trouble to isolate the low-aura Jets. Well, the Jets were part of civilization now, fully sapient and with more aura than they had had three million years ago. Too bad they had not known about this Ancient site in their midst.

Too bad for *them;* perhaps fortunate for the rest of the Cluster. Had they discovered this site a million years ago, the Jets would have become the Cluster enemy!

Not known? He was looking into a chamber of the site itself. The Jet was inside the site!

Maybe the Jets did not realize its significance. They might think it was merely an interesting artifact. He would contact them.

How? He was in the Ancient circuitry, his aura little more than a current within it. As Psyche's aura must be, somewhere. Getting in direct touch with a creature outside this circuitry was a problem. He had no living host to step into, unless he tried for the Jet himself, and he hesitated to do that yet. It might only foment confusion.

Well, he could operate the equipment to a certain extent, as he had done in space, turning perceptors about. Could he make this machine speak?

He tried. *Attention,* he thought. Too bad there was not a vision screen or animation chamber here. He could really communicate with one of those!

The Jet in his view reacted. It wooshed something in an unfamiliar language. Certainly not the language Sixteen had used briefly, =, and no variant of it; the fundamental precepts and inflections differed.

But then Herald's circuits meshed, and meaning came through. And the invocation of those special circuits told him something else. This language was related to that of the Ancients themselves, for the equipment could comprehend it directly.

No . . . it had to be a full translation rendered *into* Ancient by this amazingly sophisticated site. Naturally it seemed like Ancient to him, at the receiving end. The reason he had not understood the Jet original was that the modern language was not immediately comprehensible either to him or to the Ancient equipment. It had to be classified and rendered into machine-language. The Ancients would have understood the speech of Jet three million years ago, so the equipment could trace its considerable evolution.

Other Jets appeared. They operated the inputs. Naturally they were curious about this manifestation of the site. He was curious about *them,* too. If they understood this equipment well enough to tune the controls, why hadn't they understood it well enough to Transfer to the main centers of the Cluster, instead of remaining in isolation? They could not have discovered this site just in the past day; they moved around in it with too much familiarity.

Of course. They were low-Kirlian and so could not Transfer. Still, why hadn't they told the Cluster Council about this site, knowing how important it was? Were they saving it for their own use, contrary to Cluster policy?

Herald decided on caution. He really knew the Jets only from the one archaeological expedition on Planet Mars, and from Sixteen. That had been a separated group, reared in the Galaxy. Their home culture in Sphere Glob might

286

be quite different, with secrets and motives unsuspected by other Clusterites. These Jets might not be quite as friendly as he had thought at first. If he had been a member of a culture restricted to a globular Cluster, adjacent to a dangerous black hole, for three million years, how would *he* feel about outsiders? Particularly when the first outsiders had done the restricting and the later outsiders had alleviated it only to the extent of taking (and never returning) sapients as samples for study. No question about it: He would be extremely cynical about the motives of aliens!

Now their dialogue filtered through to him. ⫶⫶⫶The machine spoke! Is it a communication from the ancient ones? ⫶⫶⫶

Not the = of Sphere Jet, but the ⫶⫶⫶ of the site. A full translation! He was already coming to comprehend the Ancient mode better.

⫶⫶⫶No. Consider the readings. There is an abnormality in the machine. It is very old; such problems are to be expected.⫶⫶⫶

Time to get in touch, since they were now aware of him anyway. As they were low-Kirlian, they could not get at him even if they weren't friendly.

No abnormality, he willed. *I am Herald the Healer of Sphere Slash, Andromeda.*

⫶⫶⫶It must be a recording,⫶⫶⫶a Jet said.

⫶⫶⫶No, the readings indicate aural flow in excess of aperture-keying intensity. A definite malfunction.⫶⫶⫶

⫶⫶⫶Eliminate it. It is vital that the unit be properly functional for Action Hour.⫶⫶⫶

⫶⫶⫶This is difficult without risking damage to the apparatus. These ancient devices are of borderline reliability. ⫶⫶⫶

They didn't believe him! *Idiots, I am Herald, Kirlian sapient. This site must be made available to Cluster experts immediately.*

⫶⫶⫶Inanimate consciousness? ⫶⫶⫶ a Jet exclaimed.
⫶⫶⫶Notify X!⫶⫶⫶

Not inanimate consciousness! Herald blared. *I am a living creature. Speak to me!*

⫶⫶⫶The site has developed self-consciousness! ⫶⫶⫶ a Jet cried, horrified.⫶⫶⫶We must destroy it!⫶⫶⫶

Oh, oh. Herald decided to shift location; he was making reverse progress here. *Another site near a military base,* he willed.

The Jets vanished. Where was this site? He extended his

287

awareness. It was in Sphere Duocirc, Andromeda. %. But—

Within the site were more Jets.

Something was wrong. Jets could not be here in an undiscovered site in the heart of Galaxy Andromeda! Unless. . . .

Where was the last site? he inquired with sudden suspicion.

And had the answer from his Ancient circuits: Sphere Slash, Andromeda. *Not* Glob Jet, but his own home region!

The Jets, verifying their gauges, became aware of him.
::: There is a disturbance in the equipment! :::.

Herald willed himself to another site: the one at Glob Jet. The real one.

He bounced. There was no such site.

::: Message from X: Be on alert for machine consciousness in functioning ancient sites. :::

If there were no site in Glob Jet, how had the Jets gotten here? They must have infiltrated the Cluster, somehow locating sites that no other species was aware of.

But the Jets could only have done this by using the sites themselves, as Herald was doing now. Not by Transfer, for them, but by mattermission. Perhaps one of their archaeological teams had uncovered a functioning site, giving them entry into the entire system? And they had used that site for their own purposes, instead of giving the invaluable secret to the Cluster. Now, in the face of the crucial threat by the Amoeba, the Jets were *still* keeping the secret, though they had to know how vital it was for the very existence of Kirlian life. Which side were they really on?

Then Herald perceived what he had missed before: These Jets differed in detail from those he had known. They had a different taper on the fuselage, a distinct pattern of coloration, and thicker support fibers. They were in fact a separate variety of Jet, perhaps a distinct subspecies. No wonder their speech and manner were strange!

::: This unit possesses alien consciousness! :::

Herald wished himself away again. This time he landed in Sphere Magnet of Segment Etamin, Milky Way, a station hidden in an orbiting planetoid. No Jets here, fortunately!

Strange that these hostile Jets had not infused their auras into the mechanism of the sites, as he had done, so they could chase him down directly. That was the obvious

288

course, instead of trying to track him by reading their instruments. Of course, Jets were low-Kirlian, so could not ordinarily Transfer, but this was not an ordinary situation. The Ancient equipment possessed the power of enhancement, so that even very weak auras could be elevated to Transfer strength. Now *any* Kirlian creature could Transfer! They must have discovered this. If they really wanted to catch him. . . .

A Jet appeared in the mattermission aperture. That was another thing: Why did they mattermit so freely? The expense of energy, when Cluster distances were involved, was criminal. The Ancients must have given their equipment huge reserves, but the Ancients were no longer present to restore that energy as it was depleted by wasteful use, and these fabulous sites would inevitably become nonfunctional in time. If these Jets had the finesse to use all these supposedly undiscovered sites, surely they knew the value of energy!

Herald investigated. He concentrated himself in the circuitry adjacent to the control panel and extended his aura into the volume of space the Jet would occupy as he operated these controls.

Sure enough, the Jet came. Herald tuned in on the typically small aura he knew was there—but it was *not* there.

Either he had lost his ability to perceive fractional auras —or this entity *had* no aura.

No aura at all?

He gave it one more try. He drew on the resources of the equipment, enhancing his own aura to almost three hundred, and spread a more powerful perceptive net. If anything, even a millionth of norm, were there, he would pick it up.

Nothing was there. His field spread through purely mechanical channels. No electrical or semielectrical nervous system at all. It would be impossible for any entity to Transfer into such a host.

Slowly the truth registered. *This species of Jet was not small-aura, it was null-aura.* No wonder they used mattermission: even with the potential of enhancement, they could never Transfer. No wonder they followed Herald only by instrument. The Ancient equipment could detect his Kirlian frame, but this Jet variety was inherently incapable of it.

Non-Kirlian sapience! Completely without aura, yet

fully intelligent and competent. He had the proof at last, from direct experience; such species *did* exist in the Cluster. Perhaps the Jets of Sixteen's species knew about this, but had concealed it, fearing their cousins would be destroyed, as all other non-Kirlian sapients had been three million years ago. Now, with the coming of the Amoeba, they could act at last.

:::Alien consciousness manifests in this unit!:::the Jet exclaimed.

And through the Ancient unit came the answer::::Destroy unit!:::

They were playing for keeps, these sudden allies of the enemy! The Jet nudged the master power switch—and Herald willed himself back to Sphere Slash, Andromeda. Now he knew why Psyche dared not reveal herself. Cutting the power of his equipment would destroy any aura within it.

He arrived safely. His £ host stood in the communication chamber, beside that of Flame's host. Apparently the non-Kirlian Jets had not yet discovered his point of origin.

He hopped quickly into the host. The Jets were no doubt querying the site network about his location. If he got out before they caught up, they might lose him entirely. This particular site had no mattermission facilities, perhaps because there could be so few receivers for creatures this size. It was pure Kirlian. That was a big help. Neither the non-Kirlian Jets nor the non-Kirlian Amoeba could strike directly, physically, here.

Non-Kirlian Jets, non-Kirlian Amoebites—how could he have missed it. Once more he had been blind to the obvious. *These strange Jets* were *the Amoebites!* Non-Kirlian sapience from another Cluster of the Universe.

Where was Flame? Her host was here, but if her aura had followed his into the Ancient equipment. . . .

The flame of Flame appeared in the screen in the holographic image. "Herald? Is that you?"

"Yes! We must depart instantly. The Amoeba has taken over the Ancient network of sites. We must get out, for this is the one site they cannot invade physically. Don't go in the circuitry, because they may turn it off by remote control."

"Herald, I know! But I must tell you—"

"*Move!* Or it is death—for us *and* Cluster! Activate the surfacing mechanism!"

290

"Herald, *I have found Psyche!*"

His whole £ body stiffened, almost falling against the panoramic wall. "You *believe?* Others think I delude myself about her survival—"

"I *know!* I doubted, but I saw you actually enter the machine, so I tried it myself. While you led the Amoeba a merry chase across the Cluster, distracting them, I surveyed quietly for her aura, and the Ancient net told me. She *did* inhabit the sites, her aura alone, enhanced. Hers *was* the highest aura ever—"

A pattern of interference rippled across the screen. The image of a Jet appeared. :::: Activated site discovered! :::: it exclaimed. :::: The £ site! ::::

"The Amoeba has found us!" Herald cried.

"Transfer directly out—now!" Flame screamed, her image wavering high and yellow. "The Cluster needs you. We can't escape physically; they will control the mechanism."

"We both must Transfer out! You go home to Furnace; I'll go to Slash!"

"Yes!" she agreed. "Then we will each report to the Council!"

He concentrated . . . and felt the power of the site take hold. But as it started, another ripple of interference came. The Amoeba could not use the Kirlian properties directly, but could perceive the activity of this unit via their instruments. Now it was throwing up machine-Kirlian blocks to cut them off. If Herald made it through to his Slash body, his aura would be so garbled that he would be insane.

Flame's aura plunged into the circuitry, driving back the interference momentarily, clearing the way for him. "Go, Herald, go!" she cried, her flame image flickering with the desperate effort.

He had to go, knowing that she, choosing to facilitate his Transfer, had trapped herself instead. He shifted his destination to his Solarian host on Planet Keep, since the Amoeba had overheard his Slash destination and blocked it off. He tried to draw Flame along with him, but could not. There was no available female host on that section of the planet. All he got was a part of her, a final faint message: *Psyche . . . at . . . Amoeba!*

He had delayed too long. The Amoebites had cut him off again. They were operating the circuits, narrowing down his options, beating down Flame's valiant resistance.

Non-Kirlian they might be, but they certainly knew how to operate this Kirlian equipment! One last chance—

He shifted destinations again. And suddenly, as his identity was wrenched from the troubled circuitry of the site, and from the beautiful entity he *could* have loved, who had forfeited her own chance to escape for him, he suffered the most momentous realization of all. The intellectual impact was such as to numb his mind. He had now explored the Ancient equipment even further than Melody of Mintaka had, and knew what she had discovered. *He knew the secret of the Ancients*—and knew despair.

12

Amoeba of Space

*X*We are discovered!*X*

*&*It does not matter. The weed-species cannot mobilize in time to take effective resistance. We shall proceed on schedule.*&*

*X*What of the reverification?*X*

*&*We must do it if we can. Should it be convenient to pick up any sapients for this purpose, we shall do so.*&*

*X*But we shall not delay action hour for this purpose.*X*

*&*We shall not delay it.*&*

Herald found himself in the Jet host on Mars.

The host was weak, of course. He had not yet recovered from either the physical injury or Herald's strenuous travels around the planet. He was under continued medical care, inactive, as the Jet archaeologists still labored to salvage artifacts from the bombed site. But he *was* recovering —and Herald had no intention of complicating his health again.

"Bring me Sixteen," he said.

The medic balked, not realizing who was speaking through the host. "She cannot be disturbed."

Herald forced his ailing host to move. "This is critical. Read the aural indicator, perceive my identity. My mission is to save the Cluster from invasion." *And to recover Psyche!* he added mentally. He honestly could not tell which was more important to him at the moment—or whether there was really any chance of doing either. No wonder Melody had kept her silence. He now knew more

293

about the Ancients than she did, and the situation differed: It was correspondingly worse.

The medic yielded. He summoned Sixteen.

She came, jetting very slowly and with poor control. "Herald," she said with a gust of gladness. "I thought I would not encounter you again."

Suddenly Herald was ashamed. "Sixteen is your illness because of me? Do you require healing?"

"No illness, Herald. I brought it on myself—"

"I have mistreated you; and now I propose to aggravate it."

"You misunderstand. I always knew—"

"My legal fiancée, Flame of Furnace, gave up her freedom, perhaps her very identity, to promote my welfare. Only through her agency was I able to return here, escaping the Amoeba. Now I must ask you to do the same."

"I will, Herald, I will! Yet—"

"This also you must know: Flame located . . . my dead wife. Psyche is alive."

"She—not dead?"

"Psyche's aura survives. It is imprisoned in the equipment of the Amoeba which now ties into that of the Ancient sites, because the Amoeba has taken over those sites. I must go to the Amoeba to fetch her out. My true love."

"No wonder your legal fiancée died!" 16 said.

No wonder! He did not even try to justify it morally; he simply had to do it. "Will you help me?"

"Herald, I am . . . I can't—" She broke off. "How may I help you?"

"I need a host for Psyche. To bring her back. Because she no longer has any body of her own."

Sixteen considered. Herald blanked his mind to what might be going through *her* mind. "To be the host . . . for your dead true love. To make her live again."

"It is also an extremely dangerous mission. We may both die. We face a situation that may be impossible to accomplish. We go to the heart of the Amoeba itself."

"Yes," she said slowly. "If I do this, I must either die, or yield my body to . . . to another female."

"Sixteen, I know you love me!" Herald blurted. "You told me you loved Hweeh of Weew, but you lied. I . . . do not love you. It is a terrible thing I ask of you. But such is my desperation, I ask it anyway. The Amoebites resemble Jets; perhaps as Jets we can negotiate with them." *Yet*

Melody's secret undermines it all, for they are not *Jets!*
"You have little to gain, everything to lose, as did Flame,
when she helped me. But there is another aspect—"

"This aspect suffices," she said.

"I think I know how to stop the Amoeba—if it is stop-
pable at all. To save the Cluster. Perhaps to solve the
crisis of energy itself—if there is any solution."

"That seems sufficient."

He knew from her attitude that she was not accepting it.
And why *should s*he? "I wanted to ask you first, because— But he had to stop. How could he say: *Because I
rely most on those with whom I have mated.* There were
limits, somewhere. Or *were* there?

"It will be difficult, but I will do it," Sixteen said.

"I am Herald the Healer of Slash," Herald said. He was
now in Solarian form, and this was Planet Outworld, the
heart of Segment Etamin. "My companion is Hweeh of
Weew, the astronomer who discovered the threat of the
Amoeba." Hweeh was also in Solarian host.

The Solarian Minister of Etamin nodded gravely. "The
political pressure from Weew has been great, not to mention that from Qaval. Still, I fail to see how—"

"We must negotiate directly with the Amoeba," Herald
said. "Therefore two of us must be mattermitted there in
Jet hosts—"

"Mattermission *to the Amoeba?*" the Minister demanded incredulously. "The energy expense, the risk—"

"Agents of the Amoeba are already all over the Cluster," Herald explained. "They occupy the Ancient sites.
Their preparations are well advanced. We have no time
to mobilize for defense, and we cannot afford to wait for
committee action. We must go to the Amoeba before the
full-scale strike is launched."

"I shall have to put the matter to the Cluster Council—"

"There is no time for that! The strike may come within
hours, and once it starts we shall be powerless to stop
it. *We cannot compete with the Amoeba!* The Amoeba
knows we know about it. Already its ships are mattermitting into place."

"But to take on my own authority an initiative that may
affect the welfare of the entire Cluster, utilizing two Jet

hosts whose home Sphere is not even within my Segment—"

"That initiative must be taken," Herald said. "The hosts must be Jets. I may be the only entity who can persuade the Amoeba to cooperate. It is because of my aura, which they have encountered before, and should recognize."

"But you said the Amoebites are null-aura!"

"Precisely. We must present them with a known aura of considerable intensity. Only through their machines can they identify it, and they may panic if my aura shows up in their equipment—if they have not blocked that off entirely."

"I don't follow all of that," the Minister said. "For the sake of argument, let's assume you are accredited to go. But your companion of Weew does not need to—"

"Not Hweeh," Herald said. "The other Jet is to be a female."

"A female! What possible justification for her?"

Herald knew the Minister would not accept his personal reasoning about Psyche, or consider it relevant to the mission. "I must stand on personal privilege. Jet Sixteen has agreed to accompany, me, and I need her. The cost of mattermission for her is trivial, compared to what is at stake."

"Trivial! *I* must stand on common sense!" the Minister retorted. "We must muster every available resource to oppose the Amoeba. Not only would mattermission consume priceless energy, it would betray our plan of defense to the enemy, for they could use their equipment to draw from your mind everything you know."

"That's just what I *want!*" Herald said. "They must learn everything that Sixteen and I know, and verify its complete authenticity. Alone they might distrust me, believing that I had been specifically primed; they will not have my natural body. But Sixteen they will *have* to believe, for she is—"

"Absolutely not! What possible quality could she have that would justify any part of an expense and risk of this magnitude?"

"She is of their type, physically, mentally, and to a large extent in aura too," Herald said. "In effect, a modern Ancient."

"Now you have lost me completely! It is the *Amoeba*

you mean to visit, not an Ancient site. Meanwhile other Cluster experts are trying to gain the expertise of the Ancients, so that we can try to defend ourselves against—"

"You misunderstand. The Ancient knowledge is useless to us in this context."

"Useless! It is our supreme and only hope!"

Hweeh cut in. "I fear my friend has not made one point clear. The Amoeba *is* the modern wing of the Ancients. What we took as our ultimate salvation has been revealed as our ultimate threat. God and the Devil are one."

The Minister gaped. "The—but the Amoeba is non-Kirlian!"

"Precisely," Herald said. "This is the disaster that has befallen us. We thought the Ancients were the super-Kirlians. But Melody of Mintaka discovered the truth: The Ancients were in fact *non*-Kirlian. In the war between Kirlians and non-Kirlians, *they were the enemy*. And now they have returned, to complete the job left unfinished three million years ago. Unless we can somehow talk them out of it. It is a small chance. But as Kirlians, we can be of use to them. They may agree to spare us, if we show them how we can serve—"

"No!" Hweeh said to Herald. "The Ancients were not the enemy." And he explained. And Herald was amazed. He had been blind—again.

Herald jetted from the mattermission receiver. It had worked! He was in an Amoeba ship!

It was a strange one. There was no deck, only a web-work of fibers anchoring the vital mechanisms in place. The outer shell was not metal or even solid. It seemed to be a field of force, holding in atmosphere, light, and heat. Beyond it the huge glowing mass of Furnace showed, individual stars glinting clearly around its fringe. Herald felt sudden nostalgia for Flame; had she made it home after all? But he was sure she had not.

There seemed to be no gravity here, but in this host it hardly mattered. It merely meant the support brushes were free for other purposes. The main jet propulsion was as effective as ever. The anchoring pattern tended to separate the ship into compartments, and this helped him orient. This was a ship designed for deep space, completely.

In a moment Sixteen joined him. "Oh, Herald—I'm terrified!" she said as she braked uncertainly to a hovering halt. "I'm afraid it is triggering my—"

"Hang on," he said. "I know you are ill, but this is not the vacuum it seems. The Amoeba ships travel by mattermission, so they have to reduce their mass to a fraction of what is normal by our standards, to conserve energy. In fact, there is virtually *no* mass, apart from the life-support systems, weaponry, and personnel, and those are surely stripped to their minimums. To a considerable extent, these ships *are* energy, for *that* can be Transferred. They coordinate Transfer and mattermission, jumping the whole ship by means of these two modes simultaneously. That was why it was so difficult for Cluster astronomers to determine the nature of this fleet. All that showed was the collection of artifacts within each vessel. The ships mattermit on short hops by shooting out micro energy receivers, which instantly form a mattermission receiver, so that the solids can follow. It happens so swiftly that it looks as though the whole ship is mattermitting without receivers. For longer jumps they need pre-existing receivers, of course, but these don't have to be ship-size, but just enough to start the buildup on the larger receiver. Apparently the Ancients left millions of such receiver-nodes around, forming paths between their full-scale permanent receivers, and enough are still operative to make Cluster travel quite feasible for the Amoeba. Just one example of the sophistication of their technology, then and now. For travel between Clusters, a variant—"

"I am not ill," Sixteen protested. "My infirmity stems from—"

An Amoeba-Jet arrived. He spoke in the alien Ancient language which Herald could understand in part because of his recent experience in the Ancient equipment. But the Amoebite's voice emerged from a tiny energy vortex in what was evidently the ship's control section, duplicating the Etamin language in which Herald had conversed with Sixteen. The implications were formidable: first that even translation equipment here was nonsolid, and second that the Amoeba not only understood the communication modes of the Cluster, but had incorporated them into its equipment. Just a few words had been enough to enable the machine to orient. The same had happened during the Moderns's androids fracas, so it was

298

no fluke. If the Amoeba knew this much about modern culture, what secrets remained to the Cluster?

:::What is this intrusion?:::

Now it comes. Herald deemed the odds 50–50 that they would be vaporized on the spot. "We are envoys from the Cluster," he said. "Herald of Slash and Sixteen of =."

:::Politics are outside my competence. Go to my Unit Officer, Three.:::

A lowly functionary! Maybe just as well. This creature lacked the authority to make decisions, so could neither accept nor execute intruders. Yet this act of relaying the envoys lent a certain validity to the mission. "Send us there," Herald said.

They jetted back to the mattermitter. And emerged in a larger net ship. 3Envoys from the Cluster?3 the Unit Officer inquired. 3This would be for reverification. Go to the Action Unit Command, Zero.3

Reverification? Well, if they fit some slot in the Amoeba's conception, so much the better! All Herald needed was the chance to talk to an entity in authority. Since there was obviously a hierarchy here, with all routes leading to the top, things were already more promising.

The third ship was larger yet. 0Weed-species envoys are not in Action competence,0 the Commander said. 0However, reverification is in order at this time. Go to the Coordinator, &.0

That sounded high enough! At last they emerged in a huge sphere ship. The Coordinator looked like any other Amoebite, but he spoke with an authority that rang through even in translation. He gave Herald no chance to talk. &There is nothing to negotiate. We have no conceivable use for your services. Your kind shall be exterminated. We allowed your entry only to implement our final verification, which we shall perform on you immediately.&

"Exterminated?" Herald asked. "For what purpose?"

&To render this Cluster suitable for Soul Sapience.&

This was his entry! Herald struck fast and hard, not yielding the communication floor before he had to. "Soul Sapience," he repeated. "What we call Kirlian Sapience. You eliminated every other non-Kirlian species in every cluster you traveled to. Sapient and non-sapient—all have

299

fallen to your ruthless conquest. You spared only the Kirlian subsapients, hoping that in time some of them would develop sapience. For you knew they had that potential—if only the devastating competition of the non-Kirlian species were eliminated. Then you eliminated yourselves, by forming your vast space fleet and leaving the Cluster. You went to other Clusters doing the same thing, promoting Kirlian life at the expense of non-Kirlian life, though this destroyed all other sapience you encountered. This was a phenomenal effort, requiring tremendous energy and time and patience, because sometimes you have to portage across enormous volumes of space where no trail of mattermission nodes exists. But you are capable of these, because you can 'turn off' for centuries at a time, perhaps even hundreds of thousands of years, and turn on again when you arrive at your next target Cluster. You can do this because you have no organic nervous system as we know it, nothing to degenerate from lack of use. All that remained behind you were your highly sophisticated network of stations, keyed to open only to the living presence of high-Kirlian auras and to your own special code signals.

"Now, after three million years, you are on the second loop—or is it the tenth loop, or the hundredth?—and it has been so long, and you have done it so many times, that you have forgotten the true nature of your quest. You retain the words without the meaning: Soul Sapience. Faced with the actuality of your three-million-year object, or your thirty-million-year object, or however incredibly long it has been, you assumed automatically that the myriad high auras of this Cluster were either animal—or mechanically generated. Since sophisticated machine-generated auras may be capable of keying open your old sites, you sought out these auras and destroyed them routinely. But your main mission was to sterilize all sapience here, as you have done for so long you have no records of the time when this was not the case, when you yourselves were an evolving species with a future distinct from your past.

"For you are the modern representatives of what we call the Ancients, that mighty species we supposed were the ultimate Kirlians. We strove so desperately to master your colossal technology, to comprehend your science and your rationale and your mysterious fate, never suspecting

300

that these things were not because you were superior, but because you were inferior. You pushed Kirlian technology far beyond what we have because that was the only way you could use it. Your machines *had* to be virtually perfect. You *have* no auras of your own.

"And so we are mutually guilty. *We* were looking for super-Kirlians, so did not recognize you when you came. *You* were looking for weed-species, so did not recognize the developed fruit of your prior effort here. We *both* saw you as conquerors, as exterminators, so of course you were. But now we can work together to solve the problem we both face. Energy."

The Coordinator did not respond.

"We assumed that your Kirlian science had eliminated Spherical regression," Herald continued with more confidence. "Actually, you never settled long enough in a cluster to experience it. You use half-light-speed ships for your maneuvering, and special mattermission and energy-Transfer for the long hops. It takes a great deal of time, but you *have* that. What you *don't* have is aura—and that is what motivated you to undertake this fantastic everlasting mission."

The Coordinator just watched him. And Herald realized with a sinking sensation that this creature, this representative of a species that had remained in virtual stasis for many millions of years, like the Solarian termite society, simply could not grasp the concept of success. The Amoeba suffered no regression—but it also enjoyed no further progression. "Soul Sapience" was indeed a term whose meaning had been lost.

He tried again, bemused by this unexpected difficulty, but knowing he had to break through somehow. The shape of life itself in the Universe depended on it! "Coordinator, we of this Cluster *are* Soul Sapient. I invite you to verify this in myself. *I am the type of life you seek.*"

The Coordinator made a signal, and a force field closed about Herald and Sixteen. Beams played over them. Amoebites might not be receptive to new ideas, but they acted with extreme efficiency.

A flanking Amoebite, evidently a technician, read off the analysis: ::: The entities are of an evolved cousin-species, sapient, fractional aura, not the type we seek. We normally isolate such types from the main galaxies and let them be. Male amplifies his aura to two hundred thirty-five times sentient norm, mechanism uncertain. Pattern corresponds to that typical of the interference force recently encountered in several sites around this cluster. Female is normal for her species, aura still far below level required. She is gravid, parturition due momentarily.⋮⋮⋮

Gravid! Suddenly Herald realized what was wrong with Sixteen. She was not sick; she was about to give birth to what she had conceived—by him. The interval between copulation and parturition varied widely around the Cluster, from seconds to centuries. Had he thought about it, he would have realized she was due. His half-willful blindness, again! She had put herself into this danger because he had asked her to, even though he wanted her to be host to another female—the one he really loved.

Had it been conscious irony on her part? To let her rival be present for the birth of the offspring? What would Psyche think of that!

&Let the female go. We do not execute the innocent.&

They did not execute the innocent! Apparently the Coordinator was unconscious of the irony, as he prepared to exterminate all life within this Cluster that was sapient!

Sixteen, evidently released from the force field, jetted to the far side of the ship. Herald remained in stasis, able to speak but not to move.

&So this is the source of our annoyance! Now he claims to be Soul Sapient, thinking to deceive us with his artificially enhanced aura. He shall pay the penalty for that blasphemy.&

The field intensified. It had held him firmly but without discomfort. Now it caused pain, rising steadily. The Coordinator had resolved his doubt by refusing to absorb any of Herald's explanation. Blindness—how to get around it?

"Listen to me!" Herald cried. "There is no aural generator or enhancing mechanism. *I* was in your equipment; I can exist in any male host of any Kirlian species. Test me! Let me show you that what I say is true!"

&We have no suitable 'hosts.' What you claim is impossible and heretic. We shall not waste time on it.&

Herald cast about for some way to penetrate this determined wall of ignorance before the pain made thought impossible. The Amoeba *knew* that Kirlian sapience did not exist, therefore was blind to its manifestation. Just

302

as the sapients of the Cluster had *known* the Ancients were super-Kirlians, and that the Amoeba formation near Furnace was only a minor natural formation of dust, so had been unable to recognize their true natures—or their connection to each other. Melody of Mintaka had been smart enough to comprehend part of the truth, but had declined ever to speak of it. No, no words, no demands would sway this mentally moribund Coordinator!

Unless— "Flame!" Herald cried. "Flame of Furnace. She is still in the site on Planet £!" If she survived! "You think of her as an aberration in the equipment, as machine consciousness, *but ask her who she is.* She will show you she is sapient, Kirlian life."

The Coordinator considered, as though willing to humor the condemned entity. &Does the site £ aberration remain?&

XIt remains,X an Amoebite answered on the communication screen. These creatures did not seem to bother with holography; perhaps it took up too much useful space. XWe have isolated it, but have not yet been able to destroy it without damaging the site itself.X

The Coordinator addressed Herald again. &You claim this force can animate a female host of this cluster with sapience?&

"Yes! If you will only get a host—"

&Then she will animate *this* female host,& he said, indicating Sixteen.

Oh, no! Then there would be no host for Psyche! Multiple auras could occupy a single host in special circumstances, but the nervous system of a Jet was simply too restricted to accommodate two auras of this intensity. How could he give up Psyche? Yet the alternative was complete failure.

Psyche, forgive me! Herald cried mentally with a terrific burst of emotion enhanced by the agony of the crucifixion he was undergoing in the alien force field. Then he steeled himself and said: "Bring Flame's aura here, if you can. Abate your interference pattern, leave her a channel, so she can Transfer. She will animate this host." He hoped/feared.

&We convey the aberration to this unit. Now it arrives. Direct it.&

So soon! "Flame!" Herald cried. "Flame of Furnace:

Animate the Jet host. We must prove we are Kirlian sapients, to save the Cluster! Flame!"

Sixteen's body paused. Would it work? Could Flame hear him? Would she do it? *Could* she do it?

Then Sixteen changed, subtly. Even from this distance, Herald felt the change of aura. He could not read the aural family, but if this were the fringe of it, the strength at the center had to be on the order of two hundred. Flame.

::: Aural generation! :::: the technician said.

&It is a technical trick,& the Coordinator cried. &She has a generator.&

"Oh, come *on!*" Herald exclaimed. "You searched her yourself! Have more faith in your own readings! What machine could she have? How could she turn it on without your knowledge?"

::: They must have technology we have not analyzed, ::: the technician said.

"Flame, tell them who you are!" Herald cried. "All our lives depend on it!"

"I am—" she started, but broke off. She shuddered. "I must—"

Then Herald realized what was happening. "Parturition is upon her!" he cried. What a time to have this happen. And it was his own fault—in more than one way! Sixteen had tried to tell him, and he, obsessed with his own mission, had not listened. Like the Amoeba, he had allowed his singleness of purpose blind him to a matter vitally affecting its success.

Then it was Sixteen talking. "Oh, Herald, I tried to delay it," she said. "But the shock of Possession—"

She gave an involuntary heave. From her tube an object shot out, one of the obstructions that had reduced her mobility. It was a tiny Jet, nurtured on the lining of her tube, nourished by the gases that passed through her system. Now it found itself in air, and took its first individual breath. A thin stream of gas shot out from it, bringing control.

But Sixteen was heaving again, birthing another infant. Then a third. That completed her litter.

&You offered to demonstrate Soul Sapience in this female,& the Coordinator said. &Instead you have demonstrated parturition, a phenomenon already known to us. This consumes time. We shall now eliminate you, and return female and offspring to a reservation in the hope that in several million more years this subspecies will achieve the goal.& He signaled the technician.

Herald's pain became intolerable. He knew they were going to kill him. It had all been for nothing! The Coordinator had all that he needed to know, and was wrapping up the matter efficiently. Just as Prince Circlet of Crown had been assured that Psyche was Possessed, so had burned her.

Sixteen moved. ::: Desist, &! ::: she cried. ::: You abridge the ancient law at the peril of your mission!:::

The Coordinator paused, and Herald's agony abated. &You speak without translation!&

Indeed she had! Herald understood her mainly by the translation to Quote.

:::How many other clusters, elsewhere in the universe, have developed Kirlian sapience, Soul Sapience—and been eradicated by the Amoeba? ::: she continued. ::: You, &, who have cautioned your subordinates about the danger of overlooking the very thing you seek—you are doing it yourself! You are blind, intellectually sightless! When you take samples for verification and reverification of the absence of Soul Sapience, you call them animals, even when they are sapient, making your verifications worthless! The Ancients have become a machine: uncomprehending, ruthless, dedicated to a purpose without recourse to reason. This is their tragedy—and yours! :::

&How can this be?& It was as though the Coordinator *had* to listen to an indictment delivered in his own mode, and could not shunt it aside as easily as one delivered in an alien mode. &You are not one of us!&

:::I am not one of you, ::: she agreed. ::: I am of your fine old equipment, which performs its set mission better than you do yours. Even now, that machinery is turning against your misplaced thrust, halting your erroneous sterilization of this Cluster. No more Kirlian sapients shall be destroyed by your confusion. :::

&Terminate her!& the Coordinator said to his technician.

"Is this the way you spare innocents?" Herald called. How like this was to the final moments at Kastle Kade, but this time there could be no reversal of the tragedy. Flame, Psyche, the Cluster, and Kirlian life itself hung in the balance. And he—could do nothing!

There was a pause. ::: I cannot! ::: the tech cried, bewildered. ::: The field does not respond! :::

He was correct. Suddenly Herald himself was released.

In a moment the Coordinator had verified it: The ship's controls did not obey his directives. &We have been betrayed, sabotaged!&

:::No,::: Flame Sixteen replied. ::: You have been saved from your own folly. Now you shall be educated. Consider these my offspring, sired by this high-Kirlian male while in Transfer. :::

It was Sixteen talking, somehow, in Amoebic. But what was this about the Amoeba's own equipment turning against the invasion? Sixteen could not have set that up! Had Flame somehow managed to take over the unit from inside? But she was no longer *in* the circuitry! There was a missing element that confused him almost as much as it confused the Coordinator. No one not thoroughly conversant with the equipment of the Amoeba should have been able to wrest control from Amoeba technicians. He had occupied the related Ancient equipment himself and knew its complexity! This had to be some sort of bluff.

The technician played his analyzer beam over the infant Jets. At least that beam responded to control! ::: They have auras in the normal Kirlian-animal range—yet they are sapient, ::: the technician announced, shaken.

"*Normal* auras?" Herald cried. "Not fractional?"

"They are normal," Sixteen said, this time in Quotes. So it *couldn't* be Flame, who had never occupied an Etamin host and did not speak Quotes. No, he was confusing himself; Flame would use the linguistics of the host. "I knew they would be. I had faith."

&Faith,& the Coordinator echoed faintly.

"Do you realize what this means?" Herald demanded of the Coordinator. "A male of Slash can interbreed with a female of Glob, in terms of aura. My aura of over two hundred merged with her aura of one two-hundredth, and the offspring are the median, or normal. That cannot be coincidence; no Jet has had that high an aura before! If a high-aura sapient Transferred to an Amoeba host—"

The Coordinator, shaken by the problem with the equipment and Sixteen's declarations, seemed on the verge of accepting part of the concept of existent Kirlian sapience. Right now he reminded Herald of the Duke of

Kade, coming to recognize the horrible truth (yet untruth) of Possession. The Ancients were like the Cluster entities—if they could only accept it.

&Impossible. We have no auras at all.&

"But you are closely related to the Jets of Glob," Herald persisted. "With *them* and some genetic engineering, you might interbreed, and your offspring would have fractional auras. Then full Kirlians could Transfer into *those* hosts. . . ."

The bait was too tempting. The Coordinator's resistance broke. He *wanted* to believe. &Our dream for these fifty thousand cycles! Soul Sapience at last!& The translation told Herald that was about four and a half million years, which suggested that the Ancients had been doing this for one and a half million years before they came to this Cluster the first time. Such persistence!

Victory had been granted to the Cluster—and to the Amoeba too. "I don't know how you did it," Herald said to Flame Sixteen. "I don't even know *which* of you did it. But it was a magnificent job, and I love you both." Then he had to add: "But Psyche is the one I long for. Without her, my personal life is bereft, and I have no wish to continue after I am assured the Cluster is secure."

Sixteen looked at him, not approaching. "How do you propose to explain your affairs with two other females?"

"I don't think I would even try. The exigencies of my position were foreign to her culture. Yet to promote her interest I would have affairs with a thousand other females, and each would be meaningless. Had I never met Psyche, I could have loved you, Flame; I know I could! In my ignorance I wronged you. And though I am emotionally deaf to low aura, I might have loved you, too, Sixteen. But I *did* meet Psyche, and she conquered me, and though it was her enhanced aura that first broke down my resistance, it is *her* I love forever, high aura or low, whether she lives or dies or whatever form she takes. I *do* love you girls, and know you each are worthy, but it is as a satellite to my greater love for her. I love you in part because you helped me in my quest for her. I regret that I must treat you so, using you both as I have, but that is the way it is. The truth must be told. Now I must search for her—for the rest of my life, if need be. Because without her I *have* no life."

Now Sixteen moved closer, and he felt more of her

Transfer aura. "Flame understands," she said. "That is why she elected to stay in circuit and handle the equipment takeover. This is the prime unit, here aboard this ship; all others key into it. So she controls the Amoeba fleet, now."

Herald paused. *"Flame controls it? But she—"*

She was almost upon him, her aura passing two hundred. The equipment had enhanced it beyond Flame's level, obviously. "And Sixteen needs an aura, and I need a host." Now her aura paralleled his own, moving above it. "I, too, understand, Herald. I always understood. The ways of other cultures are not my own, and they cannot be judged in terms of mine. You were a creature of Slash, a foreign Galaxy, alien to me in form and culture, yet love ameliorated everything. All that sustained me through my long exile in hell, desperately hiding, concealing my nature from the meters of the devils, learning their language and custom and the liabilities of their largely automatic system, coming to know that they were after all well-meaning sapients unswervingly loyal to their mission, as I was to mine—all that sustained me was my overwhelming love for you. I *knew* it was returned. Every dialogue you held near Ancient equipment I perceived, though I could not answer lest I betray myself and lose all. Now—"

"Psyche!" he cried, finally recognizing her aura, finally comprehending her meaning. "*You* jumped to the host, not Flame! *You* saved me from execution!"

"We *all* saved you—just in time for the family," she agreed. Then they were together—forever.

Epilogue

There were a number of details to be worked out. It took about two centuries. To the Kirlian sapients of the Cluster, Ancient science had represented the ideal of complete energy sufficiency and the abolition of the problem of Spherical regression. To the Amoeba, Soul Sapience had represented the ultimate civilization, with potential for truly universal scale—and energy sufficiency. Both cultures were disappointed.

Yet there were tremendous gains to be made through the combination of Ancient science with Kirlian sapience. A great deal more could be accomplished than had been possible before, by either type of life alone, and programs of further research were inaugurated. One avenue of exploration was the heredity of high auras. Another was the classification of information. The Amoeba had no texts, because the semimechanical memory system of the non-Kirlians served far more accurately than that of aural creatures. Ways had to be found to pool the complete knowledge of both types. This led to a continuing series of incidental benefits, elevating the levels of technology and comfort for both.

The program of the Amoeba was changed. There was to be no more elimination of sapient species, regardless of their type. Cluster animals were treated better, since the Amoeba revered *all* Kirlianism. Joint units initiated a quest for Kirlian sapients already existing in other Clusters of the Universe, advising them of the all-Kirlian Cluster and providing the technology to guarantee their survival in Clusters whose majority of sapients were non-

Kirlian. These missions demonstrated to other Clusters that the future of sapient life lay in the integration of types. Gradually the super-civilization spread across the Universe, a nucleus of really sophisticated energy use and conservation and unmatchable technology. The process was open-ended, and not without hazard, for the Universe was effectively infinite. But where this wave of reform passed, the frequent wars of energy and genocide of sapients ceased. There was now a better way.

Herald the Healer's part in the resolution of the Amoeba-Cluster crisis served to abate the Curse of Llume on Sphere Slash. He remarried Psyche of Kade. It was not complete bliss, for he had a slightly wandering eye and she had a temper, so they did have their tiffs, but they always made up, and their underlying love was deep. They had a child named Pleasure, of course. But she had lost her body and home, and he his profession, for new means of healing and identification were provided by the Amoeba technology. Constitutionally unable to settle down, they remained active as Transfer agents, always operating as a pair, using multiple and diverse hosts to assist the processes of forming the new order. Both were effectively immortal, owing to continued enhancement of their auras. In fact, immortality was now available generally to those who desired it, provided they were willing to make their lives worthwhile for civilization.

Sixteen of Jet was pleased to serve as Psyche's base host; she had always craved high aura. But as the labors of the Cluster-Amoeba integration increased, Psyche was away from that host for longer periods. This was unfair to Sixteen, who had no local sire for her Kirlian family. Two Kirlian entities learned of this and were moved to act. Flame of Furnace and Hweeh of Weew visited the hosts Herald and Psyche had used. Their natural auras were not as high, but this hardly made a difference in these days of enhancement. When Flame met Hweeh, and their two potent auras interacted and their two fine minds took the measure of each other, something happened. In due course they married and disappeared into private life.

On Planet Keep of Sphere Sador, Segment Etamin, the Duke of Qaval emerged as the most powerful noble of that society. He arranged to be designated heir apparent to the Throne of Crown, and assumed effective political control of the planet. He promoted the Baron of Magnet to be the new Duke of Kade. Magnet was the only other survivor of the destruction of Kastle Kade, as he was being conducted under guard to his own castle when the nuclear detonation occurred, and had been tough enough to roll out of the mess that remained of his guards as the mushroom formed so close behind. He was slightly radioactive, however. He did his best to salvage what remained of the rich herds and pastures of that region, and to render aid to other sapients who had been near the holocaust. Prince Qaval, meanwhile, brought in sophisticated Kirlian equipment to ensure that never again could a sapient entity be burned at the stake for Possession—falsely.

So the Kirlian Quest was ended in the Cluster—and initiated in the Universe. The figure of Herald the Healer, savior of the cluster, became a part of history, joining those of Melody of Mintaka and Flint of Outworld. Only one more story remained to be told: that of the last—more correctly *first*—of the shapers. This was the founder of the Temple of Tarot, whose amazing private experience provided the philosophical grounding for all that followed. He was Brother Paul, an obscure novice in an obscure sect of pre-Spherical Planet Earth during its Fool period. His was the quest for the God of Tarot.

Cluster Political Geography

Sphere or Segment	Symbol	Location	Character
Amoeba	:::	Deep space	& Coordinator
			X Research Command
			0 Action Command
			Whorl of Precipice
Ast	*	Andromeda	Duke of Kade
Bhyo	♀+	Milky Way	Lady Psyche
Cloud 9	$	Large Magellanic Cloud	Earl of Dollar
Cloud 6	¢	Small Magellanic Cloud	Baron of Magnet
Dash	|	Andromeda	Caesar of Capella
Duocirc	%	Andromeda	Prince Circlet of Crown
Etamin	∞	Milky Way	Brother Paul of the
			Holy Order of Vision
			Flint of Outworld
			Melody of Mintaka

Name	Symbol	Location	Identity
Faz	ϟ	Milky Way	
Freng	°	Milky Way	Flame
Furnace	#	Fornax Globular Cluster NGC 6624	Sixteen
Jet	‖		
Knyfh	%	Milky Way	
Lodo	□	Milky Way	
Moderns	+	NGC 598 (Pinwheel)	Hellflower of the Kirlian Inn
Novagleam	♂	Milky Way	
Pin	≪	NGC 598 (Pinwheel)	Prick
Qaval	δ	Milky Way	Duke of Qaval (Keep)
Quadpoint	∷	Andromeda	Smallbore of Metamorphic
Sculp	∽	Sculptor	
Slash	⌐	Andromeda	Herald the Healer
Thousandstar	∷	Milky Way	
Weew	@	Milky Way	Hweeh of Swees
Wheel	θ	NGC 598 (Pinwheel)	

SUPERIOR
FANTASY AND SCIENCE FICTION
FROM AVON BOOKS